MINDSIEGE

HEATHER SUNSERI

Sun Publishing
VERSAILLES, KENTUCKY

Heather Sunseri/Sun Publishing
PO Box 1264
Versailles, Kentucky 40383
www.heathersunseri.com

Publisher's Note: This is a work of fiction. Names, characters,
places, and incidents are a product of the author's imagination.
Locales and public names are sometimes used for atmospheric
purposes. Any resemblance to actual people, living or dead, or
to businesses, companies, events, institutions, or locales is
completely coincidental.

Book Layout ©2013 BookDesignTemplates.com

Cover design by Mike Sunseri

Ordering Information:
Quantity sales. Special discounts are available on quantity pur-
chases by corporations, associations, and others. For details,
contact the "Special Sales Department" at the address above.

MINDSIEGE/ Heather Sunseri. -- 1st ed.
ISBN 978-0-9887153-5-6

To Mike
"A dream you dream alone is only a dream.
A dream you dream together is reality." ~John Lennon
The day my biggest dream entered my reality—
Kentucky Derby 1995.

ONE

....

I wrapped my fingers around the sleek handle of the knife, not in the way I'd cut a steak or chop vegetables, but white-knuckled—as if my life depended on it.

Only I wasn't about to defend my life. I was following orders.

That's right, Lexi. Take the knife. And walk. A figure hovered in my peripheral vision. His voice was deep, stern. The orange glow from the end of a cigarette brightened and quickly faded a little too close to my face. A ribbon of smoke swirled above my head and left a familiar, disgusting scent in the air.

Barefoot, I padded across the sticky kitchen linoleum and inched slowly into the hallway. I passed a living area. A mismatched sofa, a love seat, and a couple of chairs faced a flat-screen TV hanging above a gas fireplace. A lamp lit the corner of the room, casting early morning shadows on the wall.

Keep moving, Lexi. Find Jack, the voice in my head ordered.

The bathroom in the hallway was dark. With my empty hand, I pushed open the bedroom door to my left and eased into the darkness. An outside street lamp peeked through the sheer curtains on the windows, providing minimal light.

When my eyes adjusted, I stared at the bed. Jack lay right where I had left him. The familiar sound of a flicking lighter had woken me from a deep slumber, very much like it had on the night I jumped into a freezing swimming pool. And just like I'd felt that night, I wasn't sure if I was truly awake or if I was sleepwalking, or if I could touch the person behind me—Smoking Man.

Jack was stretched out on his side. His legs reached almost to the end of the bed. His face pointed toward me. His expression was peaceful, and his lips curved slightly.

Tears burned my eyes. I was drawn to Jack in a way I didn't completely understand—the way a flower always faces toward the sun. But too much had happened, preventing us from living a normal life: finishing high school, applying to colleges, hanging out with friends. I hoped someday our feelings for each other would overcome the resentment I felt at being thrown into an out-of-control situation.

Walk closer to him, the voice in my head ordered.

My grip tightened. I still wasn't sure why I had a knife, or why this mystery person was with me, leading me to Jack. The muscles around my heart constricted. Something was wrong. I knew it. But I couldn't seem to stop my forward motion.

Jack, wake up, I whispered with my mind. A tear escaped the corner of my eye.

Go on, Lexi. Kneel beside him.

I climbed up on the bed, edged closer on my knees, and leaned over Jack. The panic began to build in my chest. I could hear my own labored breaths. *Jack, something's wrong. Please wake up*, I thought to him. *Someone's inside my head.* He was usually so in tune with my mindspeak.

Lexi, do you love Jack?

"Yes." My voice was a hoarse whisper. The presence inside my head somehow prevented me from speaking louder. This stranger had a hold on me, controlling my movements and my words—everything but my thoughts. He stood close to me, as if we were inside a dream. And I couldn't bring Jack into it like I so desperately wanted to do.

The lump in my throat made it difficult to breathe. I searched my mind for this person who had invaded my head and seized control. I could feel him, but for some reason, I couldn't push him out. His ability was too strong.

But you know what he did was wrong, right?

"I don't know what you're talking about."

If it weren't for Jack, Sandra never would have found you. He led her right to you.

"What? Sandra is lying in a coma." I had never met Sandra. I'd only seen her briefly, two nights ago, when Jack, Kyle, and I escaped Wellington. I'd chosen to leave her—the woman I was cloned from—lying unconscious on a gurney at Wellington Boarding School.

I could have saved her, brought her out of the coma. But I was scared. We knew too little about this woman who cloned humans for some purpose that remained a secret to me even now.

He led Sandra, and therefore the IIA, to you. Jack is the reason your father was killed, Lexi. And he's the reason you'll have no choice but to learn to use your ability to benefit them. Or you'll be terminated, like your father. The word "them" rolled off his tongue like venom. Like he felt the same way I did about agents of the International Intelligence Agency.

Was he saying that the IIA killed my father? Why? For his research? For Jack's and my abilities? "No. You're wrong. Jack only wants to keep me safe." He loves me. And I love him.

I'm only doing this to protect you, Lexi. To protect all of us. You need to know exactly what I'm capable of... what you're capable of... and eventually, what the rest of us are capable of. That's the only way we'll be able to fight back.

Us? This person... the presence inside my head... was one of us. He was controlling my mind. And why? He wanted me to fight back? Why couldn't I see who he was? He was only a greyed-out figure to me. A shadow. "What are you going to make me do?" *Jack!* I pleaded.

Eventually, you will discover that I did this for your own good. For the safety of us all. The figure lifted his cigarette to his mouth and inhaled. After, he blew rings of smoke that dissipated as they drifted toward the ceiling. I knew that if I could wake from this strange unconscious state, his physical presence would fade like a bad dream. But I wasn't so sure about the voice, or the hold he had on my mind.

I want you to grab hold of the knife with both hands.

My free hand joined the other, both trembling.

Raise the knife, Lexi.

I raised it, slowly, until I held the knife firmly over my head, shaking uncontrollably. I stared down at my target. *Jack!* This time, I screamed with my mind.

He sucked in a deep breath and rolled over onto his back, but still slept. The scent of his shower gel reached my nose, and I craved his closeness.

Do it, Lexi. Plant that knife deep in his chest.

I shook my head from side to side. My arms strained against my own mental resistance. *Jack, I'm so sorry.*

A sob leaked from my throat. Every muscle from my stomach to my chest and through both arms tightened as I prepared to do exactly what the voice in my head ordered: drive the knife into the one I loved.

TWO

··

As if moved by a sixth sense, Jack shifted his hand just slightly to rest it at the base of my knee. The presence inside my head suddenly disappeared; I dropped the knife off the side of the bed, and Jack's eyes fluttered open.

Jack peered up at me through thick lashes. His just-woke-up, lazy grin faded. "Lexi? What are you doing?"

I shifted off my knees and sat back. My heart raced. Jack's sandy hair lay haphazardly across his forehead, messy in a good-looking sort of way, from a night of sleep. The realization that only moments earlier I had held a knife above my head pointed at his chest caused a shudder to move through my entire body.

"Hey." He sat up and cupped my cheek. "You okay? What's wrong?"

"I just..." I glanced around the room for the person who had guided me to Jack with a knife—not expecting to find him of course—then back at Jack and his dark blue eyes. "Nothing. Nothing happened. I just couldn't sleep."

Jack lay back, breaking the physical contact I craved with him.

Very good, Lexi. The voice was back inside my head, or maybe it had never left. I didn't know anymore. I could feel the unwanted presence just hanging out in my periphery. *You cannot tell him I'm in your head. I can force you to hurt him. I will if I have to. Let's keep this our little secret.*

5

I massaged the pressure point in the webbing between my thumb and index finger. It was a method I used to relieve headaches, and this presence was definitely a headache. I would find a way to tell Jack, but first I'd figure out who the voice was.

Jack smiled. "Come here." He slid his arm around me, and pulled me down to lie beside him, my back to his chest. His hand rested across my stomach. "You've been through so much." He smoothed my hair back out of my face.

"*We've* been through so much." I grabbed onto his arm and squeezed it. How could I possibly hurt the one person who had saved me time and time again?

I couldn't. I wouldn't.

Lying there, I glanced down at the floor. The knife lay there, taunting me and my weak mind. I wanted to put a face with the voice that drifted into my mind like smoke. But the image wouldn't form.

Minutes passed. My mind spun while concentrating on the voice that had entered my head and forced me to do something I would never choose to do consciously. Jack and I *had* been through so much, and he had stuck by me when he could have run. But how could he continue to stick by someone who practically murdered him in his sleep?

He wouldn't. I wouldn't let him.

Jack pressed on my stomach, tightening his hold on me. "What are you thinking so hard about?" he whispered into my hair, his voice groggy. "I can't hear your thoughts, but I know you're tossing something around. You still afraid someone is getting inside your head?"

I sat up, turned toward him, and nodded.

He pushed himself up. His face inches from mine. *I won't let anyone hurt you.*

Reaching my hand to trace an imaginary line from his temple to his jawbone, I said, "I'm more afraid *I'll* hurt *you.*"

THREE

....

The smell of coffee greeted me when I walked into the kitchen after showering. Not my drink of choice, but desperate times called for whatever caffeine option was available.

Sitting at the kitchen table, Jack held Kyle's arm out, twisting and turning it, examining it. Kyle winced from Jack's not-so-gentle touch. I looked closer, and saw that Kyle's hand and forearm were red and blistered.

"What happened?" I doctored a cup of coffee with creamer and two yellow packets.

Both boys looked up. The lines between Jack's brows deepened.

Kyle shrugged. "Clumsy, I guess. I... I fell last night while putting a log on the fire." He chuckled uncomfortably and gave his head a jerk to flip his brown, unkempt hair off his eyebrows.

"You fell," I repeated, leaning into the counter. Kyle wasn't known for his clumsiness. My eyes met Jack's.

He fell and his arm landed in the flames, Jack thought to me. I could hear his sarcasm.

I walked closer and examined the blisters. *You don't think that's what happened?*

Let's just say I'm skeptical.

Noticing how quiet the house was, I asked, "Where's everyone else?"

9

Jack tilted his head toward the back door. I followed the motion to the back patio, where the rest of the group, the owners of this house—Georgia, Jonas, and Fred—were standing in a circle. I walked over to the door. Bringing the warm coffee to my lips, I peered through the blinds. Georgia crossed both arms. Fred waved his hands in front of him in an apparent debate with the others. Neither wore the thick makeup like they had the night I'd first met them. Jonas hugged his body with one arm, and with the opposite hand, brought a cigarette to his mouth. I zeroed in on the tip that brightened when he inhaled. Something about the vision of him smoking caused me to lose my train of thought for a few seconds. There was something familiar about the movement and the cigarette, but my mind was a little fuzzy.

I gave my head a little shake and turned back to Kyle and Jack. "What are they talking about?"

Jack glanced uneasily at me before meeting Kyle's stare.

"What? Has something happened?" I demanded. We had found refuge in this house after escaping Wellington Boarding School on Friday night. Of course, I had slept through nearly two days. Now, the owners—cloned humans like Jack, Kyle and me—appeared uneasy. But they'd been the only people we could turn to.

When Jack didn't respond, Kyle brought the focus back to himself. "Can you heal it or not?"

I squinted my eyes, glaring at the two of them.

Jack ran a hand through his hair before nodding.

"I don't mean to sound insensitive, but is that the smartest choice? Won't it make you sick to heal that?"

Before I could protest any further, Jack pressed his hands around the red, blistery wound and closed his eyes.

Kyle winced again. His eyes rolled back into his head from the pain.

Jack, we can bandage the wound. He'll be fine. He doesn't need to be healed completely. When Jack didn't stop, I did what I could to get deeper inside his head. *I'm right here with you. Simply heal the wound, but try to suppress the nausea. Our minds are strong, Jack.* I continued to send him positive energy while he did what he could for Kyle's injury.

Several minutes passed. I remained inside his head, attempting to be a soothing force.

Jack's eyes opened. Kyle slouched in his chair while we studied his arm. His skin was no longer red and blistered: it was new again. Healed completely.

"How do you feel?" I asked Jack, hesitation in my voice. Setting my coffee down, I pulled some napkins from a wrought-iron dispenser on the kitchen table and blotted the blood dripping from my nose.

Jack pressed his lips together in a thin line. "How'd you do that?" he asked. "You were inside my head. More than just the mindspeaking." He pushed back from the table and stood. "I'm not dizzy or light-headed. And I'm not nauseous."

I shrugged. "I don't know. I just couldn't stand the thought of you getting sick right now. I need you well while we decide what's next."

"Your nosebleed. It seems worse than when you simply control someone's actions."

"It's nothing." I waved him off, then tilted my head back slightly while pinching the bridge of my nose. Blood slid down the back of my throat. The metallic taste mixed with the taste of sweet coffee.

Jack leaned into me. "I'm sorry. I should have thought about what that might do to you."

Kyle held his arm up. "I don't know what you did or how you did it, but thanks, man. It feels one hundred percent normal."

The door squeaked behind me. Georgia, Fred, and Jonas filed in.

"Oh, good. Look who's up," Georgia said, a little bit of irritation in her voice. Even without dramatic eye makeup, Georgia's exotic facial features stood out. She wore a deep shade of red gloss on her lips, which enhanced her dark skin.

Jonas passed by me. I crinkled my nose at the smell of cigarette smoke on his clothes. His hand brushed the small of my back as he whispered close to my head. "Don't mind her, sweetheart." My entire body tensed. "She's just cranky from lack of sleep." He continued past me.

Georgia shot icicles from her eyes at Jonas. The temperature of the room seemed to drop dramatically. "I'm not the one who suffered a colossal panic attack before dawn this morning."

"What is she talking about?" Jack asked. "What brought that on?"

Jonas shrugged. He got a mug out of the cabinet and poured a cup of coffee—black, very close to the color of his dark brown eyes. "I don't know. It just happened."

Jack took three steps closer to Jonas. "Yeah, Jonas? Is that your story?"

Jonas took a sip, crossing one leg in front of the other, and leaned against the counter. "Yeah. What's with you?"

"I'll tell you what's with me, Jonas. Your panic attacks don't 'just happen.' So, what brought this one on?"

Jack's voice boomed, and a shiver moved down my spine. I had a lot to learn about Fred, Jonas, and Georgia. Jack had known them before he found me at Wellington. The three of them lived in this house and, according to Jack, were enrolled in courses at the University of Kentucky. After watching them interact only a few times, I surmised that they trusted each other well enough. They had already been a part of The Program together, so they understood that each of them was cloned from another human.

"Back off, Jack," Fred stepped between them.

Jack backed up and leaned against the opposite counter, his arms crossed. Kyle's eyebrows shot up as he and I made eye contact.

Georgia finally spoke up, cutting the tension that was growing like algae. "So, what are we going to do? Do we move? Do we stay?"

"What do you mean, move?" I asked. And was I included in her plans to move? "Why would you move?" Of course, I didn't even know where we were. I hadn't ventured outside since we'd arrived here more than two days ago.

"Well, thanks to you, our covers could be blown," Jonas said, his mouth hidden by the edge of his coffee mug. The way his eyes drilled into me unnerved me.

"Jonas, I'm warning you..." Jack straightened, his shoulders back. A vein on the side of his neck quivered.

"What is all of this really about?" I asked. *What's going on here? Why are you yelling at Jonas?*

Jack shook his head at me.

"Friday night was a disaster." Leave it to Georgia to be the honest voice in this lot.

I agreed with her, but... "What do you mean?"

"You were supposed to run, not end up here. Jack said you would run."

Jack shook his head. "Stop it, Georgia."

"Stop what, Jack? You've protected her long enough. I don't see a fragile girl about to crumble before us."

Jack crossed the room. He slid his hand into mine. "This is all new to her. And we all still have a lot to learn."

"No, she's right," I said. "You've protected me. We got away from Wellington and bought ourselves some time to figure out what's truly happening."

Jonas let out an under-his-breath chuckle. Jack gripped my hand tighter.

What's with you? I asked.

Later.

"So, what have you decided?" Georgia asked me. "Jack must return to Wellington. What will *you* do?"

I glanced at Jack. I knew he intended to return to Wellington. He wouldn't have left if it hadn't been for me. He needed to return and watch over Addison, who was like a sister to him. I shuddered just thinking about the story of a horse crushing her skull when she was seven years old.

If Addison were to wake, Cathy and Dr. Wellington would know that I healed Addison's brain injuries Friday night—that I did exactly what they suspected I could do. And if they were to discover my abilities, everyone in this room was convinced that they'd stop at nothing to find me again. They'd force me to join their cause, whatever that cause was.

Cathy had pretended to be Jack's caring and loving mom one minute, then imprisoned us with an electric fence around our school the next. And Dr. Wellington, president of Wellington Boarding School and brother to Cathy DeWeese, had allowed her to interfere without ever explaining their ultimate intentions.

What I feared most was that they could force me to use my unnatural abilities—abilities I knew little about—against my will.

Someone was definitely inside my head this morning, controlling my actions and forcing me to hurt the one person in my life I would die to protect.

I studied the people in the room, each of them waiting for me to answer Georgia's question. My heart tightened. I knew what I had to do. I dropped Jack's hand and massaged the bridge of my nose.

A presence entered my head. A presence that was not Jack.

"Lexi?" Jack said. "You okay?"

My head jerked toward him. "Fine. Why?" Could the presence inside my head hear my thoughts? My knees began to shake. I was unsteady on my feet.

You're a good actress, Lexi. Don't let them suspect that someone's inside your head.

Georgia stared at me, still waiting for me to answer. Fred and Kyle whispered to each other in the corner. Jonas had turned away and was rinsing his coffee mug in the sink.

What do you want from me? I thought to the presence.

Tell them you'll return to Wellington.

No. I can't go back there. I wanted to go back to Wellington, to my friends, but I couldn't. I couldn't allow Cathy DeWeese, or anyone else, to control me.

You can. And you will. Do I need to remind you what I can make you do?

Why do you want me to go back there? I tucked my clammy hands into my armpits, hugging myself.

I need you to do something at Wellington. You'll find out what when the time is right.

My eyes found Jack's. A line formed between his brows. "What is it?" He pulled one of my hands free and wrapped his fingers around mine, brought me closer to him, and slid his other arm around my waist.

"Nothing. I'm fine." I dared a smile as I told a flat-out lie. I hated lying to him after everything we'd been through. "Georgia, I will not put you and your friends in danger. I won't be staying here, so you don't have to worry."

"Where will you go?" Fred asked.

"I think it's probably better you didn't know." Mainly because I didn't know where I would go. But it wouldn't be Wellington.

Jack slid inside my head and poked around. I felt his familiarity. The other presence had gone silent, but I assumed he hadn't gone far. *What are you thinking?* Jack asked.

I shrugged and swallowed hard. *That our lives are a mess.*

"I thought we always planned to stick together if and when we found others like us." Fred was obviously the more naïve of the bunch. His voice and face screamed fear.

16

"That would have been true if someone weren't trying to kill one of us." Georgia was the cynical one. But she was right. I'd put her and everyone in the room in danger if it was my ability someone was after. More likely, we each endangered the others just by being together.

"What changed, Georgia?" Jack asked. "You welcomed us Friday."

"I'm not a monster, Jack. You needed our help, and I know you would do the same for any of us. But we're going to be safer if we split up. I hate to think what would happen if the wrong people found us all in one place. We know how to get in touch with each other."

That stung. I didn't know how to get in touch with the three that lived here. Then it dawned on me. "You guys don't trust me." Georgia stood tall, shoulders squared. Fred refused to make eye contact with me. Jonas smirked.

Kyle looked offended and ready to fight. At least I had one friend besides Jack.

I pulled my hand from Jack's grip, turned, and exited the kitchen without another word. I didn't have to explain myself to my fellow freak club. They didn't want me around? Well, the feeling was mutual.

In the bedroom where I had slept, I searched for the very few things I had managed to bring from Wellington.

"They hoped you would heal Sandra." Jack's voice startled me from the doorway. "Seth led them to believe that she'd figured out a way to cure the side effects they all suffer from after using their abilities."

"They would trust her?"

"No," Jack laughed. "They were hoping Seth would restrain her and make her do what they wanted."

Seth, neurosurgeon and brother to Sandra Whitmeyer, seemed to be the one person everyone trusted to be honest about the history of our origin. He helped me tap into my ability to assess brain disease and injury, and ultimately heal. But I'd only done that once. And I still wasn't so sure about Seth.

"Don't they know how ridiculous that sounds? It's his sister we're talking about."

Jack shrugged. "Maybe. Cathy had intended to subdue her Friday night. Remember the syringe she filled?"

"What? I thought that was meant for me." Cathy had ordered me to use my healing abilities to bring Sandra out of the coma. She had held a filled syringe like a weapon the entire time. But rather than follow her wishes, I flushed some sort of drug from Jack's body and healed Addison's brain injury instead.

"No, the sedation was meant for Sandra, not you. She would have drugged Sandra if you had pulled her out of the coma."

"When I didn't bring Sandra out, Cathy tried to use it on me."

"Yes, but I was faster and turned it on her. I don't think she meant to harm you."

Not harm, maybe, but punish and control, for sure.

Jack knew I wasn't about to heal Sandra without knowing more information. I picked up my backpack from the floor and sorted through it. I had my small computer, a few clothing items, and my cell phone, which I stuffed into the back pocket of my jeans. I also had the large envelope Jack had given me buried in the bottom of my pack. Not the safest place for it, but I felt a little safer knowing I had the means and credentials to run if I needed to.

Jack sat on the bed beside my bag. "Tell me what you're thinking."

Tears welled up in my eyes at the image of me holding a knife high above him.

"Hey." He stood and reached his fingers to my face, brushing hair off my forehead and tucking the strands behind my ear. "We're going to figure this out."

I swiped at my cheek where a tear escaped. "Yes, we are. But you need to get to Wellington and fix things with your mom, and check on Addison."

"I can't leave you."

"Yes, you can. I'll be fine." I had my own agenda—which included identifying Smoking Man.

"What do you mean? Where will you go?"

"I'll call Marci. Dad obviously trusted her. And I'm fairly certain she knows a lot more than she's been telling me." I also needed time to read Dad's journals. "You can message me through the link I gave you. If my dad set it up, it's safe."

"I'm going to go talk to Jonas. He can go with you until I can get back to you." He turned to go.

"Wait!" I grabbed his arm. "Why Jonas? Why not Kyle?" I trusted Kyle way more than I trusted Jonas. "You looked like you could have punched Jonas in there."

"Jonas has a similar mind ability to yours, and he tends to get himself in trouble when he uses it. And his panic attacks can be bad. He told me he wouldn't use his ability until we knew more about the side effects. I was irritated. That's all."

"An ability similar to mine," I repeated. "As in, he can manipulate people's actions?"

"I said similar, not exactly like yours. Look, don't worry about it. You concentrate on you for now."

"Why would you send him with me if he has these issues?"

"Jonas can be a jerk, but he's loyal. He'll protect you better than anyone else out there. And Kyle needs to get back to Wellington. He and I have to play nice until we know more."

"What if all the security measures they put in place *were* actually to imprison everyone there? Isn't that why we ran? Why Georgia drove a bulldozer through the fence?" My lip quivered and my voice lowered to a whisper. "What if you get there and can't get back out?"

Jack slid his hand behind my neck. He leaned in and kissed me. "We ran because I wasn't willing to take a chance with *you*. Kyle and I won't be locked away at Wellington. I will not let that happen. Something tells me we've misjudged dear ol' Mom's motivations to keep us under lock and key."

I wasn't so sure about that. Whatever dear ol' Mom's motivations were, they had inspired our escape.

Nonetheless, I let Jack go talk to Jonas. But something wasn't right. I could feel it.

FOUR

....

A rmed with my backpack, I decided I couldn't wait any longer. I needed fresh air while Jack attempted to arrange my protection.

I didn't think I needed a bodyguard, but I *did* need a ride. I didn't even know where I was. And I definitely wanted to separate myself from Jack until I figured out who was inside my head trying to harm him. We were better off apart for now.

I opened the back door and stepped out into the October air. The early morning breeze was cool, but the sun warmed my cheeks instantly.

The safe house where Georgia, Jonas, and Fred lived was nestled among other older brick houses, very much like the house I grew up in with Gram. Autumn leaves rustled in the wind, their vivid oranges and yellows fluttering high above me. A rusty-chained swing creaked at the house next door. And beyond that, railroad tracks.

Embers in the fire pit in the middle of the patio still smoked from the night before, giving off a distinct campfire-like scent. Eight Adirondack chairs were scattered around the area. I imagined the threesome having small gatherings at their house often. I could easily picture them living a normal life together. To their outside friends, assuming they had friends, they were simply three roommates starting out in life.

A small twinge of jealousy churned in the pit of my stomach. I wanted friends, normalcy, to live on my own away from the threats that haunted me now.

I followed a line of stepping stones around the side of the house to a gate in the picket fence that enclosed the backyard. A couple of guys walked by the front of the house. Satchels crossed their chests and hung low at their hips. Another passerby sped by on a bike, a backpack strapped to her back.

We were close to a school. I glanced back at the railroad tracks again. We had to be near the University of Kentucky. There were a lot of older brick homes near the football stadium, from what I remembered from the few times I had visited campus.

I heard voices coming from the front of the house.

"Jonas, I can't send her out alone," Jack said.

I squeezed between a bush and the side of the house, positioning myself so that I could see Jack, Jonas, and Georgia standing on the front porch, and clearly hear their conversation. Luckily, they were too engrossed in their discussion to notice me.

"Take her with you," Georgia suggested.

"You know I can't do that. They'll force her to heal Sandra, and it could kill her."

"You don't know that, Jack." Jonas's tone was more serious than it had been earlier that morning. "We need Sandra. What if she can take away your nausea and how sick you get when you heal people?"

Jack and I hadn't had time to discuss whether we actually believed Sandra could heal some of these symptoms we suffered. I would argue we had these abilities *and* these side effects because of Sandra.

"Speaking of," Jack said, "want to tell me why you suffered a panic attack this morning?"

"I was just playing around." He paused and looked away, almost directly at me. I glued my back to the side of the house and out of their sight, praying he hadn't seen me eavesdropping. "There's this hot girl next door. I wanted to see if I could get her to undress in front of the window."

Ewww. Gross.

"Sounds like it was quite a panic attack for such a small request," Jack said, seemingly quite unaffected by what a pervert Jonas was.

"Now you see why I need Sandra. I can't have even the smallest tasks sending me into a full-on crazy episode." Jonas tapped his head with his knuckles.

I peeked around the side of the house. Studied Jonas. His hand shook nervously at his side, then reached into his jacket pocket and withdrew a small object.

"None of this changes the fact that Lexi doesn't want to accept that part of her genetic makeup yet." Jack—always the optimist.

He'd been so supportive of me as I discovered *what* we were. There was no doubt in my mind that he would continue to try to shield me as we searched for more information about *what it meant* to be cloned and how we were genetically modified.

"Yet?" Georgia repeated. "But you think she will, eventually? Will she become a part of The Program?"

By piecing tidbits together, I had learned that we each had special abilities, some similar, some not. Jonas had an ability similar to mine if he could force a girl to undress. And we all seemed to have certain adverse side effects—nosebleeds, projectile vomiting, panic attacks. I studied the deep lines across

Georgia's forehead. She was worried. Did she have some supernatural ability? Or even more important, did she suffer greatly when she used it?

"I don't know," Jack said. "I promised her I would help her run if that's what she wanted. Not a single one of us should be forced to embrace this life that was chosen for us."

"Fine." Jonas lifted the object up to his mouth. It was a cigarette. "I'll take her wherever she needs to go. And stay with her if necessary. It would be my pleasure." His words rolled right over the smirk that spread across his lips as he stuck the cigarette in his mouth. When he flicked the lighter and the flame sparked, I flinched at both the noise and the fire.

"It's necessary. Don't forget someone tried to kill both of us last week. And Cathy was ready to imprison us at Wellington Friday night." Jack shook his head and added, "I've got to confront my dear mother."

"If Lexi needs to come back here, we'll deal," Georgia added. "We need to watch over each other."

I stood there, my back plastered to the brick. My heart raced as a suppressed memory surfaced. Images of the previous night flashed back to me. Images of me by the fire pit. Fred had played a guitar and sung.

My eyes darted around the yard beside the house. I drilled the palm of my hand into my chest, attempting to massage my panicked heart. Jack assured me that Jonas could protect me. That he was loyal. Loyal to whom?

Events of the previous night slowly seeped into the outer fringes of my mind. Images that at first seemed like distant memories were becoming clearer. Jonas had stomped out a cigarette at my feet last night. He practically admitted to drowning me in the pool. He forced Kyle to stick his arm in the fire.

"Thank you, Georgia," Jack said, snapping me back to the present. "Kyle and I will be leaving shortly. I'm fairly certain Lexi will be ready to leave when I do."

My mind reeled through memories or dreams—snippets of reality—that I suspected were planted there by Jonas: like when he pointed a gun at my head a couple of weeks ago, and when he led me outside into the cold on the night the fire alarms were tripped in the Wellington's girls' dorm.

It was Jonas. He got inside my head the night my father died. The night he forced me to jump into a freezing pool. And this morning when...

That was why he suffered a panic attack. Not because of the lies he told Jack now.

A train whistle blew, startling me from the dark memories, the darkest of all being the one of Smoking Man—Jonas—forcing me to almost drive a knife into Jack's chest. This image had been only a blur in my subconscious, but it now came into focus.

Jonas. It was him. I remembered. And he threatened to force me to hurt Jack if I revealed his identity.

The whistle blared again, calling out to me.

The train approached slowly, running behind the houses. My grip tightened around the strap of my backpack.

I chanced a glance around the corner of the house again just as Jack passed through the front door. Jonas and Georgia traded looks, then followed Jack inside.

Would Jonas actually hurt Jack? Or was he bluffing to get me to submit to some demand of his?

Jack would be leaving shortly. And taking Kyle. He'd be safe then. Away from Jonas. Away from me.

As the train moved closer, I saw the open car. Empty. Everything that the presence inside my head had said to me scrolled through my memory like an out-of-control teleprompter. He needed me.

He would force me to hurt Jack if I didn't comply. But I couldn't hurt Jack if I was nowhere near him.

The train whistled—a signal. Or a sign.

I ran. I ran as fast as my legs would take me. I ran through the backyard of the neighbor's house, past the swing set. I ran alongside the train, the open car. I let the backpack slide from my shoulder and tossed it into the car. It slid across the metal floor.

I felt Jack's presence ease inside my head. *Lexi, where are you?*

I reached out my hand and grabbed onto a piece of metal on the open door of the car. With a giant burst of adrenaline, I sped up. I squeezed the metal and, in one motion, leapt from the gravel, lifting and swinging my legs onto the moving car. Thankfully, the rest of my body followed.

Lexi.

I'm sorry, Jack. Even my thoughts came out in panted breaths.

Where are you? What do you mean you're sorry? What did you do?

I grabbed my backpack and hugged it to my chest as I crawled over and leaned against the wall of the car. *I know who is inside my head. They want something from me that I will not give them. Not until I know why.*

Tell me where you are so we can talk. Please don't run from me.

I'm already gone.

26

FIVE

The train rattled and quivered as it crept along railroad tracks on the outskirts of the University. Though I was less than twenty minutes from Midland, Kentucky and Wellington Boarding School, I felt thousands of miles away from anyone who could help me.

I wanted Jack with me, but I wouldn't deter him from checking on Addison. I, too, wanted to know how she was and whether I had healed her. Maybe by returning to Wellington, he and Kyle would learn more about Cathy DeWeese's and Roger Wellington's intentions for the school. And for the cloned humans who lived there.

A shiver moved down my spine at the thought of a group of crazy doctors having that kind of control over a group of humans with supernatural abilities. What exactly did they hope to gain from me and the other clones?

If they hoped to use these abilities to their own advantage, why was someone hell-bent on killing Jack and me? Did someone think we knew too much? Because of Dad's journals? No one but Jack and me knew the journals still existed, even if only virtually.

God, I missed Dad.

The breeze blew wisps of hair off my face as I stared out onto the side streets of Lexington. The air smelled of dirt and gravel, and the rickety train stirred up dust.

I decided I was far enough away from Jonas. I grabbed my bag and jumped from the train, landing with a jolt and tumbling to the ground. After gaining my footing, I made my way down a side street in the direction of campus and in search of Wi-Fi.

Fifteen minutes later, I slid into a booth in the back corner of a coffee shop. The busy in-and-out-the-door activity of professors, students, and businessmen and women calmed me rather than added to my anxiety. Their comings and goings grounded me into a sort of normalcy. One could get lost in the "normal" of others' lives.

But could one also hide there in plain sight?

A short, stocky waitress approached my table. She was dressed head to toe in black and adorned with two nose rings and an eyebrow ring. "How are ya?" she asked in a high-pitched southern accent.

"I'm okay." I guessed that was true. I was more okay at that moment than I had been.

"What can I get ya?"

"Chai tea latte and a yogurt with granola?" I said in more of a question than a statement.

After writing down my order, the girl with the piercings stuck a pencil behind her ear, then eyed me curiously before spinning on her heels and skipping off.

I pulled my phone out of my back pocket. Five missed calls from Jack. He would understand why I ran—as soon as I found the right opportunity to tell him. I rubbed the spot over my heart that throbbed anytime I considered how I might have to live without him. On the run, even. I could barely swallow past the ginormous lump in my throat. I wouldn't go back to Wellington.

I had to focus. I texted Marci McDaniel. *"Marci, need your help. Can u come get me?"* Dad trusted the reporter enough to leave the puzzle box with her—the box that had contained instructions for finding his journals. Surely I could trust her.

After I hit send, I pulled out my laptop and connected to the Wi-Fi. I glanced around the coffee shop. Everyone seemed to be in a hurry to get their order, or was otherwise engrossed in conversation. No one even lifted an eye in my direction.

Deciding it was safe, I pulled up the website my Dad had created to house the years and years of journals and other information he had compiled. There was so much data. It would take weeks to read through it all. I opened the earliest-dated journals. Scrolling through page after page of scientific data did nothing but confuse me. Words like genomic DNA sequencing, somatic cell nuclear transfer, therapeutic cloning, and reproductive cloning got jumbled in my head. I couldn't make sense of any of it. Not quickly anyway, and not without a dictionary. I simply didn't have time to look up every word or phrase on Wikipedia.

Switching gears, I brought up the last journal he'd typed. At first, all I saw was an entry outlining his keynote address to the Association of International Physicians and Research—the same speech I'd heard the night I met Jack's father, Dr. John DeWeese. Dr. DeWeese was Dad's oldest and dearest friend, and his lab partner from before I was born.

Behind his speech notes was an itinerary for his stay in Lexington. The day leading up to the AIPR dinner included a tour of the University of Kentucky Hospital and a visit to the College of Agriculture. After the day of touring, he was to attend the dinner and deliver the keynote address, followed by a visit with me that never happened.

"That's strange," I whispered to no one. Why the College of Agriculture?

My phone vibrated. A picture of Jack appeared on the screen.

"Hi," I answered, keeping my voice low.

"Why'd you run?" he asked. His voice was calm. There was road noise in the background.

"I told you why. Where are you?" *Please be away from Jonas.*

"Kyle and I are on our way back to Wellington. We had to leave, but I have to know that you're okay."

Of course, I wasn't okay. The girl set my tea and yogurt in front of me. I mouthed a "thank you."

Jack continued. "Why did you run without telling me or giving me a chance to say goodbye?"

I leaned my forehead into my palm. The smell of the chai tea—the soothing scents of cinnamon bark, nutmeg, and ginger—reached my nose. "I heard you guys on the porch. You wanted Jonas to take me, and..." I paused for a minute to consider how he was going to react to the news that Jonas was getting inside my head. "It was Jonas, Jack. He's getting inside my head. He tried to drown me, and he tried to make me—"

"No way. It couldn't have been Jonas. I understand why you think that, but..."

I remained silent, giving him time to digest the information. My phone buzzed in my ear, alerting me to an incoming text. "Hold on." I read the text from Marci. "*Of course. Where r u?*"

I looked up at the picture painted on the window at the front of the shop and read the name backwards before typing: "*Big Blue Brew on UK campus.*"

With the phone back at my ear, I said, "Jack, I know you trust your friends."

"What proof do you have that it was Jonas?"

I gasped. "Proof?" My defensive instincts rose. "You want me to prove that Jonas was inside my head? Are you kidding me with this?" I broke out in a sweat. To think, I actually thought he would simply take me at my word.

"It's just that..." As Jack spoke, I imagined him running his hands through his hair. "He's my friend. He promised me he would watch over you while I took care of Addison. I'm just having a hard time believing he would do what you're suggesting."

"Do what I'm suggesting? Are you hearing yourself? He's your friend? What am I, Jack? The liar you hugged and kissed this morning in bed?"

"No, Lexi, I didn't mean..."

"You know what... never mind. I..." Closing my eyes, I squeezed the bridge of my nose. When I reopened them, I noticed movement outside the coffee shop. I craned my neck to get a better look. A black SUV had pulled up in front and stopped. Strange, since there's no parking in front of the shop. Two men in suits climbed out of the front seat. The little hairs on the back of my neck stood at attention. "Jack, something's wrong. Someone's here."

"Who? What are you seeing? Where are you?" Jack sounded panicked.

"I gotta go."

"Lexi, don't hang—"

I pushed end on the phone. The waitress who had served my breakfast several minutes ago approached my table. "You need anything?"

I grabbed my backpack and handed her some money, never removing my eye from the front door. "Is there a back way out of here?"

"Yes." She pointed behind me. "Is everything all right?"

"Fine." A man in dark sunglasses was placing his hand on the front door, pushing it open. "I have a restraining order against my abusive father, and he's entering the shop right now. If you could stall that man in any way..."

She glanced over her shoulder then back at me. "Consider it done." After a wink, she turned and shielded me while I slipped down the hallway behind her and out the door.

Tires screeched and horns blared in the not-too-far-away distance. My phone vibrated in my back pocket, but I didn't have time to look at it.

Morning traffic was thick. I crossed the street and tried to blend in with a group of students I presumed were walking to class.

Once I was a good distance away, and on the front side of Big Blue Brew, I looked back. The two men in suits stood outside the coffee shop. One was on his phone.

I pulled mine out. I had a text from Marci. "*No use running, Lexi. We are not going to hurt you.*"

Right. So, why the big black SUV and scary-looking men in suits? And Marci? My heart sank. Dad had trusted her. *I* had trusted her.

Unable to think, I simply walked. Straight through campus. I found myself at the entrance of the Arboretum—the site of my first date with Jack. I sat on a bench off to the side, behind some evergreens, but with a perfect view of the parking lot. I placed my head between my knees. I was hyperventilating, suffering a panic attack, or something.

"Get it together," I whispered to myself. My thoughts raced. It seemed that the same black SUV that had run Jack and me off the road the night of our first date was after me again. Jack and I had barely known each other five seconds before people started stalking me and trying to kill us.

And how cliché. Was it a requirement that bad government people had to drive dark SUVs? Maybe it was normal for big scary vehicles to pull up on the curb of a coffee shop in the middle of a college campus.

I lifted my head and smoothed my hair behind my ears. A couple of moms with their giggling toddlers passed in front of me. I smiled at their innocence before an uncontrollable sob escaped my throat.

Calm the hell down, Lexi, I berated myself. *Think.*

My phone vibrated with a text from Jack. *"Plz, let me know ur ok. Going crazy."*

He still cared. He just thought I was a liar. I typed back, *"I'm fine."*

Immediately, my phone rang. I declined Jack's call. What would I tell him? He wasn't even in a position to help me. He had things he needed to do.

I needed to slow my rapid pulse. Find a place to stay while I read through more of Dad's journals and waited for Jack to secure Addison's safety. I also needed to discover more information about Jack's so-called friend, Jonas.

One of the Arboretum's gardeners watered the flowerbeds in front of me. I breathed in the scent of the wet soil and the mums blooming in a pot beside the bench. My heart rate was finally slowing down. I was safe for now, but it was still early in the day.

Jack texted, *"Check front page of Lexington newspaper. Not good. Re: Marci. Call me. Plz."*

No sign of big, bad SUVs in the parking lot. Everything seemed normal around me. Quiet, even. So I ventured toward the visitors' center. Mostly workers, walkers, and some mothers with their children strolled through the gardens.

The visitors' center was quiet. A lady behind the desk looked up when I approached. "Can I help you?"

"Yes, ma'am. Do you happen to have a copy of today's paper I could peek at for a second?"

She searched the desk, and then bent down to look under the counter. "I just threw it away." She handed me the folded bundle. "You can have it."

"Thanks."

Once I was back outside, I unfolded the sections, looking for the front page. I knew I had found it the minute I saw the picture. The headline read: Local Reporter Found Murdered On UK Campus. I stared at the headline and the picture under it in disbelief. My fingers grazed the outline of the woman's face.

Tears pooled in my eyes. Oh, Marci.

Somebody had killed her. "I'm so sorry," I whispered to no one through quiet sobs.

Beside the picture of Marci was another photograph, this one of a man. The caption read, "Dr. Jeremy Porter of the University of Kentucky College of Agriculture named as a person of interest in the case."

I stared at the picture for a few seconds. "It can't be," I mumbled.

The picture was a man similar in age to my father, but who looked just like Jonas.

~~~~~

I called Jack immediately. "What does this mean?"

"I don't know."

"Marci was so scared of something the last time we talked. Does Jonas know about this Dr. Jeremy Porter person?"

"I don't know," Jack said again, his voice low, but unable to hide his frustration with so many unknowns. "Please just tell me you're somewhere safe."

I had no idea whether I was safe. "I'm okay." I looked around at the still-blooming flowers and fought back tears. Where could I possibly go? A couple of hummingbirds flitted in front of me, drinking from a feeder. I remembered my first date with Jack. My life had already turned complicated, even then, with the death of my father. But Jack was the one calming force that had gotten me through it, insisting that we do things normal teenagers did.

"I'm sorry. I never should have left you." Jack's voice was quiet.

"Of course you should have. Are you at the school yet?"

"We're in Midland."

"What are you planning? Are you just going to drive right back into Wellington?"

"No. We're meeting Cathy and Roger in town. Somewhere a little more public."

"What do you hope will happen, Jack? That Mommy Dearest will hug you with open arms and tell you everything is going to be just fine?" I knew the sarcasm in my voice had to bite.

"Is that so much to ask?"

No, it wasn't. "Just unrealistic."

"Cathy needs us, Lexi. She's never tried to hurt me."

"Just like Jonas has never meant you harm?"

"Jonas has never hurt me. Quite the opposite, really."

"What does that mean?"

"Jonas was the one who pulled us out of the car the night we were chased off the road. My car would have gone up in flames with you in it had it not been for Jonas." Jack's voice cracked a little. "He wouldn't hurt us, Lexi."

I squeezed the bridge of my nose. What Jack was telling me didn't make sense. How could I tell him that Jonas wanted me to stab him with a huge knife just this morning? "What if Jonas pulled us out of the vehicle because he needed me for something?"

"Like what?"

"I don't know, Jack," I said, exasperated. "But your mistrust in me is starting to piss me off."

Suddenly, as if summoned, Jonas's presence slithered into my head. *I could have told you he wouldn't believe you, Lexi.*

His voice made me jump. *Shit! What do you want, Jonas?*

mindsiege

Such language, Lexi. We'll get to why I need you. First, get rid of Jack.

"Lexi, I trust you," Jack said. "I just think we need more info."

"Jack, I have to go."

"Wait. You haven't told me where you are. How will I find you?"

"Don't worry about me. Call me later, when you're done with your *dear mother*. And, Jack, be careful. Don't let that woman inject you with something again."

"I'm ready for her."

Whatever *that* meant. Jack told me to be careful and hung up.

I stood and started to slide my phone in my back pocket, when Jonas mindspoke again. *Turn it off, Lexi. They found you the first time because you texted Marci. They're tracking you.*

I jerked my head toward the parking lot, scared he was right. And there they were. Two suits climbed out of the SUV; one carried a strange-looking gun in his right hand. A gun with a silencer, maybe, or a tranquilizer gun.

That's a taser, Jonas said.

I slid behind a row of shrubs and ducked down, but the two men walked in my direction. My heart sped up. I was about to make a run for it when Jonas thought to me, *Stay where you are. Help is coming.*

Jonas was here. And now I wondered if I should try my chances with the men in black. I started to stand, when a hand clamped down on my arm, stopping me. I turned my head. I was face to face with Jonas. He raised his other hand and placed a finger to his lips. Then he pointed at the men.

Georgia walked toward them and was telling them something. The gun was magically gone, tucked away. Georgia gestured to the gardens like she was some sort of tour guide.

Convince them to turn and leave, Lexi.

Why hadn't I already thought of that? I had used my mind-speak for my own benefit most of my teen years, but for some reason I froze when I actually needed it.

I concentrated hard on the suits. *Turn around and walk back to your vehicles. There's nothing you want here. What you're looking for is long gone.*

Just like that, the suits took one last look around and returned to their truck. I pulled some napkins from my backpack and held them to each nostril. The blood was a little heavier than usual.

Jonas slipped his hand into mine and tugged. "Let's go."

I pulled my hand away. "I'm not going anywhere with you."

I watched Georgia make her way to us and tried to decide if she was friend or foe. Backing away from Jonas, my eyes darted from Jonas to Georgia. "How did you find me?"

A slow grin pulled the corners of Jonas's lips up. "Lexi, Lexi, Lexi. You have so much to learn."

"Meaning?" I crossed my arms.

"Meaning," Georgia joined in, "Jonas, if he wants to, can find any of us at any time. As long as he recognizes what you're seeing." Georgia stood directly next to Jonas, united. "We better go. It won't take long before they realized they were tricked." Georgia looked at me expectantly.

I blotted my nose one last time. "It won't take who long?"

"The IIA," Georgia said, like it was every day we had International Intelligence Agency goons stalking us.

"I'm not going with you." I started to turn and walk away, but Georgia's strange look of urgency toward Jonas stopped me. She lifted her head in my direction as if encouraging Jonas to do something.

Jonas pulled an object out of his pocket—something so small it fit into the palm of his hand. He stood there a moment longer, simply staring at me, still grinning. *This is going to be so much fun.*

Apparently he hesitated a moment too long, because Georgia jerked the item from Jonas's hand. "Oh, for crying out loud, I'll do it myself."

She was on me before I knew what hit me. I felt a pinch to my neck. My legs buckled beneath me. Jonas caught me and scooped me into his arms. My head dangled back as he carried me away.

SIX

....

I woke to the sound of groaning. Mine.

I wasn't in pain, but I knew Georgia had injected something straight into my neck. I wondered how I could have been so stupid. I moaned again.

When my eyes opened, I saw mostly white. I stared up at large, popcorn ceiling tiles. I was covered loosely in a white sheet. The room smelled like antiseptic. Everything was clean and without color.

I turned my head to the left and found an empty chair. To the right—Jonas.

I sat up and analyzed my surroundings. I was in some sort of hospital room or exam room, though there were some things in the room that didn't make sense. Like the tray of surgical instruments several feet away.

Jonas leaned against a doorjamb, staring at me, far enough away that I couldn't gracefully leap off the gurney I was on and rip his eyes out with my fingernails.

"Hi, Lexi."

I was in no mood for small talk. *Jonas, I want you to walk closer to me.* Jonas pushed off the doorway, and took three steps. He was only about a foot away from the rolling cart of surgical tools. His eyes glazed over. He wasn't looking *at* me, but staring straight through me, not focusing on any one item in front of him. I had him in my control.

I gripped the sheet in my fists, preparing for a nosebleed, and concentrated hard on Jonas. *Now, grab the scalpel off the tray.*

I want you to point the scalpel directly at your heart, but don't pierce your clothing or skin yet. Then, I want you to look at me and answer my questions. Do you understand?

He nodded, then reached for and wrapped his fingers around the handle of one of the sharpest knives anywhere. Without hesitation, he pointed the blade at his chest.

What did Georgia inject me with? I brought the sheet to my nose as blood touched the top of my lip.

"A mild tranquilizer."

Why?

"You were arguing too much. And we needed to get you off the streets."

Why? I narrowed my eyes. I sounded like a kindergartner.

"To keep the IIA from capturing you," he said, and his tone sounded a lot like he wanted to say "duh" afterwards.

Where are we? I looked around again.

"The Program."

At Wellington? My heartbeat doubled in speed.

"No. At the UK Hospital, where Seth works. This is its original location, before Cathy DeWeese and Seth decided to move it to the boarding school for better security." He raised his hands and put air quotes around the words "better security."

I let out half a breath. I wasn't sure how safe I was where I was, but I knew I didn't want to be at Wellington. Georgia entered the room. Her eyes immediately went to Jonas's hands—gripping a scalpel aimed at his heart. She raised a hand out in front. "Lexi? What are you doing?"

Don't set the scalpel down, Jonas. Do not listen to Georgia. You can't even hear her. "What do you mean?" I asked Georgia.

"Don't even try playing stupid with me. I would have left you for the IIA back there, but Jonas insisted we bring you in."

I untangled from the sheet and slid to the floor. "Don't make me laugh. You're the one who wanted me to leave this morning. And then what? You drugged me? And don't even get me started on this one." I pointed at Jonas, who looked bored while following *my* orders for a change. However, sweat beaded along his hairline. He was conscious enough to know his heartbeat was one slice away from stopping.

"I made a mistake," Georgia said. "I shouldn't have been so harsh with you this morning, but I was scared."

"Scared of what?"

"The IIA. And for good reason. Once you were away from our house, they found you within an hour."

I thought about that for a second. I'd assumed the people who found me did so because of the text I sent Marci. "Why does the IIA want me so badly?" I asked, mostly to myself.

Georgia rolled her eyes. "As if I could figure that out."

"What about him?" I pointed to Jonas again. *Jonas, bring the point of the scalpel closer to your chest.* "What does Jonas want from me?" I asked Georgia.

Georgia looked away, refusing to answer.

Jonas, lift the scalpel up and hold it against your neck, but don't puncture your skin—yet.

Georgia watched Jonas with wide eyes. His hand shook just slightly.

One more question for you, Jonas. What do you want from me?

"We need you to heal Sandra. I will force you to do it."

Georgia jerked her head and gaped at Jonas.

By hurting Jack?

43

"No! I would never hurt Jack."

Then what was that early this morning? You've been inside my head, controlling me.

"That wasn't me. Well, not completely." He smirked.

Dropping the bloody sheet back on the bed, I cocked my head. *What do you mean that wasn't you?* I stepped closer to him. His hand shook just slightly. The blade punctured his skin slightly, and blood ran down his neck.

Georgia balled her hands into fists. She interrupted Jonas's and my conversation before he could answer. "Have him put the knife down, now, and let's talk about this." Her voice shook. To Georgia's credit, she at least feared my threat to force Jonas to hurt himself.

"Give me one good reason why," I said. "He's been getting inside my head for weeks."

"Because if you don't, I'll be forced to do it myself, and it won't be pretty."

That sounded like a threat, which I didn't take well to. "Do it. Be my guest."

She waved a hand, and the scalpel Jonas held fell to the tiled floor with a clank. She waved another hand at me and sent me flying backward into the wall.

I fell to the ground with a harsh grunt, the air knocked out of me. *What the hell?*

Once I caught my breath, I pushed myself up. Georgia convulsed on the ground. Jonas knelt beside her, holding her head gently. "Hand me that pillow." Jonas pointed at the gurney.

I scrambled to my feet and got the pillow. I slowly handed it to Jonas. When he jerked it from me, I flinched.

mindsiege

"I guess I deserved that," Jonas said. I assumed he was re-
ferring to being mind-controlled and held at bay with a scalpel.
His head tilted to look up at me. "The thing is... I'm surprised
you had it in you. I certainly wasn't expecting you to take control of me." He felt the side of his neck, touching the blood
that was already starting to clot and dry. "But you have a lot to
learn, Lexi."

Ignoring his insult about my apparent weakness, I said,
"She's telekinetic." He nodded. The warm look of concern he
showed Georgia surprised me. "And suffers grand mal seizures
when she uses the ability."

"Yes."

"Why would she ever risk a seizure?"

"She wouldn't. Without good reason." A thick vein pulsed
in the side of his neck. His face reddened. "She must have believed you would hurt me. Or maybe she wanted you to see
what happens to her." He sucked in a deep breath and let it out
slowly. "Like I've been telling you, you need to embrace who
we all are." There was a protective edge to his voice. Protective
of Georgia, maybe. He leaned down and kissed her on the
forehead in a brotherly sort of way.

I backed up against the wall and slid down until I was sitting. I was pretty certain I would have hurt him had she not
stopped me, and was disappointed in myself at the prospect. I
drilled my fingers into my temple.

I wanted to question Jonas further about how and why he
gets inside my head and what he meant by it not being completely him, but my head throbbed, and I couldn't handle another nosebleed right now. I was mostly sure he wasn't going
to tell me the truth... without proper motivation anyway.

I lowered my gaze as I replayed the actions—*my* actions—that put Georgia in her now-still state, but the chilling memory of her seizure heated the blood running through my veins. No one forced her to use her telekinetic power.

Caught off guard, I flinched when Jonas's presence slithered into my mind. He crossed the room and knelt in front of me, his jaw set. *Nice work, getting inside my head. You won this round, but you've got a lot to learn.* He touched a knuckle to my chin and lifted. His eyes burned into mine. *And trust me, you will learn. You can't run and hide from this, Lexi.*

"Oh, yeah?" I asked. My shaky voice betrayed me. "So tell me, Jonas: if you're not inside my head, then who is?"

I'll show you soon enough.

What makes you think I'll hang around long enough to give you the chance? Not that I believed a thing he said. He forced Kyle to stick his arm in the fire pit, then threatened me. He practically admitted that he had been inside my head.

He smiled. *Oh, you will. Like I said, you can't hide from this.* Pinning me with his gaze, he stood, and after an uncomfortable moment, he returned to Georgia.

A shiver went through me. I hugged my knees to my chest. He was right. I was quickly realizing that I would have to stay, have to learn. I couldn't live like this—with the constant threat of someone invading my mind, seizing my thoughts, and controlling my actions.

That's where we were when Jack and Seth walked in: Jonas tending to Georgia, and me watching, contemplating.

"What are you doing here?" Jack asked me from the doorway.

I didn't even look up. I just sat there, my body in a tight ball, and stared at Georgia and Jonas. Georgia slept, and Jonas watched her.

"What happened?" Seth asked. He was dressed in his white physician's lab coat. A neurologist at the University of Kentucky Hospital and head of The Program, he had been the one to convince me I could heal Addison and others of brain injuries and disease. He'd assured me I'd be begging to join The Program when the people who killed my father came after me.

Well, I wasn't begging yet.

Jack kneeled in front of me and traced his finger down my cheek. *I'm sorry I left you this morning.*

I flicked my gaze upwards. He should have been sorry he called me a liar. Besides, I had left him first. *Did you know that she's telekinetic?* I looked at Georgia, who remained unconscious.

Jack cocked his head. *She told you that?*

No, she showed me.

"Seth," Jack said, standing. "We've got a problem. Georgia had an episode."

Seth looked from Jack to Georgia to Jonas's worried face. "Was it a bad one?"

Jonas's jaw tightened. "Is there any other kind?"

"Well, at least you guys are finally getting to know each other," Seth said, as if we had all just gathered for team-building activities.

Jack narrowed his eyes at Seth. Jonas chuckled under his breath. I wanted to punch something. Or someone.

"Why are you two here?" I asked. It dawned on me that it was awfully coincidental that they showed up in the same place where Georgia and Jonas had brought me.

"Seth needed some supplies for Addison." Jack rubbed his neck.

"Which I'm going to go gather." Seth was halfway out the door when he turned. "Jonas, did you give Lexi a tour of the facility?"

I raised an eyebrow. There was hidden meaning in that question. "Where exactly is this place?"

An arrogant smirk played at the edge of Jonas's lips.

"As in the location? You don't know where you are?" Jack cocked his head toward me.

Jonas interrupted. "The Program is located in a building between the UK Hospital complex and the College of Agriculture."

That was the third mention of the College of Agriculture in one day. I couldn't think of a single reason my dad would tour that college.

Jonas crossed his arms and studied me from his position beside Georgia. Could it be that there was something to establishing The Program next to the Ag College? The hospital... I understood. But the Ag—

It will all make sense soon, Lexi, Jonas mindspoke to me.

My eyes darted to meet his, but before I could respond, Jack's voice brought me out of my own thoughts. "Something's bothering me. What, exactly, would get Georgia to use her telekinetic power?" He faced away from us. His palms were pressed against the door, his fingers spread wide.

Jonas and I traded guilty looks. We both glanced at Georgia, who had been moved to the same gurney I woke up on just hours before.

"Answer me," Jack demanded, turning and looking at Jonas. Jack was obviously well aware that Georgia didn't take her special ability or its resulting seizure lightly. He narrowed his gaze and cocked his head, analyzing something. "What happened to your neck?"

Blood along the two-inch cut just below his ear had dried into two streams running down behind the collar of his shirt.

Jonas touched the spot Jack was staring at. "It's nothing."

"It's not nothing. Who did that?" Jack's face reddened. His eyes darted from Jonas to me. His hands balled into fists. He looked ready to defend Jonas to the death.

"I did," I said challengingly. "And Georgia used her power to stop me from hurting him the way I wanted to."

Both of them looked at me like I had sprouted devil horns. "Why would you slice his neck?" Jack asked.

I opened my mouth to speak, but remembered Jonas's threat to harm Jack, and his attempt to drown me. A shiver moved through me at the thought of him—or anyone—inside my head making me do things against my will. I wanted him to stay out, but the idea that Jack thought I was lying about Jonas controlling my mind...

Jack stepped closer. "Why, Lexi?"

I ground my teeth. I wanted to scream at Jack. I wanted to tell him that Jonas was a jerk and that he was dangerous, but for some impossible-to-understand reason, I said nothing.

"It was my fault," Jonas said. "Georgia and I found her at the Arboretum. The IIA was hot on her trail. We had to tranq her."

"You tranqed her?" Jack paced.

"And then we brought her here. I didn't know what else to do." Jonas spoke like he was protecting me. I laughed under my breath.

Since I had known Jack, he'd been thoughtful, but sometimes secretive and standoffish. And overprotective at times. I wasn't sure which Jack I was seeing today. His eyes burned into mine. "What happened to you staying out of sight?"

My blood heated at his accusatory tone. "I guess with all the voices inside my head, men in black suits chasing me, and the murder of the one person I had hoped would help me, I got a little sidetracked."

His face softened. "I'm sorry about Marci."

"Yeah? Me too," I snapped, then redirected to Georgia. "Will Georgia be okay?" Her body lay motionless.

"She'll be fine. But of the seven of us whose powers I've seen so far, she has the worst side effect." Jack smoothed my hair away from my face and behind my ear. My skin tingled beneath his touch. "She's the reason I didn't want you to heal Addison. Just the thought of watching you suffer in that way... I couldn't handle it."

"But I don't suffer in that way," I said.

"Addison was the first person you healed. The *only* person so far... No one knew how your body would respond. We still don't know enough."

About many things. And we were obviously still getting to know each other, as well as the abilities each of us had. It blew my mind that I may have healed a little girl of injuries where doctors had failed. "How is Addison?"

He looked away from me. Swallowed hard. When his eyes met mine again, he said, "She's awake."

He could have punched me in the stomach and not have sucked the air from me as much as he did with those words—and my subsequent feelings of excitement and dread. I had succeeded, but what did that mean? "And?" I prompted. Could she talk? Could she walk? What does she remember?

"And Cathy knows that you cured her brain injuries."

I pulled back from him.

"Cathy doesn't understand why we ran from Wellington. Or why we wouldn't want to learn everything we could about where we came from and what we were created to do."

Neither did Jonas, apparently. It seemed I was the only one who was constantly aware of the live embryos that were murdered in the process of creating the clones who survived. Three hundred fifty-one, to be exact, according to the anonymous email I'd received before Dad was murdered. Why would I want to learn from the monstrous doctors capable of such unethical experimentation? "Who else knows that I healed her?" I whispered. I suddenly felt claustrophobic. The walls were closing in, and I had nowhere to hide. My hands shook at my side. I tucked them in my armpits and backed further away from Jack.

"Roger Wellington, Seth, and of course Kyle and myself. And now you guys."

"So, how is Addison, Jack?" Jonas asked from the chair beside Georgia. "Is she all right?"

"Well, she lost nearly two years of her life, so she's confused, and Seth ordered an MRI and some other tests, but... yeah. She seemed... for lack of a better word... normal." Jack smiled, relieved.

I wasn't sure what I felt. As much as I hated that someone close to Jack had suffered, relief was not what I was feeling.

"How did Cathy react?" I asked Jack. "What's her plan?" What I really wanted to know was what was *his* plan. Would he let his mother control him and his special abilities?

And where did that leave us—Jack and me? We were right back to where we were the moment we bulldozed our way from Wellington: me on the run and Jack taking care of Addison. I was sad to be gone from Wellington, distraught to consider leaving Jack, but nowhere near ready to sacrifice both of our lives for either. There had to be another way.

"I'm not sure. She claims that her intention was always to help us."

Right. "Any word from your father?"

"Nope. None."

SEVEN

You didn't tell him that I was inside your head," Jonas said after Jack left to find Seth. "Why?"

"How are you so sure I didn't?" I paced around the room inside The Program. Not giving him time to respond to my first question, I asked, "So, this is where Seth has been teaching you, Georgia, Jack, and Fred about how your DNA was altered?" Convenient for Seth, but not for Kyle or me. Jack had told me he Skyped early in the morning with Seth while I swam. And, as we were informed Friday night, The Program had now been moved to Wellington. Dad had expected me to apply to The Program, but something told me the application process was simply a formality.

Jonas nodded. His arms were crossed. He leaned a hip against the bed where Georgia lay.

"How long have you known you were cloned?" I asked.

"A while."

Unsatisfied with his vague answer, I faced him. His dark brown eyes pinned me where I stood. "How long?" I demanded.

"Since birth." He tilted his head side to side. "Well, since I could form and keep memories."

I gasped, stared at Jonas. "Do you know who you were cloned from?"

He shrugged. "Never met him."

"But you know who he is?" I thought of the newspaper article—the person of interest wanted in connection with Marci's

53

murder. The person from the College of Agriculture. My heart constricted a little.

"I know he's a brilliant doctor somewhere. I don't believe he knows about me." Jonas pushed away from the bed where Georgia lay sleeping. "My turn. Jack tells us that you had no idea that you had been cloned from Sandra Whitmeyer."

"Did he?" Jack hadn't known until recently that I'd been cloned. Altered like him, yes, but not cloned.

"Don't be obtuse, Sarah." He stepped closer. The sound of my real first name coming from his lips sent an ice-cold chill down my spine. It was the name I'd said goodbye to when my father hid me away at boarding school several years ago. "Peter Roslin never told you what you were created to do? That Sandra Whitmeyer orchestrated your entire life?" He stood so close I could smell a hint of vanilla from his soap, masking the cigarette smoke on his clothes.

Backing away, I shook my head. Sometimes the anger at my father for not telling me ate me up inside like a cancer I couldn't stop. Surely he knew how much danger I would be in if the wrong people found me. But what really kept me up at night and made my blood run cold was the thought that people like Sandra Whitmeyer and Cathy DeWeese had some sort of power to direct my life. That Cathy could put a fence around my school and treat me like a prisoner. That Sandra had some sort of god complex and altered my DNA in such a way as to serve her own master plan.

Or did any of them really have the ability to do these things—to imprison, to control? Could anyone truly control the life of another without permission? I could still walk out right now and not look back. I could choose my path. However,

I'd always be looking over my shoulder for IIA agents; I still didn't know how to get Jonas out of my head; and I'd miss Jack.

I'm amazed at your father's level of irresponsibility. Jonas's voice snaked in and around my thoughts, bringing me back to a reality I had to face. The reality that Jonas—someone—could get inside my head and push my buttons.

"Don't talk about my father," I said through gritted teeth. "You don't have the right."

"Hmm." The corners of Jonas's lips lifted once again. "You don't think so? That's interesting. I think I have the right to talk about any of the doctors who did this to us."

I studied him. Anger flared across his face, yet his voice remained calm. "You don't like your abilities?" I asked.

"They come in handy sometimes."

"Like when you want to control someone's actions? Have someone do something against their will? Maybe even force someone to hurt themselves? Or someone else?"

"Yeah, like that."

"What did you mean earlier? When you said it wasn't you who tried to hurt Jack this morning."

"Ahh." He rubbed his chin back and forth with his finger. "I'm not under your control now, Lexi. And you can be sure I won't be letting my guard down on my mind around you again any time soon."

The muscles in my neck tensed. I knew Jonas could get inside my head. I had felt his presence, heard his voice, and even smelled the cigarette smoke. Now, I was supposed to believe that it wasn't him? Just because he said so?

"She sure was willing to risk a lot to help you," I said, nodding toward Georgia. Jonas's eyes narrowed. He studied me, much like I studied him. "And Jack is quick to defend you," I added. Jack was ready to trust Jonas to keep me safe, and he'd left me here with him now.

Jonas's grin grew. "You *did* tell Jack about me, didn't you? Why else would he defend me?"

I turned my gaze to a stain on the tile floor.

"He didn't believe you," Jonas said. He inched forward, leaning his face downward and forcing me to look at him. *Your thoughts betray you, Sarah.*

In an unusual moment of confidence, I rotated my shoulders back and stepped right up to him—my five-foot-three-inch frame up next to his five-eleven or so. I looked up. Stared straight into his cold, brown eyes. "How's your neck, by the way?"

That was when I saw it. Although slight and brief, I saw a flicker of fear in Jonas's eyes as he touched his fingers to the two-inch slice the scalpel had left.

He wrapped his fingers around my arm, just above my elbow, and pulled me even closer. "You cut me."

I couldn't stop the sound of my shallow breathing, but forced a smile onto my lips as my eyes burned into his. "I didn't cut you. You cut yourself." I wanted to tell him that if he ever got inside my head again, I would do more than inflict a superficial wound on him. I wanted to tell him that two could play this game he started.

"You won this round, Lexi. But be careful." He leaned in and whispered into my ear. His breath was hot on my neck. "You're playing with fire. People who play with fire often get burned."

His reference reminded me how he'd forced Kyle to stick his arm into the fire pit. I pulled away from him and grabbed my backpack off the floor. "That's okay. Just so you know, if you burn anyone I love again, literally or metaphorically, the cut to your neck will go much deeper."

I turned, and had almost made it to the door when he entered my head. *Lexi, I'm going to give you a little gift. Since your father failed you in so many ways, I'm going to show you a little piece of who you are meant to be.*

I reached out and wrapped my fingers around the doorknob. My hesitation gave him the invitation he needed to continue.

What you're looking for is in the Keiser-Boone Building.

Slowly, I faced him again. "How could you possibly know what I'm looking for?"

You're not looking for the thing your dad discovered just before he was killed? And you're not searching for the reason I'm inside your head now? You'll find both inside the College of Agriculture admin building. The Keiser-Boone Building.

"I thought it *wasn't* you inside my head."

He laughed. *I never said I wasn't inside your head. I only said that it wasn't me who tried to hurt Jack.*

~~~~~

The Program was located in a wing of a building near the hospital. Seth worked as a neurologist in the trauma unit of that very hospital, which was where I'd first laid eyes on the one and only Sandra Whitmeyer. Well, not exactly one and only—seeing as I was cloned from her DNA.

57

Other than my steps echoing down the hallway, the building was eerily quiet. As I approached an exit, a fluorescent light flickered above me. *"I never said I wasn't inside your head..."* Jonas's words repeated in my mind. I pushed through the exit, thankful I had not run into Jack or Seth again. Jonas had stayed with Georgia.

I thought about checking into a hotel for the night, and planning a way out of this town first thing in the morning. Take the documents and the money Jack gave me just last week when he thought it best that I run. Would Jack miss me?

He no longer trusted me, or even believed me when I told him who was inside my head. How was it possible that he refused to think the worst of Jonas?

I rubbed the area above my heart. Had Jack changed his mind about me? The guy who'd wrapped me in his arms that morning? The person who'd risked everything to break me out of Wellington three days ago?

He'd said nothing to get me to stay when he found me at The Program. Neither had Seth, now that I thought about it. Seth was the one person who'd believed I belonged inside The Program from the first time he met me.

But now? Jack was willing to give up his life to return to Wellington? For what? To protect Addison?

Massaging the spot on my chest above my heart, I walked two blocks, wandering aimlessly from building to building within UK's huge medical complex. When I finally looked up, I was standing in front of the Keiser-Boone Building. I prepared to climb the steps to the front entrance, but hesitated when I saw the police tape to the right of the building. I pulled out the newspaper article I had saved in my backpack and read. Marci's body had been discovered outside this very building. And the police tape around a mulched landscape area proved it.

Marci had reported on the latest scientific and medical research coming out of the university, but something had spooked her after Dad was killed. She had been scared out of her mind the last time I saw her.

So, what brought her here?

And why was the Keiser-Boone Building my "gift" from Jonas?

The sign in front of the building read "Agricultural Science Center North—Administrative Offices." I climbed the steps to the front entrance and stepped inside. The front hallway was typical of many campus office buildings: poorly lit, brown walls, and tiled flooring. The musky smell reminded me of my grandmother's basement. At each end of the front hallway were double doors, the kind you find in hospitals, not in old brick buildings.

I walked toward the far doors, but stopped when they opened. Out came a man dressed in blue scrubs and a white lab coat. He passed me without a second glance.

I slipped through the doors, and found myself at the entrance of a large laboratory, lit with bright, fluorescent lighting. A long, glass partition separated me from a room filled with people doing exactly what one would expect people to be doing inside a scientific lab: peering through microscopes, studying computer screens, and taking notes and having conversations about what they were viewing through microscopes and on computer screens. I couldn't hear any of the conversations going on through the glass partition. A couple of lab techs looked up from a conversation, stopping mid-sentence to stare at me. They traded glances before speaking again. One pulled a phone from her pocket and appeared to send a message before returning the phone back to her pocket.

I heard a chatter of voices when I reached a hallway in the center of the building. But the voices were strange. They didn't come from the lab, but from inside my head. I heard them, but I couldn't see who they came from.

I looked around, confused, and unable to make out the exact words I heard. I couldn't feel Jack or Jonas inside my head. And I heard female voices as well as male voices. I ventured down the middle hallway. When I turned a corner, there was only one direction to go next: down.

The hallway behind me was empty. No one bothered to stop me. A part of me felt silly. This was a building for the study of farming, I thought.

I descended to the basement and encountered another set of doors. My jogging shoes squeaked on the tiled floor. I reached out and pulled on the metal handle, but the doors were locked. To their right was some sort of electronic panel, with a small screen and a red light moving back and forth.

"Dang it, Jonas," I swore under my breath. "Why did you send me to this building? And what did Marci find here?"

Keep going, Lexi. You're almost there.

I jumped at the sound of Jonas inside my head. *Where are you? How is it you can mindspeak to me from so far away?*

How do you know I'm far away?

I sighed. I was quickly tiring of Jonas. If I ran tomorrow, it would be because of this dark-haired, smoking man. But for today, I had to know whether what Dad and Marci found inside this building was why Jonas was inside my head now, and why Dad and Marci had been killed. I just hoped I didn't get *myself* killed in the process. It would do me no good to stop the mind games if I ended up dead. I almost laughed out loud at my own master-of-the-obvious thought. *What am I doing, here, Jonas?*

Lexi, it's time you saw more of what we are. You might not like it, but you cannot hide from it forever. You have a responsibility to learn and use your power.

Right. *You're crazy. You and what army is going to make me?* The words sounded just as clichéd and childish inside my head.

I won't need an army, Lexi. When you see what's at the end of two more hallways, you'll be begging me to help you understand everything I know about our very existence.

I'm at a dead end.

Approach the screen to the right. Look straight into it with your eyes open wide. Try not to blink.

This was insane. I wiped my hands on my jeans. Why was I even listening to him? *I'm not doing this. I can't. Why would my retinas even be recognized?*

Because you are the clone of Sandra Whitmeyer.

Just hearing that woman's name made me wince. *You're telling me that Sandra Whitmeyer was a part of whatever is going on in this building? The woman who's been in a coma for who knows how long? And that even my retinas match hers?*

More or less.

I let out a huge breath, puffing hair out of my face. "Okay. Here goes nothing. Or everything." I positioned my head close to the security panel. Inside, a tiny mechanism with a faint red light moved across the screen, much like the inside of a photocopy machine.

Seconds later, the latch on the door clicked loudly. I tried the metal handle again and gained access.

Jonas directed me down two more hallways. The chatter inside my head got louder. The walls and doors were similar to those of a hospital, but even more similar to the hallways I had just left at The Program.

I was in the bowels of the basement. There was no sign of an exit anywhere. I had turned so many different directions, I wasn't even sure where I was anymore.

Stop. To your left is a door that leads to a courtyard in the middle of the building. It's two stories down from street level, and there's no way to exit the courtyard but back through the same entrance. You might be recognized when you walk into this area, so be ready to run back the way you came. If that happens, I'll try to get you out.

What do you mean, you'll try? I asked.

Just be ready to run.

Wait, Jonas. What am I going to see?

And ruin the surprise? I don't think so.

EIGHT

....

The room was filled with tables and chairs, like a cafeteria. Light filtered down from the skylights above—outside light that was quickly fading given the evening hour.

People buzzed about: children, teens, adults. At the tables, adults sat across from small children. They read to them, helped them with what looked like homework.

Teens of all ages talked in groups of four or five.

I scanned the room. What was this? It reminded me of Wellington's dining hall between meals, when students gathered to finish homework, study for exams, or simply catch up on gossip.

I walked slowly around the perimeter. Every once in a while, a child would look up at me. One child made eye contact and smiled. She couldn't have been more than ten years old. She was wearing a navy, patterned dress and leggings, and her hair was pulled into a loose and messy ponytail. She immediately pushed away from what she was doing and ran to me.

After giving me a hug, she crooked her finger, asking me to bend down to her. I did, and she whispered, "You look different. Where've you been?"

Every muscle in my neck and spine locked up. A cold sweat broke out across my forehead. "Do you recognize me?"

She nodded, then pulled me close again. After placing a quick kiss on my cheek, she scurried back to her table.

I stood up straight, quickly turned back toward the exit—and smacked into another person.

"Oh, I'm..." My words trailed off when I stared into eyes I knew so well that I could recite their retinal pattern. Only... something was terribly wrong.

"Who are you?" the person asked.

I studied him—his cobalt blue eyes and his sandy blond hair that was cut short enough to spike in the front. Everything about him was nearly identical to Jack. *My* Jack.

"Who am I?" I repeated back to him. *Oh my gosh, Jonas. How do I get out of here?* But Jonas wasn't inside my head anymore. He had left me. He knew what I was going to find. And he left me.

Then a different presence entered my head. A very distinct presence, unlike anything I had ever felt. Instead of fuzzy around the edges, I could clearly see the person inside my head. When this person mindspoke there was no question that it was the exact person standing before me now. *Why have we never met?* the Jack look-alike asked.

My knees buckled. This person before me, with hands identical to those that have held me and brushed hair from my face. Hands that have held my own, that have grazed my lower back. Those same, but different, hands caught me as my legs betrayed me and I slumped to the ground.

He supported my back and brought me back up. My face was inches from his. I couldn't keep my fingers from reaching out to trace the outline of his cheekbone. It was Jack. But it wasn't. Everything but the way his hair was cut.

Before I could recover, a group of men and women entered the room. Some were dressed in black suits, others wore blue

64

scrubs and white lab coats. My eyes darted from them back to the person in front of me.

Come with me. Jack's look-alike grabbed my hand and led me to a group of teenagers in the corner.

When I saw their familiar faces, I stopped dead. I curled my trembling fingers into fists.

Dia! he mindspoke.

A redhead turned in her seat, and when she saw me she said, "Holy mother of all that is good and normal in this world!"

"My thoughts exactly," I whispered, as I looked at the spitting image of Briana Howard, my archnemesis from school. Everything matched, from too much makeup to those unruly red curls.

Dia, we don't have time. Make them not see her. Jack-look-alike turned to me. *Sit. Act normal.*

"Normal," I whispered. "Right." I pulled out a chair and sat. Dia moved her textbook—*Molecular Biology*—to sit in front of me.

She then turned toward the herd, who had split up and walked from table to table. Two men approached us. "Hey, Dr. Chi," Dia said. "What's going on today?" Before my very eyes, this Briana look-alike, Dia or whatever her name was, changed in appearance. She made her chest a little larger. Her hair became tamer. Loose red curls lengthened around her face.

The eyes of the man standing beside Dr. Chi roamed from Dia's face to her chest and back up again. His lips curved upward at the edges.

"Hi, Dia. Has anyone that you didn't recognize walked through here in the last twenty minutes?" Dr. Chi asked.

"Oh gosh, no, Dr. Chi. It's just been us. Has there been another breach?"

Dr. Chi and Roaming Eyes looked at every person at the table, seeming to recognize each of us, including me. Once they were satisfied, they moved on to the next table, never answering Dia's breach-of-security question.

Okay, let's go, Jack-look-alike thought.

I stood and followed, as did Dia. My heart continued to pound. I had to get out of that basement, but I also wanted answers.

Jack's look-alike led us around tables and to the door. The exit was now guarded by a man and a woman in dark suits, very much like the people I saw in SUVs that morning. As we approached, Jack-look-alike tightened his grip on my hand and mindspoke, *Don't look at them. Dia will make sure they see someone different when they look at you.* They examined us closely, but let us pass. We headed down the hallway in the opposite direction from where I had originally come in.

The second we were out of earshot and eyeshot of everyone, I let out a huge breath. Jack's twin turned and said, "Start talking."

"Yeah, who the hell are you?" Dia asked, stopping in the middle of the hallway. "Why do you look like Dr. Whitmeyer? Only in cheap clothes?" She gave me a once-over.

"And decades younger," the clone of Jack added.

I looked down at my clothes. There was nothing cheap about a North Face jacket or my two-hundred-dollar running shoes—which I was using for more and more running these days.

When I didn't speak, Dia stepped closer. "Oh, look, Lin. She's scared."

"There you guys are," another familiar voice said behind me.

I turned slowly, bracing for another clone. Sure enough, the boy behind me looked like Jonas—except clean-shaven.

"Well, well, well. What do we have here?" He even talked like Jonas—smug arrogance. "And, oh my, you look just like her." His grin didn't fade, and he didn't really seem shocked at my likeness to the doctor. He cocked his head, studying me. *Fascinating.* The word, mindspoken by this replica of Jonas, wrapped around my brain like silk.

"Ty, maybe you can make her talk before the agents at the end of the hall discover her."

"There're agents here? Dia, she can't be here." This time, Ty grabbed my hand and pulled me forward.

I jerked it away and rubbed my chest. I didn't want Jonas or this Jonas look-alike, a.k.a. Ty, touching me. Why did everyone feel the need to touch me and pull me along? "Where am I? What is this?" I finally asked. My voice came out breathy.

My eyes darted all around me: at the hospital-like walls, the white tiled floor, and the three human clones in front of me. I searched my memories. "Seven," I whispered to myself. There were seven original clones. That's what Dad's spreadsheet said. He listed other clones he knew about, but they would all be younger, I thought. The freaks before me now were the same age as Jack, Briana, and Jonas—or pretty darn close anyway.

You will follow me right now if you don't want to be turned over to IIA agents. Again, the presence inside my head was clear. Only this time it was Ty doing the speaking, and when he mind-spoke, my feet immediately began doing what he ordered.

I walked directly behind Ty. With each step he took, I followed.

"That's what I'm talking about." Dia laughed at my obedience.

Though I couldn't stop myself from complying, it felt wrong. I was walking farther into an underground facility somewhere on the University of Kentucky campus. There was no sign of an exit, and I was completely at Ty's mercy.

~~~~~

"What are you going to do, Ty?" Dia asked. She grabbed onto his arm, but he only shook her off. *She may be our only chance,* she pleaded, switching to mindspeak, which I could still hear.

Our only chance for what? How, exactly, do you think she can help us, Dia? Ty asked, irritated.

Dia considered Ty's question. We walked down yet another long hallway. I was under Ty's spell. He had told me to follow, and though I was able to process everything going on around me, all I could do was submit to Ty's command without speaking. I was helpless, and every cell in my body hated that feeling. It was not lost on me that I had inflicted a similar kind of mind control on others.

I had entered this facility to discover whatever it was Dad had found here before he was killed. Why had he toured this facility? Did he know that this existed? That there was another Jack?

At the same time, I had hoped to find a clue as to how Jonas had so much control over me. He led me to believe I'd find answers down here. Instead, I had plummeted into a raging sea of more questions.

Lin walked behind me to my left. I could see him in my periphery. Everything about him—from his furrowed brows to how he ran his fingers through his hair as he considered the situation—screamed Jack DeWeese. I missed Jack. Though I had seen him only hours before, we now couldn't be further apart.

Who are you? Lin asked me. *Why are you here?* By the looks on the other two faces, it seemed that only I heard him.

I didn't know what to tell him. Or if I could even speak, given that Ty seemed to have control over me. I tried anyway. *Someone with less-than-good intentions led me here,* I said. I was scared to say too much, but the loathing I felt for Jonas right then...

Seeming to hear me, Lin quickened his pace, now walking directly beside me. *How did you plan to get out of here?*

A knot flipped around in my stomach. I had counted on walking out. I figured the security was for getting in. It never occurred to me that I would need permission to exit, too.

I was so blinded by the desire to know why my father was killed, and why some clone could seize my mind, that I didn't stop to consider that I might trap myself.

Suddenly, Ty left my head. I stopped in the middle of the hallway. Lin's presence disappeared as well.

"Uh-oh," Ty said.

"What?" Dia looked panicked. "They've shut us off, haven't they?"

"What does that mean, they shut you off?" Now that I was able to talk to the wack jobs in front of me, I wanted answers. "What the hell is this? Where am I? You're obviously clones. What is your purpose?"

Ty got up in my face. "It's getting ready to get really ugly down here. Any second a gas is going to be released into our air that's going to knock us all out. They obviously were somewhat prepared for your arrival..."

"Not prepared enough," Dia scoffed behind Ty. "Or they'd have her already."

My heart raced. "What kind of gas?" I swallowed hard.

Ty grabbed my arm. "The sleeping kind. We have to hurry." He urged me along, and for some reason, I went willingly this time. The sounds of voices yelling echoed through the halls behind us. "In here." Ty pushed open a door to our right.

We entered a dark room. Ty held up a small flashlight that helped us see. The room consisted of many long tables with chairs all pointing in the same direction. A classroom, maybe.

Ty faced me. "How did you get down here?"

"I don't have to tell you anything," I said, crossing my arms.

The corners of Ty's lips lifted. "No, you don't. But if you don't, I won't show you the way out. And I promise, you have a matter of minutes, maybe seconds, before you're discovered."

I thought about that. Would he really show me the way out? "Fine. I got in by the retinal scan."

"Are you that stupid?" Ty asked. "Surely you know that every person's retinal scan is completely unique. Not even identical twins or humans cloned from the same DNA share retinal patterns."

70

My hands balled into fists. I was seconds away from hitting this jerk. Jonas put me in this position. And now I stared into the eyes of his cloned twin.

Ty continued. "If you were able to get through security based on your retinas, your scan was already in the system. You walked right into their trap."

I sucked in a breath. My hands began to visibly shake.

Lin moved in and grabbed my arm just above my elbow. His gentle touch made me long for Jack. "You're obviously a clone of Sandra Whitmeyer. Did you know that already?"

I stared into his gentle eyes, debating what information to trust these three lunatics with. I wasn't in too much of a position to argue. "Yes. I am aware of that."

"Are there others besides you?" I couldn't decide if it was hope or pity I heard in Lin's voice.

I looked at the three of them, one by one. Dia's eyes urged me to answer. Ty looked at me expectantly. Lin was expressionless, patient while he waited. "Yes, I said. There are others." Did I tell them that there were others who shared their very DNA?

"Do you have powers like ours?" Lin asked.

As Lin asked his question, Ty crossed his arms and widened his stance. I was caught between good cop and bad cop. But the more I answered Lin's and Dia's questions, the more they seemed to loosen up. "Yes, but I'm afraid we don't know the extent of those abilities. You seem to be more... practiced, maybe?" Of course, that was just their ability to control minds. Did they have abilities to heal in some capacity, as well? "I have a question of my own."

"You don't get to ask the questions," Dia said.

"Let her ask." Lin rubbed my elbow. I looked from his hand to his eyes. Dia stiffened next to me.

"You said they shut your powers off. How did they do that?"

Dia reached out and grabbed Lin's arm, pulling it away and holding his hand in her own. Was she jealous? Many of her mannerisms reminded me so much of Briana. Amazing how some personality traits transfer through DNA. A chill slithered down my spine as I considered my own shared DNA with Sandra. Oh, how I hoped I was nothing like her.

"You have no idea what they're doing here, do you?" Dia asked, and I shivered visibly at the coldness in her voice. She stepped closer. "They have complete control. They decide who we are, what we do, when we do it, and eventually *where* we do it."

My stomach knotted with the way she said *where*, though I wasn't sure what that meant. "And by *they*, you mean..."

"The International Intelligence Agency. The side of the government very few see or believe exists. The IIA." Ty enunciated the acronym very slowly and clearly, confirming what I suspected. "If you're down here, it was by design. And if they want you to *stay* down here..."

A hissing sound interrupted Ty. A thin smoke spewed from vents along the top of the walls.

"What is that?" I asked, staring up at the ceiling. I lifted my arm and breathed into my elbow.

"Time for a nap," Ty answered, like this was some sort of a joke.

Lin moved frantically about the room, opening drawers and cabinets in storage counters along the edges. He was much more panicked than I'd ever seen Jack. Finally, he seemed to find what he was looking for. Pulling out two gas masks, he handed one to me, and shoved the other one at Ty. "Get her out of here. We have to trust that it can only mean good things if we get this information outside of this facility. Maybe Dia's right. If she's like us, maybe she can help."

Ty put the mask over his face and gestured for me to do the same.

"But I don't know what I can do," I said. "I don't even understand what this place is."

"Put that mask on before you pass out and are stuck here." Ty's voice was muffled through the mask. I did as I was told.

At the door, I turned back. Lin and Dia slid down a wall to the floor. Lin placed an arm around Dia, letting her lean into him, and they drifted to sleep. Jealousy erupted in my heart as I imagined those two as Jack and Briana. But I shook the image away and followed Ty.

He and I ran in the direction we had come from. I heard voices and footsteps in the not-very-far-away distance. When we turned a corner, we faced a mob of dark suits. "Stop!" one of them said.

The agents were not wearing gas masks.

"This way." Ty pulled me in a different direction.

After a couple more turns, I finally saw an exit sign, glowing red in this fog that was making some people sleep but not others.

Out of breath, I grabbed onto Ty's arm. "What did Dia mean when she said she thought I could help all of you?" My voice sounded distant and echoed through the mask.

"Dia thinks she wants out of here. She doesn't know what she's talking about." He leaned closer. "There is no escape from this life. Only different levels of acceptance."

We neared the exit door. The fog grew thicker, consuming us. Another figure appeared through the mist. When his face came into focus, I practically launched myself at the person standing there. "Jonas."

NINE

....

Jonas held Ty against the wall by his throat. The two of them were identical, with one exception—a tattoo ran down Jonas's arm, but not Ty's.

Ty struggled against Jonas's grip, gasping for air behind his gas mask. "Hi, Jonas," he half-choked, half-laughed. "So nice of you to show your face."

They knew each other?

"Did you bring the tracker?" Jonas growled.

Ty couldn't answer. His air had been cut off. I shook all over with the fear of being caught and trapped in the secure facility. At the same time, my knees locked, and my feet were superglued to the floor.

The exit was only inches away. Could I just push through it?

"No, Lexi, you can't just push through it." I jerked my head, stared hard at Jonas. He had read my mind. I searched my head. Nothing. I couldn't find his presence. "Where is it?" he asked Ty.

"In my pocket," he coughed.

"Get it."

Ty reached into his pocket and pulled out a small device. Jonas took it, closing it in his palm. Then he released Ty. "Now, go." Ty stumbled twice before he disappeared into the fog.

Jonas turned to me, his look severe at first, but then a knowing grin appeared on his lips. "Did you like what you found here?"

I stared at him in stunned silence. I opened my mouth to speak, but no words came.

I asked you a question, Lexi. He moved closer. Instinctively, I backed up against the wall, and he caged me in, with his hands on either side.

My pulse raced like a horse in the home stretch of the Kentucky Derby. I turned my head and eyed his left hand, fisted beside me and still holding the small device he'd taken from Ty. "What's in your hand?" My voice was hoarse and muffled through the gas mask.

With his other hand, he took off my mask. My eyes widened in fear as I held my breath. *You don't need this. You were never in danger of being affected by the gas.* He brushed a loose strand of hair away from my eyes. A chill spread down my arms. *Now, answer my question. What did you think? Pretty scary stuff going on here, huh?* He smiled.

Sucking in a large breath, I finally asked, "What is this place?"

"This is the International Intelligence Agency's Facility for Human Cloning. We've nicknamed it The Farm."

"You knew what I would find here," I whispered.

I did. Jonas's smile faded. *They're coming. We have to go.* He snaked his hand to the small of my back and urged me to the door, where we faced a different type of security panel from the retinal scan. The sounds of footsteps echoed down the corridor. Jonas lifted his hand and pressed his thumb onto the small box-like structure.

A small click sounded. Jonas flinched. He pulled his thumb back and sucked on it before pushing the door open, keeping one hand on my back the entire time.

A finger prick for security? I wondered if my blood type matched Sandra's. My DNA wouldn't match, since it had been altered from the original, but it was close.

On the other side of the door, we climbed a set of stairs. At the top, I looked around. "This isn't the same building I entered through." How big *was* this underground facility?

"No, it's not."

To my right was all glass. Night had fallen. On the other side of the windows, the University's library and dorm towers were lit up in the distance.

Jonas pulled me along. We were obviously in a hurry to get away from whatever *that* was in the basement.

"So, that place extended beneath more than one building?"

"Yes."

Yes? That's it? I tried to wriggle my hand from Jonas's grasp, but he just held it tighter. I tried to stop walking, but he pulled and caused me to stumble into him. "Jonas, stop. Let me go."

He pushed through a glass door, and we were suddenly on a sidewalk, headed straight toward what I thought was UK's main classroom building. Students walked about in every direction, probably on their way to or from evening classes.

When a couple of men in black suits rounded a corner ahead of us, Jonas slowed. He gestured toward a bench. *Sit. Act like the other students.*

I don't know how to act like the other students. I don't understand what just happened. He let go of my hand. I opened and closed my fingers, sore from his tight grip. My pulse thumped in my ears. I was sure I was about to go into a full-on panic attack.

Jonas turned to me. "Do you trust me now?"

Seriously? The men in black walked closer. Both were scanning the area. They looked clearly out of place. *No, I don't. Not even a little. You led me into what could have been a very dangerous situation. And have given me nothing in the form of—*

Jonas cut me off by placing his hand on the back of my neck. He leaned in and kissed me just as the suits got closer. He. Kissed. Me.

And not a little kiss. A heart-stopping, deep, sensual kiss. My hands fisted against his arms, and I did not kiss back.

The two men stopped right next to us, and looked around. I wanted to shove Jonas away, but fear of drawing attention toward us prevented me from doing so.

Jonas loosened his grip on my neck just a little and pulled back. *Bow your head away from them and giggle.*

I did as I was told and shielded my face from view while giggling like a nervous little girl, but only because the suits scared me more than Jonas did. What did they want from me? What did Jonas want? I still didn't know who ran Jack and me off the road, but it was plausible that men in suits came hand in hand with dark SUVs and my constant state of danger since school started. It appeared as if they operated right here on UK's campus, in a facility that housed other clones like me.

Finally, the suits moved on. I turned slowly to verify they were really gone. When I was sure they were, I turned toward Jonas, stood, reared back, and punched him in the face, landing a sharp blow just under his left eye. "Asshole! Don't you *ever* kiss me again. I am not yours to touch or kiss."

"Why did you do that?" His fingers lightly grazed his cheekbone, wincing at the touch. "I was only helping you." He stood. "And you have the mouth of a sailor. We'll be needing to change that."

"Uh... no. You don't get to change or control me."

Jonas raised a brow, and I squirmed under his gaze. He *did* seem to have some control. He had gotten inside my head, and I hadn't felt it. Not even a little. Jack had taught me how to sense when he had been inside my head, but Jonas slipped in and out without a single flutter.

Jonas closed the distance between us. His tall, broad-shouldered frame dwarfed my tiny stature. "Did you learn nothing last night or this morning?" He reached around and placed a hand against the small of my back, bringing me closer. He whispered into my ear. "I can see everything you see. I hear everything you think. I smell your fear, and I feel your pain. I can force you to do exactly what I desire. Anything I want, Lexi. I own you."

"And you desire that I stab my boyfriend?" I struggled against his hold. "Or kill myself in a freezing pool?"

A couple of onlookers stopped and stared. "You okay?" a passing guy asked.

Tell him you're fine.

Without even thinking, I said, "I'm good, thank you." I glared at Jonas.

"I never meant you harm. I only needed you to see the extent of your powers. *Our* powers. I needed to scare you... to make you feel the impact of true mindsiege."

"Mindsiege?"

"A state of absolute mind control, where one person cuts off all logical thinking of another, and compels that person into complete surrender."

I blinked at him. "Tell me what is going on, and tell me *now*, Jonas." It had been difficult enough just to absorb the idea that both Jack and I had these healing powers and mindspeaking abilities—and then to find out, on top of that, that Kyle, Briana, Georgia, Jonas and Fred were also clones, seven of us in all... But now, multiples too? Dad's research hadn't mentioned multiple clones of the same DNA. "So, there's a facility on campus where other clones live? Are they like us?"

Jonas tilted his head from side to side. "Yes, with some exceptions. Each of those clones has the ability to get inside your head—if that's their mission. And if their mission is to force you to hurt someone..."

"Their mission? Are you telling me that it was your *mission* to make me kill Jack?"

"More or less, yes. But I already told you I would never have you hurt Jack."

"That's not an answer." When Jonas only stared at me, I asked another question. "You said it was called The Farm. Why?"

"It's a name the clones started using. They felt like animals being herded together and raised for a common purpose." Jonas suddenly scanned the area. "We must go. This place is going to be crawling with undercover agents. And they're all looking for you."

"Why would I go anywhere with you?"

"Because like it or not, you need to know exactly what you're trying to run from and why you shouldn't. And since Jack is taking care of Addison, you need me."

I wanted to laugh at that. I was definitely showing signs of hysteria. "Why exactly are they looking for me?"

"Because you're the one who can heal Sandra."

Oh, yeah. Her.

"And because you're Peter Roslin's daughter."

I closed my eyes tight. "What do you know about my father?"

"I know that he didn't live long after discovering the IIA's human cloning facility."

~~~~~

Jonas made a cryptic phone call soon after we reached his car. He refused to tell me anything further on the short drive back to his, Georgia's, and Fred's house. He was inside my head, but it didn't feel threatening. Some moments, like when I punched him, I had free will over my actions; but at other times, I did exactly as he told me. We pulled into the drive a little after nine. Only soft lighting shone from the windows. It looked like a normal home.

"You could have dropped me off at a hotel," I said, shutting the door on his small sports car. Was I even safe here? At the sound of the alarm on his car engaging, Jonas joined me on the other side of the car. Even in the dark, I could see the swelling around his eye. I silently congratulated myself.

"Jack would have killed me if I didn't bring you back here."

"How would he have known?" I asked, mostly under my breath.

Jonas's brow shot up.

"What? *He* can see where I am, too?"

"I don't think so. He's inside waiting for you. That was the phone call I received. He said you're not answering your phone."

Inhaling, I reached around and felt my back pocket where my phone was. I had ignored the vibrations of incoming calls all evening. The desire to race into the house was strong, but the anger and hurt I had suppressed most of the day now flared. Jack hadn't believed me. Hadn't trusted me. We were supposed to have stuck together. But apparently we had different agendas.

I will get out of your head if you'll promise not to run during the night.

I turned away from the house and studied Jonas. Could I promise that? "So, you knew where I was when I left this morning?"

"Yes. And before you think I'm some sort of pervert, I am not inside your head at *all* times. I didn't need to be until I thought you might run."

So, even if I did run, he'd find me. "What do you want from me, Jonas? I can't always feel your presence inside my head. Even when I know you're there."

We'll talk more tomorrow. Go let Jack know you're okay.

"Will you tell me more about what you know about my dad?"

Tomorrow. "But Lexi, be careful who you tell about the The Farm. Your father would have chosen his confidants wisely, yet he still ended up dead." He glanced down at the jiggling keys in his hand, then back up again. "Jack doesn't know."

He said it so softly, I barely heard him. How could I keep information about The Farm from Jack? At the same time, I didn't want to lose anyone else close to me. I thought of Marci. She had obviously discovered the facility, or gotten a little too close. A chill moved through me at the thought. I didn't know if Dad had told her, or if she had seen it with her own eyes.

Jonas and I entered the house together and walked toward the voices in the kitchen. I didn't feel like my life was in danger with Jonas, but at the same time, he made me want to guard my secrets. One minute, Jonas cared about Jack and maybe even me, but the next, he put me in dangerous situations. Mostly, he terrified me.

We rounded the corner. Jonas stood right behind me. Jack started toward me as soon as he saw me, but stopped. His eyes burned into me, waiting for an invitation.

"What the hell happened to you?" Georgia asked, looking past me to Jonas.

I turned and backed away. It was my turn to smirk. The skin around his eye had turned a lovely dark indigo. The dull throb in my right hand, my price for smacking Jonas, was well worth it.

"Long story," Jonas said. He didn't even look at me.

What happened to him? Jack asked. Even in my head, his voice had an edge to it.

I turned slowly, biting my lip. Jonas's stare heated the back of my neck.

Tell me, Jack said.

Georgia's expression morphed from concern to amusement. "Serves you right, idiot," she said to Jonas after what must have been their own private mindspeak.

Jack ran a hand over his chin stubble. "Will someone please tell me what happened?"

"Your girl hit me. But I deserved it." Jonas shrugged.

"She what?" Jack's voice sounded somewhere between cautious and impressed. He continued slowly toward me. He ran his fingers along a strand of hair hanging beside my face. *We have a lot to talk about.*

I peeked up through my eyelashes, trying to assess whether he would be protective of the jerk behind me, or whether he would finally believe what I'd told him about Jonas being inside my head.

Georgia grabbed Jonas's arm, forcing him to turn and exit the room. "Come on. Let's go show Fred how you finally met your match. Give these two some privacy."

Jack slid a finger under my chin and lifted. "Tell me one thing. Are you okay?"

So much had happened. I stared into those dark blue eyes, considering his question. Finally, I nodded.

His strong arms slid around me and brought my body closer. "I've been out of my mind today," he whispered in my ear. "We have to find another way to handle this. I won't be apart from you."

A tingle started at the top of my neck and traveled down the path where his arms held me. Desire bubbled up in my chest. I couldn't breathe. "Jack," I said against his chest, inhaling the scent of ocean from his shower gel. I had missed his smell. I pulled away. "We have to talk." But what could I tell him that Jonas wouldn't hear?

"I know. Come with me." He intertwined his fingers with mine and led me to the back door. The fire lit the center of the back patio. A couple of hurricane candles were strategically placed between several of the Adirondack chairs. A smaller candle sat on one of the tables. The scent of pumpkin spice laced with the smell of wood burning filled the autumn air.

It had only been last night when Jonas had played with my mind in this very spot. Exerted control over me. Made Kyle stick his hand into a burning fire. Then today, Jonas dominated everything I did, witnessed, and even thought. And then, there was Ty. It was all so confusing. Yet Jonas seemed to be the key to it all.

He had information I wanted—information about who could get inside my head and, hopefully, how to stop them. What price was I willing to pay for that knowledge?

Jack led me to a corner of the patio. A large outdoor cushion was laid out with throw pillows and a blanket. I couldn't help but wonder two things: Was Jonas really out of my head? And how was I going to tell Jack what I had to do next?

He turned to me. With a tight grip on my hand, he again pulled me close. A tear welled up in the corner of my eye. *Don't cry. I know what we need to do next, Lexi.* Jack's eyes bored into mine. I hadn't felt his presence inside my head, yet he heard me. Had I lost all ability to sense others inside my mind?

We? I replied.

He nodded. *You can't think about that next step right now, though, okay?* Something about the insistent look on his face— the way his brows furrowed, the dilation of his pupils—made me want to back away. When I pulled on his hand, he held tighter. *Do you understand? You can't think about anything other than me right now.*

Did I understand him? I studied his eyes. The lines of his face. The way his hand gripped mine. His other hand slid under my fleece jacket and burned through the fabric of my shirt on my lower back.

"You believe me," I whispered. He knew Jonas was inside my head and controlling many of my thoughts and actions.

He lifted a finger to his lips. "Shh." Something new must have happened to make him believe me.

TEN

....

When did you know?" I whispered.

Jack's fingers lightly brushed my arms. He held me close, my back to his chest, as we lay on the cushions by the fire. "I knew when I saw the cut on Jonas's neck and Georgia in the hospital bed." He nuzzled his face into my hair and kissed the back of my head. "You would never harm another human being unless you absolutely had to."

"You sure about that?"

"Positive. And Georgia never would have intervened unless she seriously thought you were going to hurt Jonas." He pulled in a deep breath and continued to feather my arms with his fingertips. "After I helped Seth, I came back to get you... to tell you I believed you. I had planned to confront Jonas. But you were both gone."

"I was so powerless when he got inside my head, Jack. My mind. My body..."

"Shhh. Not now, baby." His breath warmed the back of my neck.

"What do we do now?" I asked.

"Now, you sleep. I'll watch over you."

It wasn't quite what I meant, but sleep did sound good. My mind needed rest. We'd figure out the rest in the morning. I wriggled in his arms, turning over to face him. "What about you? You need to sleep, too."

"Don't worry about me." He lifted a hand and lightly brushed it along the skin of my forehead, down my cheek, my arms, letting it finally rest at my waist, his thumb grazing my ribs. Leaning in, he touched my lips with the lightest of kisses.

"What will we do tomorrow?" I asked against his lips. My words slurred from exhaustion.

"Shhh." He leaned in again. This time he pressed his lips firmly against mine, deepening the kiss. "Sleep. Now."

I nuzzled into his chest, and let sleep find me.

~~~~~

I woke to the sound of whispers.

I tried to open my eyes, but my lids were so heavy. And it was dark. We were outside, where Jack and I had fallen asleep by the fire. Except the fire had died out. "Jack." My voice sounded raspy.

Lexi, don't talk. Don't make a sound.

My body stiffened, now alert. *Why? What's wrong?*

I felt his hand on my neck. *I need you to sit up.* His hand slid down my spine as he helped me rise. Jack and another guy knelt beside me in the dark. I felt someone touch the waistline of my jeans. "What are you..." I started, but I was cut off by a sharp sting to my hip. "Ouch! What the hell?"

Lexi, a voice said. *Can you hear me?*

I knew that voice. That was a voice I'd heard in my sleep before. Kyle. I tried to focus. Still feeling the pain in my hip, I reached down and rubbed the spot that felt very much like the sting of a bee. *Did you just inject me with something?* My eyelids grew heavy again.

Just something to help us keep you safe, Jack said. *I need you to trust me.*

Okay. I recognized the state I was in. I was dreaming, but I was moving. And alert. Exactly the way I'd felt when Kyle helped me escape Wellington last Friday—after I'd lost consciousness from healing Addison and Jack. Kyle was able to control my actions while I was in a sleeping state.

How about a surprise adventure? Kyle asked. *I want you to come with me.*

Where are we going? I asked.

It wouldn't be a surprise if I told you.

Is Jack coming? I'm not going unless Jack is going.

Yes, I'm coming, Jack said. *I'm going to help you stand.*

I surveyed the area around the fire pit. As in previous dreams, I could focus on where I was, but the figures in front of me were a little blurred.

I pushed myself to my feet. Jack grabbed my elbow and helped me stand.

"You have complete control of her?" Jack asked, like I wasn't even there.

"Yeah. I got her. The injection I gave her should render her unconscious for a couple of hours."

"That should be plenty," Jack said.

I giggled. "Listen to you. 'Rendered.' Nice big word."

Jack and Kyle traded glances, and I realized immediately that I wasn't talking normally. But they seemed to shrug off my drunkenness.

"Okay, let's go." Jack grabbed my hand and led me, not into the house, but around to the side and out the gate. Kyle walked close by.

On the other side of the gate, we followed the fence along the neighbor's property. The swings on the neighbor's swing set blew in the breeze, the image fuzzy. The rusty chains squeaked against the metal poles. The sound echoed inside my head. With all of my senses heightened, I had to place my hands over my ears when the train whistled.

"Are we going on the train?" I asked. "I like the train. We have to run fast to get on."

Jack narrowed his brows at Kyle. "How big a dose did you give her?"

"She's fine."

They talked about me as if I weren't there. It kind of pissed me off.

"Lexi," Kyle said. "We are going on the train. Can you run fast?"

"Absolutely." To prove it, I began running in place.

Kyle laughed, holding his stomach. Jack used his free hand to shove Kyle. "Knock it off. I don't have to remind you what I'll do to you if something happens to her because of your stupidity."

"Hey, this was your idea."

"Let's just focus, okay?"

Suddenly a light shone on us. The train was coming. "There it is," I said. "I'm ready. Let's go."

Jack tightened his grip on my hand.

Kyle stepped beside me. "Okay Lexi, focus on me. We're going to run together. When you pick up enough speed, grab onto the handle of one of the cars. When I count to three, you're going to pull yourself onto the train."

"Got it."

The first car passed us. Jack dropped my hand and began to run. I followed, and Kyle brought up the rear.

mindsiege

When we picked up enough speed, Jack grabbed onto a piece of metal sticking out from the train and hurled himself into an empty car. He reached out his hand for me, but my legs didn't feel like my own. I couldn't get enough speed.

Lexi, I'm begging you, Jack said. *Run harder. Grab my hand.*

Kyle ran directly on my heels. "Grab his hand, Lexi," Kyle yelled. I reached out. Our fingertips touched, but then broke apart.

Jack ran his hand through his hair, then reached out again. *Come on, baby. Try again. Run faster.*

I lifted my hand again. The very tips of my fingers grazed his. Slowly, my entire hand made contact.

He counted. "One, two, three!"

I pushed off my feet, and Jack pulled at the same time. I landed with a thud right on top of his chest.

Kyle landed in a heap beside us.

"You okay?" Jack asked, smoothing my hair and eyeing the rest of my body.

I nodded. It was so dark inside the train car that I could barely make out Jack's face. "Why are we on the train, Jack?"

"Don't ask questions yet, okay?"

Jack pushed up and moved to sit against the wall of the car beside Kyle. I sat beside him.

"The night you helped us escape Wellington," Jack said to Kyle, "you told me you couldn't force Lexi to do something she didn't want to do."

Kyle appeared to think about that. "I don't know if it was so much that I *couldn't*, but I wouldn't want to. At the time, you both thought that I had tried to kill Lexi. I wanted you to know I wouldn't harm her."

91

"Yet here we are," Jack said. "She's going to be so mad when she wakes up."

I reached up and smoothed the line that formed between Jack's eyes. "Why am I going to be mad?"

He touched a finger to my nose. "No questions, remember?"

ELEVEN

....

"I have a chai tea latte for you," Jack whispered in my ear.

I rolled over and buried my face in the pillow beside me, breathing in the smell of fabric softener. My head ached, and I wasn't sure why. Slowly, I grew more and more conscious. I must have been exhausted the night before, because I struggled to bring myself out of the deep sleep I had been in.

I returned to my back and opened my eyes, squinting against the light. Jack was the first thing I saw. I liked that. I smiled.

Kneeling beside the bed, he was fully dressed in a navy polo and khakis. His hair was damp, and he smelled of shampoo. Lines formed between his eyes as he studied me.

The events of last night scrolled through my mind. I remembered being by the fire pit. Jack held me. We talked. Not about anything specific. Not about the clones I discovered yesterday or about Jonas's control over me. I must have fallen asleep, but not for long.

I remembered voices waking me.

I was dreaming. No.

Kyle was there.

The train.

I studied Jack's face again. His school uniform.

As realization dawned, I pushed myself up and looked around. My smile faded. "Where am I?"

"Lex," Jack said, a warning in his voice.

93

I narrowed my eyes. "What have you done?"

Calm down, please. I did what I had to do.

"What you had to do?" I pushed the blanket off of me and climbed out of bed. Still dressed in jeans and a T-shirt, I ran to the only window in the room and looked out onto... the front lawn of Wellington Boarding School. Closing my eyes, I lifted a hand to drill two fingers into my forehead. I let out a long breath and whipped around. He took a step backwards. "You brought me to Wellington?"

I paced while squeezing the bridge of my nose. I had worked so hard to get away from Wellington, a school where I'd once felt safe and had hoped to graduate from. But everything changed when Cathy DeWeese turned it into a prison for cloned freaks.

I stopped pacing and took in the room. It wasn't a dorm room. A full-sized bed stood against one wall. Beside the one window were an armchair and a small bookshelf. It was cozy. "Where exactly are we?"

"This is Coach Williams's apartment."

"What?" I didn't even know my swim coach—an ex-FBI agent hired by my father—lived on campus. That did make him closer to me, which could have been by design. For protection, maybe; protection I hadn't even known I needed.

Jack didn't move from his spot against the wall. His eyes watched me carefully as I glared at him. "Why, Jack? Why did you bring me back to Wellington?" Did Jonas know I was gone? I searched my mind. Nothing. My pulse raced, wondering what he would do when he discovered where I was. When he discovered I was right where he wanted me.

"You thought I didn't believe you."

"That's not a reason." I felt the fire spread up my neck and onto my cheeks.

"I had to get you away from Jonas. He was controlling you. He can't do that here."

Uncontrollable laughter bubbled up and out of my throat. "Is that what you think?"

"What do you mean?"

I stepped up to him. I stood so close I could hear his heavy breaths. "Jonas doesn't need to be close to control me, Jack. He can hear my thoughts, see what I'm seeing, and force my hand—anytime, anywhere. Not even the gates of Wellington are going to keep me safe from his mind invasion." Or from the other clones with a mission, according to Jonas.

"Then we have to find a way to block him." Jack reached out and slid his fingers between mine. "You block me all the time."

I did, but with Jonas, it seemed different. "That easy, huh?" I scoffed.

"No, but we'll figure it out." Jack rubbed his free hand along the back of his neck. "Seth might be able to help."

"Seth. Good ol' Seth," I mocked. I definitely wanted to talk to him. Awfully convenient that the IIA just happened to be cloning humans so close to where Seth just happened to set up the original location of The Program.

"What happened to me taking on a new identity and running so that your mom and other crazy scientists couldn't control me?"

Jack straightened, rolled his shoulders. "That was before."

"Before what?"

"Before you took off yesterday, went all rogue on me, and held a scalpel to Jonas's neck. Before Marci was murdered very

95

near The Program. And before..." He grabbed my other hand and pulled me closer. "Before Jonas controlled your mind so fully that you were willing to come back to his house with him. I don't think your life is in danger with him, but I think something strange is going on. And it's forcing you to make decisions you wouldn't normally make."

"I wouldn't have cut him badly." Would I have?

"I'm sorry I doubted you." He touched my face with the tips of his fingers, tracing the line along my cheekbone down to my chin. "It just didn't make sense. He had helped us. The night of the accident."

"It wasn't an accident, Jack. Someone drugged me and intentionally tried to run us off the road."

"I know." Pulling his hand away, he stretched and closed his fingers into fists, then reached for the chai tea he had set on the nightstand and handed it to me. "I know we thought Wellington was dangerous, but right now, this might be the only place we're safe."

"What about Georgia? Will she be okay?" We had just left her there with Jonas.

"Georgia can take care of herself. She refused to come with us. She thinks Jonas is being controlled by a stronger power and is convinced she can help him."

Yeah, that's what he kept telling me, but that didn't change the fact that every time I was controlled I saw Jonas inside my head. "How did you and Kyle know you'd be able to get me out of there last night?" Jonas had said he would stay out of my head while I was with Jack, but I wasn't sure I believed that.

"Kyle seemed to think I'd be able to monitor Jonas's invasion into your mind as long as I was touching you. I could sense Jonas there until you fell asleep. Soon after, Jonas went to bed, and Kyle came. We thought that as long as we kept you unconscious, we'd buy ourselves enough time to get out of there. Also... we tranqed Jonas."

I laughed. Served Jonas right. "How does Kyle know so much?" Until last Friday, I didn't even know Kyle knew we were both cloned.

"Kyle has actually studied supernatural abilities of the mind ever since he began entering people's dreams. And when you were able to prevent me from getting sick the other day when I healed his burns, he thought maybe our connection was stronger when touching."

Made sense, I guessed. I nuzzled my face into his chest and snaked my hands around to his back, careful not to spill the tea. Our connection *was* strong, especially when touching. "Why didn't you just tell me what you were planning? I might have gone willingly." Probably, anyway. "You took quite a chance that Kyle would be able to direct my body to leap onto that moving train."

The muscles in Jack's back stiffened. "I know. But I couldn't have you knowing or thinking about any of it. If Jonas knew what we were planning... I just couldn't take the chance that he'd stop us or hurt you." He slipped a finger under my chin and lifted my face to his. Leaning down, he brushed his lips across mine. "I do want to know one thing. Why did you give Jonas a black eye?"

I tried to look away, but Jack held my chin tighter. I swallowed hard. "He kissed me."

Jack closed his eyes. *That's all, though, right? He didn't touch you in any other way?*

"No, caveman. Jonas kissed me, and I took care of it by punching him in the face."

"Why did he kiss you?"

"IIA agents were following us." I backed away from him, breaking contact, and took a drink of the chai tea. "He wanted to throw them off. And there's some—" I started to tell Jack about the other clones and The Farm, but I couldn't form the words. Something stopped me.

Or someone.

Jonas.

Hi, Lexi. You can't tell him, yet.

~~~~~

"Are you ready for this?" Jack framed my face with his palms.

Gripping the starfish hanging on a chain just beneath my collarbone, I nodded and said, "As ready as I'll ever be."

"Just remember. You hold the power. Cathy knows what you can do. She's seen it firsthand, but obviously needs you— needs us—or she and Seth wouldn't have moved The Program from UK Hospital to Wellington."

"And she doesn't know how much we know." Especially how much *I* know.

"That's right. For now, we'll keep it that way. Once we've read more of your dad's journals, we'll confront who we need to."

"So we'll play dumb."

"And nice." There was a warning behind those two words.

"Why, Jack DeWeese, whatever do you mean?"

After a lingering kiss on the forehead, Jack opened the door to the school's large boardroom, down the hall from Dean Fisher's office.

Stopping just inside, I surveyed the people sitting at the table. President Wellington sat at the far end of the table. Beside him, Dean Fisher smiled, his expression warm and inviting. I had always gotten good vibes from that man. But today, everybody was the enemy.

Kyle sat beside President Wellington, his uncle and only family member that I knew of. His lips curved into a smirk as soon as our eyes met. I'd deal with him and his crazy train-hopping later.

To the other side of Dr. Wellington was his sister, Jack's mother for all intents and purposes, Cathy DeWeese. Just seeing her made a chill skip down my spine.

Where's your father? I asked Jack.

Still out of town, according to Cathy.

As we walked closer and stood at the head of the large table, Cathy pushed back from the table and rose.

"Sit down, Mother," Jack said. He leaned into the table, his fingers spread wide against the dark wood. "I told you yesterday that Lexi would probably never set foot on Wellington's campus again."

"I believe you said you wouldn't either." Cathy sat back down and crossed her arms.

I glanced sideways at Jack. He shrugged. He hadn't shared with me that he'd told his mom he wouldn't return to Wellington.

"Well," he started again. "Things have changed. Lexi changed my mind."

I suppressed the urge to look at him wide-eyed again, for fear of undermining whatever it was he was doing.

"Lexi changed your mind?" Dr. Wellington asked. "Was this before or after you bulldozed through my school's new fence?"

"Careful, R.W.," Dean Fisher said, then returned his attention to us. "Let them talk."

"Lexi and I have returned to Wellington on a trial basis. We—"

Cathy stood again. "You're hardly in a position to tell us what you will or won't do on any kind of basis."

Jack straightened, rolling his shoulders back. "That's where you're wrong, Mommy Dearest. I'm eighteen. And Lexi will be soon."

Dean Fisher motioned with his hand for Cathy to settle down. A very strange unspoken message transpired between them.

"So, as I was saying, Lexi and I are at Wellington to learn. We agree to abide by school rules as we always have, but we will not be held prisoner. We will come and go as we please— as we did before you added all the extra security."

"That was for you," Dr. Wellington said. "To keep you safe, not to hold you prisoner."

"Good, then we shouldn't have a problem," Jack said. "The extra security is appreciated as long as it's not used to hold us hostage."

Cathy squirmed in her seat. "Everything we've added... bringing The Program to Wellington, the extra security... that was for the two of you. And Kyle." She gestured to Kyle, who nodded in acknowledgement.

I cocked my head, eyeing Cathy. Did she not know about the others—Briana, Jonas, Georgia and Fred? What was Cathy's motive in all this?

"And, like I said, we appreciate it," Jack said. He was good at the "nice" game.

Cathy relaxed in her seat. She traded glances with Dean Fisher and President Wellington, nodding in some silent agreement.

"So," Dean Fisher began. "I guess neither of you have missed much school. A lot has happened since Friday night, though. Are you both okay, physically?"

We looked at each other, then nodded.

"One last thing." Our heads both snapped toward Cathy. "You will attend all Program classes. I'm sorry that Friday night was a shock to you. And I'm sorry, Lexi, that your father was less than honest with you about how you were created... and what you were designed for..."

My spine straightened and I stepped up to the table, ready to blast Cathy DeWeese for even suggesting that my late father was anything less than a perfect dad to me. It wasn't her place to criticize him. Jack grabbed my hand and held tight. *Just let it go. You'll get an opportunity to say your piece later. We're playing nice, remember.*

"...But if you're here to learn, you will meet with Seth as soon as possible to get The Program integrated into your schedules."

Seth nodded, still silent.

"Great. Fine." Jack pulled on my hand and started to turn.

We were just about to the door when Cathy spoke again. "Oh, and one last condition. For Lexi." We turned. I gripped

Jack's hand tighter. My other hand clenched into a fist, antici-
pating what this woman might say. "I'm going to need your
help with Sandra."

TWELVE

....

How did you turn out so amazing, when she's so... so..." Jack raised his brow at me, mid-rant. "...So *not* amazing."

"Because she and I don't share a single ounce of DNA?"

"Smart aleck."

Though it felt like I'd been away from campus for weeks, I'd only missed one day of classes and four mornings of swim practice. I wanted to go for a swim right then, but Jack convinced me that getting back into our classes was more important.

We walked toward the dorms. So far, no one even looked at us funny. It was as if Friday had never happened. To the other students, it probably hadn't.

"Remember, Cathy's syringe and drug were not meant for you last Friday," Jack reminded me.

"But she didn't tell me that. She tried to force me to heal Sandra even then. She held that syringe filled with God-knows-what like a murder weapon if I didn't obey her."

"I know, but she promised the weapon was meant for Sandra. Sandra is her enemy, not you."

"Uh-huh. I just happen to look like Sandra." And I just happen to be the one who can bring Sandra out of this coma that she put herself in.

What do you mean she put herself in the coma? Jack asked. *How do you know that?*

Seth told me she injected some sort of genetic manipulating substance into her own brain. I snapped my head toward him. "Wait. I didn't direct that thought at you. I've been blocking you."

We were almost to the girls' dormitory. Jack grabbed my arm and stopped me. "I don't understand why you're so insistent on blocking me completely, but sometimes your thoughts just slip through. I don't know."

I averted my eyes, tried to pull away, but Jack tightened his grip. A couple of freshman girls stumbled out of the dorm, giggling as they walked passed us.

"Lexi, look at me."

"What?" I sighed, finding his eyes. Did I really have to explain how I didn't want him inside my head?

"What is going on with you?"

Silence built up between us like steam trapped in a teakettle. He continued to stare. "I don't want to live like this. I live in constant fear of someone inside my head. Listening to my every thought. Manipulating my mind and my actions." I sucked in a breath. "I have to find a way to shut you and anyone else out."

"You think I'm manipulating you?"

I cocked my head and smiled. "I'm back at Wellington because of you, after vowing not to return."

"Hmmm. Good point." His forehead wrinkled. "But you do see why Wellington is the place where we might find answers?"

"No, but it's a place we can live while we search." Especially since the few people I knew outside this school were now dead.

He rubbed his thumb across the back of my hand and started to lean toward me. I thought he was going to kiss me, but his grip tightened and his face scrunched up as he pulled back.

"What is it?" I asked.

"It's Jonas."

"What's Jonas? Where?"

"He's inside your head."

I searched the edges of my mind for any sign of that tattooed jerk. "Why can't I sense him? He's said nothing."

But he's there. I can sense him right now while I'm touching you. The question is: Can he sense me when I'm inside your head?

I shivered, and Jack pulled me into a tight hug. *This is why we're at Wellington.* He kissed the top of my head. *Go get what you need. I'll meet you in class.*

~~~~~

Mrs. McMillan frantically scribbled notes across the dryerase board as I entered Advanced Biology. Danielle, my best friend and roommate, sat up straighter when she saw me. I immediately wanted to hug her, but I was late, and there wasn't an empty seat near her.

It was crazy to think that it had only been a few days since I'd seen Danielle. A long weekend, really.

Kyle, who sat next to Danielle, lifted his chin in a silent hello. I had yet to discover if my roommate knew that Kyle was the one she sketched for the art show last Friday. She claimed she had met a mystery boy in her dreams and would marry him some day. Did she know Kyle was the one she "planned to marry"? She could definitely do worse, but could I let my best friend fall for a cloned freak?

I forced a smile at them both before I slid into a seat across the room.

"Today, class, we're going to have a little quiz."

Shit! I slunk down in my seat just slightly. I'd fail a quiz for sure.

Mrs. McMillan passed out the quizzes. When she got to my desk, she handed me two pages stapled together and said, "Welcome back, Miss Matthews. Do the best you can."

All I could do was stare blankly at the questions on material I hadn't studied. I was sure most of it had been reviewed the previous day in my absence.

Want my help?

The muscles in my back stiffened at the sound of Jonas's words. *No, I don't want or need your help.*

Really? You don't think you need my help? Then I obviously didn't explain the situation you're in very well.

I searched my head, and found Jonas's presence sitting just on the edge. How can I see him so clearly at some times, but not so much at others? With everything in me, I wanted to knock him off that edge.

I worked through the thirty questions. At least they were multiple-choice. I had a twenty-five percent chance of getting each one correct.

And a seventy-five percent chance of getting each one wrong, Jonas said. *Speaking of... The answer to number five is—*

Stop. I don't want to know. I was not going to cheat on a stupid biology quiz.

That was a nice trick last night, by the way. Instead of being angry, Jonas sounded impressed. *I'm wondering if Kyle and Jack would have succeeded in getting you to leave if Jack hadn't tranquilized me.*

I smiled. *You kind of got what you deserved.*

Don't sound so pleased, Lexi.

Hey, you tranqed me first. I massaged my temples, irritated by the banter. *What do you want from me, Jonas?* My hand shook so badly, my pencil slipped through my fingers and fell on the floor.

I want you to convince Jack that I mean you no harm, and that you both need me at Wellington.

What? No way. Not going to happen.

I could force you.

If you could force me, you would have done so already.

I want you to get up right now and take your test to Mrs. McMillan. Tell her to excuse you from the quiz and class. You're failing it miserably. Force her to give you a chance to make up the quiz tomorrow.

Without even thinking, I did as Jonas instructed, and my teacher fell for my mindspeaking, hook, line, and sinker.

Once in the hallway, I dug through my bag for tissues, and treated a lovely nosebleed.

Don't you want to be rid of those nosebleeds?

Of course I wanted to end all nosebleeds forever, but I was not going to admit that. Not if it meant conceding I needed Sandra. *What I want is to know what you know about my dad and his murder.*

Ahhh, yes. Well, like I told you, your dad discovered the IIA's human cloning project facility.

How do you know this?

I overheard a conversation. Your father trusted the wrong person with this information. He discovered The Farm, told someone, and the next thing I knew, he was murdered. Find out who he told. You'll be closer to his murderer.

Was Jonas right? Did one of Dad's trusted friends murder him? Maybe not plant the bomb in his car, but set the events in motion.

Jonas, I have one more question. I searched every corner of my brain. No sign of Jonas. *Jonas!* Great. Always there when I don't want him, gone when I need him.

The bell rang. Any second now, the hallway would be filled with students. Though I wanted to see my roommate, there were many students I didn't want to talk to. Not now.

I jogged to the girls' bathroom. A face I barely recognized stared back at me from the mirror, complete with dark circles, pale cheeks, eyebrows that needed plucking, and hair that needed washing. I was a mess.

The door squeaked behind me. I turned to find my nemesis, Briana, staring at me. It always amazed me how she made a school uniform look attractive, sexy even. Her skirt was shorter than most. She wore a more fitted white blouse. It also helped that Briana spent more than the ten minutes I had on hair and makeup. Her long red hair curled into loose waves. Blush, eyeshadow, eyeliner, and gloss were applied just so.

"Where the hell have you and Jack been?"

Upon hearing her demeaning attitude, I imagined her eyeliner and mascara streaking down her face after I held her head in a toilet for a few seconds.

"Why? Did you miss me?"

"You? No," she scoffed.

Of course, she missed Jack. "We missed one day of school, Bree. What's your problem?"

She shifted on her feet and clutched a book she was holding close to her chest. "I need to talk to Jack. Where is he?" If I hadn't known Bree so well, I could have sworn her eyes were starting to tear.

I cocked my head, studied her, and thought of Dia. I wondered if Bree had similar mind trick capabilities. Did she know it? *Jack, where are you? Bree's got me cornered in the girl's bathroom. She's acting a little neurotic, and she's looking for you.*

I'm checking on Addison. Tell her you're getting ready to meet me at lunch and invite her to join us.

Seriously?

Yes.

"Well, Bree, since you asked so nicely, and because we're such great friends, I can tell you that Jack is meeting me for lunch. You're welcome to join us if you'd like."

Bree turned on her heels and headed for the door. Before exiting, she turned back. "You need some mascara or something. You look like crap."

Wow, she's a piece of work. A hot piece of work, but sheesh. Want to teach her a lesson? Jonas asked.

No, I don't. What did that mean, anyway? This didn't sound like the same Jonas I had just spoken with. This Jonas scared me. *Please get out of my head, Jonas.* Bree left while I continued my silent argument with Jonas.

No can do. I need you to do something for me.

No.

109

You don't have a choice, Lexi. Do you remember how it felt to hold a knife above your head with its tip pointed at Jack? Can you imagine what it would have looked like if you had actually rammed it into his chest? The blood. The look in his eyes when he opened them and saw that the girl he loves was murdering him in his sleep.

What do you want me to do? Even inside my head, my voice sounded small. This was definitely not the same Jonas who'd helped me evade IIA agents the previous night. I was starting to believe that it was, in fact, someone else invading my mind through Jonas's. But the fact remained: I was seeing Jonas any time this person got inside my head.

I want you to go to the infirmary, now, and tell no one where you're going.

THIRTEEN

··

You got me here, now what? I asked Jonas as I stood in the basement of the infirmary.

The walls around me were stark white, clinical. The new location of The Program looked like a surgical center, not a place for learning like I had expected. The Program was supposed to be a way for those of us at Wellington to challenge ourselves, to further our medical studies before we completed high school. No one had ever led me to believe The Program would be a crash course in how to use my brain to bring people back from near-death.

The hallway was quiet. Each movement I made echoed off of the bare walls and tiled floor.

Last door on the right. You know where we're going.

He was leading me to where we'd left Sandra and Addison on Friday night. I eased my way down the hallway. I heard no voices as I walked, only the sound of my own running shoes stepping lightly. My heartbeat quickened. I didn't want to see Addison without Jack, and I didn't want to see Sandra at all.

I pushed the door open. Memories of Friday flooded back. Of freeing Jack from the drug that had left him unconscious. Of healing Addison's brain injuries. Of Cathy, Seth, Dr. Wellington, and their mysterious intentions for me and The Program.

I had fled Wellington and the overbearing forces of Cathy and The Program to keep from being used like a pawn in a chess match, yet here I was. And now I was being manipulated by a different force.

I moved into the room slowly. Addison was gone from the bed she had lain in three days ago. Sandra still lay lifeless in a bed on the end, her brown hair tousled against the pillow. Her chest rose and fell slowly, the only outward indication that her heart continued to beat.

The door closed behind me with an insignificant click that nevertheless thundered in my oversensitive mind. Only when I was completely in the room did I notice the woman sitting at a small desk. Her eyes were wide, and darted from me to Sandra and back. "Oh, my freaking goodness," she said. She stood, took two steps, and fainted, hitting her head hard on a chair behind her as she fell.

I ran to her side. "Crap!" I checked her head for blood. Nothing. Good.

I laid her head back down gently and ran to one of the empty beds for a pillow. After placing it behind her head, I looked for a way to call for help.

Make sure she doesn't have a concussion. You know how.

Jonas was right. I knew how. I examined her brain for signs of injury, but found nothing. *I think she's okay. She probably just fainted from seeing a replica of the woman lying in the hospital bed.* I'd faint, too, if I thought it would help.

Just leave her there.

What? I can't leave her.

Yes, you can. Now pull a chair over and sit beside Sandra. We need to talk.

I rolled a chair over and sat next to my genetic original, my back straight and stiff. My knee bounced up and down as I examined the facial features of the woman in front of me. It still unnerved me to see what I would like in about thirty years. *Now what?*

I need you to show me Sandra's brain. Show me what is keeping her in a coma.

I ran my fingers along Sandra's forehead and down her cheeks. The coma she was in masked the real Sandra. Her vulnerability overshadowed the personality my father told me about in his notes. I thought back to the email someone sent me—an email from Sandra to an agent with the IIA, which implicated Dad and Dr. DeWeese in her immoral and illegal schemes.

Dad said she had sold her research to the IIA and even consulted with them. After visiting The Farm, I now knew that she more than advised the IIA. Much more.

At Jonas's insistence, I pictured Sandra's brain. Immediately the colorful patterns of neurons firing came into view. The criss-crossing of axons—the paths between neurons—were shining like multi-colored glow necklaces found at amusement parks after dark. I honed in on the pooling of liquid at the base of the brain, where cerebral fluid had leaked. This was what was causing Sandra to remain unconscious. The amount of liquid accumulating looked even worse than I remembered from Friday.

What do you see? Jonas asked.

I gave Jonas my assessment. *Seth said Sandra injected herself with some sort of genetic manipulating substance.*

The question is, What are we going to do about it?

I thought my decision to do nothing was a good one, and assuming Jonas's question was rhetorical, I decided he wasn't expecting an answer. Besides, I wasn't sure what would happen if I flushed this substance from Sandra's head. The act of bringing her out of a coma could make me extremely ill. Or what if Jack was right? What if we didn't know the consequences of my healing abilities yet? I certainly didn't want to suffer a grand mal seizure like Georgia had.

And it might not even work.

Minutes passed. Jonas had fallen silent. I searched the corners of my mind for him. Having him in my head felt like a lingering illness—like the tail end of a flu where I was mostly better, but a dull ache still hung out along my temple.

I yawned, barely able to keep my eyes open as I sat and waited for further instruction from the boy with control over me. I had barely slept the night before, thanks to the train-jumping.

I rested my forehead against my folded arms on Sandra's bed, thinking I'd just close my eyes for a few minutes, and hoping Jonas would move along and harass some other poor unsuspecting soul.

"Lexi," someone whispered in my ear.

Moaning, I buried my face deeper into the bed. The scent of cigarette smoke reached my nostrils even as I inhaled the smell of detergent from the bed sheets. I didn't want to wake up.

The realization of where I was came crashing back. I raised my head. Sandra remained comatose a few inches from me. I swiveled around slowly in my chair to find Jonas sitting, his legs crossed, on top of the neighboring bed. A cigarette hung from one corner of his lips.

"You can't smoke in here." My eyes circled the room. It was a stupid thing to say, but it was the first thought that entered my mind when I saw the person who was seizing my mind. My heart beat faster as panic set in and I remembered where I was. And now Jonas was actually in the room? I stood and backed away. The nurse remained on the floor by the desk. "How did you get in here?"

"In where?"

"Don't be obtuse, Jonas. How did you get inside Wellington?"

He cocked his head. The edges of his lips curled into a smirk. "I can get anywhere you are, Lexi."

I squeezed the bridge of my nose. "You're in my dream."

"Not exactly." He took a drag, then made smoke circles in the air. "This is my first lesson for you."

"Lesson?"

"I need something from you, and I'm willing to pay for it."

I crossed my arms. "I'm listening." Maybe we were finally getting to the root of Jonas's irritating existence inside my head.

"I need you to heal Sandra."

"No." I stood up taller.

Jonas smiled. "You haven't even heard what I'm willing to give in return."

"Why would I help Sandra?" I could think of several reasons not to: Cathy wanted me to, Jonas wanted me to, and it would make me terribly sick. Healing Addison had landed me in the bed for two days. Not to mention, why would I fix this woman with a god complex who put herself into a coma by playing recklessly with her own scientific experiments? She knew no limits.

Jonas's smile faded. "There are reasons not to heal Sandra, but the reasons to fix her far outweigh the risks."

"And those are?"

"There are two. One, I'd train you to block me and the others who are capable of controlling your mind and actions. Consider it my thank-you."

I was still hoping Jack, Kyle, and I could figure that out together. That was part of the reason Jack had forced me to run back to Wellington.

"And two," Jonas continued. "Sandra made sure the clones she created suffered consequences when using their special abilities. This was to prevent any one of us from going all rogue on her."

"That sounds more like a reason to let her rot."

"She knows how to cure your bloody noses, and your unconsciousness after you heal matters of the brain. She can remove Jack's extreme nausea after he treats injuries."

"And she can get rid of your panic attacks?" I asked, assuming that his panic attacks had everything to do with controlling me. Served him right.

"And Kyle's blindness."

Kyle longed to use his ability without experiencing temporary blindness, and I hated that Jack felt sick every time he healed someone. It would be near impossible to learn the extent of our abilities if we fell ill anytime we used our minds the way they were designed to be used.

The simple answer would be to tell Jonas no. I still wasn't convinced I would ever use these unnatural abilities—however, what my friends chose wasn't up to me. What if their destiny in life was to help others as only they could? I didn't want them to suffer if there was a way for me to help them. Who was I to think I had all the answers for everybody else?

Furthermore, I had a strong desire to learn how our minds were wired. I needed to block out Jonas—and anyone else with this mindsieging ability.

"Okay, so what's my first lesson?"

"So, you agree? You'll heal Sandra's brain?" His voice showed a hint of excitement.

"I didn't say that. I want to know what you're offering." I was willing to do just about anything to regain control of my mind from Jonas.

He cocked his head. The corners of his lips lifted. "You don't get it, do you?" He uncrossed his legs and slid off the bed.

"Get what? That you want me to do something that might very well kill me?"

He walked close enough to me that I could reach out and touch him. I was tempted to do just that. Would I be able to feel him if I did? Wasn't this just a dream?

He took another step, then reached out and grabbed my wrist. His fingers wrapped around one by one, gripping my wrist with pressure that told me he was very much right there in front of me. With a quick jolt, he spun me so that I was facing away from him and staring at Sandra. "I will not let you die," he whispered close to my ear. "But you *will* heal Sandra. I brought you here to get you used to the idea. I will be with you when you do it, and I will help you. I will make sure you live through the process."

I sucked in a deep breath. "How is it possible that you can touch me if you're not here?" How could I feel his warm breath on my cheek?

"Lexi, I am so real in your mind, that not only can you feel my body and hear my voice..." He spoke softly close to my ear. His fingers brushed along my arm on their way up my body until his hand clutched my throat. "...you'd feel pain if I squeezed just so."

His fingers tightened around my neck, cutting off my air supply. I clawed at his hand and tried to pry his fingers away. I gagged and sputtered. I couldn't breathe. "I'll be in touch, Sarah Alexandra. Jack's coming. Tell him he might want to stay away from you while you sleep." He squeezed harder, then brushed a kiss along my jawline.

"Lexi! Lexi, wake up!"

Suddenly, Jonas's hand was gone from my throat. I fell to my knees and sucked in a labored breath. My throat burned as I gasped for oxygen.

"Hey." Gentle hands touched my shoulders.

I slowly raised my head. Jack's frantic eyes searched mine. I threw myself into his arms. "Oh, Jack. I'm in huge trouble."

FOURTEEN

....

I had avoided Jack since Tuesday, which he didn't deserve, but he couldn't help me get rid of Jonas—or whoever was controlling Jonas—and I couldn't look at that helpless look on his face any longer. If I was being honest, he may have been avoiding me as well.

The library was quiet. We'd been back for four days. I sat curled up in an armchair, facing a large window overlooking the multi-purpose field where the girls' soccer team practiced in the rain. My laptop sat open. I had read the last words Dad wrote to me at least ten times in the last hour.

I stared at the droplets of water trailing down the pane in front of me, every once in a while glancing toward the girls kicking a soccer ball around, knocking each other down on the turf. Normal, everyday activity for kids at a boarding school.

"Wellington was supposed to be a safe haven for the clones we found over the years," Dad had said in his letter to me. The list of clones hidden in his research showed me there were many others, but I had yet to figure out who knew about us, or whom I could trust with the information I was discovering now.

I couldn't help but hope the other clones, the ones on Dad's list that hadn't found their way to Wellington, had discovered a way to lead normal lives. Away from the poking and prodding of scientists. Away from people who were scared and wanted the clones destroyed.

Subconsciously, my hand drifted up toward my neck. My fingers pressed lightly against my skin, feeling for any bruising from my altercation with Jonas. The skin hadn't darkened, nor shown any signs of redness, but I could feel it. Jonas had scarred me.

Now, three days later, I hadn't heard a single whispered word from him. And I was thankful. Mostly. I was starting to realize that his motives didn't line up—that he was telling me the truth when he claimed it wasn't just him inside my head. One moment he was telling me to heal Sandra or he would hurt someone I loved. And the next? He was kissing me and assuring me that he wouldn't let me die if I were to heal Sandra. The only thing that made sense was that someone, another clone, was behind the threats and the commands to heal Sandra.

But who? And why? Who was Sandra to Jonas and this mystery control freak?

"Hey, you," Danielle said, interrupting my thoughts as she plopped into the chair diagonal from me. Her long blond hair was in a low, side ponytail, and draped halfway down her chest. Based on the yoga pants and fitted top, she had been to yoga class. "Why are you hiding in here?"

I looked around. "Hiding? I'm sitting out in the open on the main floor of the library, Dani."

"It's Friday afternoon. No one studies"—she lifted the corner of the book lying across my lap—"Advanced Biology on the weekend. You're hiding from something. Or someone." She raised a single brow.

I wasn't hiding from anything. I couldn't hide from Jonas. Why bother? He'd find me.

When I didn't respond to her, she said, "Something happen between you and Jack?"

I studied her brown eyes. "No. Why?"

"I don't know. You seem depressed or something. I've never seen you depressed. And since you've never been in love before Jack, I thought maybe he was the reason." She reached out and gave my knee a playful knock. "If he did something, you know I can help. I know people." Dani wiggled her eyebrows, giving me the signal that she'd have "her people" cut his legs off if I just said the word.

Finally, I gave in and laughed out loud. "No, Jack didn't do anything." I shook my head, then focused back on my best friend and roommate for the past six years. My normal friend. "Dani, why did your parents send you to Wellington?"

Dani seemed to shift in her seat at my question. "What do you mean?"

"Well, you've been here almost as long as I have, but I don't know much about your parents." Other than that they never showed much involvement in her academic choices.

"Wellington kids don't know each others' parents. That's how it's always been." She looked down, wringing her hands in her lap. "Well, except for *your* father, I guess."

It was somewhat of an honor system at Wellington. We were never supposed to ask about Wellington students' histories or their families. I'd known Dani's parents were strict with her, but fairly absentee at the same time—like Dad in a lot of ways. Dani and I had spent many holidays and summers together at school. And when she did leave for holidays, she always traveled somewhere exotic, like Switzerland for skiing or Maui for scuba diving. Never home.

The only thing I knew for sure about her parents was that her father loved thoroughbred horse racing. "So, is your father in for the Keeneland October race meet?"

"Probably." She chewed on a cuticle and scanned the room behind me. When her eyes found me again, she asked, "So, you going to study all night?"

I narrowed my gaze when she changed the subject, but decided to back off the interrogation. Why was I giving her such a hard time anyway? She'd been my best friend forever and ever. "Uh... no," I answered.

"And nothing's wrong with you and Jack?"

"No." I shook my head to reinforce the answer.

"Good." She stood and reached for my hand. "Then we're going out." She pulled me out of my chair.

"Out?"

"Yeah. Well, sort of. Not quite *out* out, but a double date." Though her voice was upbeat, her shoulders slumped. "We *were* going to venture outside the confines of this place. Wellington lifted our security lockdown."

"They did?" I knew they had. That was the only reason I agreed to stay at Wellington. Though I wasn't sure I should be leaving the safety of the electric fence and dorm security guards just yet. I still wasn't sure who had tried to kill me. Still, it was nice knowing we could get out if we desired, yet tough for outsiders to get in. "But we're not going now?"

"No, apparently Jack squashed the idea." She raised her hand and gnawed on a cuticle, then with a slight wave of her hand said, "Something about your safety and there being more to the truck that ran you off the road last week."

"Jack said that?" I picked up my Advanced Biol, hugged it against my chest.

Dani nodded. "You don't think you're still in d. you?"

"No." I tried to put truth behind my words. "I think we're okay inside Wellington. Jack's just being overprotective." I smiled. "So... who might Jack and I be doubling with?"

She looked down at her feet. I'd never seen her so shy about a boy in my life. "Kyle and me."

I pulled her into a hug. It wasn't that I was excited about this matchup between Miss Normal and Mr. Freak-Like-Me, but she obviously felt something for Kyle. I would not be the one to erase the smile from my best friend's face.

Releasing her, I held her at arm's length. "One problem. I have an early curfew tonight because of my meet tomorrow. I'm expected to qualify for state in three events." I laughed. I had made practice only three times that week. Just enough to possibly win races, I hoped.

"I'm told they've got curfew covered."

"Okay. Well, let me finish up here, and I'll meet you back at the room."

"Perfect." Dani sashayed out the door, leaving me alone again with my computer and my thoughts about Dad, Sandra, and the IIA.

And Jonas.

I brushed my fingers along my jawline where Jonas had brushed his lips. Even though it was a dream of some sort, it had seemed so real. But he wasn't *really* there.

What *was* real? I wondered.

Jonas wanted Sandra cured, as did Georgia and Fred. The clones in the underground facility knew Sandra, and they recognized me as a younger version of her. IIA agents swarmed The Farm. Dad said in his letter to me that Sandra had always intended for the embryos to become humans, and that the IIA had funded her efforts. But Dad didn't know the location of the IIA facility until days before he was murdered—according to Jonas.

Was Jonas controlled by the IIA? And since Jonas controlled me—directly or indirectly—was I now being controlled by the same government agency?

I would not be controlled by those evil nut jobs. "I am not a puppet," I whispered to myself. I shoved my book into my backpack. Yes, a date was definitely in order. I needed normal.

~~~~~

Seated on a blanket, I leaned against Jack, who was supported by a tree behind him. My back was to his chest, and his arms circled around me, holding me tight. "This was a great idea," I said. I tilted my head up, giving Jack access to my lips, which he gladly took advantage of. We pretended all was well.

Kyle and Jack had organized and pulled off the perfect date inside Wellington. A candlelit picnic in the woodsy area behind the stables was a brilliant idea. We had privacy, ambience, and all the awkwardness of a first date—Kyle and Dani's first date.

"As much as I'd like to take credit, I can't. This was all Kyle." Jack smiled down at me, but the smile didn't reach all the way to his eyes. He rubbed a thumb across my cheek. "I'm worried about you."

I faced forward again. His words squeezed my heart. *I know.* I mindspoke because I didn't trust my voice.

You've shut me out.

I'm trying to protect you. The words were out before I could stop them. I felt Jack's body go rigid. I knew immediately I had said the wrong thing.

Jack took in a slow, steady breath. *Kyle, why don't you take Danielle for a walk?*

Kyle, who had been whispering and laughing with Dani far enough away from us that we couldn't hear their conversation, looked over at us. His face grew serious. "You guys are zero fun." He stood, then reached both hands and pulled Dani to her feet. "I'm taking Dani for a walk."

They walked toward us. "I think you're fun," Dani shrugged with a giggle.

"You..." Kyle said, pointing at Jack. "You can clean this up."

When they were gone, Jack nudged me gently away and stood. I immediately felt the heat leave my backside.

He paced in front of me, running his fingers through his hair. "I didn't bring you back to Wellington so that you would hide everything from me." I stared at the ground, refusing to look at him. *I don't want your protection.* His booming voice inside my head made me flinch. *Look at me!*

I slowly tilted my head toward him. The hurt look on his face sent a stabbing pulse straight through my heart. I swallowed hard against the lump in my throat as he stared at me in silence. Finally, I said, "Why exactly *did* you bring me back here?"

"I brought you back here because we need answers, and right now, Wellington can provide some security while we search for those answers."

I raised a brow. "You think the truth is here?"

"I do. Come on. I have something to show you." Jack pulled me up by my hands. Keeping hold of one, he pulled me after him. "Let's walk."

"What about this stuff?" I motioned toward our picnic mess.

His lips quirked on one side. "I already told Kyle he needed to come back and deal with it."

"I bet he was furious."

"He can't mindspeak to me, only hear." There was a twinkle in Jack's eye that confused me a little. We headed back toward the main part of campus.

"So, you can speak directly to Kyle's mind and choose whether I hear it?"

"Yes."

"That must take a lot of control."

"I'm learning."

"But Kyle can't speak back to you. Interesting."

Jack rubbed his thumb in circles on the back of my hand as we made our way around the stables. "When you're ready, Seth would like to start working with you."

I bet he would. I stopped and pulled my hand away from him. The smells of hay and manure from the stable wafted toward us.

He took a step closer, refusing to let a gap grow between us. "I also brought you back to Wellington because Jonas was inside your head. He was able to control your actions. I figured that since I had to be in close proximity to mindspeak with you, Jonas needed the same."

Jonas didn't have the same limitations, but for some reason I was unable to tell Jack. Jonas had somehow blocked my ability to reveal his plans. "Do you still wonder at times if we'd be better off running?"

"Of course. When I think you might be harmed, I fantasize about helping you escape. However, while I respect the fact that you're struggling with how we came into this world—"

"You aren't. Struggling, that is. You think we could use these abilities for good. That it's somehow okay. Okay that so many embryos died during the process of creating each of us."

"I don't agree with the lost lives or how our parents hid the truth from us all these years. We were lied to. But..." Jack rubbed the back of his neck. "If I thought I could use these healing abilities to save a life? I would do it. What they did was wrong, and I worry about the threats against us now. Last week, I thought the best thing for us... for you... was to run."

"But now?"

"I want you safe. I also want a life with you that doesn't require us changing our names and location every thirty days. Is that how you really want to go through life? Not knowing? Hiding? Always running? What if we run, and someone is still getting inside your head? What then? Whether you embrace these unnatural abilities or not, I'm no longer certain we can hide from that."

I looked away. A breeze blew hair in my face, and he pushed it away.

"You are so beautiful. You have the heart and the mind to do something amazing in this world."

My eyes found his. Moisture pooled, making my vision blurry. "What if I don't want to be amazing? What if I want to be... I don't know... not amazing? Average, even. What if I want to be like everybody else? Finish high school. Go to college. Get married. Have two point four kids. Own a golden retriever and a betta fish."

"If that were really what you wanted, you would have run when you had the chance. After you escaped on the train, you would have headed straight for the bus station. I know you took the money and everything to start college under a different identity. If you had wanted that, you would have gone."

A tear escaped down my cheek, and Jack wiped it away.

"But you didn't. You didn't run. And I think it's because you know you owe it to yourself and to your father to at least know who you are."

"And I owe it to you," I whispered. I sniffed hard, my nose running from crying and from the cold night air. "I didn't leave... because I couldn't leave you."

Jack crushed my body to his. His fingers laced into my hair, and he pushed my head into his polo sweater. "It's time for you to start learning more about your abilities."

I pushed back. Wiping at the moisture I left on his shirt, I said, "Okay."

He crooked a finger under my chin and lifted. "Okay?"

I nodded.

"As you learn more about your powers, I think you'll also learn how to shut Jonas out."

I *so* wanted that.

"Now, come." He pulled on my hand.

"Where are we going?"

mindsiege

"It's time you met Addison."

FIFTEEN

A girl the size of a pixie bounced up and down on the hospital bed like it was her personal trampoline as we entered. Jet black hair hung in a stringy mess. Sky blue eyes lit up the entire room.

I paused just inside the door and studied the small child, just eight years old. My eyes must have widened, because Jack bowed his shaking head. A smile reached all the way to his eyes. "Lexi Matthews, meet Addison."

Addison stopped. Her grin grew to the size of a half moon, and shined like the North Star. She jumped up one last time, lifted her legs, and bounced on her bottom before propelling herself to stand on the floor. "Oh my gosh! You're Lexi?" She ran the short distance and threw her arms around my waist in a big hug. "I can't believe you're finally here."

I traded glances with Jack. He covered his mouth and choked on his own laughter. "Hey," Jack tugged on Addison's arm. "What about me?"

"*You* didn't bring me out of that stupid coma." Addison hugged me again, knocking me off balance.

Jack visibly cringed at Addison's words.

She didn't mean that like it sounded.

"No, of course I didn't," Addison said.

I jerked my head toward her, but she had let go and was flitting back to her bed. I found Jack's eyes. "She can hear anything and everything," he said. "It's as annoying as it sounds."

"Yes, but don't worry." Addison waved me off. "I don't re-peat stuff. Unless I think you're gonna get yourself in trouble." She stared at me like she wanted to say more. Like she knew something.

"Okay, enough with the introductions. Let's sit," Jack point-ed to a chair in the corner for me. He crossed the room and got another one. "Addi, where are Cathy and your mom?"

Addison was quiet. She peered up at the ceiling. "Mom went home. I told her to get some sleep. Your *mother*"—Addison said "mother" like it left a bad taste in her mouth—"is in the dining hall with Dr. Wellington."

"You know that's exactly where they are, or that's where they *said* they were going?" I had a sneaky suspicion it was the former.

"Addison can also sense where people are at all times. If they're close by."

"Seriously?" I asked. "Where is... uh... Briana Howard?"

She considered it. "In the parking lot."

"Why is she in the parking lot?" Strange.

"Um... she's..." Addison narrowed her eyes, then gave her head a quick shake. "I don't know. She's talking to someone. I can hear her, but not... him. Yes, definitely a him."

"So, obviously not Kyle, since he's the only other guy on campus besides me who you should be able to hear." Jack sat and crossed his arms. "She can sense where anyone is, but she can only hear clones' thoughts."

"Uh-huh," she agreed matter-of-factly.

"So, you have the equivalent of a Marauder's Map in your head?" I asked.

"Marauder's Map. From Harry Potter?" She giggled. "I guess I do."

"It comes in handy," Jack said. "Like when Addison wants to sneak out of the house for one reason or another."

"So, Lexi," Addison said, uninterested in Jack's memory. "When are you going to tell Jack about Jonas?"

The muscles along the back of my neck tightened one by one. I stared at Addison while I searched my mind for any sign of Jonas. My hands shook.

"He's not there. I've looked," she reassured. "And he won't kill Jack."

"How did you..."

"Know?" she asked. "I can hear and see every one of the clones, if they're close. And I can sense where regular people are, too. I've been monitoring your conversations with Jonas since you came back to Wellington."

I swallowed that nice and slowly.

"What is she talking about, Lex? Tell me what?" He looked at Addison. "I already know Jonas, or somebody, is inside her head."

I stood and walked away from their probing eyes. Addison remained quiet while I wrung my sweaty hands.

"You can tell him. I'll block Jonas from hearing."

Despite Addison's words, I could feel the weight of that carving knife against the palms of my hands, and how the slick surface fit inside my tight grip. I would not let someone hurt Jack. Could Addison really block Jonas?

Yes, I can. Jonas can't get into your head while I'm with you.

"From hearing what?" Jack said behind me. "Someone, please tell me what you two are talking about."

I turned. "I'm sorry I didn't tell you. I wanted to." I walked close to him. He slid his hand into mine. "Jonas plans to force me to heal Sandra." Only it might not really be Jonas.

"How can he do that?"

"The same way he practically forced me to drown myself. The way he made Kyle burn his arm." I met Jack's concerned gaze. "The same way he compelled me to hold a knife pointed at your chest while you slept last week." A tremor moved through me at that memory. I tried to pull my hand away from Jack, but he gripped it tighter. I fought hard against the emotion building inside my chest as I gasped for a breath.

Standing, he pulled me to him, circling his arms around me in a tight hug. "You wouldn't have hurt me."

"I didn't have a choice," I mumbled into his chest, my body shaking. "I almost drove a kitchen knife into your heart." I shook my head, trying to free the memory. "I tried to wake you."

"You did." Jack pushed me back. He cupped my cheeks into his hands. "You did wake me. I woke that morning because I heard you screaming my name. I thought it was part of my dream, but I was hearing you. You wouldn't have hurt me."

Tears slid down both sides of my face. Jack wiped them away with his thumbs. "I'm sorry," I whispered.

"You two are cute," Addison said behind us. "But we've got to move on."

"You know, Addison talks like a thirty-year-old." A hysterical chuckle escaped my throat.

Jack smiled. He leaned in and touched his lips to mine. "I know. She's also very bossy. And has an IQ beyond something you or I can comprehend."

"And I have ears," Addison said. "I can hear you, you know."

Jack led me back to the chair. Once I was sitting, he rubbed my shoulders. "We have to figure out why Jonas wants Sandra healed so badly."

"And why he keeps threatening to make me hurt you," I added.

"That part's easy," Addison said. "Jack is the most important person in your life."

Jack's fingers slid a little farther toward the base of my neck and hairline. I was thankful he couldn't see how red my face was. But he knew how much he meant to me, didn't he?

Addison continued. "Jonas knows that, and he's using it against you."

"It doesn't make sense, though," Jack said. "He helped me rescue Lexi when we wrecked. He was so upset when Lexi ran the other day, saying she shouldn't be roaming alone. And he was mostly concerned because Lexi still hadn't admitted to wanting to know the extent of her powers."

Something didn't add up. Jonas claimed I would see everything more clearly once he had gotten into my head. He thought everything would make sense to me, not confuse me the way it had. Then he had led me to the facility near...

Addison cocked her head, her eyes probing mine. "There's something you're not telling us."

I rose from the chair and walked out of Jack's reach. Immediately, I constructed barriers around my mind. Something prevented me from revealing more.

Jack stretched his fingers wide at his sides, then closed them into fists. "She can't." He turned to me. "Can you? Jonas is there."

I looked quickly from Jack to Addison. "You lied. You told me you could block Jonas from hearing me." Defeat and disappointment tinged my voice. I had trusted this girl I had only just met. Why? Because she was like a sister to Jack?

Addison shook her head quickly back and forth. She looked more her age as she reacted. "No! I didn't lie. I *did* block him. He couldn't hear anything you've said. It's someone else." Addison squinted. "Are you sure it's Jonas?"

I shook my head. "Jonas has all but admitted he's inside my head, but only some of the times. It's Jonas I see when he speaks to me. But sometimes, his demands go against everything else I've learned or know about him. He claims he's not always in control of the mindsiege."

Jack stormed toward me. "Lexi, listen to me. You have to find a way to push this person out."

I felt Jack slide into my head. Instead of pushing him out, I let him in. *I can't feel Jonas inside my head the way I feel you,* I told him. *If I wanted to, I could push you out right now. Your presence has hard edges, ones I can get leverage against. Jonas's is like a cloud. As soon as I get a handle on him, he morphs into a different shape.*

I searched my mind further and found Addison. She was like a water balloon. I pushed on it and felt resistance. It moved with my touch, but it wasn't as easy to shove away as Jack's.

Allow me. Jack eased further in, and his hard edge knocked up against Addison's softer one. I nudged my barriers up against her too, and suddenly, she was gone completely from my mind.

"Very nice." Addison clapped like a little kid watching a circus. Fitting, since I felt very much like part of a three-ring act at times.

"So, how do we get Jonas out?" Jack asked Addison.

Why was he asking *her*? How would she know this?

Her smile fell away. "From what I've learned so far, I'm afraid you can't."

"Why not?" Jack and I asked at the same time.

"Someone else is controlling Jonas so that it always looks like it's Jonas inside her head."

SIXTEEN

....

Jonas remained enemy number one for now. He could claim someone else was controlling him; Addison and Jack tried to convince me of the same. But as far as I was concerned, Jonas was the one slithering around inside my mind like a serpent.

"You sure know how to show a girl a good time." I nudged Jack's shoulder.

He walked me back toward the dorm. Before we came into sight of the security guard that stood at the entrance, he pulled me behind a tree.

I stumbled against him, laughing, but his hand to my elbow steadied me. "We've got a few minutes before curfew." He lifted my chin. The worry I was becoming accustomed to was back on his face.

I reached up and massaged the line between his eyes. "If someone wanted to hurt me, they would have already."

His expression didn't change. "Something feels terribly wrong. How much of your father's journals have you made it through?"

"A lot, but so much of it is technical science stuff that I don't understand."

"You feel like getting away from here tomorrow? After the swim meet. We can spend the night at my house. Use a more secure Wi-Fi?" Jack tugged on my jacket, pulling me even closer. He leaned down and whispered in my ear. "Pull an all-nighter?"

I laughed. He made poring through science journals sound hot. I peeked up through my lashes. "Addison thinks Jonas and I are marionettes. Someone is pulling both of our strings. And she's right, isn't she?"

"That's my fear." Worry overflowed the trenches across his forehead. "Question is who. And why *your* strings, and not mine or Kyle's?"

"Or Bree's. Why can't someone pull hers instead?"

Jack smiled. "You don't mean that."

"No, I don't." I reached up and played with the sandy hair that lay across his forehead. He needed a haircut. What a normal thing to think about, I mused. "I better go."

"Yeah." He leaned in and brushed his lips across mine. His hand slipped under my jacket and shirt until he touched bare skin. "You better go." He pulled me closer, smiling against my face.

"That's not helping," I giggled, but made no effort to pull away.

He leaned his forehead against mine. "Part of me is sorry we didn't run Friday night. We could be spending more of our time doing this." He kissed me again.

"Shh. No regrets. We do what we've gotta do until we're on the other side of this." Whatever *this* was. "We'll have more time for other *stuff* later."

"Promise?" he asked, and I nodded. "I knew you were strong the moment I met you." His voice was almost a whisper and somewhat strained. "But I'm sorry I didn't run from you when I realized you were like me. I loved you even then, before we met. But if I had run then..."

I cupped my hand over his mouth and stared straight into those intense sapphire eyes. "Then we wouldn't have met, and I would have been left to fend for myself when the IIA and Jonas found me. And they would have." I shivered, wondering where I would be now had Jack not eased me into the truth of what we are.

"Maybe." He hugged me closer. His fingers spread wider against my back.

"No, not maybe. Definitely." I wrapped my arms around his neck. Jack lifted me in a hug so that my face was even with his. I leaned in and kissed the spot below his ear and continued down his neck. "If you hadn't found me..." My voice cracked a little.

"Shhh. You're right. There's no use playing the what-if game."

I nuzzled his neck and swallowed against the lump that formed. The warmth of his hand against my bare skin made me want to curl up inside his jacket and let him smuggle me inside his dorm.

I tried to hide a yawn, but Jack was onto me. He let me slide to my feet. "We both could use a good night's sleep."

I pulled back. "Until tomorrow then."

"Tomorrow," he agreed, then leaned in for one last good-night kiss.

~~~~~

The tingle of Jack's kiss lingered on my lips as I approached my dorm room. I touched my mouth, unable to contain a smile. How could my life be so messed up, yet so right when

Jack was near? I shouldn't have avoided him this past week, but I wouldn't be able to live with myself if I were to cause something terrible to happen to him.

Dad had called Wellington a safe haven for the clones he had recently discovered. Only, Wellington wasn't my safe haven: Jack was.

I dug in my purse for my room key. It was just after the eleven o'clock curfew. The hallways were eerily quiet for a Friday night.

No one was in the common area on my floor. The lights had already been dimmed.

Just as I lifted the key to the lock, I smelled it.

Smoke.

Not now, I thought.

I immediately began searching the edges of my mind for the invasion. If I was quick enough, maybe I could push Jonas out.

"It's no use, Sarah."

The little hairs on the back of my neck stood at attention at the sound of Jonas's voice directly behind me. When his fingers slid into my hair and grabbed the back of my neck, every muscle along my spine tightened.

"I'm not only inside your head," he whispered right next to my ear. "I'm right here." His breath warmed my neck. His fingers spread up through my hair, and he guided my head to face him.

My eyes met his. Instead of the warm amber that I sometimes found in Jonas's eyes, I faced cold black, his pupils dilated, leaving only a small perimeter of brown.

"What do you want, Jonas?" Though the grip he had on my neck made it difficult, I cocked my head just slightly. Was someone controlling him, forcing his actions the way I sometimes forced others'? "Or... are you ready to tell me who you really are?"

The boy before me smiled an evil, lopsided sort of grin. "You'd like it if you could place another name on this version of me, wouldn't you, Sarah? You like the kinder, more gentler Jonas, don't you?"

I was powerless in his grip. I could smell the fear emanating from my racing heart and my trembling limbs. But I answered him. "Yes, I do." And I did. When Jonas was being kind, he was easy to like.

He leaned closer to me, his face inches from mine. "I see why Jonas likes you, too."

I searched his eyes for his true identity, but all I saw was Jonas.

Then realization dawned. "Ty," I whispered, and the corners of his lips tilted farther up, reaching all the way to his dark eyes. His presence glided in and around my mind, leaving me drunk from the quick movements of this complete invasion. "What do you want?" I asked again.

"You will come with me." He forced me to turn, and gave me a little shove back down the hallway.

"Where are we going?"

"You'll see."

~~~~~

Getting past the security of the dorm and into The Program was not a problem for someone who had one hundred percent control over the mind of another.

Keep going, he mindspoke. We moved quietly down the hallway in the basement of the infirmary and entered the room I was becoming all too familiar with. Sandra hadn't moved. The machines around her were silent. Lights blinked to confirm that her heart still beat.

"You're going to make me heal her, aren't you?" I wiped my sweaty palms on my jeans. My heart beat so fast, I thought I might faint. "This is never going to work, you know."

Quiet.

I tried to speak again, and no sound came out. So far, I'd been unable to refuse his commands.

Lexi? It was Jack.

Jack! Help me. I'm in The Pro—

The pressure to my throat came fast and hard.

Ty, in Jonas's body, lifted his hand from my throat and placed it over my mouth. Sliding his palm to the small of my back, he brought me closer. "Try something like that again, and I will terminate you. But not until the job is complete."

The smell of smoke on his breath made me nauseated. I squeezed my eyes closed. I knew what the job was. What I didn't know was, could I do it? Was I capable? And if I was successful, would I survive the consequences?

"Now," he said, forcing me to face Sandra. "Let's get on with it."

I stared down at the woman before me. Her hair was tucked neatly behind her ears. It had been brushed recently. The nurse? Seth, maybe? Her skin was a pearly color, much paler than mine, but she *was* lying in a hospital bed. I wanted to like this woman who looked identical to me, only older. Was I supposed to? She was the reason I existed. Was I somehow supposed to respect her for that?

Before I had a chance to answer my own question, he reentered my thoughts. "Show me her brain."

Without hesitation, I pulled her brain up, just like a doctor displayed an X-ray or CT scan. As before, the fluid pooled at the base of her brain, and was most likely the culprit for keeping Sandra in a coma.

"Now, heal her."

Lexi, don't react to my voice, Jack said. *Kyle and I are on our way. Just keep Jonas busy until we can get there.*

I couldn't risk telling Jack that it wasn't Jonas who had control of me, especially since he didn't even know about Ty yet. I directed my attention back to Sandra's brain. I could see the small holes that allowed the cerebral fluid to leak. I thought I could heal her—but at what cost?

I tried to turn, but met a wall. Jonas wrapped his arms around me, keeping me pinned to the ground in front of Sandra. His presence slithered into my mind, and immediately shoved Jack out.

My hands trembled at my side at the thought that healing Sandra might kill me—if not physically, then mentally. Healing someone this way was not natural.

Stop stalling. He squeezed my body again, forcing my attention back to his commands.

There was no way out of this. I honed in on the tiny holes. As if using a blowtorch, I welded the holes shut, one by one, until the brain looked intact physically.

Amazing, the voice inside my head said.

As with Addison, pain began to pulsate behind my eyes and around my temples.

I'm here, Lexi. It's really me. It's Jonas. His voice was smoother, gentler.

Jonas? I whimpered. *I don't know what to believe anymore.*

I closed my hands into fists. My arms tightened under the hold Jonas had on me. Only, I was supposed to believe it wasn't truly Jonas hurting me and forcing me to heal Sandra.

You have to finish this. If you complete the healing and get rid of the fluid, the person controlling my mind and yours will leave.

How do you know this? I asked. I never thought I'd feel relieved to have Jonas inside my head. There was only one thing left for me to do to complete the healing: get rid of the fluid causing the coma.

They want Sandra back. Give them that, and they'll go away. For now, at least.

Fear of Sandra waking compounded the growing headache, but fear of the person controlling Jonas practically paralyzed me. I brought up Sandra's brain again. The only way I knew to get rid of the fluid was to flush it out the same way I'd flushed the drug from Jack's brain last week.

I wrapped my mind around the fluid, gathering it. I sent it through Sandra's body and out.

Liquid spewed from her mouth, spreading all over the white sheet and blanket that covered her. Like a river, it ran in the creases of the blanket, spilling onto the floor. Sandra coughed, choking on her own vomit. Jonas shoved me to the side with such force that I fell to my knees.

The pain in my head forced me to collapse fully onto the cold floor. The room spun out of control. The presence inside my head—Jonas, or the person controlling Jonas, I wasn't sure anymore—was gone. And so was the calming force that had steadied me while I healed Sandra.

I rolled onto my back and stared up at the ceiling before closing my eyes tightly. At least I hadn't passed out like last time. Seconds passed. I slowly become more aware of the other two people in the room.

"Oh my God! What happened?" the only other female in the room asked.

My eyes sprung open at the sound of her voice.

Sandra's voice.

....

SEVENTEEN

Mom, what were you thinking?" Jonas's voice came out breathy.

Mom?

My head ached. It hurt to move, but I had to. I rolled onto my side and pushed myself up on my elbows.

Jonas was bent over at the hips. His breaths came out labored. He balanced with one hand on his knee and dug his other palm into his chest.

I recognized a panic attack when I saw one.

Sandra lifted the vomit-soaked sheet and moved it to the side. Her nose scrunched up in disgust. "Where am I?" she asked. She moved her legs to hang off the side of the bed.

"Wait." Jonas moved to the other side of the bed and stopped her from moving. "You've been in a coma."

"A what? For how long?"

I sat up, scooted away from the two of them, and leaned against the far wall. If I had the strength, I'd do whatever I had to do to run from that room. Why had Jonas called her "Mom"? It wasn't possible. I pinched the bridge of my nose.

"A month. Maybe a little less."

Sandra seemed to think on that. "Then, how—" Her words were cut off. Jonas's eyes drifted from Sandra to me. She slowly turned, and I wanted to shrink to nothingness.

Sandra's eyes widened. She slid off the bed, stood, and turned to me, falling into Jonas.

"Careful," he said, steadying her.

She grabbed onto his elbow and walked slowly around the edge of the bed, hesitating at the foot. "Did you..." she paused. "Did you bring me out of the coma?"

I didn't expect her voice to sound exactly like mine—with a little less Kentucky twang, maybe. I opened my mouth to speak, but no words came. What was I supposed to say to this woman? My eyes darted around the room, then back at her.

"You don't have to be scared," she said, taking another step closer.

Scared? I cocked my head.

Behind her, Jonas sucked in a deep breath. He was slowly coming down from the panic attack.

She stepped closer. "I'm not going to hurt you."

Like I believed that. *Stop. Don't come any closer.*

She immediately stopped.

My eyes darted around the room a second time. That's when I saw the scissors lying on a counter on the far side of the room.

Jonas, grab those scissors. I directed him with my eyes. He followed my order without question. Obviously, his guard was down, much like it had been the day I forced him to hold a scalpel against his own heart. *Now, grab Sandra, and point the sharp end of those scissors into her neck.*

He pulled Sandra—this almost mirror image of me—against his chest, then pointed the sharp tip of the scissors at her jugular. Sandra's eyes widened. "Jonas, what are you doing?"

"I'm sorry, Mom." His hand shook. Jonas didn't enjoy being controlled any more than I did, as was evident after I manipulated his actions once before. "Her power is strong. Without help from *Central*, I can't stop her."

Sandra's eyes narrowed on me. "Okay, I'll play. What do you want?" she asked me.

I pushed myself up the wall to stand. Blood began to trickle from my nose, pooling just above my upper lip. I heard noises from somewhere out in the hallway.

Lexi? Can you hear me?

I pulled tissues from a nearby Kleenex box and held them to my nose. *Jack, I hear you.*

Oh, thank God. We're almost there. Are you okay? I couldn't reach you with my mind. I've been trying.

I'm fine. Who's with you? I asked.

Kyle, Seth, and Cathy. Why do you sound funny?

I walked to the three doors and locked each one. They were all heavy, steel doors, with prison-quality locks. *You'll have to wait outside.*

My hand was still on the last lock when the door handle jiggled. *What's going on, Lexi? Did you lock the doors?*

Yes. I backed away, staring at the door, and still pressing the tissues against my nosebleed.

"So, it wasn't fear I saw in your eyes, was it, Sarah?" Sandra asked.

"Don't call me that." I turned and faced Sandra. "He called you 'Mom.' Why?"

"Because I carried him for nine months, gave birth to him, and raised him."

"But he's a clone."

"That's right." She was unfazed by the scissors pointed at her neck.

"A clone of whom?" The picture of the person of interest from the newspaper article about Marci's death came to mind.

She smiled. "Is that really want you want to ask me about? We don't have time."

"Why'd you do it? Why'd you clone humans?"

"That's more like it. Now we're getting somewhere."

I stepped closer to her. *Hold her tighter, Jonas.*

He gripped Sandra and the knife tighter. Sandra tilted her head, attempting to lean away from the blade. "Because I could," she laughed. "Because I wanted to change things. I wanted to cure disease. Fight for world peace. I wanted control."

What the hell was that supposed to mean? Well, she would not control me.

"Have Jonas put the scissors down. You and I need to talk about some things before the people on the other side of that door break their way into here."

"No. You can talk just fine where you are."

She swallowed. "Okay. Have it your way, for now. I need you to join me, Sarah."

"Join you?" I scoffed. "Join you where?"

"At the IIA. I can help you. Make your nosebleeds go away. You'll never feel sick again when you heal someone. I can teach you about everything you were designed to do."

An irrational laugh bubbled up out of my throat. "And what if I don't want to learn from you? You're not the only one making that promise. What if I don't want anything to do with you or the IIA?"

"Then the IIA will continue with their plan to eliminate you and the other originals. And I will give them permission to do so."

"Because you have that authority."

"Yes, I do," she said matter-of-factly. "I have complete authority over the Department of Human Cloning. I will simply inform the IIA that you have gone rogue, and you will be terminated."

I looked at Jonas. There was something in the way he studied me. *You have something to say?*

Don't taunt her. She will kill you and the rest of the original clones.

Does that include you?

No. Remember that piece of metal I showed you? The one I took from Ty when we were in the underground facility?

Yes.

That's called a tracker. I allowed her to insert one into the base of my brain. She can terminate me and any clone at that facility—flick us off like a light switch—any time she wishes—with the push of a button. She, or the agents who work for her, can also control our every movement because of that tracker.

Terminate? Would Sandra kill Jonas? *Why are you telling me this?* I asked. If Jonas was Sandra's son, and here to free her from the coma, why would he risk telling me these things?

Because I need you. The clones need you. She knows it, but she wants control over you first. She can't kill you with the push of a button. She'd have to murder you in a more... traditional sense.

That doesn't explain why you would warn me. Whose side are you on?

I'm on the side that gets this tracker out of the back of my head and lets me live my own life. But I'm also on the side that will allow me to use my abilities without bowing down to a bunch of ruthless scientists. That's what Dia was trying to tell you. Those of us who know Sandra know that we cannot cross her. But we also know there has to be a way out of the hold Sandra and the IIA have on us.

I walked two more steps and stared straight into Sandra's green eyes. I stood close enough to hear her breathing, her pulse just slightly higher than normal. "What's stopping me from killing you right now?" For a split second, a tiny bit of fear flashed over her face—her cheeks fell a fraction and the lines of her forehead twitched.

Her lips quirked. "You don't have it in you. You and your friends need me. I have the cure for your ailments—which will only get worse, by the way. Why do you think you get those nosebleeds, Lexi? Because you've used some special power?" A laugh escaped her throat. "Those nosebleeds are a sign of a bigger... problem. Your dad knew this. We'd struck a deal just before his death."

I narrowed my eyes. My nosebleeds had been worse recently, but I had assumed it was because I had used my mindspeaking ability more often. "You're lying. My father would never negotiate with you."

The turning of the lock on the door sounded behind me. In walked Jack, Bree, and Cathy.

Lexi, don't give up control of my mind, Jonas thought. *If you do, the IIA will just take control of me again. I've been trying to tell you that I'm on your side. That I wasn't the one who tried to kill you.*

I'm starting to believe you.

"What is going on here?" Cathy asked, interrupting Jonas and me.

Jack strode past Cathy and me. He grabbed Jonas by the shirt, then punched him. "What did you do to her?"

Jonas pressed his fingers against his now-bloody lip. Chuckling, he said, "I guess I deserved that. But you're making a mistake. I didn't do the things you think I did."

"You didn't kiss her?"

That was the thing he chose to punch him over?

"Well... I did do that," he laughed. Jack lunged at him again, forcing him to take a step backward with his hands raised. "But I haven't been controlling her. Not completely, and not alone, anyway."

Cathy stood between the two adolescents and held Jack back. "Would you two stop it? Lexi, where's Sandra? Did you bring her out of that coma?"

I turned a complete circle. Sandra had vanished. Still, only one door was open. "Where's Bree?" My heart began beating at an uncontrollable rate. Something wasn't right.

"Bree was here?" Jack asked.

The laughter from Jonas started out as a low chuckle from deep within his chest, but erupted into a hysterical fit. He braced himself against Sandra's hospital bed.

I stared at Jonas, then turned quickly to Jack. I could barely get in a breath. "She came in with you," I said in a barely audible whisper.

"No she didn't. It was always just me, Kyle and Ca—"

I lunged at Jonas, punched him in the chest, and growled, "Why are you laughing? Tell me what just happened." Although I was pretty sure I knew.

Jonas swallowed his laughter. He looked down into my eyes. "That wasn't Bree. That was Dia. That was Sandra's rescue party."

EIGHTEEN

....

I f that was Sandra's rescue party, why are you still here?" I
asked, noticing only then that all humor had vanished
from Jonas's face.

He walked across the room to the sink and grabbed a couple of paper towels from a dispenser, running water over them.
His lip was starting to swell.

Cathy and Jack stared at the two of us, their mouths slightly
agape.

Jonas leaned against the counter. He crossed one arm while
dabbing his lip with paper towels in the other hand. I raised
my brows at him in a will-you-freaking-answer-me way.

"It would appear they left me," he said.

"They left you. Your own mother,"—I put air quotes around
the word "mother"— "the crazy scientist who has toyed with
our lives—the same mother who I'm feeling some severe feelings of hatred for right now—left you inside the school with
people who no longer trust you and could easily justify killing
you in self-defense for just standing there and breathing the
same air we breathe. You're telling me *she* left you?"

"Yes. Something tells me my lovely mother no longer be-
lieves I'm on her side. Or doesn't care." Jonas touched his lips
gently. "Did you have to hit me?" he asked Jack, ignoring me.

Jack ran a hand through his hair. "You're lucky I only hit
you once. I should have—" He stopped himself mid-sentence,
letting out a frustrated breath. He approached me and grabbed
my elbow gently. "Did *you* bring Sandra out of her coma?"

157

"It would appear so."

"Are you okay? You don't feel sick?" Jack asked, studying me.

I shook my head. Should I tell him that Jonas actually helped me? Would he be happy about that, or would he punch Jonas again?

"This is a disaster. How could you let her leave?" Cathy asked. Her voice had an angry edge.

"Wasn't like I was given a choice, Cathy," I said. I found Jack's eyes again. "I didn't want to heal her. Not until I knew more about her. But..."

"She had no control over her actions," Jonas said. "This was the work of The Farm. This is what I've been trying to tell you."

I whipped around to face Jonas. "Oh, yeah? Well, your communication skills suck."

"I'm going to go check with Security to see if they saw where Sandra went," Cathy said.

I watched her leave, then directed my attention back to Jonas. "Start talking. How are we supposed to believe *you*—the son of that maniac of a woman?"

"Sandra is your... mother?" Jack asked, as if finally catching up.

Jonas nodded. "I couldn't come out and tell you. Someone within the IIA would hear me. It wasn't just you being controlled. Some cloned freak was inside my head, too. Ty, mostly."

"But he's not there now?" I asked.

He shook his head. "No. I can tell without a doubt when someone or something is controlling me."

"Something?" Jack asked.

Jonas turned around and lifted his hair to reveal a round scar at the base of his hairline. "A tracker was placed inside my head to give the IIA full access to my mind and body. Sandra and the IIA can manipulate me and track my every move."

"Are you trying to tell me that someone was inside your head when you tried to make me kill myself? That someone else is trying to force me to kill Jack? That someone is inside your head now?"

Jonas faced me. His eyebrows further darkened his brown eyes. "Not exactly." He swallowed hard, then looked away.

"What *are* you saying?" I crossed my arms, losing patience.

"Some of that was me. I was getting inside your head after your dad died. I wanted to know more about you, and Jack was being very secretive. And when I thought you would ignore what you were created to do, I tried to scare you into needing to find out more."

Jack charged forward and stood in front of me. "It's true then?" He grabbed Jonas by the neck. "You put our lives at risk?"

Jonas gagged. "No," he squeaked out. "Let. Me. Explain."

Jack, stop, I pleaded.

No, he'll answer to us, or he'll find himself in his own sort of coma.

I touched Jack's arm. His blue eyes were on me instantly like two thick storm clouds. The pain that shot out of them was like a knife to my heart. "Let him explain," I pleaded. When Jack didn't immediately let go, I pulled harder on his arm. "He did keep me from going unconscious while I fixed Sandra's brain. We need to hear what he has to say."

Jack let him go with a shove backwards. Jonas massaged his neck. "I wasn't trying to kill either of you."

"What were you trying to do?" Jack asked.

"The clones need Lexi. We need her to accept who she is and embrace her abilities. And you were just going to let her go." Jonas was talking directly to Jack now. "You know she's the key to our survival."

I took in a breath, watching them both, but mostly Jack. "What's he talking about, Jack? What's he mean 'She's the key to our survival'?"

Jack stepped to me. He brushed the back of his hand down my face. "We know that Sandra altered our DNA to give us these supernatural abilities. My mother thinks Sandra also made sure that those abilities wouldn't come without consequences."

"You mean the nasty side effects?"

He nodded.

"What does that have to do with me and our survival?"

"Seth disagrees with Cathy. From conversations he's had with his sister over the years, he thinks Sandra made sure your DNA was equipped with the ability to heal each of us. Seth doesn't think Sandra planned on being separated from you. But your father hid you all these years."

"Is this why your parents and Seth are now at Wellington? Did they know all this?"

"Probably. Cathy's not really talking, still. And my father is nowhere to be found."

As if on cue, Cathy stormed in. "Jack! Addison is gone."

~~~~~

"Security cameras caught a female helping a child into the back of a sport utility." Cathy paced. "Then she and a second female, a teen, climbed into the front seat. When I questioned the officers at the front gate, they claimed that I had left with Roger in my Mercedes at about the same time."

"That's Dia," Jonas said. "She can make anyone believe they're seeing whatever she wants them to see."

"Who is Dia?" Jack asked.

"She's an identical match to Briana." I spoke with my eyes closed, massaging the bridge of my nose with my thumb and forefinger.

"And you know this how?" Jack asked.

"I met her." I looked down at my hands. Jack would never forgive me if I could have prevented Addison from being taken. "There are others, Jack. There's one that looks like Bree, another like Jonas..." I inhaled deeply before squaring my shoulders and facing him. "And one like you." I'd spent all week trying to forget what it looked like for Jack to hold Bree in his arms. Only it wasn't Jack and Bree.

"And you're just now telling me?"

"I couldn't. My mind was restricted by Jonas... or whoever was invading me."

Jack raised his hand. "We don't have time for this right now." He turned to Jonas. "Where will they take Addison?"

"I guess to The Farm. She's the one that got away."

What did *that* mean?

On the other side of the room, Cathy had slipped out. "Jack," I pleaded. "We'll get Addison back."

"*We* won't do anything. *I'll* get her back. You'll stay here. And you," he said, pointing at Jonas. "You're going to help me get into the IIA."

Jack turned and walked out. He slammed the door, causing me to flinch. I stared after him. "He'll need our help to break into that stupid facility." My voice cracked. I started after him.

"It's not breaking in that's the problem. It's getting back out." A chill danced down my arms at Jonas's words. His fingers circled my wrist, stopping my forward motion. "You and I have unfinished business."

I looked down at his hold, then at his face. "Let me go, Jonas."

"Not until you hear everything I need to tell you. Besides, he can't go tonight. He knows that. Let him cool off."

~~~~~

"What do you want me to do with that?" I stared at the gun lying on a table between Jonas and me.

"I want you to learn to use it." He backed up against the wall of Coach Williams's apartment, crossed his arms, and studied me. Coach had said Jonas could sleep on his couch. I figured an ex-FBI agent was the perfect person to watch over the boy who *kind of* tried to kill me.

I raised my hand very slowly. My fingers hovered just over the metal before making contact. The texture was partly rough, partly smooth. The steel was cool to the touch.

Pick it up, Lexi. His voice moved through my mind like an old friend looking for a place to relax for a while. It was confusing.

I didn't trust him, yet he seemed to want to help me. Jack was off dealing with his own issues. I needed someone.

I slid my fingers under the handle and lifted. "It's so heavy."

"That one's pretty light. It's perfect for a girl."

I glared at Jonas. "What? Because I'm a girl I'm weak?" I held the gun in front of me, getting used to the feel of it in my hand.

He chuckled. "Uh... no. 'Weak' is not a word I would use to describe you. But you are small, and you've never used a gun before. This is a good start."

I set the gun back down and moved away from the table. "Why do I need to learn to use a gun?"

"Because, although I was trying to get your attention by getting inside your head, I did not drug you, I did not run you off the road, and I did not put those marks on your neck. I also am not the one who murdered your father or his friend. I couldn't hurt you, Lexi."

Not that a gun would have stopped some freak inside my head from hurting me. "What do you know about my father's death?"

Jonas stared down at the floor before looking at me again. "I saw your father in person for the first time the night of the talk he gave last month to that group of physicians."

"You were there?"

"Mom... Sandra attended the event."

I thought back to that night. I would have remembered seeing an older woman that looked just like me. That was the first night I saw Seth.

"I followed her there," Jonas continued. "I remember thinking how strange it was that she wore black pants and a white button down shirt, until I watched her go through the employees' entrance. She hid among the workers, making sure to keep her distance from your father. But I knew immediately that she was watching him. She was acting so strange."

Unable to stand still, I circled the apartment, wringing my hands. "Didn't you already know Jack? How did you spy on Sandra without Jack seeing you?"

Jonas cocked his head. "I can hear her thoughts. See what she's seeing. Just like I can hear and see what you're seeing."

"How is that possible?" I asked. "I thought the only reason we have these strange supernatural abilities is—" I stopped myself. How *can* I speak to someone's mind? Force them to do what I want? I turned away from Jonas. I had refused to learn this information. Seth wanted to tell me. Jack had tried to convince me to attend The Program lessons with him. I whipped back around. "Unlike me, she has no idea that you're inside her head. Am I right?"

"Until now, maybe." Jonas's voice took on a regretful tone.

"Because of whatever it was she injected herself with?"

He nodded. "She has watched, studied, and manipulated human clones for the past eighteen years."

"But she's your mother? She raised you? What does having her as a mother even mean?" Absentmindedly, I touched my fingers to my lips, remembering Jonas's lips on mine. I bowed my head so that he couldn't see my face. As mad as I had been at Jonas for kissing me, it had never felt like kissing my brother or anything.

Jonas pushed away from the wall that he'd been leaning against since we started our conversation. He hooked a finger under my chin and lifted my face so that I had no choice but to meet his probing gaze. "We are not related in any way. My DNA is of some doctor I've never met. I share no relation to Sandra Whitmeyer, or to you." His brown eyes looked almost black as his pupils dilated. One could get lost in the darkness and danger he emanated.

I blinked twice, three times. If I hadn't been completely in love with Jack, I wondered what kind of pull the boy in front of me would've had on me.

When I pulled my face from his grasp, a grin spread across his face. He walked to the table where the gun lay, picked it up, and rested it against his palm. Never really closing his fingers around the handle, he stepped to me.

My pulse quickened. I stared at the dark metal, then up at Jonas. He watched me expectantly. I was sure he could hear the beating of my heart, feel the shaking of my limbs.

My eyes returned to the gun. Jonas let the gun slip and turn until he held it by the barrel, pointing the handle toward me.

Take it!

I shook my head and backed away a step.

He followed. He reached out with his empty hand and grabbed my arm, giving me no choice but to stand close. I followed the line of tattoos running up his arm until they disappeared beneath the sleeve of his shirt. He breathed heavily, like me.

Hold it, Lexi. Now!

I jumped at the boom of his voice inside my head. Slowly, I took the object from him, lifting it with extreme caution. I squeezed the handle without putting my finger anywhere near the trigger.

"I can smell your fear," he whispered. His hand slid down and circled my wrist. Goosebumps spread up my arms. "I can feel your pulse racing underneath my fingers. And I can hear your short breaths like you've just finished a sprint." He leaned closer to my ear, and I was sure I would pass out from his closeness and the fear of him I still felt. "The way you feel right now... that's what having Sandra Whitmeyer as a mother meant. Being poked and prodded. Being observed, studied, and held prisoner in a life that you can't escape." Jonas's eyes glassed over.

"Why didn't you run when you had the chance?" I asked.

The corners of his lips lifted slightly. "Naïveté really isn't attractive on you, Lexi."

That's how I knew. *You couldn't run. Just like I can't, now.* I pulled away, backed up, and sat on Coach's sofa. I lay the gun gently on my knees and rested my hand across it. As easily as I could have sunk to my knees and cried myself senseless, I knew that was not the answer.

"When I led you into The Farm, then helped you escape, I pretty much signed my death warrant."

I cocked my head. "What do you mean?"

"I showed you the most top secret government experiments in the world. I showed you into the devil's lair and provided you with all the ammunition you needed to expose the government for playing with human life. How do you think the public will react if they discover just how many human lives are lost for each cloned human they've produced? Even worse, how do you think Americans will react when they learn that the government had discovered a way to control minds?"

I stared at him; my heart practically stopped. "You think they'll murder you for showing me the facility and the other clones?"

"No. They'll kill me for showing you the exit."

"I thought their goal was to cure disease." My breath got caught in my throat. *I thought Jack and I were created to help people. Cure illnesses. Fix fatal injuries.*

"That's what they'll want the public to believe. Think about it. If the government tells the mother of a child born with a brain defect that they can now make that child normal? Or what about someone who's in an accident and wakes up paralyzed from the neck down? You think they'll fault a government who's discovered a way for that person to walk again? Even if they have to overlook the fact that the government uses that same technology in other ways."

I stared at the gun in my lap. The heat of anger spread up my arms, across my neck, and to my face. Would the government truly do something that deceptive? And where did I fit into this?

Jonas knelt in front of me and covered my hand with his. "You get tonight to mentally prepare," he said, his voice taking on a harshness that contradicted the gentle touch of his palm.

I lifted my eyes to study him. "Prepare?"

"Tomorrow, you'll learn to shoot that gun, and you'll learn to protect yourself. Both physically and mentally." *That's where we'll start, anyway.*

NINETEEN

....

aturday morning's swim competition came way too
quickly.

Somehow I managed to win each of my races and
put up times good enough to qualify for the next meet, but I
didn't score a single personal-best time. Not surprising, since I
had spent so little time in the pool the past week.

The meet finished around lunchtime. I stuffed my goggles
and swim cap inside my bag, grabbed my water bottle, then
threw my bag over my shoulder. When I turned toward the
locker room, I ran into a wall of a body.

Every muscle in my stomach tightened. "Jack, hey." Feeling
naked in my swimsuit, I crossed my arms across my chest.

"Hi." His voice was so quiet I barely heard him.

"I'm surprised you're here." His stormy eyes sent a chill
down my arms. I was shocked to see him after what had happened the night before.

"Jonas made me see the risks of barging in on the IIA before we're ready with a plan." He turned his head toward the
crowd that was thinning behind him. Jonas stood near the
door—waiting for Jack, maybe. Or possibly he was waiting to
show me how to use a gun. I suppressed a roll of the eyes just
before Jack turned back. Keeping his voice low, he said, "We
need to talk."

"Okay." I shifted on my feet. Why was I so nervous in front
of him? "I need a shower."

"Meet me behind the stables?"

I nodded. The stables were always fairly deserted on Saturdays and a perfect place to relax with Jack. I first started to fall for Jack when he introduced me to his passion for horses and to Cheriana, his cloned quarter horse. I craved alone time with him. Time to tell him how sorry I was. About Addison. About our recent argument. Would he ever look at me like he had the night of the gala? Like I was the only woman left on this earth and made especially for him? Did we even have time for that?

We also needed to discuss everything I'd learned about The Farm and what Jonas had shared. "Give me thirty minutes."

"I'll get you something to eat." He slipped his hand behind my neck and leaned in, kissed my forehead. "Hurry, okay?" He turned and left me staring at the back of his concert tee and admiring the well-sculpted muscles underneath. Wellington really should get rid of uniforms during the school week. I smiled, but it only lasted a moment before someone knocked into my back.

"Oh, sorry," Briana said, but I knew she wasn't. "Who is that?" She nodded toward Jonas. Jack spoke to him for a second, then pushed through the door, leaving Jonas alone.

Jonas had been watching me during my entire conversation with Jack, and he continued to stare now.

"That's no one," I said, my gaze still directed at him.

Briana moved to stand directly in front of me. "Why is 'no one' practically eating you for lunch with his eyes?"

I peeked around Briana. Sure enough, Jonas was smirking. His eyes pointed at me like a missile locked onto its target. He could hear Briana through my mind, and see what I was seeing. "Don't be ridiculous. And by 'no one,' I meant no one you need to concern yourself with." In other words, none of her business. "I have to shower."

I moved to get around her, but Briana cut me off. "What are you not telling me? Who is he?"

I sighed. "He's a friend of Jack's."

Briana moved beside me again, not bothering to hide the fact that she was openly staring down Jonas. "Introduce me."

"What? No." I lifted my water bottle and took a huge gulp.

Yes, Lexi, introduce us. Jonas's words filled my head. I had enjoyed an entire morning without him there. *I'm thinking this Briana is much prettier than Dia.*

They're identical, you idiot. I took another drink as I glanced sideways at Briana. When I saw her, this time I spit my water all over her.

"What the..." Briana brushed the water off of her chest. "What is *wrong* with you?" she screamed at me.

"Me? What is wrong with *you?*" I looked directly at her chest. She had always been well-endowed. Compared to me, any girl was. But looking at her now, I practically burst out laughing.

She followed my gaze. Looked down at her chest, then back at me. She gasped. Her cheeks turned red. "You can see, can't you?"

Briana had obviously discovered her ability to alter what others saw. Dia had used the same trick when I'd first met her at The Farm. "If you mean the 34DD breasts you suddenly have packed inside that tiny piece of lycra, then yes, I can see."

Briana didn't say another word. She spun on her heels and sped away from me.

Jonas no longer contained his laughter. Instead, he bent over holding his stomach. When he lifted his chest again, he thought, *Well, that was interesting. I guess we don't have to wonder anymore whether she knows she has some sort of supernatural ability.*

Shit, Jonas! Are you kidding me? Did you see her face? She was scared to death. Briana may have discovered enough of her ability to play around with the power, but confusion and panic were evident in the way she fled.

All traces of laughter left his face. *First of all, don't curse at me. It's not attractive. And secondly, I know Dia well enough to know that Briana doesn't have an ounce of DNA lending itself to fear. That was a girl that was well aware of her ability to enhance her looks. She's just shocked that you saw through the charade.*

~~~~~

I raced through my shower, anxious to meet Jack. As I dressed in jeans and a fitted cashmere sweater, I kept an eye out for Briana, but she was nowhere to be seen.

My hand rested on the door handle leading to the hallway when I heard three distinct pops from the hallway. I yanked my hand back. I might've had no desire to use guns, but I'd watched enough TV to recognize gunfire. Every muscle in my body tightened, from the back of my neck all the way down to the arches of my feet, cementing me to the floor.

"What was that?" I heard a girl from somewhere in the vicinity of the showers yell.

"Who's letting off firecrackers?" another girl asked.

I stared at the door handle.

"Were those gunshots?" someone whispered close behind me.

Finally, snapping out of my paralysis, I turned. Briana stood in front of me in her sweats. Her red, curly hair dripped down the front of her chest.

Lexi! Where are you? Jonas was inside my head. I jumped.

"Lexi, answer me. Was that gunfire?" Briana asked again.

I could only nod.

A few girls came around the corner to inquire. When I saw their faces, they appeared concerned, but so far, they remained calm.

Lexi, Jonas said to my mind. *There are IIA agents on campus. They're armed, and they're coming for you—and any other clones they might find.*

My heart rate sped up, but my mind finally began to work. I stared right into Briana's eyes. "Yes, that was gunfire. Help me get the others away from the door."

Briana didn't ask questions. She began shushing the twenty or so swimmers and instructing them to move into the showers and to "Shut the hell up!"

I kept walking, past the showers to the door that led to the pool. Briana grabbed my arm. "Where are you going?"

"I'll be fine. Let me go."

"No, Lexi." Panic surged across her face, her eyes.

I pulled my arm from her grasp and placed my hands on her shoulders. "Listen. I'll be okay. I don't know how much you understand about what you did out there by the pool, but I have abilities of my own. I need you to trust me. And I need you to keep them quiet." I lifted my chin in the direction of the other girls. "Actually, I want you to try something. Do you know how you... uh... enhanced your figure? I need you to imagine those girls and yourself as invisible. Can you do that?"

Her eyes doubled in diameter. She shook her head. "No. I don't think I can. I don't even know how I did that. Not really."

"Just try. Okay? I know that you can do this. I've seen it done."

Briana nodded, seeming to understand. She and I would be having a little chat sometime very soon about how much she already knew.

I turned and opened the back door just wide enough to slip through. A headphone-wearing custodian picked up trash in the bleachers on the far side of the pool. I stayed close to the wall as I crossed toward the main exit. A few stragglers from the swim meet were huddled in the bleachers. Some lay flat, unmoving, between rows. My eyes traveled to the other end of the pool to a single door—an exit very rarely used and away from the direction of the gunfire. Just as I opened my mouth to yell at the remaining spectators, a door to the main exit flew open and in walked a group of men and women holding guns, very much resembling a SWAT team.

I quickly ducked inside Coach Williams's office undetected, a little shocked that it was open. The room was dark. The only light came from the pool area. *Jack, I've got trouble.* I dropped to my hands and knees and crawled under Coach's desk. I curled into a tiny ball.

Where are you?

I'm in Coach Williams's office. Trapped. I heard gunshots. Jonas says it's the IIA.

I'm on my way, he said.

I heard voices approach. I thought my heart would explode.

Jack, just in case, I want you to know I'm so sorry about Addison. I never meant to put her at risk. I didn't want to heal Sandra, but I couldn't control—

Shh. I know. You're going to be fine. We're going to be fine. I don't blame you about Addison.

The way he said "we're" sent a spark through my blood. It was near impossible to see a future beyond this school anymore, beyond the predicament of being a clone with abilities these murderers and scientists wanted to use—and more to the point, abuse—but I knew one thing for sure: I did not want to imagine a life where Jack blamed me for some part of this mess. I had to find Addison and make everything right.

The voices got louder. I tilted my head back, closed my eyes, and said a silent prayer. When I reopened my eyes, a dark metal object stared me in the face—a handgun of some sort was fastened to the underside of Coach's desk. I pushed further into the oak desk, unable to distance myself from the deadly weapon.

Jonas? Where had he gone? He hadn't spoken to me since he warned me of IIA agents. *Are you seeing this? Boy do I wish I had taken you up on your offer to teach me to shoot.*

Additional voices joined the small group. There had to be a dozen agents just outside the office.

Lexi, reach up and unsnap the strap holding the gun, Jonas said.

Just as I put my fingers on the strap and began to pull, Jack said, *What gun? No, Lexi. Don't. You don't know how to use a gun. You'll only put yourself in greater danger.*

Great. Now, I had both of them inside my head, contradicting each other.

Do it, Lexi! Jonas screamed.

"Did anyone check the pump room and the offices?" one of the agents asked outside Coach's office.

They're coming in! I screamed inside my head so that both Jack and Jonas could hear. Jonas could force me to grab the gun. He hadn't, though, and I needed to act.

Keep calm. I'm coming. Jonas, where are you? Jack asked.

Jonas said nothing. He'd gone silent. I searched my mind and found nothing. Great. When I wanted nothing to do with him, he gave me no privacy. Now that I needed him...

Whispered voices came closer. "Can you imagine the reward for finally capturing Sandra Whitmeyer's clone?" a woman asked.

"It's hard to believe the great and powerful Peter Roslin trusted the wrong person in the end," a male voice answered.

An audible gasp escaped my lips and tears stung my eyes.

"I'd heard Dr. Roslin had information to destroy the IIA labs, but someone killed him before anyone found it."

A gunshot, followed by crashing glass, shattered my thoughts. "What are you two just standing there for?!" a third agent joined the conversation.

"Awaiting orders, sir," the woman answered.

"Check that office."

My pulse lurched. I reached up and unhooked the small strap on the holster. I pulled the gun from the leather. It was much heavier than the one I'd held the previous night. Heat spread across the back of my neck. Muscles clenched in my shoulders just thinking about the lethal object that was three times the size of my hand.

Another loud explosion of glass pierced the air, followed by the high-pitched squeal of the fire alarm. *What was that?*

Tell me what's going on. Jack said. *I'm just outside the building. Which freaking entrance should I use?*

Jonas remained silent.

I placed the gun in the waistband of my jeans, praying with everything in me that the gun had a safety and that I wouldn't shoot myself in the leg. Slowly, I began to crawl from under the desk just as the door to Coach's office squeaked open.

Lowering my head to the ground, my eyes widened at the sight of two sets of feet entering the office. By the size of them, it was one female agent and one male. To make matters worse, the voices of at least six others stood just outside the office.

Mentally calculating my options, I realized I didn't have many. I was trapped, and had only two weapons: a gun I didn't know how to use, and my own mind. I drew the gun from my waistband and eased up from my squatting position behind the desk.

I faced two agents. The female agent wore a black baseball cap with her hair pulled through the hole in the back in a ponytail. The male agent was a fit man. I could just make out sculpted muscles beneath a plain black T-shirt. Before the agents could react, I pointed the gun straight at the woman's head and flooded both of their minds, something I had never done before. *Do not speak. You will both lower your weapons.*

They each instantly did as I commanded.

Turn back toward the door. I eased around the desk and stepped to their backs. *You will protect me at all costs as you lead me to the main exit. Tell me you understand.*

In unison, they said, "We understand."

Now walk.

The three of us exited Coach's office. My heart leaped to my throat as I realized there were more agents than I had thought.

Agent Ball Cap stuck out a protective arm as she shielded me from agents to our left. She pointed her gun directly at them. "Drop your weapons." Their eyes widened as they traded glances, but they did as they were told.

Agent Sculpted Muscles directed agents to our right to clear a path as we walked slowly toward the exit.

"You two are making a mistake," another male agent said. I recognized his voice as the one that had handed out orders a few short moments ago. He was an older man, cursed with unfortunate thinning hair. His eyes focused in on mine. "Sarah, we are not here to hurt you. Sandra would like to spend time with you."

A hysterical laugh escaped my throat. *You're an idiot. I want you to turn and jump in that great big pool behind you right now.*

Blood that had only dripped lightly now poured from my nostrils. I leaned forward, letting the blood drip to the floor. The metallic scent of blood mixed with chlorine. Agent Thinning Hair did as he was told and leaped into the pool, making a great splash. With a satisfied grin I ordered Agent Sculpted Muscles: *Give me your shirt, please.* With one hand he hunched his shoulders and pulled his T-shirt over his head, sliding the gun through the opening until he tossed the shirt to me. I wiped the blood off my face and applied pressure to my nose.

Agent Ball Cap had four agents on their stomachs, faces to the ground, and disarmed. As I maneuvered around their bodies, a hand reached out and snaked around my ankle, sending me sprawling across the wet pool deck. I screamed as my jeans

tore and skin ripped from my knee. My ankle twisted unnatu-
rally. My gun pinched into my back.

Agent Ball Cap took two giant steps and hit the woman
who still held tightly to my ankle with the butt of her gun.

I stared at the woman, grasping my foot and breathing
hard. Her eyes watered, but she looked directly at me and said
with a hoarse voice, "Your time is up. Sooner or later, you'll
have to come in. He'll force you to."

"Who? Who will force me?" I asked. When Agent Ball Cap
pointed her gun at the woman's head, I reached out a hand. *No,
don't shoot her. Leave her be.*

"Dr. Wissss..." She hissed as she slowly loosened her hold
on me. Pain seared through my ankle and from the skinned
knee. I crab-walked backwards away from her with much discomfort, then turned over and crawled the rest of the way to
the door, careful to only allow the one knee to touch the
ground.

When I reached the doors, I pulled myself to my feet by
holding onto the metal door handles. Agent Sculpted Muscles
and Agent Ball Cap stood behind me. *Thank you for your help. Go
jump into the pool with your guns, now.*

Amused, I pushed through the exit and limped into the
hallway.

I started in the direction of the women's locker room when
several agents entered the hallway in front of me. Switching
directions, I darted around the corner in the opposite direction.

My back against the wall, I breathed through the pain of my
injured ankle. Slowly, I peeked around the corner. The agents
reached the pool doors and stopped.

I squinted and focused on a woman pushing through the group. Sandra.

"Find Jonas," she said through gritted teeth. "And find Sarah." She ushered the SWAT team forward. "Remember, I want both of them unharmed. We're not leaving without them."

TWENTY

··

I was unsure about a lot, but I knew one thing for certain: I would not allow my DNA donor to capture me for her wack job experiments. And I worried about my school-mates trapped in the locker room. I had to get help. I started to back away from the corner, but was stopped.

A hand slipped around my waist. Another cupped my mouth. I sucked in a deep breath through my nose. "Shhh. Don't scream."

Every muscle along my spine tensed until I recognized Jack's scent and voice.

I turned and threw my arms around his neck. He circled his arms around my waist. *You okay?*

I nodded, breathing into his neck, but tensed as his hands continued around until they came into contact with the gun tucked into my jeans at the small of my back.

He pulled away, taking the gun with him. "What the hell, Lexi?" he asked in a loud whisper. "Are you crazy?"

I only shrugged, then leaned my head back and looked down the hallway. When I met his angry gaze again, I mind-spoke, *Seriously? You want to debate my mental state right now?*

Let's go. After tucking the gun into the back of his own pants, he grabbed my hand and pulled.

I grunted in pain. Jack turned and looked down at my leg, then released a heavy sigh. *Can you walk until we get to the next building over?*

Yes. What about the girls in the locker room? I asked. *Bree has them corralled in the shower.*

They'll be fine. His facial expression did not reflect the certainty of his words.

Instead of going outside, Jack led me down the steps to the building's basement.

"Where are we going?" I had never gone into the basements of the school buildings. Not until last week when Kyle led me to The Program.

"To the tunnels. We'll cross over to the classroom building and find a spot to hide out while I heal that leg."

And ankle.

His grip on my hand tightened. "What happened to Jonas?"

"I don't know. One minute you both were inside my head telling me what to do, the next... he was gone."

We made it most of the way across the tunnel. When I stopped a second time from the pain, he reached down and scooped me up into his arms.

"You need to save your energy." I leaned into his chest. I knew he needed every ounce of strength to heal my ankle. Unless I could somehow take on some of the negative side effects like I had when he healed Kyle.

He hugged me close. "I'll be fine. Let's get to a bathroom, though, so we can clean up your knee."

And hide. "There, on the right," I said when I saw the ladies' restroom sign.

We were ten feet away from our destination when we heard a voice behind us. "Put her down, Jack."

Jack stopped. He slowly turned. Jonas pointed a gun at us.

"Why, Jonas? I thought..." I didn't know what I thought. I studied the straight edge of his set jaw and the lack of emotion on his face. My eyes traveled over his body, landing on the smooth, pale skin of his arms, void of any ink.

"Jonas, she's hurt. I need to heal her." *When I set you down, I want you to reach behind me and get the gun out of my waistband.*

Jack slowly set me on my feet. I pretended to steady myself by hugging Jack, allowing my right hand to slide down to his waist. I wrapped my hand around the handle of the gun and lifted it from his jeans. I looked up into Jack's concerned eyes. *This isn't Jonas. Meet Ty. Notice the lack of tattoos on his arms.* Jack's face softened upon hearing that it wasn't his friend who had betrayed us, but the relief that fell over his face was soon replaced with deep trenches of worry across his forehead.

"Turn around, Lexi." Ty's voice sounded somehow off to me. "You had to go and make everything so difficult. I told you what would happen if you didn't cooperate. I told you I'd force you to hurt Jack."

Leaving my right arm behind Jack, I faced Ty. He was going to see through my awkwardness or hear my thoughts. Then it dawned on me. He wasn't hearing my thoughts. At least he hadn't reacted to any. "You're not going to force me to do anything," I said, with much more conviction than I felt. I hopped in front of Jack on my one good ankle and bent my right arm behind me. Jack took the gun.

Keep him talking, Lex. Jack fiddled with the gun at my back.

"What kind of coward has to hide behind the face of someone else to exert control over little ol' me?"

His lips quirked up. "It was definitely more fun when you couldn't tell us apart. What's the use in having a clone if you can't use them to do your dirty work?"

I cocked my head, studying Ty. "You came with the IIA? They're controlling everything you do. You know that, right?" I broke my contact with Jack and hobbled away from him. Though Jonas practically strangled Ty that day at The Farm, Ty *had* helped me find my way back out. His actions now didn't make sense, nor did his desire to harm Jack.

The clones inside the IIA facility were simply pawns.

Ty's lips quirked. "Controlling me? No." *And we are most certainly not pawns.*

I flinched at the sound of his mindspeak. Why was he in my head now? And not before?

"Jack is your shield," he said, as if the brightest lightbulb in the world just clicked on in his head.

I looked nervously at Jack. "My shield?"

Ty shook his head. "Never mind."

But he had said it—shield—and it all became clear. When Jonas... or Ty... forced me to lift a knife high above Jack, I had nearly plunged it into his chest. But Jack had rolled over, grazing my knee with his fingers... and it was then that the mind invader had vanished, and I was able to drop the knife.

There were other times, too, like now, that Ty hadn't heard my thoughts. And now I knew it was because Jack had been touching me.

"It was you who tried to make me kill Jack." I had accepted that it wasn't Jonas, but staring at Ty now, it all made sense. The IIA used Jonas's look-alike to force Jonas into my head.

That's why I had been so certain that Jonas was the one manipulating me.

"Me. Jonas. What's the difference? It's all part of the IIA's plan," Ty said.

Finally catching up, Jack moved closer and placed his fingers on my arm. *I can't believe there're two of them.*

I met Ty when Jonas led me inside The Farm on campus.

Ty cocked his gun. "Step away from her."

No, don't, Jack. He can't hear my thoughts while you're touching me, and he won't kill me. So stand behind me.

How do you know? Jack asked.

The IIA is here for me. They want something from me. I heard Sandra tell the agents not to hurt me.

Was this before or after you sprained your ankle?

"I said, step away." Ty waved the gun at us haphazardly, which made me more nervous than the possibility that he might actually pull the trigger on purpose. I had read somewhere that most shooting incidents are from a gun accidentally going off.

"Look, Ty. Tell me what it is you want. Maybe we can work something out."

"We'll work something out all right." He smirked. "Tell your knight to step away. I've got something you want. Information I've been instructed to tell you and only you."

I looked back at Jack with a raised brow and nodded.

"Fine," Jack said. "I'll lower my hand, but I won't step away. Tell her quickly." The warmth of his hand left my lower back. But his close proximity remained.

Okay, Ty, out with it.

You will come with me, and I promise to return Addison to Wellington.

My heart picked up speed just hearing Addison's name. *How can you promise that?*

I'm not promising it. Sandra is. They haven't done anything to Addison yet, other than insert a tracker into her brain, but they will program her tracker soon if you don't come. And if you'll come, Sandra promised to return Addison to Jack, here, at Wellington.

Frightened of what Sandra might do to Addison through a tracker, I was tempted to take Ty up on his promise, but I didn't believe him. I reached my hand behind me. Jack immediately grabbed it, silencing Ty from my head while I searched for Jonas. *Jonas, can you hear me?*

Been waiting for you to get Ty out of your head. My plan backfired on me. I tried to reason with that crazy clone of mine. He rewarded me with a blow to my head.

Did you hear what he said? I asked Jonas.

Yes. He's lying. They would never let Addison go now that they have her.

"What's it going to be?" Ty asked, becoming impatient.

What's he want? Jack held more tightly to my hand.

I gave my head a small shake. *He wants me to return to The Farm with him.*

Fat chance of that. When I remained silent, Jack stepped closer, careful not to lose contact with me while continuing to hide the gun in his hand. *That's not all, is it?*

What do you mean?

I mean, you're silent. You're considering whatever it is that he offered in return. Jack's heat on my back made it even harder to concentrate. His hand left mine, traveled up my arm until it reached my cheek. Applying pressure, he turned my head, forcing me to look at him. *What are you not telling me?* When I didn't answer again, he slid his hand down my body and pushed the small of my back, bringing my body flush with his. His eyes burned into mine.

Jack. I squirmed under his gaze.

Don't "Jack" me. Tell me.

I took a deep breath. *He said the IIA would trade Addison for me.*

Jack's face reddened. *No! Not even an option.*

Jack. Be reasonable.

I. Said. No. I'm not trading one person for another.

"Okay, time's up." Ty's footsteps sounded behind me until I felt something hard press into the middle of my spine.

I lowered my eyes to the gun Jack still held between us, then peered up at him.

Duck to your right! Jack said in my head. *Now!*

With no time to think, I darted right, falling to the floor. Jack's arm swept upwards, hitting Ty's hand and knocking the gun loose. The metal made contact with the hard tile floor and the gun slid against the wall.

Jack pointed his gun directly between Ty's eyes. "Tell me who is in charge at the IIA." A vein in Jack's neck was pulsing as he held Ty's neck with one hand and the gun with the other.

"Sandra," he choked.

"Who else?"

I crawled across the floor and sat beside the gun, just in case I needed it. My ankle throbbed.

Though Ty struggled for air, a smirk filled with arrogance spread across his face. "That is the question, isn't it?"

"Answer me." Jack pulled back the hammer on the gun.

Jonas appeared at the entrance to the hallway. "Jack, don't." He then looked at me, scanned my body starting at my face, and stopping when he saw the blood seeping through my jeans and the unnatural way my ankle stretched out in front of me.

"Tell me who," Jack yelled.

"Who what, Jack?" Jonas moved closer. "I don't care for Ty either, but killing him isn't what you want to do."

"Oh, yeah? Why not?"

"Because he's just another victim."

A gagging noise escaped Ty's throat. "I'm no victim."

"That's not helping, Ty," Jonas said.

Ty laughed again, and a chill moved down my spine. "Tell him who Sandra's partner is."

Jonas stared at Ty. Jonas's face was unreadable. Did Jonas know what Ty was talking about? Did he already know who was helping Sandra? And what prompted Jack to ask?

Your boyfriend forgot one small detail in this plan of his to make me talk, Ty mindspoke to me. *He forgot that without touching you...*

My head snapped to attention.

Now, don't even think about mindspeaking with Jack. Grab the gun.

I glanced sideways, and without a second thought, slid my fingers under the handle of the gun and brought it to my lap.

Stand and walk toward me.

I did as I was ordered. I limped toward them. Jack yelled at Ty, but I couldn't hear the words any longer.

Shoot him. Now! Ty yelled.

I lifted the gun and pointed it at Jack's chest. Sweat formed along my hairline. The throbbing in my ankle was almost unbearable. I held the gun tightly. My finger curled around the trigger and began to squeeze.

Lexi, no! Jonas's presence filled my head. He bulldozed his way through Ty and Jack and tackled me to the ground. A gun went off, but I didn't know if it was the one I held, or Jack's. Pain erupted through my shoulder.

Before I even had a chance to get my bearings, I heard another small explosion. Smoke filled the hallway.

I tried to push myself up. Jonas lifted his shirt over his head and thrust it at me. *Breathe into this. I'm going to take some of your pain away while you and Jack get to that bathroom.* He pointed twenty feet away at the door we were originally headed for.

Whether it was from adrenaline or the strength in Jonas's words, I managed to hobble over to Jack, who was hacking from the smoke. I took in a deep breath through the T-shirt, then placed it over Jack's face. We supported each other, ran for the bathroom, and didn't stop until we were safely inside.

Jack helped me to the floor, then stood to assess all of my injuries.

~~~~~

Jack only threw up twice after healing my injuries. I had done my best to enter his mind and lessen the side effects of the healing process.

I lay against the wall, out of breath and lightheaded. "What do you think is happening?"

"I don't know, but I'm feeling better. I'm going to check it out." He grabbed the gun from its resting spot on the sink and brought it to me. "Here. Hold this. Anyone enters this bathroom, I want you to shoot them."

I gaped at him. "Jack, no." I moved to my knees and pushed myself up. "I'm fine. We'll go together."

Jack stared at me for a few seconds before finally agreeing. "Fine. Stay behind me."

The hallway was quiet. We heard shouting in the distance, though. We eased our way down the hall. Jack held the gun in front of us with one hand, and held my hand with his other. The smell of smoke was still intense. As we approached the stairwell, Jonas appeared.

"They're gone," he said, out of breath.

I let out a huge sigh of relief.

"Gone? Are the police here?" Jack asked.

"Yes, and so is the fire department." Jonas glanced down at my ankle. *All better?*

I nodded. "It was Dia, wasn't it? She got them into Wellington without sounding any alarms."

"That's right. And they set off a small bomb to throw authorities off while they escaped."

"Why didn't you tell me that Sandra was your mother?" Jack asked Jonas.

"Would you have trusted me if I had?"

Jack looked at me. "No, not once I met Lexi." He reached out and cupped my cheek. "But I would have put some of our background together much faster. Made different decisions, for sure."

I knew what he meant. He might have refused to come to Wellington. To meet me. *We were meant to meet, so don't even go there. Sandra would have found me eventually, anyway.* I leaned my face into his palm. *We have to find a way to protect each other.*

"What's next?" Jack asked.

"Next?" Jonas sucked in a deep breath. "We train. We become stronger than the IIA. We rescue Addison. We take charge of our own lives."

A certain darkness shaded Jonas's eyes, and his shoulders slumped forward. I couldn't be sure, and I definitely didn't understand it, but I thought a part of him had to be feeling betrayed by the woman who'd raised him.

TWENTY-ONE

....

I t didn't take long for parents to learn of the small explosion on campus. But since few students were hurt, and even fewer witnessed IIA agents with guns, Dean Fisher and President Wellington were able to minimize the level of hysteria.

Parents who lived nearby showed up that day to remove their children. Cathy, Dean Fisher, and Dr. Wellington spent the afternoon on the phone. I began to suspect a trend. Armed with my computer and knowing no parent was coming to get me, I escaped to a spot on the top floor of the library. I scooted a club chair close to a window overlooking the main loading zone between the two dorms. Tucking my legs beneath my body, I curled up with my computer and began comparing Dad's list of human clones with the parents who were arriving at Wellington that day.

Just as I suspected. The kids whose parents had arrived so far were not on Dad's list. Just how many clones were at Wellington? I wondered. I scanned Dad's records. He had noted names, aliases, and known locations. By my count, there would be about fifty students left when "regular" students were gone.

"Lexi."

I turned in my seat at the sound of Jack's voice. He looked dejected, tired. His face drooped, his shoulders hung forward. Shifting my computer to the chair, I stood. "What's happened?"

"You need to come with me."

"Where?"

"The infirmary."

My heart sank. "Who?"

He didn't answer. Just stared at the spot on the floor in front of him.

I packed up my computer and followed him wordlessly out of the library. His silence was all the proof I needed that something devastating had happened, and I knew not to ask questions.

The upstairs of the infirmary was equipped with twenty beds, all separated by curtains. About a dozen students injured by flying debris from the bombing were being treated by Wellington nurses and Midland EMTs. The murmurs of students recounting what had happened to them sounded like nothing more than a low hum.

"You're scaring me," I said to Jack as he led me past the injured.

He squeezed my hand and pulled me to the last bed on the left. Jonas stood off to the side and out of the way. Kyle leaned over someone in the bed, but I couldn't see who.

"Kyle. Lexi is here," Jack said.

Only when Kyle turned did I see the person in the bed.

"Dani?" I rushed to her side, opposite where Kyle sat. Her face was tear-stained. She glanced from Kyle to Jonas to me. "What happened?" I asked.

"I'm sorry, Lex." A tear ran down her face.

"What are you sorry about? Are you hurt? Have they called your parents?"

"Show her," Jack said.

I glanced back at Jack. Jonas stuffed his hands in his pockets. "Show me what?" I asked, confused. Danielle wiped the tears from her face with her bare hand.

Kyle helped her lean forward. She turned her head to face him. Slowly, Kyle lifted her hair to reveal the back of her neck.

There, at the base of her hairline, was a small incision. My heart jumped into my throat. My hand flew to my mouth to smother my gasp. Reaching out my other hand, my fingers hovered just above what looked like two stitches. I looked at Jonas.

They inserted a tracker inside her, he said.

The air was knocked from me by that punch to the gut. "Who did this to you? When did it happen?"

"I found her unconscious on a bench outside the aquatics center after the meet was over." Kyle rubbed Danielle's hand while he talked. "She was on the side leading to the boys' dorm. I carried her here. A few minutes later I heard the explosion."

Jonas, who did this?

Had to be Sandra.

We can remove it, right?

He shook his head. *Removing it will kill her instantly. I'm sure Sandra counted on me informing you of that.*

"There's more," Danielle whispered. She reached into her pocket and handed me a folded piece of paper. "It's addressed to you."

Jack took three steps forward. "You didn't tell me they gave you something." He tried to snatch it from my hands, but I quickly shielded it.

195

After glaring at him, I unfolded the piece of paper and read the contents to myself.

"I found it in my pocket when I woke up," Danielle said. "What does it mean, Lexi? I didn't understand it."

What does it say? Jack demanded.

I raised my head and stared at him through a waterfall of tears. *They'll kill Dani if I don't turn myself over.*

~~~~~

I raced down the stairs to the basement of the infirmary like I was running from another bomb. Only this time, the bomb was embedded at the base of my best friend's skull, and I didn't know how long the timer was set for.

Down here was The Program. And I wanted to know everything. About my true identity and purpose. About the other cloned humans. And about the adults calling the shots.

If I was going to turn myself over to Sandra Whitmeyer, I would go armed with the information that had been hidden from me most of my life.

I ran from door to door, attempting to open each one. When I tried the fifth door and it was locked, I kicked and pounded on the hard steel. I stepped back and looked up at the ceiling. When I saw the small camera above me, I began waving. "Hello. You wanted me? Well, here I am. So open the doors." I wanted inside these rooms. I wanted to know—no, I *needed* to know— what The Program was all about. Why did everything come back to me learning about my creation? Why did Sandra want me so badly? Why had Seth insisted I be a part of The Program?

Unable to contain my rage, I screamed, then pounded on the door in front of me again until I could do nothing but sob.

After one last weak punch, I leaned my head against the cold metal, my hand still fisted against the door. Tears ran like a river down my face. My body convulsed. Arms circled my body and pulled me backwards. "Shhh. It's going to be okay."

I crumbled into Jack. He didn't let go as he sank to the ground with me, pulling me into his lap. I shook my head adamantly. "No, it's not going to be okay."

He held tighter, burying his face into my neck. "I promise, it will be."

"I just lied to my best friend, Jack." I sobbed, turning into his chest. He rubbed my back and let me cry. "I told my best friend that everything was going to be fine. But it's not going to be fine." How could it be? She had no idea what had just been done to her.

I pushed back and stared into his eyes. "They're going to kill my best friend. And they're going to kill Addison." I sucked in the shakiest of breaths. "Unless I hand myself over."

Jack ran his hand over my hair, smoothing loose strands behind my left ear. "They won't. And no, you absolutely are not turning yourself over to them. Don't even go there."

"They will, Jack. They will kill them."

"We're not going to let them. Do you hear me?" He brushed his lips across mine. "Now, listen to me. I wish we had all the time in the world to be angry and talk about how unfair this all is, but—"

"But we don't." I swiped at my drenched face. He was right. My tears would not help Danielle. She needed help reaching her eighteenth birthday and beyond, and I was the only one who could get her there.

I pulled back and stared up into Jack's eyes. "We have to fight."

"Yes."

"All of us."

"I know."

"We have to decide who we can trust. Who's on our side. And then we have to trust them. And we have to fight." I was repeating everything, maybe in an effort to convince myself more than Jack.

Jack placed his hands on both sides of my face and kissed me hard on the lips. He pulled back, locking eyes with me. "I know."

"You know."

"Yes." He was as calm as I'd ever seen him. That calmness transferred to me in a wave. He was my rock. We'd face this together. This was what love was. When you're faced with your deepest despair, a hole you're scared you'll never climb back out of, the one who loved you most would lift you out and be your strength.

I stared into Jack's eyes, each one a raging sea being rocked by a hurricane. "Thank you."

"For what?" he whispered, running fingers along the strands of hair framing my face.

"For coming to Wellington. For not running. I wouldn't have survived everything that's happened had you not been here with me."

He kissed me lightly on the lips, which felt funny, soft after a hard cry. "You're strong." He leaned his forehead against mine. "We'll face this head on, together."

"Well," Jonas clapped his hands together behind me. "Glad that's all cleared up. What's the plan?"

I spun around and faced Jonas. Jack stayed close to me. Protective, while I regained my bearings.

"Let's find a place to sit," Jack said. He reached down, grabbed my hand, and led me two doors down. When he turned the knob, it opened immediately. Of course it did. I rolled my eyes.

"Tell us about the trackers," Jack said, entering the room and pulling a couple of chairs together.

Jonas followed us in. I wasn't used to him looking nervous, but in that moment I knew he had bad news. "Like I told you before, Sandra inserted a tracker into the base of my brain mainly to track my whereabouts. I couldn't live my life trapped in The Farm. And she allowed me some liberty to leave The Farm as long as I didn't fight the tracker." He walked over and leaned against a table, crossing his arms and one leg in front of the other.

"Why do you think she's allowed you to live?" I asked. "I mean, didn't you say she could kill you with a couple of keystrokes on the computer?"

Jonas shifted and rubbed at the stubble on his jaw. "I don't know why. Unless it's because she thinks they actually have control of me. Through Ty. Or by programming the tracker in my own head."

"Did you know back then that the tracker was permanent?" I walked over and slid into the seat next to Jonas. Jack sat beside me. He propped his elbows against his knees and clasped his hands together. His leg brushed against mine, keeping constant contact.

"No, I had no idea. And I didn't understand how much power that tiny device gave the IIA. More specifically... Sandra."

"What kind of power?" Jack asked.

"Initially, the tracker was used for knowing where the human clones were inside the IIA. It gave the clones a way to walk around the facility. A little more freedom."

"And then?" I prompted.

"Then, as with anything Moth... Sandra did, the device became another way for her to manipulate whatever it was she wanted control of. In this case, she wanted more mind control."

"And you *knew* this?" Jack asked. "Why would you let her put one of these inside your brain?"

Jonas's face hardened. "Because, Jack, I had to get out of that prison. And I didn't have a choice."

A shiver moved through me. I thought about what Jonas had said when he'd laid the gun in my hand and explained what it was like to grow up with Sandra as a mother. I touched Jonas's arm. "Go on. So, what happened?" Jack stiffened beside me.

"I already knew I had pretty intense mind control of my own. I constantly practiced getting inside the heads of others—inside the non-cloned when I didn't want to be detected, then, as I got stronger, inside the clones. Before long I could tell any time Sandra's machines altered my tracker, and I knew any time another clone entered my mind." Jonas narrowed his gaze on me. "I made one mistake, though."

"Ty."

He nodded. "That's right."

"What do you mean? Why was Ty your mistake?" Jack asked.

Jonas shifted his gaze to Jack. "Ty is my DNA twin. By practicing, I became stronger. Ty picked up on this. And he followed in my footsteps. He became just as good, if not better, at the mind tricks."

"But Ty seems so different from you most of the time."

"Ty became distant from me. I caught Sandra whispering to him in corners over the past few months." Jonas stopped, stared intently at me. "I knew, that morning when I had the most intense panic attack I'd ever experienced, right after having just had an unexplained panic attack the night before: Ty had learned to get inside my head, undetected."

"Ty was controlling you the night you forced Kyle's hand into the fire," Jack confirmed.

"And, of course, the next morning when you practically forced me to stab Jack." I glanced regretfully at Jack.

"The good news? I'm already another step ahead of Ty."

"How?" I asked.

"Once I had Sandra's trust, I was able to leave the facility. She was too busy in her own little scientific world to monitor everything I did, so when no one paid attention, I worked to strengthen other areas. And for some reason, she hadn't made me return by the time she fell into a coma."

I remembered how Jonas pinned Ty to the wall by his neck. "You built up your physical strength."

"And I studied. I got into many forms of self-defense: guns, knives, martial arts."

"Which is why you wanted Georgia, Fred, and me to take those classes." Jack's leg shook next to mine.

Jonas nodded. "At the same time, I borrowed your books and studied biology, DNA mapping, genetic engineering and manipulation... you name it."

"And when Seth came along and started The Program..." Jack looked like he was understanding everything Jonas was saying.

"I jumped at the chance to find out what he knew and grow closer to you, Georgia, and Fred. I thought we could help each other. And I no longer trusted my mother." Jonas said the word "mother" with more than a hint of disgust.

"And I led us straight here. To Wellington. To Lexi."

I stared at a spot on the floor in front of me, trying to make sense of Jonas's reasons for being at Wellington and for telling us everything now.

"I want you to know I'm on your side. You can trust me."

I snapped my head in his direction.

"Yes, I hear almost everything you think, Lexi. You're too new to all of this, but I've also been on the receiving end of your mindspeak." Jonas's lips curved up. "And let me just say, the moment you had me hold a scalpel to my own jugular vein, I knew it wouldn't be long before you caught up to me in terms of mind strength."

"What about Ty? Is he still in your head?" I asked.

"Not at this very moment." I heard uncertainty in Jonas's words.

Jack threaded his fingers with mine and rubbed his thumb across the backside of my hand. "Are you still in Lexi's head?"

Jonas smiled. "Not at this very moment."

Jack shifted. I squeezed his hand. *Let it go for now. The least of our worries.*

"Look, Jack," Jonas continued. "You and I both know we can't escape our fate. It's been laid out before us. Lexi was never going to be able to run from this. I think you knew that."

Jack pulled his hand from mine and stood. He paced across the room, running a hand through his hair. He faced me. Without taking his eyes off me, he asked Jonas, "Can you give us a minute?"

Jonas pushed off the table and exited the room. I had no idea if he gave us privacy or not. I couldn't find him in my head. "I don't think he's reading my thoughts or listening in right now," I said to Jack.

"It doesn't matter. I don't like that he's been tapping your thoughts, but that's my problem to deal with. At least until you can shut him out." Jack glanced at the door Jonas exited through, then brought his eyes back to mine. "I definitely don't like the way he looks at you. He's protective of you in a way that makes me want to punch him. At the same time... he can help make sure no harm comes to you."

I stood and stepped close to Jack. I brushed the back of my hand down his face. "You have nothing to worry about."

"Hmmm. There's plenty to worry about. You're right about one thing, though. Jonas has different motivations than the two of us. He embraces the healing aspects of our DNA-tweaking, and he thinks that you will, too, eventually."

"He's wrong. I will still find normal some day."

203

Jack smiled. "I'll be right there with you. Right now, that's the least of our concerns. You need to meet with Seth. It's time to learn more. We can decide later which parts of our powers to embrace, which parts to ignore, and whether we want to have anything to do with some of the people in our lives."

"Where is Seth?" I asked.

"He's waiting for us across the hall."

"He's been here the entire time?"

"That's right. Since he heard about his sister bringing a SWAT team on campus, he's been ready and waiting. That man is nothing if not patient."

I took a shaky breath. "Does he know about Dani?"

Jack slipped his arm around my waist and pulled me close. "Yes. And I'm sure he and Jonas are discussing it now." He smoothed my hair back behind my ears.

"What if something happens to her because of me? Or Addison... what if..." My voice cracked.

"Shhh. Stop. You didn't do these things. None of this is your fault."

I swallowed hard against the giant lump in my throat. "I can't let anything happen to either of them, Jack."

"Nothing will. Think about it. If something happens to them, they've got nothing. We'll run. If they don't have bargaining power, they've got nothing."

"You know that makes no sense, right?" I smiled weakly.

"It makes a little sense. Now, come here." He lifted me up so that my face was even with his. He pressed his lips to mine. "We *will* figure this out." He kissed me again, deeper this time. When he released me, he let me slide back to my feet, out of breath and slightly lightheaded. "I'll meet you across the hall. I have something I need to do first."

I cocked my head. "Secrets?"

"I want to know where my father is."

TWENTY-TWO

....

I found Seth and Jonas in a room across the hallway. It was set up like a classroom, with tables organized in a circle for open discussion. Seth and Jonas spoke quietly in a corner as I entered.

When they saw me, they immediately stopped talking.

"Hi, Sarah," Seth cleared his throat. "I'm sorry. I mean, Lexi." He sounded genuine. "Old habits," he added.

"It's okay." It wasn't okay.

"I'm glad you're here. I know this is hard for you. I—"

"Do you?" I interrupted. "You're Sandra's twin brother. You and I are related by DNA. How am I supposed to believe that you aren't going to drug me with something? Or insert a tracker into the back of my neck? Or force me to heal someone I don't particularly want to heal? Or worse?"

"All fair questions." He gestured toward a chair. "Please. Let's sit."

Jonas led the way by taking a seat first.

After deliberating for a brief moment, I followed.

Seth sat at the same table, facing us. "Where's Jack?"

"He's checking on his father."

Seth clasped his hands on the table, stretching them out between us. "First, you know I'm here to help you, right? Or you wouldn't be back at Wellington in the first place."

Wasn't like I chose to return to Wellington. "I'm mostly certain of that."

"You also believe I *can* help you, or you wouldn't be sitting here."

"Yes." I guessed that was correct.

"We're just going to talk tonight. I promise I will work hard to earn your trust, but I need something in return."

I raised a brow, looked sideways at Jonas, then back at Seth. I didn't owe either of them squat at this point.

Jonas snickered. I hated that I had no idea which of my thoughts he heard and which he didn't.

When I didn't answer, Seth continued. "I need you to give me the benefit of the doubt for now." He got up and walked to an easel with a super-sized pad of paper attached to it. He flipped the pages over until he got to a list. "I've suspected there were seven original clones for a while now. But I was only starting to figure out what you were created to do before I got a call that my sister was in a coma. Since then, I've been piecing bits of information together. Some of the information had come directly from my sister, as she'd been trying to persuade me to join her at the IIA. Other information has come from the various clones I've met so far."

I stared at the piece of paper in front of me where Seth had listed the following: mind-altering abilities, mind control, physical strengths and abilities, and supernatural healing powers.

"That's why you initially formed The Program away from Wellington. You learned from Jonas, Fred, Georgia, and Jack under the guise of 'teaching' them?" I made air quotes around the word "teaching."

Seth shifted. Raised his hand to his face and massaged his jaw. He stared at me, thinking. "Yes, I formed The Program close to where I work, until it was time to bring it here on campus. I've learned from each of the clones I've worked with so far. From you, even. I like to think we've learned from each other." He paused. I thought he would say something more, but he turned to the easel and pointed to the items there. "We have to figure out where your strengths lie within these areas, and how we can use these strengths to defend who you are as human beings—not the scientific experiments Sandra and the IIA want you to be."

He talked a good talk, that was for sure. "So where do we start?"

"I'll ask you the same question I've asked every member of The Program. What one thing do you desire from The Program more than anything else?"

I didn't even have to think. "That's easy. I want to *not* need The Program."

Jonas remained expressionless.

"Can you explain further? Because I'm pretty sure you do need The Program. What do you want from me, Lexi?"

I stood and leaned across the table, my face a few inches from Seth's. "Everything." Seth's face drooped slightly. "I need to know everything you can teach me about your evil sister. I want to know what she created me to do, and what she created the other clones to do. I want to know why she joined forces with the IIA. I want to know where she's been since the explosion of my father's original lab. I want to know who else you think's working with her. After I know everything about her, I will make her wish she never played around with her own DNA. She will regret messing with people I love. Maybe after I've made her pay for her selfish choices and saved my friends from her Frankenstein-like ways I'll be free to lead a normal life. When Sandra no longer exists in my world, I will *not* need The Program. That's what I want from you."

With no humor in his face, Seth said, "Fine. We'll start first thing in the morning."

~~~~~

Jack and I faced each other, circling, like boxers in the ring. Jonas watched from his spot along the wall. He hadn't moved in the past fifteen minutes. Only stared. Analyzed.

Jack insisted on being the one to do self-defense training with me. "Remember what I showed you. How to block. How to strike." He spoke in a low voice. He intended for only me to hear, but I knew Jonas was listening.

Seth watched from across the room. A phone was glued to his ear. I was hyperaware of everyone in the room. The tension was high, and all eyes were on me.

How did I go from not wanting anything to do with this world—this life of medical experimentation—to needing to soak up everything I could in order to protect those I loved? How was I suddenly wanting to learn martial arts? How to shoot a pistol? How to block genetically engineered freaks from slithering into my mind and interjecting control over my actions and decisions?

How did I go from doing the controlling to being controlled?

I saw Danielle this morning. She's getting stronger, Jonas mindspoke. *I think it will do her some good to get in here and learn some self-defense.*

Jack switched directions. I was a microsecond behind him. His arms were up. He and I had practiced movements in slow motion earlier. He taught me to strike and to block. It all fit in well with the kickboxing classes Dani had dragged me to in the past. *Are you kidding? Dani can put almost anyone on his butt, including you.* She *should be teaching us.* I was never very good at any of this. It should be Dani in here, and me in the hospital bed.

Seth wasn't sure Dani would be able to control the effects of the tracker on her mind. She wasn't cloned with the DNA enhancements that the rest of us had. So far, Dani showed no signs of feeling any effects of the tracker. Possibly because Sandra or the IIA hadn't activated the tracker yet.

It was up to me to watch for the slightest change in Dani in order to protect my best friend.

Jack made his move. He took one step into the middle of our imaginary circle, swept my feet from under me, and sent me to the ground.

I grunted hard when my back hit the mat, and gasped for air.

Slowly, I rolled to my side and coughed.

Jack stood and walked away from me, grasping the back of his neck with interlocking hands. Through his form-fitting T-shirt, I could see the muscles in his back tighten.

I'm sorry, I mindspoke.

Jack came back and offered me a hand. He pulled me to my feet and pinned me in place with a furious gaze. "Where were you? You weren't concentrating at all."

"I... I don't know." Even I could hear the weakness in my voice.

"I'll tell you where," Jonas said, stalking toward us. "She was letting me in. I was talking to her. She concentrated on everything but the danger in front of her. Her mind is weak. This isn't working."

Heat flared on my cheeks. Maybe my mind *was* weak. Maybe I wasn't meant to do any of this. I glared at Jonas.

"What can we do differently?" Jack asked, his voice calm.

"For one thing," Jonas started, "you can stop babying her. She needs tougher training. She needs to be able to fight even when people are in her head, especially the dangerous ones. She needs to be able to multi-task. She needs—"

"Stop! Stop with the 'she needs.'" I rotated my shoulders back and looked up into Jack's eyes. "I said I was sorry." I turned to Jonas. "You have no idea what I need, so stop pretending to know me. You. Don't. Own. Me." I spun on my heels and stormed out of the room.

~~~~~

The cool water soothed my sore muscles and hurt feelings from the earlier training session with Jack. I glided through the deep end of the swimming pool after pushing off the wall with my legs. This was my kind of workout. The water was the perfect temperature. I was alone. And I needed an escape. An escape to a time when I was just a senior in high school planning which college to attend next year, which boy I hoped would take me to prom, or what movie to see this weekend.

Swimming relaxed me. But even the hardest workout wouldn't expunge the memories of the last few days. And forgetting wouldn't prepare me to face Sandra.

I *would* confront Sandra. It was just a matter of time. And it was important that I be prepared.

I touched the wall, out of breath. I had been swimming for over an hour. I ripped my goggles and swim cap off my head and threw them up on the deck. Eyes closed, I ducked back under the water and smoothed my hair back. When I surfaced and reopened my eyes, I stared at bare feet in front of me.

Glancing up the length of the legs and body above me, I found Jack staring down at me. I leaned my head back in the water to get a better angle on his incredible body and smiled. "Up for a swim?"

He didn't smile back.

He turned and kicked his shoes off and away from the pool. Next, he pulled his shirt over his head, providing me with quite a show of his ripped upper body. Facing me, he yanked the snap of his jeans and pushed them down, stepping out of them and tossing them aside so that they joined his shoes and T-shirt.

Wearing only his boxers, he walked the few steps to the edge of the pool and sat. His legs dangled in front of me.

Slowly, I ran my hand along his ankle, up the length of his shin, and around to his calf. Holding on to both calves, I positioned my body between his two legs.

He stared down at me, but still hadn't spoken. I wanted to tell him that everything was going to be okay. That I loved him. That when this was over, we would go on to graduate from high school, go off to college, and just be together. But I couldn't tell him those things. I wouldn't make promises I might have to break.

I looked away from him. We were alone in the aquatic center.

He reached out and placed his palm on my cheek. Closing my eyes, I leaned into his gentle touch. Cool air touched my cheek when he pulled his hand away. He used his hands to shift and ease his body into the water.

We were face to face—me in a swimsuit and he in his boxers. The strong scent of his shampoo mixed with the smell of chlorine. My hand shook as I reached out and touched the hair on his forehead. His other arm snaked around my waist and pulled me to him. My face was inches from his. His breath was hot against my lips. He held me so tightly I was sure he could feel my heart beat against his chest. My eyes were glued to his. My mind—blank.

I saw and experienced nothing but the beautiful person in front of me.

He leaned in and kissed me just under my earlobe. Electric impulses traveled from that spot and spread down my arms, my chest, and into my stomach.

His hand began to roam up my back until his fingers spread wide, two of them slipping under one of my straps.

"I love you," he whispered in my ear. "That will never change."

I pulled my head back and looked at him. At the emotion in his eyes. His hand roamed further up my body until it was intertwined in my hair. Then, all at once, he crushed his lips against mine. The electric current running through us exploded like a thousand active neurons.

We stayed like that until we both needed a breath. He trailed additional kisses along my jawbone until he breathed into the crook of my neck. My hand roamed his back and massaged the base of his neck.

Eventually, he loosened his hold and pulled his head back to gaze at me. "You're shaking," he said.

"Am I?"

He nodded, his face serious. "You're cold. Let's get you into a hot shower."

After climbing out of the pool, Jack wrapped me in a large towel.

I stared at the gold specks in the blue of his eyes. "Where will we be in eight months?"

His brows furrowed, casting a dark shadow over his face. "I'll be wherever you are, and you'll be wherever I am."

I smiled a little at that. His face remained as serious as it had been when he'd entered the pool.

He grasped at terry cloth with both hands and brought me closer. He leaned in and kissed me with soft lips. Once. Twice. Three times. Then, he let me go. "Shower. I'll see you at lunch."

"Come with me?" I asked with a distinct playfulness.

Finally, he smiled. Closing the distance between us again, he whispered against my cheek, "That's not what you really want. Timing is off."

"No, but it got you to smile."

TWENTY-THREE

....

The dining hall was empty compared to a normal day. Most of the noise came from the workers trying to keep a routine for the frightened students who remained on campus—other cloned humans who I assumed were unaware of how they were created. Seth claimed he would be talking with them soon. I recognized most from Dad's list.

They were young. Seventh and eighth graders, mostly. I couldn't help but wonder if they had spoken to their parents. Would their parents tell them the truth about being clones?

I massaged the bridge of my nose. As much as I wanted to do something to help the unsuspecting students left at Wellington, I couldn't. I had to concentrate on Dani and Addison. They needed my help more at the moment. Maybe by helping them, I would also do something good for the others.

I continued to look around. A few teachers huddled at their usual table, no doubt discussing the bombing. How much did they know? Cathy, Dean Fisher, and Dr. Wellington weren't present. And I hadn't seen Jack's dad since before the art gala.

Over by the windows was my target group: Kyle, Jonas, Briana, and Jack.

Jack was already staring at me when I made eye contact. He smiled, but it didn't reach his eyes. Not like the smile I got out of him after our "swim." Turning in his seat, he reached behind him, grabbed a chair, and brought it to the table beside him.

Briana and Kyle appeared to be having their own private conversation at the other end of the table.

I sensed Jonas in my head. *Hi, Lexi,* he said without even turning to see me. I concentrated hard on finding his presence on the outer perimeter of my mind where he liked to hang out. As if my hand could reach inside my head, I imagined wrapping my fingers around that presence, and I squeezed hard with all the rage I could muster. Then I expelled him from my mind.

Jonas flinched in his seat. He turned and looked at me, serious at first. Then a lazy grin spread across his face. "Very good."

I closed the remaining distance between me and the group. I leaned down next to Jonas, my mouth next to his ear. "Stay out of my head, Jonas, or I will make it my mission to learn to use a gun next. I'm getting tired of your constant invasion. You never know when I might just snap." As I said the last word, I snapped my fingers for dramatic effect.

Jonas laughed.

Asshole.

Language, Lexi, Jonas scolded.

I took my seat next to Jack.

"Did you eat anything yet?" When I shook my head, he stood. "I'll get you something." He glanced over toward Briana, then back at me. *She could use a friend.*

Briana looked like she had been crying, something I had never seen. *I know. I'll try.*

Jack walked toward the lunch line. Out of the corner of my eye, I knew Jonas was watching me. I jerked my head in his direction. "What?"

He leaned forward in his chair and spoke softly. "If you continue with this pissy attitude and never-ending anger, we'll get nowhere."

I studied Jonas's eyes. The amber specks flickered in the dark brown, producing a warmth I wasn't used to with him. He looked nothing like the woman who produced him. Or like me, I guessed, since we didn't share a single ounce of DNA. My heart, which had felt frigid before my swim, thawed slightly. Amazing how a good workout calmed me, especially one in the water, where I could be alone and shut out the rest of the world.

Jack returned with a cheeseburger and fries for me though I had zero appetite. Despite the earlier swim and make-out session, reality had flooded back the moment I had entered the dining hall. Jack sat and placed a palm on my knee. I covered his hand, sliding my fingers between his. I glanced between Jack and Jonas, then mindspoke so they could both hear me. *I'm sorry for earlier today. This is going to be harder than I thought.*

That's why you're not going to do it alone, Jonas said.

Jack leaned in and kissed the side of my head. "Now eat. You need strength."

Briana and Kyle slid down closer to us. I poured ketchup on my burger and all over my fries. Briana squinched her nose up in disgust, which made me want to eat the entire plate.

"Bree knows everything," Kyle announced.

Bree leaned in, her arms tucked under the table. "How could my parents keep this from me?"

"I had a decent relationship with my dad, knew he worked with stem cells, and even knew he once cloned a goat, and I still didn't have a clue what I was." I took a bite of my burger, suddenly realizing I was starving. After swallowing, I added, "How long has it been since you took the pills?"

"I ran out a couple of weeks ago, and forgot to get more."

That explained how she was able to enhance her appearance by the pool. The small pills were all the evidence I needed to know that Dr. Wellington, President Fisher, and who knows how many others knew everything about the clones at this school well before I'd discovered the truth. The school doctors prescribed the pills to me under the pretense of helping me with chronic headaches and nosebleeds. In reality, the pills suppressed my healing abilities and the strength of my mind-altering capabilities. "What did you think you were taking them for?"

She glanced nervously around the table. "I thought they were regulating my periods."

The boys smartly stayed silent.

"Bree, what do your parents do?" I asked.

She shifted in her seat. The whole conversation was making her uncomfortable. "My dad owns several restaurants around Lexington, and my mom owns thoroughbred racehorses."

I had never heard that. It didn't sound very high-profile. Danielle's dad also worked with thoroughbreds. Maybe they knew each other.

Can you hear my mindspeak, Bree? I took another bite of my cheeseburger.

Jonas looked curiously from me to Bree, as did Jack. Kyle didn't seem to catch on, but I hadn't directed the words at him.

Instead of a quick jerk, Bree's head rose slowly, her eyes a vibrant color through a layer of moisture that never fell. "Oh. My. Gosh."

"Well, that answers that," I said, and took another bite of my burger.

"Answers what?" Kyle asked. The other two laughed.

We didn't all have the same powers or abilities, yet many of our mind capabilities overlapped. And so far, I had yet to witness the same healing powers in the others that Jack and I had. Unless I counted Jonas's ability to ease pain and sickness.

"Where are Fred and Georgia?" I asked.

"Georgia freaked after the incident at The Program on UK's campus," Jonas said. "She and Fred left the morning after I brought you back to the house."

"What do you mean? What happened on campus?" Bree asked.

Jonas's lips quirked on one side. "Let's just say Lexi and I had a power struggle, and Georgia had to step in."

"Ahhh. I totally get that. Lexi and I have a power struggle on a regular basis." She threw a mischievous grin my way.

Just like that, Bree cut through the tension with brutal honesty. The whole table laughed. Except me.

I think I'm gonna like her, Jonas said.

I had a strong sense that he already knew he liked her. *Good. Maybe you can get inside her head for a while.*

Anyone ever tell you you're no fun?

I chuckled. *All the time.*

~~~~~

"They said to meet them in Room 201. That's all I know." I linked my arm with Jack's. His anxiety level had grown since lunch. We were all a little on edge. "I wanted to visit Danielle first, but Kyle insisted I didn't have time."

"We'll see her after," he reassured me.

All of Wellington Boarding School had been transformed in less than twenty-four hours into The Program—a school for the genetically enhanced human cloned. According to Jack, his mother and Dr. Wellington were planning to hire additional science teachers to add to the extensive curriculum for all of the students who remained at Wellington and needed an education into whom they were designed to be. This was what Cathy DeWeese and Roger Wellington had desired all along, I supposed, but I still wanted to understand why.

While school personnel scheduled meetings and classes for the younger students, Seth and Coach Williams had arranged for a special presentation for me, Jack, Jonas, Kyle, and Briana.

Apparently, with the majority of the students gone from the school, we were able to spread out into a classroom building that had not been damaged in the explosion.

Jack and I entered the room to discover a variety of different guns strewn about two large tables. My heart constricted. I should have seen this coming.

The first person I saw was Danielle. She wore her signature yoga pants and a pretty wrap-around cardigan. Her blond hair was tied into a loose ponytail that hung down her back, covering the incision at the base of her neck. I let go of Jack's arm and crossed the room. Throwing my arms around Danielle's neck, I pulled her into a giant hug. "Hey," I whispered. "I'm so glad you're here. How're you feeling?"

Kyle turned his head toward us, smiling. That was why he'd discouraged me from seeing her. He knew she'd be here.

"I feel fine. No different, really." She stepped back. "Kyle and Jonas have explained a lot of crazy things to me."

"Have you noticed anything... strange?"

"You mean have I felt someone invade my mind and turn me into a robot?" She wrung her hands in front of her. "No."

"Good. I'm glad." I hugged her tightly again. "I'm going to get that thing out of you."

"I hope so. Kyle explained some of the things you've been learning." She cocked her head at me. "Why didn't you tell me what you were going through?"

The others standing around us had gone quiet. "I... I don't know." I glanced nervously around the room. Briana was watching me expectantly. This was all new to her, too. "Well, because I've really struggled to grasp the magnitude of what it all means. And until recently, I had no idea how many of us there were. It all happened so fast, you know?"

She nodded. "And your father? He had something to do with cloning you and Jack? And Kyle, Jonas, and Briana?"

"It would appear he knew about it. I'm still trying to understand just how much. Although I'm not sure it matters anymore. He's not responsible for the predicament we're in now." No, we had others to thank for that. "I think he was trying to protect those of us that he could. So much so that he got himself killed in the process."

"Okay," Seth interrupted. "Let's begin. Everyone have a seat. Coach Williams is going to get us started."

We all sat. Jack scooted his chair close to me. It suddenly dawned on me that he was constantly touching me. And I didn't mean by holding my hand, or placing his palm in the small of my back. It was less obvious than that. Sometimes, if we were sitting, he would position himself so that our knees knocked together, or he would interlock his ankle around mine. If we sat at a table, his pinky finger would graze mine ever so lightly.

Are you purposely touching me every chance you get? I asked him.

He met my gaze. *Well, yeah, of course. That's what guys do when they like girls.*

I smiled. *That's not why you're touching me, though, is it? You're shielding me.*

I don't know what you're talking about. Now pay attention.

I faced Coach. He was going on and on about gun safety and why one gun was better than another for various reasons. How he and Seth planned to teach us to protect ourselves, but more than anything, how to be safe.

I raised my hand. "What other options are there?" Everyone looked at me strangely. "What?" I shrugged. "I am not going to use a gun."

Jonas looked up at the ceiling and sighed loudly. *You're killing me, Sarah.*

Don't call me that. My name is Lexi. "Why does that surprise you? You saw how I reacted to a gun."

Jack watched Jonas and me. But if the blank look on his face was any indication, I wasn't sure he was listening to the conversation.

"What do *you* think?" I asked Jack.

"About what?"

Are you even paying attention? Are you planning to carry a gun around?

I already do. He shrugged. *Sometimes.*

I stared at him. How did I not know that he carried a gun?

224

That was when I felt it. I had pretty much blocked Jack from reading my thoughts and I trusted him with my life, so I had stopped watching for his presence inside my head. But there he was, hanging out along the edges of my mind.

I moved my leg away from him, breaking his contact with my body. I stared across the room at Jonas. He cocked his head.

"Lexi, why don't you want to learn to use a gun?" Seth asked.

I stood and walked over to the table where half a dozen guns lay, mainly to get out of reach of Jack. "Because, Seth, guns scare me. And if I'm scared of guns, and if I'm caught with a gun, I'm pretty sure it could be used against me."

I searched my mind. Jack was definitely there. His presence, like always, was solid with concrete edges, comforting and protective. I kept searching.

"While I agree with you in theory," Coach began. "I think you should at least learn how the different types work, where the safeties are, and how to clear them of ammunition." He held up a bullet. "You can rest a little easier knowing these are rubber bullets. Getting shot with one of these would sting, but wouldn't break the skin."

Somehow, I was able to keep up this debate about guns while I searched my mind for other foreign presences. "I guess you're right. I should at least learn. But I'd like to learn other weapons, too. I want to know other ways to protect myself that my enemies wouldn't see coming."

Jonas smiled. "So, can Seth continue? There are others here who aren't such scaredy-cats."

After glaring at Jonas, I spun around and returned to my seat. "Yes, please continue, Seth."

I sat back down and kept all parts of my body out of reach of Jack's while I searched through my mind again. Bypassing Jack's presence, I found what I was looking for. It was like finding a few specks of pepper in a shaker of salt. Jonas was sneaky, hiding in the tiny crevices of the outskirts of my consciousness.

I immediately stretched my foot back out and made contact with Jack. He pressed the length of his leg into mine. While I could still see the tiny granules of Jonas's presence, I blocked his mind games with Jack's help.

"So, the gun you're holding now," I said, trying to prove I was listening. "Is that a typical issue for IIA agents?"

Coach held it loosely in his palm. "This one? This is a Glock 19, and yes, some law enforcement would carry this or something very similar. But IIA agents would also carry backup weapons of their own, so it's good to know different types."

I liked the idea of backup weapons.

Briana and Danielle both paid close attention to Seth's and Coach Williams's lessons. Kyle seemed to hang on every word as well. Jonas was more interested in watching the others in the room. Something told me he purposely avoided my glares, but he did not avoid looking at Briana, and often.

Jack continued to shift in his chair. His gaze shifted from me to the classroom door to Jonas. His anxiety seemed to grow. I wanted to know why, but I didn't want to ask now when we would have to mindspeak. I didn't want to risk Jonas hearing our conversation.

Toward the end of the lesson, Seth and Coach handed each of us a Glock and showed us how to unload and reload a magazine of bullets, while making sure a bullet isn't left in the chamber.

While I practiced with one of the pieces, Jack wandered over to Coach and spoke with him privately. Jonas helped Briana, Seth discussed something with Kyle, and Danielle and I unloaded and reloaded our own firearms.

The guns definitely made me nervous, but the fact that the bullets were rubber eased my worry somewhat. I unloaded and reloaded the Glock three more times while I stared daggers at Coach and Jack. What were they talking about? Jack had been acting nervous all afternoon, and now he was having private conversations.

After the fifth time I successfully reloaded the gun, I set it down not so gently on the desk in front of me. Every head in the room jerked toward me. "What?" I asked with a shrug.

Jonas shook his head.

Jack's lips stretched into a thin line. *Will you please remember that you're handling a deadly weapon? For someone who claimed to be scared of guns not one hour ago...*

I started to answer him, when Danielle stood and turned toward the rest of us. Backing away from us toward the door, she brought the loaded Glock up and pointed it directly at her temple.

"Dani?" I stood slowly, my hands stretched out as if for balance.

She held her free hand out. "Don't come close." A tear formed in her eye.

"Danielle?" Kyle was on his feet, too. "What are you doing?"

"It's not me," she said.

I shot a panicked look to Jack.

Someone's in her head, Jonas mindspoke.

"Dani, can you feel someone in your head?" I asked.

She cocked her head and squinted her eyes at me. "Feel them? What kind of question is that?"

A crazy one, I guessed.

Suddenly, she stood straighter. Her eyes darted all around, not focusing on any one thing. "There's a voice inside my head." She listened for a moment, then her eyes focused on me. "I have a message for you."

I stood straighter, grabbed onto the desk.

Danielle brought the gun down, cocked it, then pointed it at her head again.

My pulse raced. I felt lightheaded.

A lone tear ran down Dani's cheek. "You have until tomorrow."

To do what? I threw out to anyone who was listening. But no one had time to answer, because of what Dani did next.

She pulled the gun away from her head and pointed it straight out in front of her, aiming it at nothing at first. She twisted her body to the right. To the left.

Jonas started moving. Racing in front of Briana, he motioned for her to get down. He signaled likewise to Kyle. Jack and Coach already had guns cocked and in their hands. "Please don't shoot her," I pleaded.

I won't do anything I don't have to do, Jack replied.

Jonas got closer to me, and another tear escaped Dani's eye as she met my frightened stare, took aim...

Jonas leapt.

mindsiege

Dani fired.

···

TWENTY-FOUR

Why are you not freaking out?" Jack asked.

"You would rather I did?" I stood on top of my dorm building and looked out on the entire front half of the campus. I kept one eye on the infirmary to my left, and another on Wellington's front gate.

"I'm just surprised, that's all."

"Did you get Jonas all fixed up?" I asked.

"His shoulder is fine. I healed the torn labrum around the joint. He cried out like a baby." I heard the smile in Jack's voice.

"Dani was so upset. I left her sleeping. Kyle is with her."

"Good."

My eyes studied the lack of movement around the front gate. Yesterday, Sandra physically broke through the security barriers of Wellington, and today, she proved she was capable of powering through mental barriers, too.

Four guards stood at Wellington's front gate—two inside the gatehouse monitoring security cameras, two in front of the actual gate. They didn't appear to be armed, but according to Coach, they were each equipped with more than one firearm, a police baton, and most likely a knife of some sort.

I lifted my chin toward the front gate. "Did you know that before you arrived... I'm pretty sure the one or two security guards who stood at Wellington's front gate were unarmed? Didn't need the security."

"Hmmm." Jack moved closer and leaned his back against the railing, watching me.

"Did you also know that until about a month or so ago, I had a simple routine? I swam. I went to classes. I visited my Gram. I hung with my best friend. I drew and painted." I sucked at the art thing, but it was therapeutic, giving me a creative escape when I needed it. And looking back on it all now, I liked my boring, normal life.

"That was before you met me. Now your life is exciting, unpredictable, and adventurous." Obviously joking a little, Jack's voice sounded upbeat for the first time all day. The warmth of his gaze begged for my attention.

"No, I didn't know you," I said. "What a distraction you proved to be."

"Hey!" He knocked my arm playfully. "Are you saying you wish I hadn't been there to heal your broken arm? Or to talk my friends into bulldozing the school's brand-new security fence to break you out of here?"

I couldn't help but smile at him. "Technically, I'm not sure I would have broken my arm if you hadn't been in my way when I flew out of the girls' locker room. And as far as helping me escape Wellington?" I cocked my head. "Have you looked around lately? We didn't make it very far."

Jack's grin faded, taking the momentary light mood with it. "I know. I'm sorry."

"It's okay. Wellington wasn't the problem, only the people that had moved in." I moved closer to him and ran my fingers along his chest, tracing the design on his concert T-shirt. "You also know that Sandra and the IIA want something that they apparently can only get from me."

Jack circled his arms around me and brought my body flush with his. His chin rested on top of my head for a moment before he bent down and nuzzled his face into the crook of my neck. "I know," he whispered.

"These mind games... the IIA... Sandra... They won't stop until they get what they're after, or we're dead."

Jack's hands began to roam. He pulled my body closer, if that was even possible. Cool air seeped under my sweater as his right hand slipped under my shirt. I wanted to curl up and escape until I only existed inside his arms. His breath tickled my ear. "I won't let anything happen to you."

Though Jack attempted to distract me with his wandering hands, I played back today's incident in my head. "Something doesn't add up with the way Dani took that shot, or the way Jonas leapt in front of me." My body tensed as I said out loud what I had been thinking. Hopefully, Jack's touch shielded Jonas from hearing my thoughts.

Jack sighed, releasing me a little. "What did Dani say?"

"She was too upset to talk about it. And I'm scared to put her in further danger. I can't know for sure who's listening in on our conversations."

Stroking my hair absentmindedly, he kissed the top of my head again, then held me out just slightly, one hand still resting at the small of my back, skin on skin. "I've been spending a lot of time inside your head the last few days."

I feigned shock.

"You knew?"

"Of course I knew."

"Did it bother you? Why didn't you say something?"

I shrugged. "Because it comforted me. I could have shut you out."

"I know, but—"

"When you first explained how you could hear my thoughts, it bothered me, but then I learned how to shut you out. So, it was my choice." I looked away again. "Having Jonas inside my head isn't comforting at all. And the thought of Ty or anyone I don't know inside my head is making me crazy. I don't know what they're doing or when they might make me do something against my will. Dani is so upset. They made her shoot a gun at someone, Jack. I know how she feels. I have to find a way to get that thing out of her."

"Well, I've been studying your mind. I've studied how neurons fire and how brain activity behaves when I'm inside your head. I've seen how it's different when I'm touching you versus when I'm not. Or even when I'm across campus. I can tell when you're sleeping. I know when you're freaking out and when you're happy." He paused.

Bothered by the silence, I glanced up at him. "Go on."

"I also know when Jonas is inside your mind."

"You do? Because I can't always tell. It takes quite a bit of effort to monitor my own mind. I sense when you're there. I sometimes sense when Jonas is there, but mostly he slips in and out undetected."

Lexi? I could hear a huge tension in his words. *Jonas is always inside your head.*

My eyes widened. But then I remembered Jonas's presence earlier at the same time Jack had been touching me and roaming around in my brain. Jonas's invasion had looked like tiny specks of darkness among lots of light. My pulse began to race. *Is he there now? Can he hear everything we're saying?*

Jack shook his head. "I'm almost positive he can't."

"Almost?"

The pressure of Jack's palm to my back intensified. He reached down with his other hand and threaded his fingers with mine. "He gets visibly frustrated when I touch you. At first, I actually thought he was trying to get close to you. After you two returned from campus that night, and he had kissed you..."

"And after I gave him a black eye," I reminded him.

"Yes, that, too." Jack shifted feet, keeping physical contact with me. "But I noticed him looking at you differently, and I couldn't figure it out. He reacted to you differently after that. Thankfully, I had already decided to get you away from him. But then he showed up at Wellington."

"Ty or the IIA was controlling his mind. I was forced to heal Sandra."

"Exactly. Jonas began acting like he knew what was best for you. I was insanely jealous at first. I'm pretty sure that's exactly what he wanted."

"Wait a minute. Are you saying that you no longer trust Jonas?"

Jack looked away from me. "Not exactly. I just don't know. I'm wondering if we can afford to trust him if we're not sure."

"But how do you know he can't hear everything we're saying right now?"

"Ty. He made a huge mistake when he told us I was your shield. Now Jonas is being more careful and less obvious with how he invades your mind."

"You're wondering if Jonas has truly been deserted by Sandra and the IIA." I said the thing I'd been thinking ever since I'd healed Sandra and she'd fled the facility.

"Exactly. So, I've been watching. And today—"

"Maybe that bullet was meant for Jonas." Jack's expression remained unchanged as I said out loud exactly what he was thinking. "Just maybe... whoever controlled Dani's mind ordered her to shoot Jonas, not me. And that person knew the bullet would not kill or even hurt Jonas badly." Maybe it was even Jonas who was inside Dani's head. He had proven he could get in and out without the host body knowing.

"I think he knows I'm starting to not trust him. I also think he staged saving your life in order to win it back."

I stared out across campus again, mentally exhausted from wondering who was manipulating my mind and who was my friend. "What do we do?" I asked. "I can't ignore Sandra's demands to give myself over to her by tomorrow, and I'll need Jonas to get me inside."

So, we get closer to Jonas. He won't be able to hide his true intentions forever.

~~~~~

Jack held my hand, rubbing his thumb over my skin. We walked along the sidewalk behind the bombed classroom building. I was amazed by how well Dean Fisher and President Wellington had kept knowledge of the incident covered up. Had this been a public school, Wellington would've been a media circus.

Eventually, Jack would have to let me go, therefore breaking his protective shield. We couldn't spend the rest of our lives joined in some way, as nice as the prospect of him touching me forever sounded now. But we had to push forward with our plan to get Addison back and rid both Addison and Dani of the trackers embedded at the bases of their brains.

We went over my part of the plan one last time.

"Your job is to learn more about the trackers. Who has them? How are they inserted? How are they manipulated? Who controls them?"

The more I thought about the plan, the more nauseated I became. Not to mention my goal of getting Jonas and everyone else out of my head.

"You cannot mindspeak to me once our plan is put into place. So when I let go of you outside the next building, you're on your own until we meet up later tonight. Do you understand?"

I cocked my head. "Of course I understand. I can't mindspeak to you if I have any hope of learning what I need to from Jonas without him getting suspicious. Like I told Seth, since I can't escape this crazy, stupid situation, I want to know everything. Maybe then we'll find a way out."

Jack stopped and turned to me. He pulled me close and whispered, "I hope so." He brushed his hand down the length of my cheek, then leaned in and pressed his lips to mine. After two light touches with his lips, he pressed harder, deepening the kiss and taking my breath with it.

I pulled away first, swallowing hard. My heart constricted, but I had to ignore the ache for now. "You haven't told me your part of the plan."

His lips tugged downward. "I can't. We can't risk Jonas reading your mind once the shield is broken, and learning what I'm up to. But I will tell you that part of my job is to find out why my mom is keeping Father's whereabouts a big secret."

Jack was scared I would blow the entire plan, and for good reason. I would never forgive myself if something happened to Addison or Danielle—or anyone—because of my vulnerable mind. "When will I see you again?"

He rubbed his thumb across my lips, my cheek. He tucked a strand of hair behind my ear. Anything to keep touching me. "You'll see me soon. I promise. Try not to anticipate that moment though. The plan will work better, the less you know." After one last kiss to my lips, Jack stared into my eyes. *Promise me you won't take any unnecessary risks. You'll call out to me if your life is in danger in any way. I will come immediately.*

I lifted his hand and brushed my lips across his knuckles. *You know I can't promise that.*

He countered with a lingering kiss to my forehead. *I love you for your courage and your honesty.*

I love you for seeing things in me that aren't there. I gave him a weak smile.

Then, he let go.

TWENTY-FIVE

....

I found Jonas at the gym where Wellington's boxing and wrestling teams worked out. I was pretty sure no one from those teams remained on campus. Regardless, we were alone.

He worked the speed bag as I approached. The room reeked of leather and sweat. I searched my mind, and didn't see his small presence there at first, but remembered that Jack had said Jonas was always there. I examined the darker corners. That's where I found him hanging out, practically dormant. I tried to watch how the small specks representing Jonas's invasion into my mind reacted when I spoke. *Hey, Jonas.*

The specks came alive as if just awoken. Jonas reached up and stopped the bag with both hands. "Where've you been?" he asked, keeping his back to me.

"Checking on Dani. Seeing if she got as much pleasure out of shooting you as I would have." I forced a smile.

He turned in time to see the smile. "I definitely expected more of a thank-you for taking a bullet for you."

I cocked my head. "*Did* you take a bullet for me?"

A smirk spread across Jonas's face. "What do you mean?"

"Maybe you only thought she was going to aim at me? I've been wondering if Dani was actually aiming at you. Maybe she hit her target."

"Why would Dani be firing at me?" he asked.

"Why would she want to shoot me?" I countered, then continued. "Let's back up. Let's say that someone from the IIA was

239

sending me a message through Dani. And the message was giving me less than twenty-four hours to turn myself over to the IIA. If that were the case, why would the IIA then shoot me?"

Jonas's grin grew. "Hmmm. Well thought out. But you forget one thing. The rubber bullets most likely would not have hit you in a body part that would have seriously hurt you, let alone kill you. What if the IIA wanted you to feel pain? What if they wanted you to know they were serious about making your beloved best friend do something she'd rather die than do? And of course, they knew your boyfriend would heal you anyway."

He was right. Dani said so herself. She'd rather die than hurt me. And I felt the same way.

"Also good points." I walked around him and punched the speed bag while avoiding eye contact. I could barely reach the bag at the height it was set, but it was something to hit. I needed Jonas if I had any hope of saving Dani. I turned back to him. He was closer than I expected. My breath caught. Searching his eyes, I wondered if it was truly lack of trust that made me nervous around him, or something else entirely. My eyes slammed shut. When I reopened them, he remained inches from me. Willing my pulse to slow, I asked, "What do you think I should do?"

"About?"

He smelled of a hard workout mixed with the hint of deodorant. Moisture seeped through his gray T-shirt. "Should I turn myself over to the IIA? Would that save Dani?"

Jonas's grin disappeared. "Are you asking if I think the IIA would leave Dani alone and not use the tracker inside her head? Not try to remotely control her again? I can't answer that." He reached up and stopped the speed bag I had set in motion. He looked everywhere but at me. "As far as turning yourself over to the IIA... I don't know, Lexi." He sighed while wiping his forehead on the sleeve of his shirt.

I roamed around the gym. I tried out the large punching bag with a side kick, all the while keeping thoughts of Jack out of my mind. I would have to turn myself over to the IIA—to Sandra. That was the only way. For both Dani's and Addison's survival. I threw a punch and another kick.

"Very nice. You up for a workout? Maybe we can work on concentration techniques while practicing some self-defense."

I shrugged. "Okay." I massaged my chest where panic slowly swelled in my heart. I had to keep my thoughts in line. The last time I tried this, Jonas took over my mind, and Jack put me on my back. I had to focus on learning everything I could about the trackers, while keeping a constant lookout for signs of Jonas and Ty. Somehow I had to convince Jonas to take me back inside The Farm.

We began with a regular kickboxing workout. Instead of punching and kicking air, Jonas wore thick gloves. I kicked and punched his hands, taking out pent-up frustration on innocent pieces of padded leather.

Eventually, our workout morphed into Jonas showing me what to do if someone grabbed me from behind. He also reminded me of the various vulnerable parts of the body. My hands and feet, and other parts of my body, became weapons.

As we worked, I practiced erecting walls and barriers around my thoughts. I attempted techniques Jack taught me for keeping him out of my head. I had used all of these techniques before, though. And they hadn't worked with Jonas.

"You're going about this all wrong, you know," he said, sliding the padded gloves back on.

I aimed a side kick into Jonas's left hand. He grabbed my leg and twisted. I went down hard.

He let go immediately, and I sprung back to my feet ready for a fight. "Why did you do that?" I wanted to kick him again, this time straight to the face.

"Because you were concentrating so hard on keeping me out, you stopped paying attention to the opponent in front of you."

I used my forearm to push hair out of my face. "So, what am I doing wrong?"

"Remember earlier when you found me inside your head, and you squished me out? You imagined crushing me with your bare hands, and that's exactly what you did with my invasion into your thoughts."

"Okay, but that took work. I need to be able to keep you and others out at all times. Even when I'm physically busy with something else."

"Right. And you're fully capable of doing so. You've proven this. You just don't know how to shut others out on command."

"And you do?"

"Of course I do." He tilted his head side to side. "Well, except people controlled by the IIA. But I'm getting better at it."

"What do you mean by that?"

"Well, the more I study your thoughts, Jack's ability to shield you, and my power over you..."—he winked at the last

part, sending an angry fire straight up my back and neck—
"...I'm convinced that the tracker at the base of my skull has intensified my ability to control you. And that's exactly what Sandra wanted. But it has also allowed Ty deeper into my mind." He took in a deep breath, letting it out slowly. "Until I figure out a way to remove the trackers and destroy Sandra's path into our minds, we have to do our best to block access, or at least recognize when another invades, so we can choose not to follow."

"The deeper Ty gets into your mind, the deeper you get into mine," I said, mostly to myself. I leaned against a metal pole and massaged the bridge of my nose while processing what he was saying. I wasn't sure who was responsible for manipulating my mind more: Sandra, Ty, or Jonas. "Why haven't you shown me how to keep you out? You said you would."

"Maybe because I like being inside your head and experiencing what you're thinking and feeling."

Maybe it's because you still want to kill me. This was exactly why Jack didn't want me with Jonas. I was sometimes too honest.

Jonas laughed. Then his face softened, his eyes narrowed. "If you really believed I wanted to kill you, you wouldn't be here. Besides, Jack might not trust me, but not because he thinks I might kill you." Pulling the gloves off and tossing them aside, he stepped closer to me.

I held up a hand to stop him, and he pressed his chest into it. My heart leapt into my throat. My mouth went dry. I was not getting into this subject with him while he could read all of my thoughts. I couldn't even admit to myself what I was thinking for fear Jonas might hear me. "You're not going to teach me how to shut people out of my head, are you?"

"Why would you say that, Lexi?" Jonas frowned. His hand traveled up and covered my hand resting on his chest. "You still believe I'm trying to hurt you?"

"Maybe not harm me physically, but every time you... or Ty... force me to do something against my will, you hurt me. Every time you sneak in and around my head, you hurt me." The muscles in Jonas's face drooped. Maybe I had said too much. "I'm sorry, Jonas. Sandra expects me to surrender to her tomorrow. It would be nice to know how to block Ty and anyone else trying to get inside my head." *And yes, that includes you.*

Fifteen seconds passed. The amber specks in Jonas's eyes reflected the overhead lights. Pulling my hand away, I shifted under his scrutiny.

He backed up and scrubbed both hands over his face and into his hair. When he finally looked at me again, I saw a vulnerability I'd never seen in him before. "Fine. Let's get started."

I was working with Mr. Multiple Personalities. I could barely keep up.

"To start with, instead of erecting walls the way you do to keep Jack out, you need to form pockets."

"Pockets?"

"Yes. We all compartmentalize our thoughts and fears." Jonas motioned me closer. He bent over and grabbed the training gloves, sliding them back on. "Imagine someone who has just lost someone close to them."

Easy enough. I knew how that felt.

"Now, while this person might be grieving a terrible loss, they're able to place that despair within a pocket inside their mind and heart. This is how they're able to continue in their everyday life without being paralyzed by sadness."

I remembered how quickly I was able to return to school after Dad died, despite overwhelming grief. "Okay, I'll buy that."

"Take a look inside your own mind. Can you imagine different pockets there? Maybe one for love. One for the deep affection you feel for Danielle. Another for whatever thoughts you have when you think of Briana. One for grief."

"Yes," I whispered. I was completely buying into this. I could see different imaginary compartments forming in my head.

He lifted his hand and waved me forward. "I want you to practice a series of uppercuts, side kicks, hooks, front kicks, and crosses. Any pattern you wish, but at the same time, imagine placing different thoughts and feelings inside these pockets."

I began a sequence of punches and kicks, then I did exactly what Jonas ordered. I placed my love for Gram inside one pocket—a feeling that filled me with warmth in one moment and a longing to see her that tore my heart apart in the next. I didn't like anyone knowing that vulnerability.

Jonas moved to the side. I switched back to slamming my fist then my foot into his gloved hands. "Now, think about Briana. The thoughts you have of her are often ones you'd rather her not know, right?"

"I suppose that's accurate." I remembered some of the cruel things she'd done to me, the anger I'd felt, the jealousy of seeing her flirt with Jack when he first arrived at Wellington. I stuffed my own unkind thoughts inside a pocket in my mind. Jonas was right. I didn't want Briana to know these thoughts, mainly because I wasn't cruel. She made me angry, but I didn't find cutting her down worth how that might make her feel.

"Next, think of Jack. I'm sure you think of him in ways you don't want him... or anyone else... to know."

Fire flared across my cheeks. I did have some pretty powerful thoughts where Jack was concerned. I went to work on them, stuffing them quickly inside a too-small pocket, like a teenager overstuffing her dresser drawers, unable to keep clothes or socks inside while trying to close the drawers.

"Nice. Not much leaked out while you did that. Now think of me."

I stopped punching and stared at Jonas. I was sure my mouth hung agape. Jonas raised a brow and stood straighter. Immediately, I snapped out of my trance and closed my mouth. I transformed my face and attempted to swallow all expression.

Jonas's lips tilted up. "Not the reaction I expected, but not completely disappointing."

I rolled my eyes, and kicked his right hand hard. "You surprised me, that's all." My mind filling up by this point, I pocketed the many conflicted thoughts I had of Jonas—fear of what I still didn't know about him, admiration for turning his back on his mother, confusion, curiosity. Was he my friend or my enemy?

"You're so easy to read, Lexi."

I stopped and turned away from him. This was never going to work, though hiding my face was not going to keep this guy out of my head. Frustration and anger at my own inadequacy invaded my thoughts, and I added those to the many compartments I wished would protect my mind from siege.

Seth had asked me what I wanted from The Program. My first answer, had I concentrated only on myself, would have been to learn complete control over my mind at all times. I wanted control of every aspect of my future and how my abilities would be used—*if* they'd be used. At the same time, the idea that my own thoughts and actions were not safe inside my own mind invoked the desire to run. To escape this life and not look back.

This wasn't just about me anymore. I needed The Program to teach me not only how to help myself, but to help others affected by Dad's, Dr. DeWeese's, and Sandra's years-ago experimentation into human cloning.

How could I help others, though, if I couldn't keep this one person—this one confusing boy—from reading my every private thought, desire, or dream?

Jonas's hand touched my shoulder. "Lexi," he whispered.

I spun around. "Please don't touch me." I was afraid a single touch would reveal every secret, every insecurity, every fear I ever had.

He dropped his hand to his side. Both gloves gone, he flexed his fingers wide. "What I meant, Lexi, is that I read your emotions all over your face. And I read your body language as you turned away from me, but..."

I wrung my hands. I was never able to hide my feelings well, especially the strong emotions that grief, confusion, and Jonas invoked. "But what?" I asked weakly.

"But I couldn't read your mind—your specific thoughts." He crooked a finger under my chin and lifted. "Congratulations. You successfully pocketed most of your thoughts. I only heard a couple about Briana, probably because the two of you have such a long past filled with so many powerful emotions. A few more about Jack, which isn't surprising given how intense the two of you are." Jonas cocked his head, eyeing me like he wanted to figure something out. "And I didn't hear anything about me, although your reaction has me quite curious." He smiled.

My face must have reddened from the fire that flared there. I took in a long breath and let it out slowly, studying the quizzical look in Jonas's eyes. How would I know if he was telling me the truth? Was I capable of hiding thoughts from him? Could I, for example, pocket the thought that I was wondering where that tracker that Ty gave him went? Could I hide from him my constant questioning why Sandra allowed Jonas to live if she had the ability to terminate anyone with an implanted tracker? Maybe she still had a use for him. And maybe he knew it.

"Let's take a break."

"What? No. I can't afford to take a break. Dani and Addison need me."

"You need a break. We also can't afford to keep going while you still don't trust me."

"What do you mean?" I looked down at the floor, focusing on a used band-aid wadded up against a floor mat.

"Don't even bother denying it." Jonas sighed. "You did a great job just now, and I'm positive you'll only get better and better at pocketing your thoughts. But you're afraid I'm not being completely honest with you." He stepped close to me. He slid a hand behind my neck, and forced me to look up. "And you're definitely not being honest with me. Tell me you're not afraid of me."

I blinked. Stared into those dark brown eyes, dilated to the point of total darkness. "I'm not afraid of you, Jonas," I whispered. My mouth ran dry. "I..."

"Are you sure?" He wrapped a strand of hair around his forefinger, while simultaneously rubbing the skin beneath my long hair, a touch more intimate than I was comfortable with. "I'm not here to hurt you, Lexi. Only to help you." He tilted his head. His eyes narrowed, and I was certain he saw straight through me.

"Help me what?"

The expression on Jonas's face changed ever so slightly. Had I blinked, I would have missed it.

"Help you realize the fate you'll eventually face. You know I can make you accept it as well."

"What fate would that be?"

His lips twitched, lifting upward at the corners and sending a chill over me. I concentrated hard on the pockets I had just formed and immediately tucked away my latest observation: Ty had just slipped inside Jonas's head and taken over. I pulled Jonas's brain up as an image inside my own mind, and examined the fiery neurons ablaze there. I knew what Jack and Jonas looked like inside my head, but what did Ty look like inside Jonas's head?

"What *is* going on in that head of yours?" Jonas/Ty stood close enough that his breath warmed my cheek, and I could see my reflection in his eyes.

"Welcome to the party, Ty."

His grin grew. "Very good, Lexi. I wondered when you'd finally learn to recognize me." He suddenly leaned in and kissed me, forcing my lips to open. His arms hugged me close, and I squirmed to get away. My eyes widened.

A growl vibrated from my throat as I brought my hands up and pushed hard against his rock-hard chest, but failed to budge him at all. Suddenly, he shoved me away hard enough that I stumbled backwards into a body bag and fell to the floor. The breath was knocked out of me. I gasped for air.

Jonas's chest rose and fell in rapid movements. He bent over at the waist as if catching his breath. When he looked up, pain filled his eyes as he examined me where I fell. "I'm sorry. That wasn't me."

"I know."

Wrinkles formed across his forehead. He approached me slowly and reached out a hand. My gaze lowered to it, then back up to his bright amber eyes. "Please take my hand."

Without thinking, I slid my palm into his. He wrapped his fingers tightly around mine and pulled me up, our eyes never leaving each other. "Looks like we both still need a little practice," I said, my voice low.

"Yes, but... it's time we shut my mother's operation down."

I studied the look in Jonas's eyes—the look I had been searching for since I left Jack and found Jonas. The look that said, "I'm on your side—not the side of the crazy woman running the IIA." This was the Jonas that Jack swore existed. "Good. Then you can start by teaching me more about the trackers." I tried to drum up enough saliva to swallow, my heart still beating from the hold Ty had had on me. "And you can teach me how to get inside The Farm. Alone."

"I'll teach you more about the trackers, but there's no way in hell I'm allowing you to enter that IIA freak show alone."

TWENTY-SIX

....

I cocked my head and examined the tracker from a different angle. The small object made from a combination of metal, plastic, and wire was lodged at the base of the skull where the cerebellum meets the spinal cord.

"Oh, my," I said, staring at the eight lit-up MRI images in the basement of the infirmary. Jonas and I were alone. Only one nurse was on duty, and she was upstairs on the other side of the building. Jonas was giving me a lesson in trackers. "It's practically touching the spinal cord. I could paralyze her if I tried to remove this thing."

"That's what I've been trying to tell you." Jonas stuffed both hands in the front pockets of his jeans. "Mine is in the same spot."

"Why there?"

Jonas shrugged. "Maybe to make it near-impossible to remove. It runs on tiny electric impulses." He approached the screen. The images of the skull glowed a bright blue color against the black background. Very pretty, actually. Jonas pointed a finger at the back side of the device. "There's a microchip right here. That's the data center."

"Data center?"

"Sandra or her agents are able to send out instructions over any cell network. The messages are collected here. The device itself then sends out radio waves throughout the brain."

"Giving them complete control of whoever has one," I whispered.

Jonas tilted his head side to side. "More or less."

"But in your case, she doesn't have as much control as she wants."

"More like as much control as she *thinks* she has. She uses Ty or another clone to get to me fully and to disguise the invasion. Fortunately, she hasn't realized that I'm learning to detect when another presence tries to take over my mind."

"You've found a way to keep Ty out."

"Mostly." He flashed me a weak smile, one with an unspoken apology for the uninvited kiss earlier. "That doesn't mean I'm not constantly watching out for him. And sometimes I miss him. Like earlier."

"So, you pocket your thoughts—but when you do detect him, how do you keep him from forcing you to act against your will?"

"That's a little trickier. Like I said, I'm always on the lookout for anything foreign entering my brain. If I don't catch the person inside my mind, things like Kyle sticking his arm in the fire happen. And let's not forget how you've seized control of my mind—twice now."

Oh, I hadn't forgotten. I walked closer, analyzing the actual device. I pointed to the opposite side of the object from where the microchip was located. "What are the little prong-like things on this side?"

"Exactly that. They only come out when the tracker is implanted. Those little legs, or prongs, weren't there before the tracker was implanted."

"Strange. What do they do?"

"That's what holds the tracker in place." He glanced side-ways at me with a grim look. "Those small prongs are what keep us from removing the tracker."

"What do you mean?"

"If you tried to take the device out, the prongs would pull and scrape at the base of the brain. Those tiny legs are de-signed to puncture the cerebellum and cause massive brain hemorrhaging. Or they'll slice at the spinal cord, or the many tiny nerves along the spinal cord, causing paralysis."

"Neither outcome would be good." I backed away from the pictures and leaned against an exam table. "What if when I removed the device, Jack was here to heal the spinal cord?"

"Can he heal spinal cords? Has he ever done that?"

"No, not that I know of," I answered, slightly deflated. Was I capable of removing the device and healing the brain? What if I passed out in the middle of it? Dani or Addison would die for sure. "There has to be a way to remove it without harming the host." I needed to see an actual tracker. "What happened to the tracker that Ty gave you the day we were on campus?"

Jonas walked over and turned off the monitors. "Why? What are you thinking?"

"Not sure. But I'd like to hold one of those in my hand and see how those prongs come in and out." I refused to believe that removing these tiny objects and freeing victims of San-dra's invasion was impossible.

Jonas slipped inside my head and poked around.

I narrowed my gaze. "That was obvious. Why are you in-truding when I'm standing right here?"

"That was no more obvious than I've always been. You're just becoming more aware."

"Huh. Interesting."

"So, are you going to tell me what you're thinking, or do I need to keep sorting through your thoughts?"

I smiled. "How about we see if you can figure out what I'm thinking as you hunt down that tracker, and I'll put my plan into motion while you're gone."

I needed to find Jack. I had to tell him that I was pretty sure I knew how to extract the trackers from Addison and Danielle, not to mention from the other clones and from Jonas. Surely he wanted to be rid of that thing. I was almost certain that once I removed the tracker, Ty would no longer have access to Jonas's mind, therefore blocking Sandra from further manipulating Jonas.

I walked closer to the MRI images. I tilted my head while I analyzed the device and the tiny prongs further. Removing the tracker wouldn't be an option if I couldn't find the one person I thought could help me.

"Lexi, there's one more thing." Jonas stood directly behind me; his voice was low. "You have to know why Sandra needs you."

The muscles in my neck tightened. Turning slowly, I narrowed my gaze at Jonas. He stuffed his hands in his pockets and stared intently at the floor between us. "Okay..." I said, hesitating. "Why?"

"You hold the key to her entire life's research. The ability to control and manipulate her little monsters is important."

"No shit."

Jonas took a deep breath. "Can I continue?"

I quirked both brows and motioned with my hand for him to continue.

"She figured out how to control and manipulate people with these little devices."

"Okay, but what does that have to do with me?" I reached up and fiddled with the starfish and key hanging around my neck.

"The reason she cloned and manipulated her own DNA to begin with was to create a healer of all disease and injuries. You, Lexi, were designed as the perfect healer. And Sandra plans to replicate that ability inside one of those tiny trackers. She will stop at nothing to make sure you join her inside The Farm."

I stood up straighter and thought about the other clones and kids inside the IIA facility. She was creating an army of clones—raising them like caged animals to do exactly what she trained them to do. Little workhorses she could manipulate with these small gadgets. "Sandra's too arrogant to realize that I'm nothing like her. I'll never help her." I would never join her cause.

If you turn yourself over to Sandra, you might not be given a choice.

~~~~~

"So, do you think it'll work?" I asked Jack, unable to hide the worry from my voice.

Jack rubbed the stubble on his chin, and analyzed the MRI pictures Jonas and I had stared at for over an hour. "It might. But Lexi—"

"You don't think Georgia will risk the seizures, do you?"

"It's not that. If she thinks she might be saving a life, Georgia will do whatever we ask her to do."

Jack's admiration for Georgia cut right through my heart. Not in a jealous way. I knew Jack respected the other clones and what they were willing to do for each other—the clones he knew well, anyway. But I wasn't like that. I wasn't sure I'd ever sacrifice my own life for others. Or use these abilities created by the devil herself. "You're scared I won't follow through with it, aren't you?"

He whipped around. His eyes found mine instantly. "What? No, of course not." He stepped up to me and placed a hand on my cheek, heating my entire body with a look that came close to tearing me apart at the seams, so much so that I had to look away. "Don't look away," he whispered. When I looked back, he continued. "I know you'll save Addison and Dani as soon as you know how. And as soon as it's safe. We know too little, though. What if it's riskier than anything you've done so far?"

"It won't be. I'm stronger." Jonas taught me to pocket my thoughts. I *was* stronger. It had to be enough, because I was out of time.

"What if removing the tracker weakens you? What if someone sees you at The Farm?"

There was that. And the thought of Sandra capturing me for her own mad-scientist uses frightened me to my core. While Jack attempted to convince me that he thought I could do it, I had my doubts—but I wouldn't let him see those. "I can do this. Especially if I have help."

"Wow. Did that hurt?" He leaned in and kissed me. "I'm not sure I've ever heard you admit you needed help."

"Har har," I scoffed, but wrung my hands in my lap at the same time. "So, do you think it could work?"

The door flew open behind me. Jonas's voice was in my head instantly. *Absolutely not!*

Well, that answers the question of whether I could keep him out of my head. I turned. Jonas's face was a deep shade of red. I kept my voice calm. "Don't be so dramatic."

"Dramatic? You haven't seen dramatic. Did you tell him?"

I cringed, closing my eyes tight. *Please don't, Jonas.*

"Tell me what?" Jack asked.

"Tell him, or I will."

I rotated my shoulders back and stared up the nine or so inches into Jonas's eyes. Fury met fury. I inhaled and let out an exaggerated breath. "Fine." I turned back to Jack. I reached out and linked my fingers with his in order to block Jonas out.

"Say it out loud," Jonas ordered.

Jack raised his eyebrows. He stood taller. The muscles in his arms tightened, bracing for what I had to say.

Fine. "Jonas thinks Sandra figured out how to project supernatural mind abilities through these small tracker devices, but she needs me in order to replicate healing powers. He's afraid Sandra will be able to custom-design these trackers with all kinds of special powers—and then have complete control over whoever is implanted with them. In other words, Sandra wants to play God."

Jack's eyes iced over. His expression hardened. *You weren't going to tell me this, were you?*

There was nothing to tell. It's one hundred percent speculation on Jonas's part. I am no miraculous healer.

Bullshit! Jack boomed inside my head. *You're exactly what Sandra cloned you to be. It all makes sense.*

Pulling on his hand, I urged him to look at me. "I have to do this. I have to go to The Farm and find Addison before it's too late. Jonas thinks one computer server controls the trackers. If I can find the machine that gives Sandra and the IIA access to innocent minds with these tiny implants—I can shut down her entire operation. I have to try."

"Why go there first? Why not remove Dani's tracker first before you risk entering the devil's lair?" Jack asked. His fingers stretched wide at his sides then rolled into fists.

I glanced down at my hands, then back at Jack. "Because if I extract Dani's first, Sandra will know. I don't even want to think about what she'll do if she realizes I'm a threat to her entire operation of tracker clones. She can kill any one of them with a few keystrokes. But if I can shut down that server—"

"And exactly how do you plan to do that? Do you know anything about computers?"

I was hoping to take a fire axe to it. "I haven't worked that part out, yet."

He stared at me for what seemed like an eternity before turning to Jonas. "What do you think about this crazy plan? Surely you're not on board with this."

"Oh, you're ready to trust me now?"

"When have I not—"

Jonas raised a hand, cutting Jack's words off. "Don't."

Jack's chest fell. *Look at her,* he mindspoke. *You of all people know how I feel about her. I will do whatever I have to do to protect her.*

Jack's words were directed at Jonas, but I heard them. Did Jack mean for me to hear him?

So will I, Jonas responded to Jack, then looked intently at me.

He'd meant for me to hear both his and Jack's words even if Jack hadn't.

"Look," I said, squeezing Jack's hand. "I'm going to The Farm. You both can either help me, or you can sit here and hope for the best." Jack glared at me, as did Jonas. "You two are ridiculous. Each of you, at one time or another, have wanted me to be more in tune with who I am as a clone with freakish healing abilities. And I wanted nothing to do with any of it. Plus, you both are responsible for me landing back at Wellington.

"Well I'm here. I didn't want to be, but I am. That has to mean something. And two innocent people are in a dire situation because of me." I took a deep breath. "And my dad and a reporter he trusted are now dead because of all this."

"About that," Jack said. "Something keeps nagging me about the IIA, something we need to think about if we're actually going to sneak into The Farm."

I was excited he was finally listening to me, but my decision to enter the IIA became more real at his words, making my head ache a little. "Yeah?"

"Marci told you that your dad was planning to move you. I think he figured out what Sandra was doing and knew she was getting closer to finding you. He didn't want you to be a part of this. And for good reason," he added.

"You think Sandra killed him," I whispered. "And Marci knew too much. When she discovered The Farm—"

"They murdered her, too."

"One question keeps bothering me, though," Jack said, and I knew immediately what he was thinking.

I nodded in agreement. "Who knew Dad well enough to know he was about to move me away from Wellington?" There were few people he might have told this information.

"I've got an even more important question," Jonas said. "Who knows Sandra well enough that they kept the facility running while she was in a coma, and who was capable of operating the implanted trackers? And why don't I know who this person is?"

"Are you sure you don't know?" I asked.

Jack stood close to me, a warm hand to my lower back. "I'm afraid whoever it is has us right where they want us."

"Along with many other clones we know nothing about," I said. "With your father out of the country, I know who my guess is."

"Cathy."

I cupped his cheek with my palm. "Which is why we have to try this plan. We have to get into The Farm. Tonight, while they're still unsuspecting. And Cathy and Dr. Wellington can't know we're gone."

Jack's face softened. "I'll take care of distracting Cathy."

Jonas sighed. "I'll work on Georgia."

And I needed a weapon.

TWENTY-SEVEN

....

What's this do?" I pointed to a strange gun-shaped object that was obviously not a gun.

"That, my friend, is a Taser. It will drop your attacker to their knees in an instant." Jonas pretended to touch his neck with the end of the Taser, then faked a massive convulsion as he fell to the ground like someone having a seizure.

I rolled my eyes then took the weapon from him. *Idiot.* The Taser was smaller than a gun and very light. If it did what Jonas demonstrated, it could be very useful. But it might also be used against me if a thug wrestled it away from me.

Jonas pushed himself up. "I still don't understand why you won't pack a gun."

I shrugged. "Just don't want one." I knew I would never kill another human being. And I simply didn't want to risk having a weapon that could be turned on me. "But I'm not opposed to defending myself or others I love. So, I'm open to other options. What else we got here?" I gestured to the table of weapons before me.

Jack entered the room with Seth and Coach. Whatever they had been discussing, they stopped the second they entered the room.

Keeping secrets? I asked Jack.

From you? Absolutely not. "Coach has something I think you'll like."

"Oh yeah?"

Coach set a small, hard case on a table in the middle of the room. He flipped up the metal clasps and opened it up. Inside, a dozen or so rings were displayed—ladies' diamond rings, other less-flashy women's rings, and even simple men's rings.

I looked around at the other faces. Everyone, except Coach, looked as confused as I was.

"Are these some sort of James Bond spy gadgets?" Jonas asked, only half-laughing.

Coach pulled one of the daintier rings out and handed it to me. I held it in front of my face and gave it a little shake. It made a strange sloshing noise. I shook it again. "This has liquid in it."

Coach watched me examine the ring. His eyes couldn't hide his excitement. "This is something very new. Not many know about it."

Jack sat on the edge of the table beside me. "Therefore, few would know to look for it if someone, let's say, was searched for weapons."

"Slide it on." Coach took the ring and helped me slide it onto my middle finger. "It tightens a little, like this." He proceeded to slide something and tightened the ring on my skinny finger.

I held it up in front of my face. It was a simple silver design with a large pearl on top.

"The pearls are hollow but not empty. The liquid inside can pack quite a punch. Twist the pearl clockwise by only touching the sides," Coach said.

I twisted it like he said, and a tiny pointed tip slid out from the top of the pearl. I reached out my finger and was about to touch it when Coach grabbed my forearm. "Don't touch that."

I jerked my head up. "What does it do?"

"That pointy tip is a small needle. It's very sharp. If you were to touch that needle to someone's skin... even the tiniest graze... the liquid from the pearl would be injected into that person's body. Just a small amount is all you would need."

My heart rate sped up. "Need for what?"

Jack rubbed his stubble, shifting beside me.

"A few drops of that in someone's bloodstream will buy you about ten minutes. The entire container will buy you about twenty-four hours."

"What does it do?" Jonas asked. He held my hand up and examined the pearl.

"It acts as a paralysis drug. When injected into a person's bloodstream, within five seconds the person will be unable to move any part of their body."

"Paralyzed," I whispered.

Coach nodded. "Able to breathe and maybe move their eyes, but they'd be limp as a rag doll."

I held the ring in front of my face, examining it the way a newly engaged girl might stare at her engagement ring. This would totally work. I wouldn't kill anyone, yet I could incapacitate someone if I needed to.

"To close and reseal the chamber holding the drug, twist the pearl again in the opposite direction."

Seth had been standing against the wall. He pushed off and paced around the room. "Okay. So, let's say you get into the IIA's facility. What then? You just going to roam the halls looking for Addison, paralyzing people you come in contact with and hoping they don't shoot you before you get close enough?"

Jack and Jonas traded looks. It was Jack who stood tall and spoke first. "No. I'll be armed, as will Jonas."

I fiddled with the ring around my finger.

"And you're okay with that?" Seth asked me.

I scanned all of their faces. "Yes. However, with Jonas's and my mind-control tricks, I'm hoping to avoid injuring any of the agents. And I've asked someone else to come along."

"Who?" Jonas asked.

As if on cue, the door opened, and in sashayed Briana. She wore black leggings, a fitted black sweater, and black ballet flats. She looked like a stylish cat burglar. I wasn't sure if anyone else noticed whose face Briana found first, but I sure did. It hadn't taken long for Briana to set her sights on Jonas. And by the look on his face, I was pretty sure he was soaking it up.

I shook my head. "Hi, Bree. You think you're up for this?"

"I think so. Between what Jack has shown me and what I've practiced, I think I can at least help."

Jonas cleared his throat and stood. "I've shown Bree how to operate a Taser. She's armed already."

And when did you have time to do that?

Jonas shot a quick glance at me. *Jealous?*

Uh... no. "What about Georgia?" I asked.

Jonas's face fell slightly.

"Nothing?"

He shook his head.

"What?" Jack asked, as if just understanding what we were talking about. "No one has talked to Georgia?" He looked me straight in the eye. "We can't go in there without her. I won't let you."

"You won't *let* me?" My eyebrows shot up.

"Lexi, be reasonable. If you can't remove the tracker..." Jack stared at me until I squirmed. "You're planning to go in anyway."

"Yes. And maybe it's for the best. I'll go in alone, find the tracker server, destroy it, grab Addison, and get out. With that computer destroyed, the other clones with trackers will have a fighting chance."

"Absolutely not. You realize what that would mean?" Jack ran a hand through his hair.

I reached up and grabbed both of his hands in mine. "I know exactly what it would mean. It will be better this way." I lifted one of his hands up to cup my cheek, leaning into his touch. "One way or another, you're getting Addison back. And if I can't extract the trackers, I'll figure out a way to work with Sandra until I can."

Jack turned to Jonas. "And you're okay with this?"

"No, but her mind is made up." He looked down at his feet. "She won't be going in alone, though."

I eyed Jonas. "Oh, yes I will. You're not going back in there if we can't remove the trackers. If Sandra thinks you're part of some plan to destroy her operation, she'll kill you for sure."

"If Sandra wanted me dead, she would have done it already." He stuffed his hands in his pockets. "I'm fairly certain she thinks I'm still working to bring you in to her. When she sees that I have, she'll trust me. She obviously needs me for something."

"This is crazy." Jack came close to yelling. "What do we think has happened to Georgia?" He grabbed my forearm and turned me to him. His furrowed brows shadowed his already dark navy eyes. *This was not the plan. You were supposed to take Georgia, find Addison, get rid of her tracker, and get out.*

"I left her a dozen or so messages on our very private voicemail," Jonas said. "She hasn't answered a single one. She and Fred have gone completely off the grid. Which is where we all should have gone."

I'll be fine. I promise. I prayed I could keep that promise.

"So, there's a chance she'll get in touch with you."

Jonas nodded, but it was not a convincing nod.

"So, back to the plan." Seth began packing away some of the weapons that weren't chosen. "Cathy and Roger are out of town."

I glanced at Jack.

They received an email from my father explaining that he had information about the journals, and asked them to meet him at the Louisville airport.

I raised an eyebrow. Was it really from your father? Or did you send that email?

He smirked, confirming that he, in fact, had sent the decoy. He still had no idea what had happened to Dr. DeWeese.

"Coach and I will be with other select FBI agents on campus," Seth continued. "We cannot interfere. The FBI has their own investigation into the IIA going on... but the feds know nothing about you. They've asked for our help in a case against my sister, and it just so happens they have a temporary mobile office set up in the middle of campus."

So the FBI was obviously watching the IIA. "How much *does* the FBI know?" I was sure there had to be Americans who predicted the existence of cloned humans, but I'd always hoped it was the same type of people who were certain aliens lived among us and that the government hid the aliens' spaceships in Area 51.

"So far, they don't seem to have hard proof that the IIA is doing anything illegal, let alone harming Americans," Coach explained. "And the federal government offers quite a bit of leniency to this rogue agency."

I couldn't decide if that was a good or a bad thing. I wasn't ready for the public to become obsessed with the idea that people existed among them that "might" have the ability to cure their every ailment or injury.

"So we're ready, then?" I was asking everybody in the room, but only looking at Jack, who remained stoic.

~~~~~

It was after two a.m. when we arrived on the University of Kentucky campus. We parked next to a bar that had closed an hour before. Beside the bar was a twenty-four-hour diner. It was packed.

We climbed out of the SUV Seth had allowed us to borrow. The sounds of kids just slightly older than me were loud on the other side of the restaurant's glass windows. I felt a sudden pang in my heart—the same twinge I got when I longed for normalcy that I'd never known, and just might never experience.

Jonas laughed.

"What are you laughing at?" Briana asked.

"I was just thinking about what I would give to taste a good old-fashioned grilled cheese right about now."

"And that's funny?" Briana didn't look like she understood, but I sure did.

"Not funny, but something most of the kids in there won't even remember in the morning. Yet I'd cherish it."

"Okay, let's go." Jack placed his hand on the small of my back. "We need to keep moving. Hopefully, The Farm won't be heavily staffed in the middle of the night. Maybe we can get in there, find what we need and get out."

You mean, hopefully we can find Addison, trash the IIA's tracker server, talk as many clones as possible into leaving with us, and high-tail it back to Wellington before crazy woman Sandra kills us all?

A guy in love with you can hope, right?

I reached around and grabbed his hand. I lifted it to my mouth and kissed each of his knuckles.

He pulled on me. "You guys go ahead. I just need to say one thing to Lexi."

Jonas grumbled something unintelligible, then urged Kyle and Briana forward.

I studied his eyes. He and I had already had a long talk. We both had refused to say goodbye, and I wouldn't say it now. This could go well—or this could go very, very badly. Neither of us wanted to put odds on the outcome.

He brushed hair back off my face. "Promise me," he whispered. "You'll at least try to make it back out of there. If things get bad... if we get separated... I don't know. Promise me you'll do what you can to make it back to me."

I can't believe you're even saying these things to me. I mindspoke to hide the shakiness and fear in my voice. *I will fight with everything in me to make it back out to you. If not tonight, then tomorrow. And every day after that.*

He reached down and planted a kiss on my lips, closing his eyes tight. *I'm holding you to it.*

~~~~~

The University of Kentucky campus was beautiful at night. Ornate street lamps lit the sidewalks. Spotlights were strategically placed against buildings and under trees, providing additional aesthetic light. Shadows danced off leaves blowing onto sides of buildings in the cool autumn wind. Limbs creaked against each other, creating an eerie ambiance so close to Halloween.

As we neared the agriscience building, we attempted to stay off the main sidewalks, walking along dark and less-traveled paths at this late hour.

I reached down and zipped my fleece snug around my neck. Jack wrapped his fingers around my hand.

How is it possible that a group of über-intelligent doctors are playing with human life right under so many people's noses? I asked him. *What is the FBI actually waiting on? Why not destroy this operation?*

The FBI doesn't have enough proof that the IIA isn't working on science or medical advancements that will help Americans—and the world for that matter. Jack squeezed my hand. It was no secret that he and Jonas were closer to embracing their identities and their special abilities than I was. They wanted to believe that our abilities to heal were part of something good—and while they hoped to destroy Sandra's mission to hurt anyone who got in her way, they wanted me to embrace my capability to heal, too.

Stop! Jonas yelled inside my head. We all froze mid-step.

What is it? What's wrong? I asked.

Georgia.

Is she here?

Jonas nodded. "She's close," he whispered. "She doesn't want to go in."

I squeezed Jack's hand hard, and turned my frantic eyes on him. "We need her," I said.

"Where is she?" Jack asked Jonas. "Tell her to meet me."

"If you go," Jonas said, "you won't be here to shield Lexi from Ty or anyone else who wants inside her head."

Jack held onto both of my hands. "I'll be back. And I'll bring Georgia with me." He pressed his lips to mine before staring hard into my eyes. *Jonas will protect you.*

Jonas looked from Jack to me, then nodded.

TWENTY-EIGHT

....

We can't wait much longer," Jonas said. "We don't know how long it'll take to get in there and find Addison."

Jack had taken Briana with him. Though she was just learning to use her supernatural abilities, she would still be a second set of eyes in case they ran into trouble.

"Can Briana speak telepathically to you?" I asked Jonas.

"I'm not convinced she can't. She just doesn't know how yet."

"So, you think I might be able to as well?" Kyle asked. He lay on a bench behind Jonas, an arm draped over his forehead. I was pretty sure this was his way to relax, while Jonas and I paced and fidgeted.

"I don't know." Jonas sounded harsher than usual.

I walked over to the bench and nudged Kyle. He raised his head, letting me sit, then placed his head on my thigh. "It would be nice to have some time when no one was trying to kill us to explore these abilities," I said.

Jonas raised a brow. "*Now* you're interested in learning more?"

"I've never been opposed to knowing, I'm just not convinced I want to use the unnatural powers."

Kyle lowered his arm. "What if we're capable of healing people of some horrific illnesses?"

271

I thought about that for a minute. Before I could answer, Jonas added, "We could possibly help people in ways that doctors and scientists have only dreamed of doing."

"I know, but how do you suppose we do that? Just hang up a sign that says, 'Doctor Is In—Can Heal All That Ails You'? Do you realize the masses of people that would show up? Our lives would be in significant danger." I almost laughed out loud at the irony of that statement. Our lives were already in danger.

"I think that's why Cathy is at Wellington." Jonas continued to pace. "*You* think she's trying to force us to do certain things against our will—"

"I think she's the reason my dad is dead," I said through gritted teeth, interrupting Jonas with as much calm as I could drum up, which wasn't much.

"I'm just not convinced of that. I think she wants to protect us so that we have control over who knows we even exist. I also think that may be what your father had wanted. Then, we could use the powers for good, without the masses overwhelming us."

"If that's the case, she sure went about it all wrong," Kyle said.

"Thank you," I agreed. Cathy was at best an overbearing wacko.

"You both are missing the point, though." Jonas stopped and stuffed his hands in his pockets. This conversation was simply a diversion from what we were all truly worried about—getting in and out of The Farm alive with Addison. "The ball is in our court. We hold all the power. All the con-

trol." He faced me. "Lexi, when you, Jack, and Kyle left Wellington, you opened their eyes. You opened *my* eyes in a way."

"Go on," I said. See? I could be reasonable and listen.

"When you guys bulldozed through their security, you told
Cathy, Dr. DeWeese, and Dr. Wellington that they're not in
charge. You are." He kneeled in front of me. Locked eyes with
me. "*We* are in charge."

Kyle sat up and faced forward. "He's right. We *are* in charge.
And like it or not, our life's purpose was put in place way before we were born. Now *we* get to choose how we embrace our
destiny."

Lexi.

At the sound of Jack's voice, I stood and walked away from
Kyle and Jonas. *Yeah. I'm here.*

*Georgia says she can see inside your head when Jonas lets her.
They practiced this the day they found you on campus. But she has to
be touching Jonas.*

What? They had no right—

*You can be mad later. Right now, I need you to focus. She refuses to
enter The Farm. I'm going to see if she can see what you're seeing by
touching me.*

I gave my head a little shake. He was right. It wasn't like she
was the only one invading my mind these days. *Okay.*

Jonas was standing practically on top of me when I turned.
"I heard."

Of course he heard. *I'm examining the tracker inside Jonas's
head right now,* I mindspoke to Jack. The inside of Jonas's brain
was lit up with firing neurons. Unlike many of the other brains
I had examined, Jonas's head was filled with red fiery neurons.
His tracker was lodged at the base of his brain, much like Dan-

ielle's. The tracker looked like a robotic spider. The prongs curved like thin, fragile legs, but I knew the device was anything but fragile.

I'm seeing what you're seeing, Lexi. Georgia's voice was quiet inside my head.

Do you see the thin prongs?

Yes. They look like they would break off easily.

Well, I've held one of these in my hand. The prongs are very strong and gripping, especially when the device is moving backwards against resistance. If we pull this device out while the prongs are extended, it will grab hold of whatever it can. Those prongs could pierce the brain or the spinal cord in a millisecond.

Georgia went silent. I still sensed Jack. *Jack?*

I'm here. Georgia is freaking out a little. She doesn't want to risk Jonas's life.

Well, it's not up to her. And we're not removing his right now anyway. I need her to help me remove Addison's first.

Jonas nodded. He had already insisted that Sandra would not terminate him yet.

I'll make sure Georgia's ready.

Jack wasn't coming with us into the facility. I massaged the spot on my chest where my heart beat furiously. I could do this. I just had to focus.

"I'll be with you the entire time," Jonas whispered. "I'm not going to let anything happen to you. It will be better with fewer of us anyway. But we'll need Briana."

I had no idea how Jonas could sound so calm. He was at risk of dropping dead any second with a single key stroke if Sandra chose. Also, Jonas was my ticket in and my ticket out of the facility. And I wasn't completely confident in Briana's abilities yet. "Why do we need her?"

"She can confuse the agents. When they look at us, they'll think they're seeing Ty, Dia, and Lin. And with your mind-altering abilities, you can convince them that that is exactly what they're seeing."

I turned the ring on my right hand round and round, careful to avoid twisting the pearl. I could do this. I had to. And if Georgia and I could figure out how to get the tracker out without killing or paralyzing the hosts, we'd be able to do serious damage to at least part of the IIA's cloning program.

"So, we're good?" Jonas asked. I answered with a slight nod. "We can do this. *Georgia* can do this." *Besides you, I'd say she's probably the most powerful of us all.*

Yes, but with the most severe side effect.

~~~~~

"Last chance to turn back," Jonas said. He, Briana, Kyle, and I stood at a back entrance to the agriscience building. "This is where I used to sneak in and out. Back when Mom..." His voice trailed off.

I touched his arm. "It's okay. She's the only mother you ever knew."

"Right. You don't really believe that it's okay."

No, I didn't. I decided it was probably better if I said nothing. He probably heard my thoughts anyway, despite my attempt to pocket them.

"Anyway," he continued. "This is where I snuck in and out of the facility back when Sandra trusted me. I was fairly certain they monitored my every move. Or they were too busy with crazy experiments that no one noticed my comings and goings."

Briana slipped a hairband from her wrist and pulled her thick red hair into a low ponytail. "Well, here's hoping they don't monitor this entrance tonight."

Kyle and I traded worried glances. I then directed my determination at Jonas, who stood directly in front of the retinal scanner. He looked at me for permission to continue.

I nodded. "Let's do this." He had better do it quick, before I changed my mind.

But I wouldn't change my mind. Addison was in there somewhere, and I had to find her. And I had to locate and destroy the server controlling the trackers. Without the ability to alter the trackers, Sandra's ability to manipulate minds would be lost, and we would have time to remove the remaining trackers.

Jonas leaned down, aligning his eyes with the scanner.

My heart sped up immediately, and my stomach began to churn.

The latch on the door clicked. Jonas wrapped his palm around the handle and pulled. Just like that, we were in.

The four of us entered a dark hallway. The lights immediately flickered on. I felt exposed by the brightness.

We were in the basement of the building. Jonas led the way. We walked wordlessly behind him, careful to make as little sound as possible. The walls of the hallways were a light gray. The doors alternated between a deep gray and navy blue. Nothing like the white hallways of The Program.

I wasn't sure if it was my imagination, but I thought I smelled the scent of the gas the IIA had used to put Lin and Dia to sleep the first time I entered The Farm. *Jonas, is that—*

I smell it, too. I'm the only one who might be affected by it because of the tracker, but my device has never been programmed to react to the gas before, so we'll just have to be careful. He glanced over his shoulder. "Does everyone remember the plan?" We all nodded. Jonas zeroed in on Briana. "You up for this?"

Is she up for what? Strange time to be asking her that.

Briana nodded. The features of her face were tight; her eyes were deer-in-the-headlights big. "I'm already one step ahead of you."

What does that mean? What is she doing?

She's already altering what someone would see if they saw us.

I looked behind me at Kyle. Only it wasn't Kyle. It was Jack. *Okay, that's weird.* When I turned back around, Jonas's tattoos were gone. He was Ty. Briana looked like herself, I supposed, but she and Dia were identical. *Who do I look like?*

You look like an older version of yourself.

"What?" I asked in a loud whisper. "She made me look like Sandra?"

Will you keep it down? It had to be someone Briana's seen before and who's supposed to be here. She couldn't very well make you look like Dia, now could she?

I sighed. *I guess not. But what if Sandra sees us?*

Jonas closed his eyes for a moment. *We're only in disguise in case guards or agents see us. Hopefully, it will throw them off. If Sandra sees us, it won't matter what we look like. She'll know it's us.*

Well, especially if she sees her twin. Shit!

Jonas furrowed his brows at me. *Can we continue?*

I gestured with my hand for him to lead the way. The overhead lights hummed—the only other sound besides our light footsteps.

Jonas led us down two halls, each one dark until our motion was detected and lights above flickered on. I suspected armed agents would jump out any minute. I couldn't imagine how it was possible that we were wandering these halls undetected. Jonas stopped in front of one of the gray doors. The window at the top—at Jonas's eye level, but not mine—was dark. He reached down, turned the knob, and pushed it open. I raised a brow, surprised that it was unlocked. After looking both ways down the hallway, he ushered us in.

He flipped a light switch. Instead of an overhead fluorescent, two lamps glowed—one beside a full-sized bed, and another on a small black dresser on the other side of the room.

I turned in a circle. Besides a bed and a dresser, there was just a small desk with a laptop and a desk lamp. A couple of textbooks were spread across the end of the bed. A guitar stood in the corner of the room on a stand. This was a teenager's room. I jerked my head toward Jonas. "This is your room, isn't it?"

"You lived here?" Briana asked, a little taken aback.

"Of course. Well... until I got my tracker and was allowed to leave the facility. But that was after we moved here to Kentucky. Where did you think I lived before I moved in with Georgia and Fred?"

"I assumed you lived with Sandra. Just not inside some laboratory."

"I've lived with Sandra most of my life. Usually at some research facility." He sat at his desk and opened the laptop. His lips tugged downward in a look of sadness I'd never seen on him before. "She lived wherever the work was. I was just part of that work."

Kyle stood watch at the window.

It was too quiet. Why hadn't agents descended upon us? Standing over Jonas, I watched him click around on his laptop at what appeared to be some sort of floor plan. "Is that this building?"

"Yes." He continued to click.

Then, suddenly, a video image popped up on the screen.

"Holy crap!" I leaned in closer.

Briana joined me. "Who is that?"

"That's Addison," I said. Addison sat in the middle of a bed, hugging her knees and staring straight ahead. Nothing like the little girl that had jumped on her bed like a monkey back at Wellington. "What is she doing?"

"Watching TV, maybe?" Jonas answered, unsure. He clicked some more and was able to show us a panoramic view. She *was* watching TV, and she wasn't moving. At all.

"How are you able to tap into this camera?" Briana asked.

He smiled up at her. "I'm a man of many talents."

She slapped at his shoulder playfully. I rolled my eyes.

"So, you've somehow hacked into their security system? How did you know where she'd be?"

"There were only a few rooms I thought they'd place her in. The residential wing of this facility isn't that big. And it's fairly full."

Addison remained motionless while I continued to study her. She was not the energetic eight-year-old that I remembered. She looked... sad. Even more childlike and innocent than

279

I recalled. I had to get her out of here. A woman walked into her room, her back to the camera. Addison didn't even look up.

Why was someone walking into her room at this hour? Normal people slept at this late hour.

Then I realized what was bothering me. It was something Jonas had said after I healed Sandra, after Addison had been taken. "Jonas, why is Addison in the residential wing?"

Jonas wouldn't even look at me. I drilled holes into the woman in the video. *Turn around. Let me see your face.* As if she could hear me, she turned, walked back toward the camera, and, I assumed, out the door. It was Anita, Addison's mother and the DeWeese's housekeeper. She was here.

And I knew what Jonas had meant when he'd said, "Addison was the one that got away."

TWENTY-NINE

....

S he lived here, didn't she?"

"Well, not here," Jonas said. "But she was born in one of the previous research centers."

Did you know this? I asked Jack. I had pretty much left my mind open to him since he had left me to find Georgia.

No, but it makes sense. I didn't meet Addison until the summer she came to live with us. I had been told she lived with her father before that. I never questioned it.

Interesting. So, Addison probably didn't have memories of the research facility where she was born. "Who's her father?" I asked Jonas.

"None of us really have fathers, Lexi. You and Jack are two of the lucky ones who feel as if you were raised by a father, and in Jack's case, a mother, too. Most of us simply have the one person our DNA originated from, and a surrogate."

"I have parents," Briana said.

Kyle looked over from his spot by the door. "My upbringing is definitely... complicated."

Complicated, I stifled a chuckle. That was too nice of a word to describe how each of us was raised. I was raised by an absentee father and by my grandmother, who was the mother of the woman who carried me for nine months then disappeared soon after I was born. It would be a disgrace to give her the title of Mom.

Jonas closed the laptop and stood. "I've got what we need. Let's go."

"Go where, exactly?" There was a heaviness in my chest. So far, our adventure into the building had been uneventful. Way too easy.

Jonas grabbed a piece of paper off of his printer and crossed the room to the door. He taped the paper onto the back of the door and pointed to a square at the bottom left corner. "We are here." He stuck the end of a red ink pen in his mouth and pulled, leaving the lid between his teeth. After placing an "X" over his room, he traced a line down what appeared to be a hallway, made one left turn, and then placed an "A" over a square on the right. "This is where Addison is. That's where Lexi and I are going."

"What? They're not coming?" I lifted my head toward Briana and Kyle.

"No. Too many people. Too dangerous." He placed his hands on Briana's shoulders and stared straight into her eyes, pausing a moment before he spoke. "If I give you the word, you and Kyle leave. Georgia and Jack are at this door." He pointed. "You knock three times slowly. Georgia knows how to open it from the outside."

"What if you need help?" she asked, her eyes searching his.

"Yeah," I agreed. "What if we need help?"

"Then we'll mindspeak to them." Jonas replied. *I can control Briana. She doesn't know it. And Kyle can hear me, he just can't answer back for some reason. To any of us.*

Please promise me that I'm around when you tell Briana that you can control her mind. If you thought I was upset... I laughed.

"Let's go," he said, ignoring me.

Briana looked from Jonas to me and back. "Be careful." She pulled me aside and lowered her voice. "I promised Jack I wouldn't leave you." She wrung her hands and glanced nervously toward Jonas.

I grabbed one of her hands and squeezed. "I'll be fine. We'll alert you guys if there's trouble." I didn't believe we'd be fine. Not for a second.

Is Georgia ready? I asked Jack.

She's ready. We're ready. Use your ring if you need to and run like hell if something goes wrong, okay? Promise me.

I didn't.

~~~~~

Jonas and I crept down a hallway farther away from the door through which we entered, and farther away from Jack. All was quiet: nothing other than the light sound of the rubber soles of our shoes.

We just have to round the next corner, Jonas said. *Addison is the second door on the right.*

Lexi, something's wrong. Jack was in my head. *Three government cars just pulled up to the curb at the back of the building. Strange for the middle of the night, don't you think?*

I rubbed my chest. My heart beat so loudly I was sure Jonas could hear it in the middle of this silent hallway. I began concentrating on pocketing information, attempting to keep him out of my head—even though my previous efforts to do this had been mostly unsuccessful.

I watched the back of his head. He didn't react. I could only assume I'd been able to shut him out. For now. I simply couldn't risk Jonas aborting our mission when we were this close to Addison.

Anyone getting out of the cars?

Not yet. We're tucked behind some bushes.

Jonas and I continued around the corner and stopped in front of a dark blue door. I heard distant sounds of a horn or something. An alarm, maybe. *What is that?*

Don't worry about it. Let's keep going. The look on Jonas's face didn't comfort me.

We slipped inside the room. Addison still sat in the middle of her bed, staring straight at the TV—but the TV wasn't turned on. I looked from the TV back to her. "Addison?" I whispered.

She didn't move. What had they done to her? This was not the little girl I met last week.

Lexi! You've got to get out of there, Jack yelled. *They know you're there. An agent just rushed by us saying your name into his wrist microphone.*

I couldn't leave. I wouldn't leave Addison. Not like this.

I don't believe it. Jack said, panic behind each word. *We were wrong. It wasn't Cathy. It was... Lexi, listen to me. Stop whatever you're doing and turn around.*

What is it? What's wrong?

Jonas stiffened. The movement was slight, but he obviously heard me.

Sandra just got out of one of the vehicles with... Jack's voice trailed off.

I stretched my fingers, then curled them into fists at my side. *Who's with her? Talk to me, Jack.*

Jonas turned and stared at me. My eyes darted from him to Addison, who looked so tiny, just sitting there as still as a statue in the middle of a hospital bed.

mindsiege

My dad, Lexi! My dad is with Sandra.

I cringed at Jack's words. I squeezed my eyes tight. Was there no one we could trust?

Jonas slipped his hand into mine and squeezed. "We're here. This doesn't change anything."

I knew getting inside The Farm had been too easy. I'd have to help Jack with this latest shocker later. Jonas was right. We were here and Addison needed us. I had to focus. *Jack, I need Georgia to pay attention. Something's wrong with Addison. I'm going to see if I can dislodge her tracker right now. She's not moving. It's like they've shut her down, mentally. She won't even speak to me. She's comatose. And Jack?* I closed my eyes tightly for a moment. *Anita is here.*

Silence.

Jack? I'm sorry about your father, but I need you to stay with me. I'm not leaving without Addison.

I'm here. And so is Georgia. She's ready. She can hear everything you say. Please be careful. And hurry. There are six agents entering the building with my dad and Sandra.

Jonas grabbed Addison's hand. "Her hand is freezing."

I brought up the image of her brain. The same brain I had studied and healed all too recently. Instead of brightly colored neurons firing like fireworks, the activity in her head was slow and the coloring of the neurons and surrounding tissue was dull, almost brown in color. I moved around in her head. A strange coating covered many of the surfaces I knew to be responsible for processing information. I kept searching. When I reached the spot at the base of her brain, I saw it—the tracker. The tissue around the tracker, and along a path from the tracker to the back of her neck, was bruised. I would need to extract the tracker the same way it went in.

Georgia, you with me? You see the path we need to take?

Yeah, I see it. But what happens if we fail?

I studied how the tracker was lodged. If I were to move it as it lay, the prongs would puncture her brain and spinal cord in several locations. I couldn't predict how much injury that would cause, or if I could heal her fast enough to prevent long-term damage... or death.

We won't fail. Can you see each of the prongs? There are eight of them. Just like a spider.

Yes, I see them.

The prongs all come from tiny holes in the tracker, I explained. *I need you to slide each prong back inside the tracker itself.*

I watched silently. It was slow going. It took more than a minute before the first prong was hidden inside. While I witnessed Georgia working a miracle, I smoothed Addison's hair and tried to pocket all of my emotions and thoughts.

I heard the commotion of approaching footsteps. I looked at Jonas, who was typing away on the computer.

When the footsteps registered with him, he met my gaze. "They're coming."

Lexi, I can't see Addison's brain anymore, Georgia said.

Sorry. I pulled up the visual of Addison's tracker again, while I spoke to Jonas. "You have ten seconds to convince me that you didn't know John DeWeese had been working with Sandra. If you're not honest with me, I can't promise how hard I'll work to make sure you make it out of here with me." With my thumb, I fiddled with the ring on my middle finger. I imagined the paralyzing liquid sloshing around inside the pearl.

"What are you talking about?" I felt his eyes studying me. I continued to monitor Georgia's progress. "Of course I didn't know."

I didn't take my other hand off of Addison. Georgia had managed to tuck in five of the prongs. *Keep it up, Georgia. You're doing great.*

"What are you up to?" Jonas asked.

I felt the intrusion into my head, different from Jonas's normal entrance. This presence blew in like a thin fog, elusively sliding in and around crevices. This was not Jonas, but Ty. I immediately began moving pockets around, hiding thoughts and feelings. I tried to categorize and pocket the image of Addison's brain the way Jonas had taught me.

He grabbed my arm and jerked me up. "What have you done?" He shoved me hard across the room, then turned to Addison, who remained still.

I scrambled to my feet and ran to the door. Instead of swinging it open with my shaking limbs, I turned the steel lock, locking us inside. I wasn't leaving without Addison. And I couldn't take Addison in her current state.

Ty, in Jonas's body, grabbed Addison's head roughly, lifting her hair and examining the back of her neck. There was a bandage covering the spot where the tracker had been inserted.

Kyle, Briana, you guys have to get out of here. Try to make it to the back door. Use whatever force you have to use to get out of here.

Jonas/Ty turned. He tilted his head. A slow, sly grin spread across his face. At the same time, I felt the stabbing presence of his mind invasion.

I had to focus. I kept one mindful eye on the tracker inside Addison's head, and one on the contents of my own head.

Lexi, I want you to stop what you're doing to Addison, right now.

This time it was my turn to grin. I was tired of these mind games, and for some reason, by concentrating hard on his presence, I was able to shove his demands to the side. I had full control over my actions. For the moment, anyway. I pushed away from the door, and stepped closer to him instead of backing away. "No... Ty... I won't."

Georgia had seven of the eight prongs tucked safely away. Addison still hadn't moved. Not even when Jonas/Ty had shoved her head forward.

Behind me, the door rattled. *Hurry, Georgia.* I wasn't about to let Georgia, and therefore Jack, know that I was now with Ty, or that others were trying to get into the room. We knew this might not go well. It was the risk we took. It was the risk *I* took.

Lexi, you do not have a choice. He slithered in and around my head like the serpent that he was. *You will stop what you're doing.*

I didn't know how, but I was completely capable of choosing not to follow Ty's orders. Maybe because Jack and Georgia were taking up the bulk of the guest space inside my brain. I was able to sense Ty's presence and at the same time keep charge of my own mental faculties.

Keys rattled. Whoever was on the other side of the door was coming in. I was in trouble.

Finally all eight prongs were tucked neatly inside the tracker. *Georgia?*

It's me, Jack said. *Georgia's out for now. Tell me what's going on. Did she succeed?*

Yes. The prongs have been tucked away, but the tracker is still there. I searched my mind. Georgia was gone. Was she suffering a seizure? Jack was there, my constant. Ty was searching frantically. And there in tiny hidden spots was Jonas. Was he hearing my thoughts? Was he capable of shutting Ty out? Or had Ty taken over?

Jonas?

Nothing.

The door flew open behind me. I whipped around and backed up. Sandra entered, followed by two agents. I skirted around the bed to stand on the opposite side from Jonas/Ty.

Sandra is here, I said to Jack.

We've got to get you out of there.

Take care of Georgia. You know I'm not leaving without Addison and some answers.

Don't do anything stupid, Lex.

'Kay.

"Why hello, Son," Sandra said.

"Hi, Mom."

Jonas? I begged.

I'm here.

I let out a large breath. *Thank God.*

She's speaking to Ty. Ty thinks he's got control of me.

How does she know he's controlling you?

She assumes Ty's inside my head and controlling me—and there-fore you—because that's what she programmed his tracker to do.

I don't understand.

You will in a minute. We don't have much time. You need to extract the tracker from Addison, if you can.

I don't know if I can without Georgia. I'm not telekinetic.

Sandra walked over to Jonas, only I was pretty sure Ty was in control, and cupped his cheek. "You've done really well, Ty. Do you have control of Lexi?"

He shook his head.

"What do you mean? Why not?"

"I'm controlling Jonas, but she's not responding."

"Go get me Ty. Now!" Sandra ordered the agents. One reddened. He wheeled and left the room.

Lexi, listen. You can do this. You'd be surprised what you can do, Jonas said. *I watched how you got the drug out of Jack's head—the one that rendered him completely unconscious. And how you removed the fluid from Sandra's brain. Heal Addison the same way. I'll work to block Ty from seeing exactly how you work your magic.*

This was impossible. I'd had Jack and Sandra puke out the foreign substance. This was not the same.

Sandra turned to me. "After everything I've heard, I'm surprised to see you here, Sarah."

What was that supposed to mean? "Are you disappointed or pleased?"

"Oh, I'm pleased. Very pleased. And when Ty gets here, I'll show you just how pleased I am. I thought for sure you'd be a coward like your mother."

THIRTY

....

I had too much to focus on to consider Sandra's latest riddle. What could she possibly know about my mother? I spun the ring round and round on my finger. Keeping one eye on Sandra, I brought the image of Addison's brain up as if I had a projector in my head. The tracker rested at the base of her brain, right where I had left it. The prongs were inside the device.

Her neurons were still a drab brown. Amber, but with no shine.

"I thought you would have Jack with you." Sandra stared at me from beside Jonas. "Where is he?"

"I left Jack back at school," I lied. "He would have slowed me down." Jonas, standing behind his mother, nodded in approval.

Closing my eyes briefly, I tried to move the tracker. It shifted slightly. My heart began beating out of control. Could I be telekinetic on top of everything? Would removing this tiny metal object make me sick? If I became as sick as I'd been the night I healed Jack and Addison, or if I suffered some sort of seizure like Georgia, I was doomed. Sandra would have me.

Who was I kidding? I was trapped already. Hopefully Briana and Kyle were already safely on the outside with Jack and Georgia. No sense all of us going down.

An agent entered the room, walked straight to Sandra, and whispered into her ear. Jonas lifted his chin, urging me to concentrate on Addison.

Keep talking to her, I mindspoke to the agent. *Keep Sandra busy.*

While the agent kept Sandra occupied, I went to work. Closing my eyes, I wriggled the device through the tunnel in Addison's head that hadn't yet healed from the recent insertion.

When I had it at the edge, I opened my eyes. Sandra had walked to the corner of the room to listen to the agent. I sat on the edge of Addison's bed, pretending to look tired. I leaned into Addison. Lifting my hand, I brushed her hair around to hang down in front, exposing the bandage on the back of her neck. I peeled the edge of the bandage back to reveal a red and scabbed-over wound held together by a few stitches.

Again, I squeezed my eyes tight, and with one final push, I urged the tracker out of Addison's skull, through the scab in her neck, and into my bare palm.

The wound began to bleed. I had no way of stitching it. Instead, I willed the skin to cover the bloody area. And it did heal—somehow. Flesh formed over the raw wound, leaving no sign of the scab or the stitches that were there moments earlier. I had never done that before. Healing superficial wounds was Jack's department.

Blood dripped from my nose, and my head began to burn like a slow-burning campfire as I fought back feelings of nausea. But no seizure, thankfully.

Jonas watched me with concern. *You okay? I can't come over there, or I'd try to remove some of that pain.*

I wiped my nose on the sleeve of my fleece jacket and replaced the bandage on the back of Addison's neck, despite there no longer being a wound.

As I pressed on the bandage, Sandra suddenly shoved the agent. "You idiot, she's controlling you."

I slid off the bed while discreetly stuffing the tracker into the coin pocket of my jeans. The agent gave his head a shake as if he could rid his mind of my voice. Sandra crossed the room and stood directly in front of me, eye to eye. I fiddled with the ring on my finger. How quickly could I paralyze her? And if I bought myself ten minutes, was that enough time to grab Addison and get out of there?

It felt so strange to look at a woman who was the image of what I would become. Yet at the same time, I couldn't see past her monstrous actions. I straightened, stared deep into her green eyes. Was I capable of being like this woman?

No, you're not. Jack was in my head.

Jack.

You think I was just going to leave you?

The door opened, and Sandra spun away from me. The real Ty appeared, with two agents close behind him. The female agent had one hand on the gun at her hip.

"Great. You're here," Sandra said.

Ty remained silent. No grin played at his lips. His arms, clear of any ink, hung loose at his sides.

Jonas's nervous eyes darted between his mother and his twin clone. "Mom, what are you going to do?"

Ty and Sandra didn't break eye contact. He was so much taller than her, but the vulnerable look on his face made me want to help him.

What's she going to do? I asked Jonas, but he didn't answer. Only watched. His hands balled into fists.

"What happened, Ty? How did you lose control of her?" Sandra asked.

"I don't know. At first, when I was inside her head, I was able to be Jonas. Not even Jonas knew it wasn't him toying with her. Jonas was even sure he was falling in love with her." Ty stifled a laugh, but only for a moment before all humor was gone from his face again.

I glanced toward Jonas. He cocked his head, staring at his look-alike. Did he think he loved me? No, that was crazy.

"Are you admitting that Jonas is stronger than you?" Sandra asked. "That he now knows when you're calling the shots inside his head? And that he can now refuse your orders?"

Was Jonas stronger than a clone being operated by some computer-generated mindsiege? Surely.

"And are you telling me that you can no longer control Sarah? Make her see exactly what we want her to see?"

I was not liking where this conversation was going. Ty's eyes widened with fear. He rotated his shoulders back and stood tall. He did not look away from Sandra.

"Mom?" Jonas said.

"Jonas, say goodbye to your brother."

Brother?

"Mom, don't do it. It's my fault, not his. I can help him. Help you work out the flaws of his tracker."

Don't do what? I looked from Ty, to Jonas, to Sandra. She looked up at the camera in the corner of the room and gave some sort of hand signal.

Ty's eyes popped open. He gasped—and then fell to the ground.

His eyes remained open. Still. Glassy.

"Is he..." Dead? Tears flooded my eyes.

Two agents gathered up Ty's limp body and whisked him out of the room.

My heart beat out of control. I swallowed against the taste of bile in my throat. "You killed him?" My mind reeled. Addison still hadn't moved.

Jonas's face was red with fury.

"Jonas, if you don't want to face the same fate, you will come with me," Sandra ordered, then turned to the remaining agent. "Show Miss Matthews to her room. She gives you any trouble, tranquilize her."

Jonas? What's going to happen?

Don't fight it. Even inside my head, I could hear the devastation in his voice. I felt a strong need to reach out and touch him. To console him. *They won't do anything to you. Remember, they want you here more than they want you dead.*

That's reassuring.

The agent grabbed me by the arm.

I resisted the urge to mindspeak or to paralyze the man. I would listen to Jonas and not fight. For now.

Just before the agent led me from the room, I looked back at Addison. She still hadn't moved, but when I focused on her eyes, they shifted and looked directly at me.

~~~~~

We made three turns before the agent unlocked a door and shoved me into a room. I spun and lunged toward him, but he easily deflected my attack. He closed the door and locked it with a key hanging around his neck.

The agent was not a large man. No more than five foot eight, but he looked solid, and his biceps threatened to bust through his white button-down.

"Turn around," he said, his voice brusque.

"Why?"

He pulled a syringe from his pocket that held a few milliliters of a bright yellow substance. Holding it up, he stuck a needle on the end and pulled the cap off. "I don't want to use this, but I will."

I turned. The room was empty except for a single bed and one swivel chair typical of a doctor's office.

"Where were you, Sandra, and Dr. DeWeese coming from so late tonight?" I glanced over my shoulder at him.

"What?" He capped the syringe, tucked it in his back pocket, then forced my arms out to my side and proceeded to pat me down. "That's none of your business." I eyed my special ring—a ring I wanted to use, but the time wasn't right. Not yet.

But you want to tell me anyway. Where'd you go tonight?

"We spent the afternoon at the track and then dinner," he answered. The agent continued to search my body—for weapons, I assumed. I was thankful I hadn't brought a gun. When he reached my bottom, he stopped, pulling my phone out of the back pocket of my jeans. "You won't be needing this." He stuck my phone inside his other pants pocket.

Dang. "You got back awfully late. Why?" *Where else did you go?*

"We had dinner at Palmer's, that lasted until just before—" He stopped, grabbed me by my shoulders and spun me around. "You're mind-controlling me."

No, I'm not. No one is inside your mind. Who else was at Palmer's? What were they discussing?

"Just John, Sandra, some investors, and other IIA agents. They were discussing final evacuation and destruction of the labs."

"Evacuation? Sandra's moving the labs?"

The agent's shoulders straightened. "You *are* controlling my mind." He pulled the syringe from his pocket.

"No, I swear I'm—"

He jammed the needle directly into my neck. I faded fast.

~~~~~

I awoke with a massive headache. Not sure if it was from removing the tracker from Addison or the drug the stupid agent injected me with.

I was alone. And I had to pee.

Welcome back.

Jonas. What time is it?

Six a.m.

I drilled my fingers into my temple. I wished I had a needle to stick straight into my eye to release the pressure building there. *Where are you?*

I'm not far. I'm trying to get back into Sandra's good graces. Convince her that I've been working for her all along. That I brought you here like she wanted.

How do I know that's not exactly what you did?

You don't. Jonas sounded sad. Tired. *You'll have to do something completely out of character and have a little faith.*

Ouch. I had faith. Just not in people very often. What's the plan? Besides finding a bathroom. I scanned the room. No doors other than the one I entered through.

The plan is to sit tight until I tell you otherwise. And try to behave. Don't control any minds. Sandra has ordered all agents to keep you under if you give them any trouble. They all have trackers in the backs of their necks and have been trained to know when one of us is inside their heads. They only take orders from two people.

Sandra and John DeWeese. I squeezed the bridge of my nose. *Did you know about Dr. DeWeese?*

I suspected.

Jack? I asked. *Did he know?*

He has suspected as well. But that didn't prepare him for seeing it with his own eyes.

He said nothing to me. A tinge of anger flared across my cheeks. Anger with myself, I thought. For not being someone Jack could trust with his suspicions. *Where is he?*

He returned to Wellington. To regroup.

Regroup, huh. I pocketed my thoughts the way Jonas taught me. Trust no one—my father's words from the letter he sent me after his death. Sit tight? No way. I pushed myself out of the very uncomfortable bed and walked to the doorway. It was locked, of course, but only with one simple bolt. Still, it was a steel bolt.

What about Georgia? I asked Jonas. *Where is she?* I wondered how bad her seizure had been the night before.

Seth has her at the hospital, one building over, recovering. Kyle is with her. Why?

No reason. I worked quickly to hide what I was thinking.

Lexi, I mean it. Don't do anything stupid.

Whatever. *I'm locked inside a room with nothing but a bed and a chair, Jonas. I can't even go to the bathroom. Which I need to do, by the way.* I looked up at the camera in the corner and waved. "Hey, assholes. I need to use the bathroom."

Jonas laughed.

I sat in the chair, crossed my legs, and twirled my ring round and round. I'd give anything for a gun right now. Except they would have taken it, right along with my phone.

We need to remove your tracker.

We will. At the right time. I can't chance Sandra figuring out that we've discovered how. She hasn't noticed Addison's tracker missing yet, but she will. And when she does..." His voice trailed off. He didn't need to take that thought further.

So, Ty? I asked. *Were you close to him?*

There were several seconds of silence before Jonas mind-spoke. *He was my brother. Sandra carried us both. My DNA was altered, much like yours and Jack's. Ty's DNA wasn't changed from the original. He was given a tracker soon after birth that artificially altered his DNA, giving him almost identical mind-controlling capabilities to mine. The idea was to see if the scientists could manufacture the trackers with the mental powers.*

By placing the special abilities inside an electronic tracker, they could have complete control over any human being, I clarified.

Right. What you witnessed yesterday was Sandra realizing that I was stronger than Ty. In other words, the genetically engineered clone—me—was stronger than the manufactured form of the same person—Ty. And Sandra wanted to prove a point.

Which was?

That we are expendable when we're no longer necessary to her experiment. Ty let her down, and she killed him—to show you, and probably me, what she's capable of.

I shivered. Either someone had just turned on the A/C or the memory of Sandra's action cut right to my heart, freezing the blood being pumped through my body. *And Sandra needs me because she can't get the medical healing part correct.*

Exactly.

I sat up straighter. Seemed to me she couldn't get the mind-control part right either, or Ty wouldn't be dead. I knew what Sandra was after: the most important thing Dad gave me before he died. I reached for the starfish and key hanging around my neck underneath my T-shirt. She wanted the information Dad had encrypted on the website—the DNA mapping that could be translated into what Sandra needed to create her army of healers. So, did Sandra need me, or information she was sure I had access to? At what point would Sandra decide I was no longer necessary?

The door clicked, and in walked a woman in a white lab coat. Beneath the coat she wore a short black skirt and a dark purple silk blouse. Her jet black hair was slicked back into a tight ponytail, and she had an air of snootiness. She had to be a doctor of some sort. "Come with me."

I wiped my hands on my jeans, stood, and followed her. "Could I possibly use a restroom?" I mean, did they really expect me to hold it forever?

"Yes."

"That's it? Just yes?"

We didn't walk long before she ushered me into another room. This one was quite different. Very much like a dorm room and like Jonas's room he had shown us the night before, except this one was decorated for a girl. A bed decorated with a lavender comforter was pushed into the corner of the room. There was a desk and a small dresser.

"What's this?" I asked.

"This is your room, Sarah."

"Since my friends call me Lexi, I'm going to assume you and I aren't friends." We stood just inside the small room—a room much more decorated than the last one I was in. I fiddled with the ring on my finger and studied the lady in front of me. "So, are you a nurse or something?"

"I am a clinical neurophysiologist." She enunciated each syllable. I could have sworn her nose rose further into the air as she spoke.

"Well, that must have taken quite a bit of education. You must not have done very well in school."

She pursed her lips, and inhaled through her way-too-pointy nose. "Why do you say that, Sarah?" She said Sarah like it was a bad word.

"Well, I just assumed that only the bottom students, or maybe doctors that were fired from hospitals that helped people, would end up at a research facility that experimented on innocent children. I didn't mean anything by it." I shrugged and walked farther into the room.

"Mmmm-hmmm."

She closed the door and left me in this room that had a much more homey feel to it. And a more *permanent* feel. A chill galloped down my spine. Nothing about my situation would be permanent. I promised myself that. Thankfully, it did have a bathroom.

After I took care of my needs, I explored the room. Opening the top drawer of the dresser, I discovered clothes exactly like the ones Dia had worn the first time I visited this facility. Gray scrubs were not my thing. I slammed the drawer closed.

What on earth did a clinical neurophysiologist actually do? I wondered. Whatever it was, she wouldn't be doing it to me.

THIRTY-ONE

....

I stared up at the plain white ceiling tiles. The more bored I got, the madder I became at Jonas.

My stomach growled. I hadn't eaten since early the day before. And it was past ten a.m. I hadn't heard from Jonas in more than an hour. At this point I didn't even know what Jonas's mission was. Were we forever trapped inside this prison of a facility? Would I be forced to submit to my psycho twin of a DNA donor?

Well, twin except for the wrinkles. And Sandra was heavier than me.

I made a mental note to continue swimming later in life and wear good anti-aging cream. Or do the opposite—refuse sunscreen and eat fast food every day. Either way, I would not look like that evil woman as I aged.

I also planned to dye my hair as soon as possible and get purple contacts. Or something.

I sat up and rubbed my face in my hands. What was I doing? *Jack, where are you?*

Nothing. I felt lost without him, but I was thankful he wasn't trapped along with me.

I couldn't stop remembering Ty's expression as he fell to the hard floor. Lifeless. Unplugged like a malfunctioning toy robot that had its batteries yanked out by a petulant child. No longer useful to the cold, heartless scientist who created him.

I didn't even know if Briana had made it out okay. Was she still here somewhere?

I didn't have time to consider that rhetorical question because just then Sandra entered the room, along with the obnoxious clinical neurophysiologist.

"Lexi, you will come with us, now."

I scooted off the bed, stood, and crossed my arms across my chest. "No, not until I get what I need."

"And what do you need, my dear?" Her condescending tone made me want to plant the entire load of my ring's paralyzing drug into her jugular vein.

"I want reassurance that Dani will not be harmed. That's what you promised."

Sandra poked her head outside the door into the hallway. "Jonas, we will need you after all."

Jonas rounded the corner. Worry swam in the trenches that formed across his forehead and in the "V" between his eyes. *Don't fight this, Lexi.*

Don't fight what, Jonas? I said his name in the same fatherly tone in which he'd said mine. *Don't patronize me. And don't you dare assume I'm going to follow your every command just because you have the decency to walk in here with pity on your face. Look where I am.*

"Force her to cooperate," Sandra ordered Jonas.

Don't make this harder than it has to be. I have to convince Sandra that she can trust me and that I'm following the commands coming to me through the tracker. Now, walk toward me.

Are you telling me that you're getting commands, but you're able to defy them? I asked.

Apparently—ever since Ty was removed from my head.

But you could still force me to do whatever it is you order?

Yes. Walk toward me, now. This time, his voice wove through my mind like silk ribbon, and I immediately stepped to him. The muscles in my legs tightened and my knees grew weak as I did exactly what he ordered, again with no control over my own body.

He slid his fingers around my upper arm. His touch was gentle. I almost welcomed it. I had felt so alone the last twenty-four hours.

"Great," Sandra gestured toward the door. "Let's go."

The neurophysiologist led the way. Jonas squeezed my arm a little harder.

Did you find the server controlling the trackers? I asked.

Maybe.

Who do you think is pushing the buttons?

Sandra and Dr. DeWeese, for sure.

We followed the two doctors down the hallway. Sandra looked back just once. I was sure we had only two ways to escape this underground world: kill Sandra and Dr. DeWeese—the way they'd most likely killed my father; or destroy the trackers, and the computer server operating them, and run like hell.

I was pretty sure that I was not capable of murder, and I lacked hope that the other option was even remotely possible while under heavy security.

~~~~~

"What are those for?" I asked, eyeing the tangle of electrodes and wires snaking their way from some kind of computer.

"Dr. Mendez is going to perform an electroencephalogram, or an EEG, to monitor your brain activity." Sandra stood in front of the computer and began typing. "Once you have submitted to this test, and I receive the reports and information I need, I will release your friend Dani."

I didn't believe a word this witch of a woman said. "What does that mean? What information? Information from the actual test?"

Sandra turned. "That and your father's journals, of course. Lie down, please."

I tensed. How was she planning to obtain information from Dad's journals? I would die before handing them over. I crossed my arms. "No. You tell me exactly what you're about to do to me, and I will consider cooperating."

Sandra smiled—one of those really scary smiles that caused my body to shiver from the iciness of it. "Jonas."

One word from her and he was inside my head. *Lexi, you will climb up on that examination table. You will cooperate and allow the test.*

Without thinking about it another second, I did as Jonas ordered. I hopped up on the exam table, as ordered, and lay back against the headrest. "What will this test tell you?"

"It will map the activity in your brain. That, along with the details of how your DNA was altered, and a few other pieces of information we'll get from the journals..." Her voice trailed off.

Dad's journals. The muscles in my neck and back tightened. I grasped at the edge of the leather chair where my hands rested. Jonas furrowed his brows, studying me. I had full control of my body and mind again. Jonas wasn't keeping control, only exerting control when Sandra ordered it.

I said a silent prayer that I was successfully keeping my thoughts to myself. When I thought I could speak without incriminating myself, I asked Sandra, "Do you know where the journals are?" No one had ever found the hard copies of Dad's research. I had assumed they'd been destroyed.

Dr. Mendez began placing the electrodes on my forehead, around my face, and in my hair. I wanted to fight it, but I knew I couldn't. And I was still biding my time.

"No, but I will." Sandra reached into the pocket of her lab coat and pulled out a syringe. "I need a small amount of blood from you." She grabbed my arm and turned it over.

Instinctively, I jerked back, though I had nowhere to go, and I had no intention of stopping these tests—yet. How much of this would I allow before I fought back? Could I even fight it? Would Jonas stop getting inside my head when I told him I was done with all of this and wanted out?

Sandra motioned for his help. Jonas approached from the other side, reached across my body, and held my hands against the arms of the chair, exposing the vein Sandra needed to draw blood.

You know where the journals are, don't you? Jonas asked.

I looked up into his eyes. *I can't tell if you're on my side or not anymore.* I was not about to confide in him about the journals.

His eyes softened just slightly. His face was inches from mine. *I am on your side. I will not let her hurt you.*

But you got inside my head. You controlled me.

Are you kidding me? Don't act like I've hurt your feelings. You asked for this. Coming here was your choice. We could have approached this another way, but you took the risk. He looked at Sandra. "Could you please hurry?" Jonas pleaded.

The movement was small, but I felt it. The slow graze of Jonas's finger against my arm—the arm farthest from Sandra, and out of her view. I found Jonas's eyes. He didn't look at me at first, but when he did, his eyes were an inferno.

Sandra tied a rubber armband around my upper arm, pressed two fingers into the crook of my elbow, then stuck a needle into one of the veins. "Why? You don't like being close to a younger version of me?" Sandra winked.

She.

Winked.

Like this was some sort of fun and games to her. Like I was some sort of toy. For her. Or for Jonas.

"I thought you liked the most precious and most protected clone ever created." She pulled the needle out. After slapping a band-aid across my arm, she untied the armband.

"Of course not. It's creepy. You're my mother, and she looks just like you."

A vein popped out on the side of Jonas's neck. He was lying about something. When he turned his head back to me, I studied him. Heat flared across my cheeks when his eyes met mine. *I've got to get out of here. She's going to figure out how I really feel about you.*

My eyes darted sideways. Sandra typed, and Dr. Mendez pointed at the computer screen. I looked back at Jonas, whose face was too close. He rubbed his thumb across my arm, the arm he continued to hold, only much more loosely now.

My heart sped up. My pulse was going to register in the brain activity they were about to measure. *How do you feel about me?* I had no idea what made me ask that. I didn't want to know the answer.

Let's just say, I'm starting to understand why Jack was ready to whisk you far away from all this.

I narrowed my gaze. *But you've always been against me running.*

It's just that I feel protective of you. You're not my sister. And I don't see myself as being related to Sandra or to you by blood. So, don't look at me like kissing you or having feelings for you is incestual. I'd like to blame Ty for getting inside my head and playing mind games with my feelings for you, but I could have stopped those feelings from happening. I could have fought them harder the way I did yesterday in the gym. And I will. For Jack. And for you. I don't think I can turn off the protectiveness I feel for you, but I will try to think of you more like a sister.

"Okay, I think we're ready," Sandra said, and Jonas jerked backwards away from me. I stared straight ahead, practically tuning Sandra out, as I digested Jonas's latest revelation. "Dr. Mendez will take it from here. I'm going to check on Addison." Sandra started for the door.

After giving my head a little shake, I reached out and grabbed Jonas's arm before he could follow her. *You have to get Addison out of here,* I begged.

A sly grin spread across his face. The moment of awkwardness between us was gone. *You don't know much about Addison, do you?* He leaned closer, his mouth next to my ear and whispered. "Now be a good little girl." *I've got a surprise for you later, and I don't want to come back and find you tranqed.* He pulled his arm free and followed Sandra out, leaving me alone with the snooty Dr. Mendez.

~~~~~

The EEG was painless and uneventful. Afterwards, Dr. Very-Uptight led me to a cafeteria. Teenagers my age and younger sat at long, picnic-style tables. Dr. Mendez pointed to the start of the lunch line, then turned and left out the door through which we'd entered.

Strange. She trusted me to do exactly as I was told? Even I wouldn't trust me to do that. I went straight to the door and pushed. Locked. A woman with spiky blond hair and teeth too big for her face approached me. "Miss Matthews, can I help you?"

She wore a dark suit. I immediately spotted a Glock on one hip and a Taser on the other. An agent. "No. I'm good." Identification hung around her neck, along with four keys.

I turned and walked toward the start of the lunch line. I didn't even pay attention to the food I grabbed. Someone handed me a plate of something. I managed to grab a banana and a bottle of water.

As I searched for a place to sit, I felt several pairs of eyes on me. I scanned the faces of several kids sitting by the windows. Dia and Lin.

And Jonas.

I weaved around several tables to where they sat.

Dia's eyes practically shot fireballs at me.

Lin picked at the chicken on his plate. He looked sad, and my heart ached for Jack.

"Sit down, Lexi," Jonas said. "Dia, stop looking at her like that."

I raised an eyebrow. *Why is she mad at me?* Bree and I were finally getting along. I guessed her clone didn't get the memo.

She thinks you're the reason Ty is dead.

My head snapped in Dia's direction.

I'm glad you came back, Lin mindspoke. *Dia will realize that you're only here to help. Eventually.*

Was I here to help them?

I thought about that while I peeled my banana and took a bite.

Don't look now, Jonas said. *But about a dozen agents just entered the cafeteria with rifles.*

My back was to the door and the agents. Lin and Dia both looked over my shoulder. The four of us traded glances around the table.

"I won't save her this time," Dia said, her voice curt.

She assumed the agents were looking for me? And that I had just casually waltzed in, grabbed some lunch, and sat down to chat it up?

"She's not the one they're looking for." Jonas's eyes found mine.

"Who are they looking for?" I whispered.

He smiled. "Apparently Jack didn't tell you much about our sweet Addison."

"Addison?" Dia said a little too loudly, because several heads turned suddenly in our direction. She tucked her chin, and lowered her voice. "Addison is here?"

"Shhh." Jonas stuffed a bite of chocolate cake in his mouth. He stared down at his plate like it was the most interesting thing he had seen in days.

I felt something hard poke into the back of my neck. My muscles tensed. "Who's this?" a man asked behind me, while practically bruising me with what I assumed was the barrel of a gun.

Jonas stood. "Take the gun off of her," he ordered.

The agent laughed. "Who's going to make me?"

I turned in my seat. Jonas reached out, grabbed the barrel, and lifted it toward the ceiling. It went off with a boom, causing part of the ceiling to crumble and shower dust down on us. Children and adults screamed and dove under tables.

"What is going on over here?" A female agent rushed over to us. She lowered her rifle when she spotted Jonas. "Oh, you're here, Mr. Whitmeyer."

I looked quizzically at Jonas.

"Mr. Whitmeyer, you'll have to excuse our newest agent. He probably thought you were Ty."

"All is forgiven. I'll let you explain to him that my brother is now dead, so there should be no confusion in the future. Now, if you'll excuse me, our newest guest and I have some business to take care of."

"Of course." Both agents bowed their heads.

I stared in shock.

Jonas slipped his fingers around my arm and tugged me forward. "We need to talk," he spoke close to my ear. "This might be our last chance. Sandra is freaking out about Addison's latest escape act. She's watching videos leading up to Addison's disappearance. It won't take long for her to figure out that you were the last to touch her. Or that you removed her tracker."

THIRTY-TWO

···

W e have to hurry." Jonas pulled me down yet another hallway.

"We always have to hurry." I stopped. Yanked my hand from his. "I want to know everything *right now*. No more bullshit, Jonas. I want to know about Addison. I want to know where Jack is. I want to know what your plan is. I want to see the machine that controls the trackers. And I want to know what an agent meant when he told me that The Farm was scheduled for evacuation and destruction." I poked him hard in the chest. "It's show-and-tell time, Jonas. And if you don't lay it all out right now, we're done."

"Wait. Back up. What do you mean evacuation and destruction? Who told you this? And when did they say it would happen?"

"No!" I whispered loudly. "I'm not telling you anything until you come clean. And by clean, I mean *ev-er-y-thing*." I crossed my arms.

Voices and heavy feet sounded behind us. "This way," a man said.

"Come on." Jonas grabbed my hand again. A low growl of frustration erupted from somewhere deep within my throat.

Despite my irritation, we ran. I would give him one more chance, though I was exhausted from allowing him inside my mind. I might not be able to block him out every time, but I sure would try harder. I might use my ring on him just to prove a point. And I couldn't be sure I wouldn't enjoy it.

I wanted Jack. I missed him. His touch. The promise of a future. I wouldn't hesitate to escape to a new life far away from here—if I ever got another chance.

The next time Jack gave me the opportunity to run, I was one hundred percent in.

Jonas darted around one more corner, then to a door on the right. He stuck a key in the lock, opened it, and we both slipped inside, closing the door quietly behind us. I leaned my forehead against the steel door. The coolness helped the fire that had spread across my face.

Jonas placed both hands on my shoulders and rubbed. I couldn't help but replay his confession of feelings for me from earlier. I think I knew he felt something for me, but with his and Ty's mind invasion, I never knew what was real. I couldn't help but like Jonas at times, but it was never anything more than friendship. And other times, like now, Jonas infuriated me.

I drew my head back, then pretended to beat it against the door several times before he stopped me. "Hey. Remember I said I had a surprise for you?"

"I don't want any more surprises," I said. I jerked my shoulder from his grasp. "I'm done with surprises. Especially from you." I swallowed hard. "I just want to paralyze that evil woman that gave us life, destroy the server, and run far, far away from here where the IIA can't find me."

A tear ran down my cheek. I was definitely losing it. Jonas had stopped touching me. I didn't know if he had backed away to let me have my moment of pity, or was he standing right behind me?

I didn't care. I no longer cared about Jonas. I only cared about finding my way back to Jack. And saving my best friend from a fate that she never should have been a part of.

"Does your plan to run from the IIA include me?"

I whipped around at the sound of his voice. "Jack!" My knees buckled a little. He caught me. "You're here." I slipped my arms around his neck. He wrapped his strong arms around my waist in a hug, lifted my body, and carried it farther into the room.

"I'm here," he whispered into my hair, his breath warm on my neck. "I'm sorry it took me so long. We had complications." He kissed me lightly behind my ear.

I pulled back. "Why are you here? You shouldn't be. She's awful, Jack. She'll kill you. She'll kill me when she figures out I'd rather die than give her what she wants."

"Shh." He smoothed my hair. "I'm here. And we have a plan."

"Thank goodness." I noticed the room we were in for the first time. "Where are we?"

"Sandra's apartment," Jonas said, his voice quiet.

A growl rumbled in my chest. I glanced at him. "Isn't that a little risky?"

"It was my idea." Addison popped into view out of nowhere. "You know. Hide in plain sight."

I jumped backwards. My hand flew to my chest. "Where did you come from?"

"That's what I've been trying to tell you," Jonas said. "Addison is our little gen mod version of the invisible girl. She can vanish in the blink of an eye, and reappear whenever she wishes."

My eyebrows jumped up. "Gen mod?"

"Genetically modified," Jonas answered.

"And she's discovered how to make herself invisible?" This was too much.

"Well..." Jonas tilted his head side to side. "It's really about mind trickery. Similar to Dia and Bree. Where Dia and Bree can make people believe they're seeing something or someone else, Addison can make a person see nothing at all. Her own invisibility cloak. It's quite useful." Jonas smiled.

I could feel my own eyes widen. "If she can do that, why didn't she use that trick while at Wellington when Dia and Sandra kidnapped her?"

"Dia," Jonas said.

I raised a brow, "Meaning?"

"Dia is very well aware of her surroundings, including the people around her," Addison explained. "She has to be, in order to manipulate what a person sees or doesn't see. And she can be sure to see things, including me, even when I try to disappear. She had no trouble finding me in my weakened state—so soon after I'd recovered from my brain injury."

Jack brushed up against my back and circled his arms around me. His hands interlocked against my stomach. I laid mine on top of his. "Briana will most likely have the same powers as Dia," he said. "She just hasn't tapped into them completely yet."

Addison went on. "The day you visited me for the first time, Dia was already manipulating what I was seeing. I told you I found Briana in the parking lot, only it wasn't Briana. It was Dia. She was already throwing me off. I didn't even see her coming. She was how Sandra escaped unnoticed."

I squeezed Jack's arms with my fingers, drawing his arms tighter around me. I had craved his touch, and now he was here.

Jonas eyed us from across the room. "I hate to break up this little reunion, but we have work to do if we want to get out of here. And I don't want Sandra to find Lexi and me here. Together. She needs to trust me a little longer. If she turns on me, she'll reprogram my tracker, and I won't be able to control what they force me to make you do. I don't ever want to be her puppet again."

"Good point," I said.

"Wait a minute," Jack removed his arms from me, and moved to stand between me and Jonas. "What kinds of things would you be able to force her to do?"

Jonas stood up straighter. Shoulders back. "Anything. Unless—"

"Unless what?" Jack squeezed his hands at his side.

"Unless Lexi figures out how to block me. She was able to block Ty in the end."

"Which is why Sandra terminated him," I said with great sadness. Jack relaxed his protective stance and moved so that he wasn't blocking me. "Which is also why I need to destroy the server, or remove every tracker." I was convinced that if I could remove the trackers, that even Dia and Lin would be safe from Sandra's wrath. That they wouldn't follow her orders. They could come with us. "Where's Georgia?"

"I don't know." Jack rubbed the back of his neck. "We're in touch, but she's in hiding. She says she'll help remove the tracker from Jonas, but that's all she's agreed to for now. She had quite a reaction after Addison."

Addison nodded. "We have to shut down their system and get the trackers out of everyone we can. When they brought me here and put that stupid thing in me, it was like I was un-plugged. One second, I was fighting with Dia, the next, I felt a sharp sting to the back of my neck. Then, nothing... until I woke up and saw Lexi." She lunged at me, throwing her arms around me and practically knocking me over. "Thank you for coming to save me."

Addison was such a little girl at times, but her disappearing act was pretty cool. And would come in handy.

Addison backed away. I looked from her to Jonas to Jack. Worry swam in Jack's eyes.

"So, it's the four of us?"

"Actually, five of us," Jonas said. "Briana's here."

"When Briana and Kyle came to the door last night, Kyle took Georgia to The Program to get help from Seth." Jack glanced sideways at Jonas. "Briana stayed with Jonas."

"But they got zero sleep last night while they studied the complete layout of this building." Addison snickered. "She's sleeping in Jonas's closet."

"His closet?" I wanted to laugh, but the situation was far from funny.

Jonas shrugged. "Thought the agents might stay out of my closet."

"What's the plan?"

Jonas pulled a packet of papers folded lengthwise from his back pocket. "I have a copy of a map of The Farm for each of you." Unfolding the packet, he laid one across a table. We all gathered around. "We are here." He pointed as he explained the layout. "From what I can tell, the tracker server is somewhere in this control room, which is connected to this lab. Lexi, your job is to get to the control room, which can only be accessed through the lab. I won't be with you, but I can see everything you see."

"What do they do in that lab?" I asked.

"That's where DNA is studied, I think."

I remembered the lab I saw when I first entered The Farm last week, but this lab was at least one floor lower.

"You'll know the control room by the equipment around it. I saw it at one of the previous facilities. There'll be at least three computers around the server. There will probably be some biometric security required to gain entrance to the lab, but the door to the control room will have even heavier security."

"Like the blood kind?" I asked. I hated having my finger pricked. I much preferred when no one had to get hurt to open a door.

"Yes, like the blood kind. Or the eye-scanning kind. Or a thumbprint *and* blood kind. A key might be required. I just don't know. Whoever discovers this room first will need to mindspeak to the rest of us. I'm pretty sure Briana is the only one who can't actually speak to us, but she can hear the chatter when you direct it at her. I should be with her and will make sure she's informed."

Jack slipped his hand in mine again. The constant touch gave me hope that we would be together outside this facility eventually. He pulled me closer, urging me to turn to him. "I'm worried about you."

I want you to come with me, but you can't. I squeezed my fingers more tightly around his. *If Sandra were to discover you here with me, I'm afraid she would stop at nothing to ensure we remained here. And I have no idea what it means that your father is here with her.*

It means he's a part of some plan of hers and probably has been for a very long time. Jack's furrowed brows cast a certain darkness over his already stormy eyes.

"You don't have to worry about Lexi," Jonas said. "I'm not going to let anything happen to her."

Jonas has become very protective of you.

I glanced down at our joined hands. Jonas had helped me understand a lot about who I was the past week. *I've had to really work through a lot of trust issues where Jonas is concerned.* I met Jack's eyes again. *A lot of my well-being is based on blind faith right now.*

We wouldn't be standing in this very spot if I didn't feel it was necessary for our future, Jack said. *And I would not have left you in Jonas's hands if I didn't trust that he had control over his own mind. However, if something seems even a little off, I want to know immediately.*

I nodded. *I think Jonas's protectiveness of me is real. I'm lucky to have two strong people looking after me.*

Jack dropped my hand and reached behind him. He pulled a small handgun around. "I want you to carry a gun."

I backed away. "Absolutely not."

"Listen to me." He grabbed my forearm, stopping me from getting too far. "It's loaded with rubber bullets. Unless you hit someone in the eye or in another weak spot, it won't seriously harm them. But it could save your life and give you the chance to escape."

I looked at Jonas. "What if they search me again and find it? They'll know someone gave it to me."

"You need to carry it. We'll deal with that if it happens."

I wrapped my fingers around the handle and lifted the gun in front of my face. I had such a horrible feeling about this.

"Take it," Addison said. I turned and faced her. She was so young, but I had no idea what her childhood had been like. "Sandra is crazy. She came to Kentucky for one reason—you."

Jonas stepped forward. "Well... and to get Addison back." He stuffed his hands inside the front pockets of his pants. "The biggest thing we have going for us right now is that they think they have you, Lexi, even if only physically. Sandra is just arrogant enough to think you'll join her team simply because you were created from her DNA."

"Well, they don't have me," I declared. The gun slipped perfectly into the waistband of my jeans. It was small enough not to cause much discomfort against my skin. I made sure my shirt came low enough to cover it.

"Where will you and Addison go?" I asked Jack.

"Our job is to find the other trackers—the ones not implanted. And to stay out of sight. We can't risk Addison being caught again."

Or you. Please be careful.

Jack nodded.

"We have one last thing to talk about," I said. "What will happen if they begin evacuating?"

Addison's head snapped in Jonas's direction. Jonas rubbed his face. "I haven't seen any signs of packing up, but this place is like a circus."

I cocked my head. "What does that mean?"

"If you'd ever seen a circus come to town, you'd know. They arrive in slow motion—one truckload at a time over several days. When the circus is over, they're gone before the last jug-gling clown unicycles out of the main tent. Not a trace of this place will be left within an hour of being told to evacuate."

"How will we know?"

"Oh, you'll know."

THIRTY-THREE

··

The announcement, along with a piercing alarm and an intermittent strobe light, came over an intercom speaker less than an hour after I left Jack and Addison. "LAB WILL SELF-DESTRUCT IN ONE HOUR."

A sharp pain had erupted in my chest when I'd first left Jack back in Sandra's apartment. We should be doing this together, but risking the two of us being caught together wasn't a risk I was willing to take. Not to mention, we had little time to find both the trackers and the server controlling them—as the computerized female voice made clear.

Jack and Addison were by now roaming the facility in search of additional trackers; we all agreed the trackers wouldn't be stored in the same lab as the server. And Jonas had left to check on Briana.

According to the map Jonas gave me, I was in the hallway near the main lab. People rushed about. Most didn't even glance my way as they passed, which was strange. Either this entire place was built on the arrogant assumption that I would decide I wanted to be a part of this, or they already knew for a fact the one thing I refused to accept—that I was trapped inside The Farm with no way out. Every once in a while I'd get a strange look or a double-take. Probably because I looked scarily like the barracuda heading up this strange underground laboratory.

Similar to the lab I saw the first time I came here, the room I'd been looking for was behind a wall of glass windows. Inside, men and women in white lab coats typed away on computers, lifted equipment onto rolling carts, and boxed up supplies.

The IIA was moving their operations.

But why?

Maybe they knew that the FBI and police were getting close to something like Marci's murderer. Maybe the university discovered the illegal experiments that were occurring inside this secret laboratory.

I stood in front of the glass, scanning the sea of doctors and scientists. Behind rows of microscopes, medical equipment, and computers was a door tucked away in the back right-hand corner of the room. If Jonas was right, that was the room I was looking for.

I ran my fingers along the ledge of the interior window as I walked toward the entrance to the lab. The double set of sliding doors only required an ID badge.

A woman in a lab coat and scrubs exited the lab in a hurry. She was alone. The doors closed behind her too fast for me to slip through, though.

I followed her around the corner and watched her enter the women's restroom.

Looking both ways down the hallway, I snuck in after her.

The bathroom was quiet. It was only the two of us.

I waited for her to finish inside the stall. My hands shook at my side as I waited in the neighboring stall, the door open. I didn't want to hurt anyone. That wasn't what I was about.

The toilet flushed, and I knew what I had to do. I spun my ring halfway around so the pearl was on the palm side of my hand. I twisted the pearl, and the small needle appeared. I would have simply mindspoken to get her badge and clothing items, but this way, she would be unable to run after me and get help.

She walked slowly past, oblivious to my presence as she adjusted the lanyard around her neck.

I stepped out, made three quick steps, and caught her by surprise with a bear hug with one arm. My other hand went straight to her neck and made contact, but not before I took an elbow to the stomach.

I grunted loud, the breath knocked out of me. She made an "oww" sound. I had definitely grazed her with the tiny needle. But was it enough?

I held my breath as she started to turn, but her body went limp. Thankfully, she was a small woman. I caught her as she slid to the ground and softened the landing of her head on the concrete floor.

I righted the ring so as not to paralyze myself. Leaning down, I whispered, "I'm sorry." I then took her lab coat, her ID, and her glasses. Maybe the glasses would help disguise me a little.

A minute later, I was at the door of the lab. No one noticed me; everyone was completely focused on packing up the lab.

Jonas, I'm inside the lab.

How did you manage that? he asked.

Don't worry about it. Point is, I'm here, and I'm making my way over to the control room. Everyone is too busy packing up to even notice me. Where are you?

I'm calming Dia and Lin down. Trying to talk them into coming with us when we leave here. Trying to convince them that we can remove the trackers.

Have you mentioned this to Georgia? I don't know how to remove the trackers without her.

We'll figure it out.

I stayed to the outer perimeter of the room, not making eye contact with anyone. I wished we could remove every clone within this facility tonight, but there wasn't time.

When I reached the door to what I believed to be the room housing the tracker server, I studied the panel just outside the door. It was a square panel with a keypad next to it. I held up my palm to test the size. It definitely would measure my entire hand. Maybe it scans each fingerprint. Right about the spot where my middle finger would go was a tiny hole in the otherwise flat surface.

This room looks to have a combination of security measures.

You've got to get out of there, Jonas said. *Sandra just stormed past me. She's headed in that direction. I don't know how you got inside that part of the lab, but she won't be happy.*

Yes, Lexi, Addison said. *Sandra is headed right for you. And she's moving quickly.*

I turned on my heels and walked back the way I came. I could use a Marauder's Map right about now.

I slipped outside the lab and walked in the opposite direction from where I hoped Sandra would be coming. I shed the lab coat and left it on the floor, then stuffed the ID down my shirt.

"There she is."

I jumped when I heard the voice of Dr. Barracuda herself. I slowly turned toward her. The young lab tech I had assaulted stood beside Sandra, picked up her lab coat, and began dusting it off.

"Sarah, come with me." Sandra did not look like she was having a good day. And the lab tech was downright pissed.

I debated internally whether I should make a run for it. Where would I go? "Why?" I asked her. I fingered the ring on my finger. The gun pushed against the small of my back, tucked in my waistband.

Sandra looked sideways at the lab tech. "You may go. If no more little girls attack you, you might make it out alive."

The woman evil-eyed me as she approached, reached up and snatched the glasses still perched on my nose, then spun on her heels and stalked off.

When she was gone, I redirected my gaze back to Sandra. I had swallowed all fear back in Sandra's apartment when Jack had looked me in the eye and promised we'd make it out of here.

Sandra's shiver-inducing grin spread across her face. "You think you've got this all figured out, don't you?"

I cocked my head. "Figured out? Are you kidding me? I don't think I'll ever have this all figured out. That wasn't my intention when I turned myself over to you."

"What *was* your intention?

I almost laughed. What was my intention? I didn't have just one. To do the right thing. To save my best friend. To get Ty and Jonas out of my head forever. To discover enough about this facility and Sandra to escape and live some semblance of a normal life. But instead of confiding all that, I simply stared at Sandra. She looked exhausted, like she hadn't slept in days.

"What if I told you my dream is to have you, Jonas, and Jack working alongside me? I want you to know what Peter, John, and I created you to do. The three of you are very special, Sarah."

"My name is Lexi. My dad renamed me when he hid me from you. If he had created me to do something so special, why didn't he tell me?"

"I can't answer that." Sandra actually had the gall to appear remorseful when she spoke.

"That's because you killed him before he had the chance," I answered for her.

Sandra placed a hand over her heart, a gesture very similar to one I've done many times. "I'm sorry your father was killed. That was unfortunate. But I didn't kill him."

"Unfortunate? Unfortunate is dropping an iPhone in the toilet. My father was murdered because he was trying to protect me. You expect me to believe you had nothing to do with it?"

"Yes, actually. I was in a coma by the time your father was killed."

I blinked. Two, three times. "Then, you ordered him killed."

"You're smarter than this, Sarah." Sandra turned and began walking away from me. "Come with me. I have something you need to see."

Above me, a voice said, "LAB WILL SELF-DESTRUCT IN FORTY-FIVE MINUTES."

~~~~~

We found the blueprint for the trackers. Jack mindspoke to the group. *Lexi, where are you?* His voice sounded panicked.

I stared at Sandra's back as we passed the lab. Jack was not going to be happy. We turned a corner and continued toward the interior part of the building. She scanned her ID at a door, then placed her palm onto a scanner similar to the one I saw outside the control room.

I heard a small click. Sandra pulled her hand back and sucked on her middle finger for a second. She didn't even flinch. The door slid open.

I'm with Sandra. I closed my eyes and braced for Jack's response. *We're entering some interior room around the corner from the lab.*

Turn around. Run. Do whatever you have to do. Get away from her.

Why?

We were wrong. Addison says you're entering the main DNA lab right now. The tracker server is located on the other side of that room. I've got a list of trackers in front of me and who they've been designed for. Lexi, there's one with your name beside it.

THIRTY-FOUR

....

I stopped. Refused to enter the room. "What is this?" *You will not make me enter this room. You will tell me now what is inside.*

"Your mind tricks won't work on me. You will come with me now. When we're done here, you'll know who was responsible for your father's death." Sandra's voice was one hundred percent calm, like she had no doubt I would follow. But when I hesitated, she added, "Come now if you want to keep Danielle from meeting the same fate as Ty."

A shiver started at the top of my scalp, moved to the base of my neck, then traveled throughout my body. I had no idea why she was immune to my mindspeak. The woman before me truly was a descendent of the father of lies. Getting close to her was like getting drawn into a forest raging with an out-of-control fire with no chance of escape. She might not have been responsible for my dad's death, but she had no problem killing those who got in her way.

Yet I couldn't say no to her. She tempted me with things I desired so deeply, I couldn't turn away. Sometimes a person had to move forward to find her way out of a scary place.

I walked the few steps through the door. It slid closed behind me, making me flinch.

The room was a semicircle. A larger lab than the one down the hall, but with fewer people rushing about. Sandra and I were separated from lab technicians by a glass wall. Beyond the partition, the techs were dressed in white protective suits, including blue surgical gloves and white hoods over their hair.

This was the DNA lab. I recognized the large machines around the room designed to analyze and store DNA and blood data. Like in the previous lab, the people were rushing about, packing up equipment and preparing to move. A few of the machines were on rolling carts ready to be transported.

"Dr. Whitmeyer." A young African-American man approached. "The device is almost ready. We have customized it to your latest specifications. It will be ready in plenty of time for you to make the last truck out of here."

"Thank you, Daniel. Is the main server ready for the switchover? I don't want the tracker system down for even a second longer than absolutely necessary."

"The server is ready. There will be very little down time. We'll only need the hard drive with this last tracker synced to it. Once that's plugged into the new server, you'll be operational again."

The muscles in my neck and shoulders tightened. It wouldn't matter if I shot up the computers here with a machine gun; Sandra would just continue to manipulate the trackers from the next location. Unless I somehow got my hands on that hard drive—that would slow Sandra down a little while we removed Dani's and Jonas's trackers.

"This way, Sarah." Sandra barely acknowledged the man's instructions. She continued around the half-circle to another door. This door was equipped with another palm scan and finger prick.

The door opened. And my heart stopped when I saw John DeWeese. Sandra stepped behind me and gave me a shove inside.

"What took you so long?" he asked when he saw Sandra, then he looked at me. "I'm so thrilled you could join us, Sarah."

Why did everyone insist on calling me by that name? I remained silent and just stared at the centerpiece of the room: an exam table of some sort with leather straps at both ends.

I suddenly couldn't breathe. Jack, Jonas, and Addison chatted inside my mind about possible ways to get me out of the situation I was now in—a position I had put myself in. I barely listened as I watched Dr. DeWeese type on a keyboard, producing a graphic design of a tracker on a large retractable screen on the far wall. It rotated in different directions in 3-D. I drew in a labored breath. My hand clutched at my throat. *Jonas!* I finally mindspoke, letting him enter my mind fully.

It's going to be okay, he whispered. *Breathe. I promise I'm going to get you out of there.*

What is it? Jack asked.

Don't tell him that his father is here. It will kill him, I said, speaking only to Jonas. Jack would have to face this sooner or later, but later was better.

It's your father, Jonas said.

Fine, don't listen to me. It wasn't like Jonas ever had before.

"Show her," Sandra ordered Dr. DeWeese.

"Gladly." Dr. DeWeese smiled.

A video played on the screen. A movie of my father, Sandra, and John when they were younger. They appeared happy. It reminded me of the picture Jack showed me the night he informed me I had been cloned. Images of the three of them. All smiling. Sandra looking up at the two men as if they were her heroes.

"Sarah," Sandra began. "I once thought your father, John, and I would cure every disease and injury known to man. We would find a way to promise every human on this earth... well, those with the means..."—she smiled—"...the opportunity to live a long, healthy life."

I watched the screen change from an image of the three scientists to pictures of brains, neural activity, and DNA mapping. It was picture after picture of their research. Pictures of the goat they cloned. And of Cheriana, Jack's cloned horse at Wellington.

Sandra continued. "No one would ever question the intelligence of your father, John, or me. Nor would they doubt the intelligence of the original owners of the others' DNA. What we did was study the most brilliant medical minds of our time. We studied my brain activity. Your father's. John's. And many others. We cloned those human beings multiple times, hoping for as many successes as possible. Then, within a control group, we enhanced parts of the DNA and brain that we felt would produce a sort of supernatural healer."

"Seven of us," I whispered mostly to myself.

Dr. DeWeese's face turned toward me. "What did you say?"

"I said 'seven of us.' There were seven in the control group."

"Seven of the control group survived. That's right." Sandra smiled. "Oh my God. She knows."

I tilted my head, studying the monster in front of me. What riddle was she spewing on about now? "I know that you're the devil."

"How did you know there were seven?" John asked.

If it was possible for my heart to beat any faster, it did. My eyes went in and out of focus. I willed my heart to slow. "You told me," I squeaked. "That day we talked at Wellington."

"No, I didn't. I told you that I had no idea how many of the original clones had survived." He cupped his chin. Rubbed the stubble across his jaw. "You have the journals, don't you?"

"I don't know what you're talking about." This was bad.

Dr. DeWeese tilted his head backwards, stared up at the ceiling, and let out an enormous laugh.

I didn't see anything resembling humor in the situation. The female voice overhead reminded us, "LAB WILL SELF-DESTRUCT IN THIRTY MINUTES."

Neither Sandra nor Dr. DeWeese seemed the least bit panicked.

"Where are the journals, Sarah?" Sandra asked.

It was my turn to laugh. "Your lab is going to blow up or melt in acid or whatever in thirty minutes. You've got me locked inside a high-security room. No one knows where I am. And you think I'm going to hand over the one thing my father left behind to protect me? You both are seriously demented." I turned to Dr. DeWeese. "Does Jack know what an a-hole his father is? Does he know that you're behind all this?"

His face fell just a little before he recovered. "My son will understand. It's time you both grow up." He inhaled deeply, then took a step forward. He had such a kind face, like Jack, yet when I looked deep within Dr. DeWeese's eyes, I saw something that was completely unlike Jack. Something profoundly corrupt. "Lexi, my son loves you, and for good reason. You were created for him. To complement him. You both are beautifully cloned to be better than Sandra and me. To accomplish miracles Sandra and I have only dreamed of." He glanced side-ways at Sandra, who smiled. I wanted to puke all over both of them. He continued. "You two could change the world. Join us, Lexi."

I rotated my shoulders back and stepped toward this vile man. "We *are* better than you, but not because you altered our DNA to be smarter. We are better than you for a reason that is beyond your understanding. You... you..." I lifted my hand and drilled my forefinger into my temple. "You two are crazy."

"You haven't seen crazy," Sandra said. She no longer had the calm tone she had when we first entered the lab. "You will tell us where the journals are."

I walked over to a swivel chair in the corner of the room and sat. Though the blood in my veins raged like a mad river after a storm, I willed myself to appear calm. "I don't think so." I had no way of getting out of that room without help, and I was not about to hand over the one thing Sandra needed from me. I had meant it when I'd said I would die first. "Question. If you designed us to be these über-healers, how did the other supernatural aspects of our abilities come about?"

Sandra shrugged. "Those were unintended side effects of the genetic manipulation. But a most welcome bonus." She smiled. "Not the first major scientific breakthrough based on unintentional consequences."

"You mean you have no idea?" I asked.

"Well, it seems that some of the abilities are extensions of your personalities," Sandra said. "From what I've heard, you, like me, are somewhat of a control freak." She glanced at Dr. DeWeese. "Therefore, it makes sense that you can manipulate people's actions with your mind. Jack, like John, is extremely aware of those around him. So, he can get into peoples minds, talk to them, hear them. According to John, he has been very aware of you since the moment he knew you existed. The fact that he can hear your thoughts and communicate with you so easily makes sense. I could go on, but we simply don't have time."

Dr. DeWeese wiped his palms on his khaki pants. He was nervous. He had disappeared before the night of the gala. Did Cathy know that he was with Sandra? Was she part of this? Instinct told me the answer to both of those questions was a big fat no.

"I think it's time you knew who the real enemy is, Sarah. We are not your enemy." She pointed back and forth between Dr. DeWeese and herself. "You have an opportunity to be a huge part of American history. To be a great service to your country and the world. We want you to thrive, not run from your true destiny."

"What are you babbling on about now?" I raised both brows.

"We are not the only country developing genetically modified ultra-intelligent humans," Sandra said. "We were just the first. And the IIA is responsible for assuring that the United States continues to be the best. Other countries have already developed genetically mutated animals and insects that are being used in counterintelligence missions. Spiders, for example, mutated to slip through cracks in the walls with microchips in their bodies designed to spy on important military and political meetings."

Dr. DeWeese typed on the computer in front of him. A little boy playing in a very dusty street appeared on the large screen. "See this child? He is one hundred percent boy when he's playing. But when his handlers activate the chip embedded in the center of his brain, he becomes approximately sixty percent robot. The forty percent of him that is human gets him near a group of military generals. The sixty percent of him that is robot records everything those generals say and reports back the location of the terrorists protected by his country... which in turn leads us to launch military attacks at those locations."

"That genetically engineered boy was created by the IIA," Sandra said.

"Get to the point," I said.

"Friends of the United States are willing to pay unbelievable amounts of money for genetically manipulated human beings who can be controlled by a single computer program." Her voice started to take on an angry edge. "That boy was sold to another country for enough money to fund our future facility for a decade or more."

I swallowed against the taste of bile that rose to the back of my throat. "You're running a freak show that grows robotic children so they can be controlled by a computer." They were growing spies for the international community. "For what? For money?"

"Of course for money. You think the type of medical research and healing miracles we're working toward comes cheap? You could be a part of this. You and Jack. You would want for nothing."

Money? She thought I would bow down to her highness for money?

I eyed the computer in front of Dr. DeWeese. "So, that machine controls every person with a tracker?"

"The ones I'm in control of, that's right." Sandra looked pleased with herself. "Look how easily Ty got inside your head. And his manipulation was completely from a computer program." She pointed to the computer Dr. DeWeese had been typing into. "He wasn't cloned to do so. As you saw, I had complete control over him."

Well, not *complete* control, I wanted to argue.

"If I wanted him inside your head, he was inside your head. If I wanted him inside Jonas's head, who then got inside your head and forced you into a freezing swimming pool, then that's what happened."

"All because of the tracker?"

"That's right." Sandra was starting to use her hands a lot to over-explain some grand point. "And you'll be a part of this. A part of something so huge. Or..." She tilted her head side to side. "Or you'll be eliminated by those who will not risk information about our division of the IIA being released into the world."

An imaginary darkness fell over my entire existence. I didn't want the world to know that we were magical healers. But how could I knowingly allow these people to grow children to be used in this way? To be manipulated beyond their control? Was human life no longer sacred? "Terminated? Like you tried to do the night you ran Jack and me off the road?"

"That wasn't me. You think I want my most prized creations murdered in a car crash?"

That almost sounded sincere. But if what she was saying was correct, then others had tried to kill Jack and me, and would continue to do so. I tried to suppress a laugh, but couldn't. It bubbled up and out of me, but quickly turned to an escaped sob. "What about Ty?" I remembered the image of Ty's glassed-over eyes when Sandra decided he was no longer useful. He was just a machine to her. I swiped at a tear that had escaped. "Is it true you birthed Ty and Jonas? You carried them as your own babies?"

"That's right."

"Yet, you felt nothing when you killed him in cold blood. Premeditated murder in the first degree."

"I needed to prove a point."

"Which was?"

"That I could."

The speaker crackled overhead. "LAB WILL SELF-DESTRUCT IN TWENTY MINUTES."

Dr. DeWeese's face paled. I wasn't sure if it was because he wasn't aware that Sandra murdered her own son, or because this lab was set for some sort of death in twenty minutes—with him still in the bowels of The Farm.

"As you can see, we are about out of time. You can join us voluntarily, or I can force you. But it's time you decide. Surely with everything I just told you—"

"That's what all this was. You making your case to get me to join you?" I stood from my swivel chair. *Jonas, Jack, are you seeing this? Could it be that one computer is controlling every tracker?*

It gets better than that. Jonas said. *The hard drive in the computer behind Sandra pops out of the computer from the back of the machine. If we can destroy that, we destroy the database of trackers currently in existence. There's probably a backup, but getting that one will buy us some time.*

"You will join us. We can protect you. We have no intention of keeping you locked inside one of our facilities forever. You can have freedom to roam, just like Jonas."

"Freedom. Just like Jonas. You mean your other son that you admit to controlling with one of your trackers? So, you want me to give you permission to place a tracker at the base of my brain? Stuck to my spinal cord? So that you can what? Control my every move? My thoughts?" I circled the room. The two doctors watched me. Their eyes never left me. I understood what it felt like to have a laser pointed at the middle of my forehead.

"It's not like that. Jonas is happy. He's always had the liberty to live his life and learn how to use the incredible powers I gave him. We would be a team."

I almost laughed. She had no idea how little she was able to control Jonas.

"Did you make this offer to my father? To join your team?" I asked Dr. DeWeese. "That night he came to you because he thought Jack and I were in danger. He trusted you. It obviously wasn't you that he was afraid of, was it?"

"No, he's always known this day would come. He knew the international intelligence community would eventually demand that you and the others help with the IIA's cloning program. But don't you see? We are able to protect you here the way he would have wanted."

"Your wife was trying to protect us in her own way, by placing a secure border around the school and hiring extra security. You *need* Jack and me. You need all seven of the original control group and Dad's journals to know how to reproduce the technology you created nearly eighteen years ago—

before your original lab went up in flames and all your records with it. Must have been a real bitch starting from scratch."

"Dr. Whitmeyer," a voice said over an intercom by the door.

"Yes, Denny," Sandra replied.

"The tracker is ready."

"Time's up, Sarah." She walked to the door, lifted her palm to the scanner, and opened the door. Denny stood on the other side of the door and handed Sandra the tiny device I assumed was meant for me.

"Doctor, the labs and children have been evacuated." He passed Sandra. "This room is sound. Even if you don't make it out of here, you're protected."

"Thanks, Denny, but we'll make it."

Denny continued to the other side of the room and proceeded to lift a hidden panel in the floor. He turned and climbed down two steps before pausing. "Would you like for me to wait for you and Dr. DeWeese?"

"No, Denny. We'll be along in ten minutes."

"Don't be much longer than that. Things will start to get a little dicey beyond that point."

What did that mean? *Jack?*

"Thank you, Denny," Sandra said, irritated by Denny's warning.

I'm almost there. Stay strong. Jack sounded somewhat panicked. What was taking him so long?

Sandra set the tracker on the small tray beside the dental chair. "I need you to tell us the location of the journals."

"Or what? You're going to jam a tracker into the back of my neck?" I crooked my elbow and felt for the gun stuck in the back of my waistband. It was still there. I twisted the pearl on my ring, forcing the paralyzing compartment of my ring into ready position.

Sandra smiled. "No." She walked to the computer. "I know your father recorded the journals on the internet. You will tell me how to access them, or say goodbye to Danielle."

THIRTY-FIVE

....

I lunged at Sandra, but Dr. DeWeese caught my arm and stopped me. Tears blurred my vision. I pushed them away. "You can't." I would not let anything happen to Dani. But could I give Sandra access to the journals?

Lexi, give her what she wants, Jack said.

My heart sank.

I'll be there in five minutes. The last of the agents and lab techs are vacating the lab. We have what we need to enter that part of the lab. You only need to open the door to the room you're in.

How was I supposed to do that? More importantly, how could I give her the journals? But then again, how could I not?

A picture of my best friend and roommate popped up on the screen. "Dani," I whispered to myself. "I won't let anything happen to you."

"Give me access to the files, Lexi. Now." She punched on the keyboard. The screen changed from being a picture of Dani to being a picture of a brain. I recognized it as Dani's. I had seen the inside of her brain.

Like Addison's, Dani's tracker sat at the base of her skull, all eight prongs extended.

I squeezed my eyes tight. I wondered if Sandra would even need me after she had the journals. Could Jack and I escape and go into hiding? Without us around, maybe our friends would be safe as well.

"All I have to do is push this one key, Lexi, and Dani drops." Her finger hovered over the key.

"Don't! I'll give you the information you need." My heart beat wildly out of control as I died a little. I rattled off the URL, the username, and my password. The taste of bile rose once again in my throat. How could I possibly live with myself if I had just handed this monster unlimited access to play with human life?

But my life would be meaningless if I didn't save my best friend.

"You made the right decision." Her eyes widened when dozens of named files displayed on the screen. An evil smile lifted her entire face. I recognized the files. The spreadsheet of all the clones. The years and years of journals. And the file with the DNA sequences needed to reproduce my own special abilities—exactly what Sandra needed to enhance the power of the trackers even further.

Sandra closed the website and saved a document with the login information. The display of files was once again replaced with a picture of Dani's brain. The glint in Sandra's eye when she turned her cold, emerald eyes on me sent an avalanche straight through my core. Then, Sandra did the unthinkable.

She pressed the key on the computer she said she wouldn't push if I gave her what she wanted.

"No!" I sobbed. I struggled against Dr. DeWeese's hold. My eyes fixated on the screen. The differently colored neurons that fired in and around Dani's brain suddenly dulled, until no color was left—nothing but different shades of gray. All spark and flare gone.

"What did you do?!" I screamed. A rage not even I recognized exploded inside my chest. I stared at the lifeless brain. All activity had ceased. Uncontrollable tears streamed down my face. My mind reeled with murderous thoughts. I'd never felt such intense emotions for a living soul. Dr. DeWeese held tightly to my arm. I reached my other hand behind me and wrapped my fingers around the handle of the gun in my waistband, but didn't pull it out just yet. "Let go of me right now."

"Put her on the table." Sandra sounded bored.

"There's not enough time," Dr. DeWeese said. "Let's just take her to the truck. We can do the implant there."

"There's plenty of time for this tracker."

"What does that mean?"

Sandra picked up the tracker and held it close for me to see. "This is the newest generation of my greatest creation—a tracker designed especially for you, Sarah. Designed to fit with what I know of your powers already. I'll be able to modify it further once it's synced with our computers. But this tracker will give you the power to cure your friends of the side effects they suffer from after using their powers. And your nosebleeds will be gone. There will be nothing you can't cure."

That's what Seth meant when he told the others that Sandra had the ability to take their side effects away. Did Seth know that this was how Sandra could do it?

Sandra continued. "And best of all? This is a self-guided tracker. I'll make one tiny incision at the base of your neck. The tracker does the rest. It will scan the surrounding tissue, then guide itself to its final resting spot while doing no harm to the delicate nerves around your spinal cord or your brain. Once the tracker finds the most optimal location, the prongs will deploy and burrow into place.

"Then, a quick stitch or two, and we're done. Two, three minutes, tops. Now," she motioned Dr. DeWeese with her hand. "Put her on the table." Sandra turned and set the tracker back on the small tray.

I struggled in Dr. DeWeese's arms, but he pushed me forward.

"Once she has the tracker implanted, we'll link the tracker to the server, and she'll have no choice but to submit. Then we can grab the hard drive, get the hell out of here, and move on to the next location." She turned to me. "You're going to love the new facility. It's by the ocean. Given the username of "mylittlestarfish" you just gave me, I assume you like the ocean, Sarah?"

I squeezed my eyes closed. I hated this sociopathic killer.

"LAB WILL SELF-DESTRUCT IN TEN MINUTES."

Dr. DeWeese closed his arms around me and lifted. My back was to his chest. I tried to kick and fight my way out of his arms, but he only held me tighter. "Let me go," I cried.

"No use fighting it, Lexi. There's no way out of this now." His voice in my ear sounded so similar to Jack's. But he and Jack were nothing alike.

Lexi, we're right outside the room. But we have no way in, Jack said.

Dr. DeWeese guided my body toward the exam table. The tracker that had been created specifically for me sat on the stainless steel tray. I glanced back at the screen, at the frozen image of Dani's brain, a horror film paused with an image of the final scene before the hero swoops in and saves the day. Only there was no hero in this film. This film had been generated by Sandra's very own dark imagination from a computer she'd created to have ultimate control over her freak-clones.

348

Dr. DeWeese urged my body closer to the table. With one final look at the screen, my body went limp. *It's useless, Jack. Dani is gone. They've got me. They've got the journals. You guys need to get out of here before this lab goes up in flames.*

Don't you dare shut down on me, Jack yelled.

I heard banging from somewhere on the other side of the door.

Are you freaking kidding me? You're going to give up now? Jonas joined in. *Get your ass moving. Stick that ring in Sandra's neck and fight your way out of there. I didn't train you to be strong only to have you quit at the first sign of trouble.*

First sign? What world was he living in? Dr. DeWeese forced me onto the table on my stomach and held me down. I tried to struggle, but he was so much stronger. I rested my forehead against the cold leather of the table. Sandra leaned over me, brushed my hair to the side, exposing my neck, then started to strap down my left arm. Jonas slipped into my mind, and I immediately began pocketing my thoughts, clearing my mind from his invasion. I used my own brain to wrap imaginary fingers around his presence and squeeze it until it didn't exist.

Oh, that's just great. Now you toughen up and learn to squash my direct orders. Jonas pushed back, but I was somehow able to ignore his presence.

Listen to me, baby. Jack's voice was soft, soothing. *Don't give up on me. On us. I'm right here. I'm on the other side of the door. You just have to meet me halfway.*

Halfway, huh? I just let my best friend die, Jack.

349

But think about how many people you've saved. Think about me, baby. Think about Gram. Think about your father. He did everything he could to protect you.

Protect me? He kept me in the dark, I practically whined, and I don't do whiny. I was starting to hate the sound of my own mindspeak.

No, he protected you until you were ready. Now, you have all the information you need to make whatever choice you desire.

You mean the information I just handed over to Sandra?

No, I mean the information Sandra thinks you just handed her.

What are you saying?

Did you really think I would let you hand over your dad's life's research to that mad scientist? Jack's voice cracked in my head with a mixture of humor and fear. *I was scared to tell you with all the crazy mindreading going on around us: we moved the real files and replaced them with meaningless data. She needed to think you were sincerely handing her what she wanted.*

My body relaxed into the table; relief engulfed me upon hearing Jack's words. Sandra continued to struggle with the restraint around my left wrist. Dr. DeWeese leaned over me still. *Oh, my, how I love you, Jack DeWeese.*

I know. Now fight. You promised me you wouldn't give up. Fight like crazy. Time is running out, and I don't know what's going to happen when it does.

With a burst of adrenaline, I yanked my left arm free, so incredibly thankful for the years of swimming that gave me strength. I quickly turned over on my back.

"Don't let go of her, John."

Also grateful for the rigorous kickboxing workout Jonas had put me through, I brought my foot up and made contact with Dr. DeWeese in a beautifully vulnerable spot. He grunted and pulled back just enough to give me my opening.

Sandra grabbed for one of my arms, but I was faster.

I gave the pearl a quick twist then slid my fingers around her neck and gathered her hair in my fist. She grunted. Bringing her face just inches from mine, I smiled. I was suddenly the one with the evil thoughts. An anger I had never known before pulsed through my veins. I stared into eyes identical to my own as I rotated the pearl around my finger with my thumb, careful not to touch the already exposed needle. "I'm terminating this program, bitch." I flattened my palm against the side of her neck. The needle from the pearl made contact with her skin, and she flinched. I snaked my left arm around Sandra, hugging her next to my body while I continued to press the ring into her skin.

Almost instantly, her body went limp. I let her slump to the ground beside the chair.

Dr. DeWeese lurched for Sandra, catching her head in his palm. "What did you do to her?" Her wide eyes stared up at him.

I reached over and grabbed the tracker from the tray, then rolled off the table and backed away. I pulled the gun from my waistband and pointed it at Dr. DeWeese. "She'll be knocked out for twenty-four hours or so. So she might need a little help out of here."

"LAB WILL SELF-DESTRUCT IN FIVE MINUTES."

He laid her gently on the ground and stood. "You're not going to shoot me. If you had it in you to kill someone, you would have shot Sandra after she killed your best friend."

Talk to me. You okay? Jack asked. *We're running out of time.*

351

I waved the gun at Dr. DeWeese, motioning him toward the door. "Unlock the door."

"No." He walked slowly toward me.

I cocked the gun. He paused, but then took another step toward me.

Lexi, you have to open this door, now. This time it was Jonas. He was inside my head completely. *Shoot him.*

It was a direct order. I pointed the gun down at Dr. DeWeese's kneecap. And fired.

His eyes widened. He fell to the ground on the opposite knee.

The gun was at close enough range that the rubber bullet had to have shattered his kneecap.

"You shot me," he said, shock in his voice. He fell further to the ground, beside Sandra.

I leaned down and peered directly into his eyes. "You can thank Jonas for that. He ordered me to shoot you." I smiled.

"LAB WILL SELF-DESTRUCT IN THREE MINUTES."

Jack, Jonas, I'm coming. I bent down and slid my hands under Sandra's shoulders. I pulled her limp body backwards toward me. Toward the door.

Dr. DeWeese grunted. He reached for the exam table, trying to pull himself up.

If he starts limping toward you, shoot him again, Jonas said.

"Gaaaahhhh!" I screamed as I hauled Sandra's dead weight. She was completely paralyzed. At the door, I lifted her up further, sliding my arm around her back, and held her there, propped up against the wall. I took her right hand and pushed it flat into the scanner. The click of the finger prick sounded, verifying her DNA.

The door slid open and Jack rushed in. I let Sandra fall to the ground, and I fell into his arms. Jonas, Addison and Briana stood just outside the door.

"Let's go," Briana urged.

"Wait! The hard drive." I pointed to the computer on the other side of the room.

Jack held me in the doorway while Jonas rushed over and ejected the hard drive from the computer. "They'll have a back-up of this information, but I'm sure they were counting on this one. So we'll at least slow them down a little."

Dr. DeWeese held himself up by leaning against the table. "Jack, don't leave me here. You have to help us."

I looked at the open hatch in the floor, then at Jack's face. His eyes were glued to mine, his message clear—his father would have to fend for himself. He didn't even acknowledge his father. Sandra's eyes, the only item on her body capable of moving, fluttered as she lay splayed across the floor beside me.

When Jonas had rejoined us, he looked down at his mother. I thought he might spit on her or kick her, but he simply looked away. "We've got to get out of here. Briana, dear, you're going to need to work your magic on Lexi and me. Addison, can you help Jack disappear?"

Addison nodded. "Gladly."

"LAB WILL SELF-DESTRUCT IN ONE MINUTE."

Jack leaned in and kissed the side of my head. "Let's go home."

THIRTY-SIX

....

hree days later...

I drew lazy circles with my forefinger at the base of Jack's clavicle on a peaceful, sunny afternoon. He reclined on a large stadium blanket in the rose garden of the UK Arboretum, looking up at the sky. One arm was bent behind his head. I lay partially on my side, partially across his chest. With his free hand, he feathered fingers along my arm. The scent of jasmine drifted from the nearby herb garden.

"Look," he said. "That cloud looks like a rabbit."

"Uh-huh," I mumbled, my eyes closed, and he continued on about cottontails and long, floppy ears.

We were trying to take the day off from Wellington, The Program, and watching the endless news reports of the "strange lab fire that occurred on the University of Kentucky campus." According to reporters, a small explosion caused a fire in a building that had, until recently, been mostly empty. A private organization had rented the space from the university for an exorbitant amount of money after receiving a grant for stem cell research and therapeutic cloning. So far, no reports had been made of fatalities or injuries from the fire.

The destruction of the lab began right after we walked away from Sandra and Jack's father. I shivered at the memory of the fire that broke out and threatened to trap us in the basement of the University building. Jack hugged me tighter.

The other thing my mind refused to take a break from was remembering my best friend—her laugh, her never-ending habit of doing yoga anytime we talked, and her unconditional love. I didn't know what I would do without her. And I couldn't stop wondering if her death had been my fault. Could I have stopped it?

"You did everything you could," Jack whispered.

I had given up on blocking Jack from my mind the last few days. Jonas promised to stay out. Georgia and I removed his tracker, but he could still get in if he wanted. The tracker allowed Ty to control me in ways that Jonas never would have—but Jonas was still capable of manipulating my thoughts and desires.

"They just took her," I said. My voice shook. "Her parents just swooped in and took Dani's body before I even got to see her one last time. I didn't get to say goodbye. No closure. Nothing. Why? And how did they find out so fast? It was the middle of the night—" My throat burned with a lump I could barely swallow past, yet my eyes remained dry, incapable of producing another tear.

Jack tightened his hold on me. "I don't know, baby."

I breathed in deeply, exhaling as a shudder moved through me. The school had organized a candlelight vigil in honor of Dani, but Dani's parents planned a private funeral—family only.

"I was family to her. She would have wanted me at her funeral. Don't you think her parents' actions were strange?"

"Yes, but Wellington Boarding School is the ideal school for strange families."

I chuckled even though it wasn't really funny. "What do you think Sandra will do when she discovers Dia and Lin didn't make it to the next destination?"

"You're assuming that Sandra and my father got out alive."

"Yes. I have to assume that. Someone would have helped them through that trap door. Sandra was so calm. She had a plan for everything. I will not let them sneak up on us again." I flattened my hand against his chest. "I hope Georgia and Fred are being hospitable to Dia and Lin." I smiled. Dia and Lin had more of a chance at a normal life by staying here in Kentucky with us, but my heart tightened just thinking about how little we knew about them. Would they be missed? Or were they just as expendable as Ty was to Sandra? And what about the rest of the clones inside The Farm? I would have freed them all if there had been more time.

"Hmm. I'm sure they're fine. Probably experiencing a little culture shock being outside the lab."

"Do you think Sandra will come after us again when she discovers that we stole the trackers and the hard drive? Should we destroy them? Where did Jonas put the trackers anyway?"

Jack covered my hand with his. "Lexi, stop. We agreed to take the day off from worrying about all this."

"You're right. I'm sorry." I wriggled my fingers from his grasp and trailed them down his chest, his stomach, and let them slide beneath the hem of his Bastille concert T-shirt until I found skin.

His hand followed suit by slipping under my shirt and up my back. "I'm sure there's gotta be something we can do to free your mind of all that junk." His free hand cupped my chin and directed my head toward his. When my gaze met his, he said, "Come closer."

I moved further up his body until my head was even with his. "What did you have in mind?" I offered my best coy smile.

He tilted his head as he slid his fingers around to the back of my neck and guided my face nearer until he claimed my lips with his. He pulled back. "A little of this." He kissed me again. "A little of that."

After a long, deep kiss, I trailed my lips to his cheek until they found the spot behind his ear. His hands roamed all along my back and neck. I smiled against the skin of his neck, breathing hard. "Someone's gonna see us."

"No they're not."

I pulled back and studied the sly look on his face. "Why do you seem so sure?"

"Because I rented this side of the arboretum out for the afternoon. It's been blocked off."

"Can we stay here forever?" I asked.

"No." He brought me in for another kiss. His hands were relentlessly convincing me to forget about everything outside the here and now. His fingers ran down the side of my body, causing me to shiver in his arms. "I promised Briana I would have you back by tomorrow morning."

Tomorrow? What were we doing until then?

"The rest of the day is a surprise." He had read my thoughts again. "For now, we're going to make out on this blanket in this very private garden." His words took on a playful tone, yet his eyebrows drew together, casting a dark shadow over his eyes.

He attempted to distract me with gentle kisses, but something bothered him. I let it go for now.

"Why does Briana need me back at school?" I said against his lips.

"She needs your help. A Halloween party or something. Said it's a big event every year."

I bent my neck and buried my face into his chest, and I immediately cut off all thoughts from him. I hadn't told him that my eighteenth birthday occurred this Halloween. Wellington had always allowed the students to make a big deal out of the holiday. I think it was their way of keeping students on campus on a night that could easily get out of control. "What if I don't want to go back to Wellington?"

He crooked a finger under my chin. "Then we won't go back."

I stared at his serious face for a moment before I spoke. "You'd do that?"

"Haven't I convinced you yet? I'd do anything for you. For us."

I nodded. "In that case, I think I'm ready to see the safe house my dad left instructions for."

"I'm already one step ahead of you."

What does that mean? I mindspoke to hide the accusatory tone in my voice. I hadn't told anyone where the safe house was. Not even Jack. And except to swim, I never removed the starfish and key from my neck. Even then, the necklace was locked inside my locker.

"Remember when you thought I was looking for my father? Questioning Cathy about Father's whereabouts?"

Yes.

"That wasn't the only thing I was doing."

I pushed up to my knees so that I could better see Jack's face when he told me what he had been hiding from me.

"Don't freak out."

"Why is it that every time you tell me not to freak out, you immediately tell me something that I, of course, will freak out about? What is it? Just tell me."

"I'd rather show you."

~~~~~

Jack insisted that we take a long motorcycle ride on the back roads of Kentucky in the heart of the Bluegrass before we went to the safe house.

Late that afternoon, we pulled down a long drive lined with a plank fence. A chestnut horse ran alongside the black fence. I hit Jack's arm, signaling for him to stop, which he did.

After climbing off the bike, I lifted my helmet off and set it on the seat. "If I didn't know better, I'd think that was—"

"Cheriana?"

I whipped my head around to look at him. "How did you know where this house was?"

"How did *you* know where this house was?" he retorted. "Your dad didn't mention it in any of the documents online. It's not in any of your school records. It wasn't in any of the papers my dad had on you from the time he hired a private investigator."

I remembered how Jack spoke with Coach Williams privately during several classroom and weapon sessions. He disappeared to "check on things" and never told me what.

"Coach knew. Dad gave him access to everything. But he never told me anything," I said mostly to myself.

"He didn't think you were ready." Jack averted his gaze from me to glance up toward the house at the end of the drive. "I got permission to move Cheriana here."

My hands turned clammy. Panic began to build in my chest. "Permission from whom, Jack?"

Jack closed the distance between us. He reached up and cupped my cheeks with both hands. "You know I love you with every cell, every neuron, every fiber of my genetically modified being, right?"

"Tell me who I'm going to find at this house, Jack."

"You know who's here—who's waiting for you at the end of this drive."

I had faced so many obstacles in such a short period of time. More than one person should ever have to. Could I face one more challenge?

I walked slowly over to the bike and put my helmet back on. And debated. Stay. Or go.

"Want to know my opinion?"

I faced Jack. I did not need his opinion. "Let's do this."

He drove me the rest of the way up the driveway. Handing him my helmet, I locked eyes with Jack—the love of my life. His lips curved slightly, but the smile didn't reach his eyes as he nodded in encouragement. I turned slowly and made the short trek to the front door alone. I reached my hand up to knock, but the door opened before I made contact.

And I came face to face with the one person who had managed to elude the messed-up events of my childhood—yet whom I could blame for them all.

Mom.

A Note From the Author

Thank you for spending time with Lexi, Jack, Jonas, and the rest of the cast from *Mindsiege*. Now that you've finished reading *Mindsiege*, please consider leaving a review on Goodreads and/or bookseller sites such as Amazon and Barnes & Noble. Reviews are the greatest way to help other readers discover new books. I would truly appreciate it.

Don't forget to sign up for my newsletter—*A Piece of My Mind*—at http://heathersunseri.com/newsletter and be the first to hear about what's next in the *Mindspeak* series and other stories that might be in the works.

Happy Reading!!!
Heather

ACKNOWLEDGEMENTS

To God—Jeremiah 1:5. Thank you, God, for knowing and loving me before I was even formed and for having a purpose for me that is specific to my life.

Thank you to...

Mike—for the infinite ways that you love and support me in all my neurotic craziness.

Maggie—Your clever zaniness inspires me every day.

Robert—for always being patient and understanding when "Mommy has to work."

David Gatewood—I'm thankful to Hugh Howey for "introducing" me to your superhero power of making my words into a better story. (Are you sure your DNA wasn't altered as an embryo?) Your sense of humor and especially your Star Wars quote got me through what you initially called a "light copyed-it."

Taryn Albright—for your bravery of tackling a very early draft and asking tough questions. Your insightful suggestions enriched the story. And to that, I'm grateful.

Jessica Patch, Laura Pauling, and Katie Ganshert—my beta readers. I couldn't have done this without your honest feedback and willingness to read a story before it was fine-tuned.

Connie Boyce and Jenny Kays—for finding those pesky typos.

Kentucky Independent Writers—You are a talented and supportive group of writers.

My friends and family—for your encouragement in the form of texts, Facebook messages, and phone messages. Sorry for all the times I said no to lunches and other meetings while working on this story. Love all of you.

ABOUT THE AUTHOR

Heather Sunseri was raised on a tiny farm in one of the smallest towns in thoroughbred horse country near Lexington, Kentucky. After high school, she attended Furman University in Greenville, South Carolina, and later graduated from the University of Kentucky with a degree in accounting. Always torn between a passion for fantasy and a mind for the rational, it only made sense to combine her career in accounting with a novel-writing dream.

Heather now lives in a different small town on the other side of Lexington with her two children and her husband, Mike, the biggest Oregon Duck fan in the universe. When she's not writing or working as a CPA, she spends her time tormenting her daughter's cat, Olivia, and loving on her son's Golden Retriever, Jenny.

Heather loves to hear from readers. Please sign up for her newsletter—*A Piece of My Mind*—on her website to hear when future novels are released. You can also connect with her in several other ways:

Heather Sunseri
P.O. Box 1264
Versailles, KY 40383

Web site: http://heathersunseri.com
Blog: http://heathersunseri.com/blog/
Email: heather@heathersunseri.com
Facebook: http://www.facebook.com/heathersunseri.writer
Twitter: @HeatherSunseri

Photo by Candace Sword

Made in the USA
San Bernardino, CA
24 August 2015